The GENTLEMAN

THE
Kinkades

The GENTLEMAN

BESTSELLING AUTHOR
DR. REBECCA SHARP

The
GENTLEMAN

PROLOGUE
MAX

THEN...

She was beautiful—and I really needed to stop staring.

I checked my watch again. Now, fifteen minutes past the hour. Todd was late, and I wasn't surprised. Punctuality wasn't a suit, let alone a strong suit, in my best friend and business partner's deck of personality traits. From the time we were kids, he'd always been the one sprinting to my house in the morning because he missed the pick-up at his. The one knocking at the classroom door five minutes after the exam started, begging to be let in.

"Max?"

The call caught my attention, and I went to the counter for my coffee. "Thanks."

The Brew Bar barista smiled back at me as I picked up the mug. "You're welcome," I heard her say, but I was already looking away and taking a sip, my attention drawn to the woman sitting at the table by the window again, the light catching her profile and setting her hair into golden fire.

She had me in a daze. I stiffened at the thought, the scribbled note like a weight in my pocket from earlier, but I couldn't look away. Couldn't stop staring. Describing her as beautiful was like calling the sun bright—true, but entirely lacking.

Whoever she was, she wasn't from around here. I was born and raised in Stonebar Harbor. I'd grown up working at my aunt's jam business, Stonebar Farms, alongside my dad almost every summer until I was old enough to work full time. If I hadn't sold or delivered jam to every local in the area, I was now delivering fresh flowers to them. Or would be soon, as soon as Maine-Stems took off. *As soon as my best friend and business partner started pulling some of his weight.*

Forcing my eyes back to my phone, I took another draw from my Americano and checked Todd's text again.

> Meet me at the Brew Bar at nine. I've got news!

He was now twenty minutes late, but if "news" was *the* news on the one task I'd given Todd to handle on his own—investor funding—then I'd let him slide.

While I'd grown up picking fresh berries and watching the ins and outs of growing a business unfold at Stonebar Farms, Todd had grown up rubbing blazered elbows with vacationing senators, congressmen, and businessmen. Todd McCormick *Senior* was a senator for most of Todd McCormick *Junior*'s formative years. So while I'd learned the value of hard work, my best friend had been taught how to "play the game," and I'd lost count of how many times I'd had to walk him back from "breaking the rules." How many times I'd stopped him from doing reckless things just because he wanted to "get away with it." *How many times he was let in late to those exams, not because he was remorseful, but because every teacher knew who his family was.*

I saw it for what it was. A cry for attention from Todd and Mary McCormick, who were born to be politicians, not parents. It was only their pronounced absence that let any of my guidance sink in, filling some of the voids and course-correcting Todd's trajectory from becoming a total thoughtless prick.

The coffee shop door opened, but it was only Ella who came rushing inside. Ella owned The Pastry Queen a few doors down. Ukrainian by heritage, she specialized in all kinds of international pastry delights, and I assumed she was here to refuel after the morning breakfast rush.

I tracked her toward the counter...but only so I could take another look at the golden goddess by the window.

The petite blonde looked like a vintage pin-up in her ripped jean shorts and strawberry-patterned blouse that cinched at her waist and ruffled over her breasts. Her hair fell in loose waves down her back as she sat at one of the backless stools, her sandaled feet resting on the top rung because she was too short for them to reach the floor. She tipped forward, her eyes drifting shut as she put her nose to the bright pink peonies in the vase by the window. *Peonies proudly provided by local florist, MaineStems.*

Her lips parted as she inhaled, and the look of pleasure on her face—*dammit.*

I pushed away from the counter and adjusted my cock in my slacks. *Twenty-five minutes.* Todd was twenty-five minutes late, and I...I wasn't going to miss my shot.

I needed to meet her. Needed to know who she was. What she was doing here. *How long she'd be in my orbit.*

I reached her side in a couple of strides, but she didn't notice. Her eyes were still shut, one hand cupped around the bloom as she let out a soft sigh, the sweet sound burrowing straight to my cock. *Damn, what I wouldn't give to be the man to harvest each and every one of those exquisite sighs.*

When I cleared my throat, her eyes fluttered open, big brown orbs taking a second to focus on me.

"Most beautiful," I said, shoving my hand in my pocket to obscure the stretch across the front of my pants. Between that and my jacket, it should hopefully keep my attraction to her from making this awkward.

Pink colored her cheeks, a lighter version of the shade of the peony petals. "Excuse me?"

"Peonies were originally cultivated in China, and the Chinese word for them means 'most beautiful.'"

Her bright smile blossomed between full red lips. It was stunning. A welcome punch to the gut.

If the Chinese had been witness to this woman's smile all those thousands of years ago, they certainly would've reconsidered giving the accolade to a flower.

"They're my favorite," she said and looked back to

the bouquet. "I love how there's just so much flower inside the bulb..."

"They open up to three times their original size." *Not unlike my dick at the moment,* I thought as the pink tip of her tongue slid across her lips.

She was a pixie goddess.

Setting her book on the table—*The Lion, the Witch, and the Wardrobe*—she turned to me, head tipped and brows lifted, and rested her hands on her knees, saying, "You know a lot about flowers."

There were a lot of replies to that, not the least of which was offering up that the bouquet she was admiring was one of mine. But I didn't. I didn't reply with anything about me because none of it mattered.

"When I like something, I want to know everything about it," I murmured and extended my hand. "I'm Max."

And I wanted to know everything about her.

Her lashes dusted her cheeks, her eyes hooding as she looked at my hand. *Hesitation.* But only for a moment.

"I'm—"

"Daisy!" Todd's voice detonated through the coffee shop, and he strolled in like he'd just rolled out of bed—and smelled like he'd just rolled out of a beer can.

The big brown eyes of the pixie goddess flashed with what I swore was guilt before my best friend, my oldest friend, strode right beside me—in front of me—and kissed the woman of my dreams.

Daisy.

Pain shot like a hot spear straight through my chest. Impossible, my mind argued. I'd just met her—*hardly* met her. I couldn't ache for someone I barely knew.

My bright-eyed goddess laughed as he tipped her almost off the stool until she was forced to cling to him. And then I saw them, the bouquet of white-petaled blooms hidden haphazardly behind his back that he drew out as he sat her upright.

"For you, doll." Todd handed her the bouquet of daisies. They were beautiful. They were her namesake. *But they weren't her favorite.*

And that was Todd in a nutshell—thoughtful but thoughtless at the same time. Moving through life, trying to fit everyone, including—especially—himself into the picture his parents had laid out for him.

I watched Daisy smile and thank him, but it wasn't the same smile as before. It wasn't the *most beautiful.* But Todd didn't notice that either.

"Sorry, I'm late," he said, already focused on me with a wide grin—the same smile he'd had when he'd pulled out front of my house in the brand-new Mercedes his parents bought him for his sixteenth birthday. The *look what I got* smile. "It looks like you guys already met, but doll, this is my best friend and business partner, Max Hamilton." He motioned to me. "And Max, I want you to meet my girlfriend, Daisy."

I held my smile like there was a gun pressed to my back. *What other choice did I have?* The woman I couldn't stop staring at was my best friend's girl.

If only that meant I'd stop looking at her the way that I was, but I knew it didn't. I already knew that for the time she was his, I'd look at her and wish she were mine.

Unfortunately, reality was even worse. What it really meant was that for the next four years, I'd continue to do what I'd always done—save Todd from himself. *And spare Daisy from his genuine thoughtlessness.* She deserved a man who knew what her favorite flower was and who brought out her most beautiful smile.

Even if that man wasn't me.

CHAPTER 1
MAX

NOW...

"Todd?" I called as soon as I saw his tux hanging off the bathroom door. "What the hell..." I ripped the hanger down and tore off the plastic, opening the door to the grunt of his acknowledgment.

Shit.

My oldest friend sat in the tub in the bathroom of his hotel room, drinking what looked like the last bottle from the minibar. The others spread like confetti inside the basin. Or maybe like hollow graves inside a porcelain tomb.

"Dammit." The metal hanger clanked on the shower rod as I crouched and ripped the nip from his hand.

"Hey!" Todd's protest died on a deep groan as he tipped forward and hung his head in his hands.

My best friend looked like shit, and it was his wedding day.

His hair was a mess, tangled in every direction. He reeked of the unholy union of fresh and stale alcohol. And the circles around his eyes made it look like he hadn't slept a wink.

A second glance over him, and I confirmed he hadn't. He still wore the same clothes he had on last night at the rehearsal dinner at his parents' house.

"What the hell is wrong with you?" I growled and dumped the last drops of liquid down the sink, tossing the bottle in the trash.

"Me?" His head shook, defeated. "I don't know, Max. What the hell is wrong with me?" He started plucking through the other empty bottles, searching for another drop.

"Come on, Todd." I swiped my hand through the tub, taking away the rest of his litter. "Talk to me. What's going on? You were fine last night..."

Fine was a relative term when it came to time spent with his parents. Time hadn't dulled the weight of the McCormicks' expectations on their one and only son, and neither had it dimmed the consequences.

"I was...I don't know who I was last night. Not a McCormick, apparently."

"What are you talking about?" I grabbed a wash-cloth and went to the sink, dousing it with ice-cold water.

"My dad..."

I slapped the cold cloth on his neck, marginally enjoying his flinch and hiss of shock.

"Fuck your dad, Todd. How many times have I told you that?" I opened the cloth and laid it over his head. Moving back to the sink, I filled one of the glasses with water and took it back to him. "Drink this."

"I thought he'd understand," Todd muttered before downing the whole glass, probably wishing it were vodka.

I wished I understood why he still listened to—revered—his parents like he did. For all the time I'd known him, they'd either been absent or made him feel inadequate, and still he kept trying. Trying and failing and drinking. Trying and failing and drinking. *And drinking and drinking and drinking.*

"Todd." I put my hand on his shoulder, filled with equal parts fury and pity. "Listen to me. Forget your dad. Whatever he said...forget it. Today isn't about him. It's about you. The future you're making. You decide what happens after today. What kind of life you're going to make with the person you love, the person you want to spend your life with."

These blow-ups with his dad were a tale as old as time. They started when we were in school and continued when Todd didn't do as well as was expected. When Todd decided to help me open a start-up business. When Todd started dating Daisy, rather than one of the wealthy socialites on his mother's marital menu. *When Todd got Daisy pregnant.*

Every time Todd tried to be himself—do something for himself—they argued until legacy inevitably pulled Todd back in line. Legacy, or the fear of not having one.

"Come on. Clean yourself up and get ready," I said, giving him a little shake, his head bobbing like it was attached by a single tenuous tether. "Daisy deserves better than this."

She deserved better than my troubled friend, who remembered her birthday but asked me to send her a birthday bouquet of daisies every year because he was too busy—*and never remembered that peonies were her favorite*. Better than my friend, who would've forgotten their anniversary if I didn't say something, if I didn't line up plans and gift suggestions like I was his butler rather than his best friend.

Better than my friend, who got annoyed when Daisy continued to work at the Stonebar Country Club, where he'd met her, to pay for school. Who continued to get frustrated, no matter how many times I explained Daisy's reluctance to rely on him, given how her father had abandoned her mother. And who refused to understand why she wanted to get her degree in chemistry when, as his wife, she wouldn't need to work.

And so much fucking better than the man who knocked her up and made her drop out of her master's program, proposing to her and promising to take care of her, and then had cold feet every step of the way.

But it was a whole hell of a lot of guilt that kept me from telling her that.

No matter how I'd helped Todd over the years, Daisy loved him, and it wasn't dependent on whether or not he remembered her favorite flower or their anniversary. Or whether he fully understood or appreciated her need for independence. *At least, that was what I told myself.*

"Daisy..." Todd said her name like he'd already forgotten who we were talking about.

"Your daughter deserves better than this." An edge sliced into my voice.

"Better than me." He corrected bitterly and pulled out of my hold, swaying as he rose. "Better than a McCormick."

There were plenty of people who would hate Todd

McCormick at this point, but knowing him for as long as I did—knowing the trauma that apathy and constant disapproval can do to a person—I didn't fall for the bitterness aimed at her, but instead heard the bitterness aimed at himself.

Todd wanted his parents' approval, but the only way he'd learned to get that was to fit himself into their picture of who they expected him to be, even though it wasn't what he wanted. And that meant dragging Daisy along with him.

"Come on, man." I tucked my arms to my sides with a deep sigh. "You deserve better than this too."

How many times over the course of our lives had I watched him get to this point? To this fork in the road that split what his parents wanted from him and what he wanted for himself? How many times had I watched him reach this split and let it tear him in two?

The last time, he hadn't ended up drunk in a hotel bathtub but in a venture capital presentation for Maine-Stems. It almost cost us the investment, but Todd fixed it because his father was a senator. And that was how he was raised to fix all of his problems. Money. Connections. Power. Rather than thinking before acting.

But the more I pushed him, the more he pushed back. The same way he did with his parents. I learned the hard way that people only change when they want to, and Todd didn't want to. That was why, as soon as I was able, I'd bought out his shares of MaineStems, and he hadn't protested. He looked at it as proof that the only path he belonged on was the one laid out by his parents. But he didn't want to change that either. Not enough.

"I don't have a choice anymore, Max. Dad already

has everything lined up. All the steps. All the players. I'm going to have a wife and a kid. A house. Be a second-generation senator, and that's the end of it. That's my story."

I hated that he'd lumped Daisy in with the rest of it like he hadn't picked her, like he wasn't in love with her. And he was. He was just struggling. That was all. *How many times had I told myself that over the last six months? How many more times would I continue to believe it?*

I didn't know what he had argued with his dad about last night, but it didn't matter. It probably had something to do with the massive party his parents announced at dinner that they were going to host at the country club to celebrate the wedding. They'd been furious when Daisy stood her ground on a small, intimate ceremony. But in the end, they figured out how to get their way.

"You always have a choice," I said and filled the cup again from the sink, handing it to him.

Todd downed the second glass the same way as the first, like he'd been stranded in a desert for the last twenty-seven years, and finished it by setting it on the counter with a thunk.

"You don't need them, Todd. You have Daisy. You're going to marry the woman of your dreams this morning." *And mine.* The thought no longer stabbed my chest, the knife perpetually buried there, but twisted it instead. I wished I were a worse man. One who would let this spiral happen and separate him from Daisy. But I couldn't—I wouldn't—do that to him. Or her. "And in a few months, you're going to be a father. It's never too late to be better. To pick a different path. To walk away from your parents' plan."

I caught the hard flex of his jaw. "You don't understand," he muttered and gripped the edge of the counter.

"Me? How long have I known you?" Sometimes, it felt like I understood Todd's demons more than he did. Especially the ones that made him drink. "I understand this—the baby wasn't part of your plan. Or your parents' plan. But Jesus, man, do you know how lucky you are?" I turned away and raked a hand through my hair, feeling my own demons start to claw up my throat. "Daisy is smart and funny and genuine and gorgeous. Do *you* understand just how fucking *lucky* you are that she picked you? That you get to have forever with a woman like her?"

I bit into my tongue then, tasting the coppery tang of a confession about to go too far. For a beat, I wondered if I already had.

There were so many times over the course of their relationship that I swore he had to see it. He had to see the way I looked just a little too long at his girlfriend. *His fiancée.* That I knew all her favorite things to help him grovel when he came up short. But that was Todd, perceptive only to the perimeter of ignorance. He noticed only his best friend having his back, the way I'd done for the entirety of our friendship.

But right now, the way he looked at me...the haze in his eyes...Did he realize? *No.* He was drunk. He could hardly follow the tether of what we were talking about. There was no chance he could hear all the things I wasn't saying.

I cleared my throat, and whatever clouded his

expression was gone in an instant, convincing me I was right. *He had no idea I was in love with his soon-to-be wife.*

"You're right." His shoulders slumped.

"Come on." I patted him on the back. "Shave. Rinse off. Fix the rat's nest on your head."

His gaze found mine in the vanity mirror. "She deserves better."

"So get ready and give her a better man."

Todd stared at me for long enough to make me question what I'd said—to make me question what was going through his mind—but then he nodded.

"Get dressed and brush your teeth. I'm not letting you be late." Todd reached for his toothbrush and rinsed it in the sink. I let out a slow exhale of relief. We'd made it through the storm. "I'll be outside."

"Max." He stopped me.

"Yeah?"

"I need a favor."

I folded my arms over my chest. "Name it."

"Daisy's bouquet..."

"You didn't drop it off this morning?" I looked over my shoulder. The bright pink peonies I'd hand-picked for Daisy were still in the vase on the small table in his room.

"No." Todd scratched the back of his neck, looking guilty but not apologizing. "Probably wouldn't have been a good idea."

"I'll handle it," I told him, feeling my throat grow tight. "Get dressed. I'll be back for you in an hour."

I didn't want to see Daisy before the wedding. I didn't know why I was afraid I'd do something stupid like confess just how much I loved her—how much I'd always loved her—when I'd had the better part of four years to do so. I guessed there was something about the finality of her and Todd getting married. Something that gave me the same instinct I'd had at the Brew Bar the day we met—the one that screamed to get up, to do something before I missed my shot.

But now, like then, I buried the instinct and the way I felt about her, and did everything I could to make sure my best friend's wedding went off without a hitch.

THE TOWN OF FRIENDSHIP STARTED TO GET QUIET this time of year. While Stonebar Harbor still drew in visiting crowds through September, the smaller seaside town to the south had already begun to shed the dregs of its tourist season.

My car rumbled over the cobbled, aptly named Maine Street and pulled up out front of the Lamplight Inn. My cousin, Elouise—Lou—had bought the historic landmark of Friendship last year, renovated it back to its bed-and-breakfast glory, and officially opened the inn to guests early this year.

When Todd told me he and Daisy were getting married, he'd said they were just going to go to the courthouse, and I could've punched him. I understood he thought this was just an inevitability. That Daisy got pregnant, and therefore they had to get married, and the courthouse was the most efficient way to do that. It was logical, but it was also incredibly stupid.

"Daisy said the courthouse was fine."

"Of course, she did. She's the most easygoing person on this planet. That doesn't mean she doesn't deserve more than the courthouse."

"But what's the point? No one but us is going to be there. My parents are going on vacation, and Daisy doesn't have family."

"You're her family, Todd. You're going to be her family. That is the whole point."

"Max?" Wade climbed down off the ladder where he'd been hanging the pink and purple peony garland—also provided by MaineStems—over the entrance.

Wade Stevens was Lou's fiancé and older brother to the infamous Hollywood heartthrob, Blaze Stevens. Blaze had stayed at the inn earlier this spring, and after taking a fall down the main stairs, Wade had come up to check on his brother. He met Lou, and he'd never left.

I grabbed the bouquet from the front seat, holding it up as I approached. "Special delivery."

Wade smiled and nodded. "They're upstairs in the first suite."

"Thanks." I ducked inside, wondering how questionable it would've been to ask Wade to deliver the flowers.

My hand tightened around the stems. I couldn't do it. I was a glutton for punishment—for the torture of giving the woman of my dreams her bouquet so she could marry my best friend.

CHAPTER 2
MAX

The entrance and main stairwell of the Lamplight Inn were covered in cotton candy peonies on every surface, on the railing for the stairs, and most impressively, the floral arch I'd constructed last night in the inn's communal living room for the ceremony. I'd left the rehearsal dinner early, before dessert, to come here and start setting it up. My younger sister, Harper, and I worked until two in the morning to get it perfect.

The pink blooms climbed like ivy—*with* ivy and baby's breath—above the fireplace and up the chute, turning it into a floral waterfall. It was almost too much. If this wedding hadn't come so dangerously close to not being *enough*, to not being what Daisy deserved, maybe it would've been overdone.

But I was the one who noticed the glimmer of sadness in her eyes when she insisted to Todd that the courthouse would be fine. I was the one who cataloged every downcast stare when Todd complained about one thing or another, even though I'd stepped in to handle everything for him. *And let him take credit.*

I let Todd tell Daisy that having a small ceremony at the Lamplight Inn was his idea. I let him take credit for the blueberries and cream wedding cake that I picked out because I was the one who'd gone to the tasting. Daisy had too much morning sickness, and Todd, who'd gone out the night before with one of his friends from college because Daisy was studying, was suffering from a different kind of morning sickness.

I wanted this day to be special for her. I wanted to see that most beautiful smile one more time when she saw the flowers. When she tasted the cake. When she kissed her groom. There was no overdoing the promise of forever, no matter how it killed me inside.

I took the stairs two at a time, my heart starting to beat a little harder in my chest. Just before I got to the top, Daisy and Lou's voices filtered out from the suite at the top of the stairs, the door partially cracked.

"I look like a white whale."

"You look beautiful, Daisy," Lou chided.

"I agree with Lou. You look gorgeous, Dee," Harper joined in.

I slowed and stopped on the landing. I didn't realize my sister was here too.

"Maybe I just feel like a whale because I can't see my ankles. Are my shoes even going to fit?" A pause. "Maybe we should just go to the courthouse. Then I could wear my sweatpants."

"You're not going to the courthouse," Lou insisted. "First, because there is no world where you don't look gorgeous, and second, because Max would cry if you didn't get married in front of his flower arrangement."

My jaw tightened. The irony of how wrong she was didn't escape me.

"I'll cry too," my sister chimed in. "I left at twelve-thirty, dead on my feet, but Max was here until two. He sent me a picture when he finished."

There was a long pause followed by Daisy's soft voice again. "He's done too much."

"I'm pretty sure there's nothing my brother wouldn't do for you—"

I knocked loudly, *very loudly,* on the door and stepped back.

Not everyone was as oblivious as Todd to how I felt about Daisy. Then again, Harper was probably the one person who was around us the most. *Too busy to date* was my excuse for dragging my younger sister to rounds of golf or an afternoon out on Todd's parents' boat or to one of their fancy society parties.

Half the time, it wasn't because I couldn't stand to spend hours watching Todd and Daisy together, but because it meant hours I'd spend talking to Daisy alone. Todd always barricaded himself with friends at any event involving his family—me, our frat brother from college, Scott, and Daisy. He claimed it was so I wouldn't be the third wheel, except he and Scott would end up going off socializing and gallivanting. Meanwhile, Daisy and I would be left to quiet moments alone.

Those quiet moments with her most beautiful smile were death by a thousand cuts.

Knowing she was marrying Todd—helping it unfold —was the final nail in the coffin I'd willingly climbed into, making today both a wedding and a funeral.

I knew I had to move on—knew I had to find some

way to get over her. But even distance couldn't work. Not when Todd started slacking on the simple wedding plans. Apparently, climbing into a coffin wasn't enough. I decided to dig my own grave, too, by stepping in to help.

"Oh, Max." Lou opened the door and stopped short. "I thought it was Wade. What are you—" Her brow furrowed just until her eyes found the bouquet. "Oh."

"What is it? Is Todd—"

"Max just brought over your bouquet," Lou answered over her shoulder. "Here. I can take it. You shouldn't see the bride—"

"It's okay, Lou," Daisy called, and I saw her move from where she'd been lying on the bed. "I think that superstition is only for the groom."

Which you aren't, the reminder buried like a barb under my skin. No matter how I made myself bleed, I'd never get it out.

"Okay, I'm going to go down and check on Wade and refill your water." She hugged a giant water bottle to her chest and stepped into the upstairs hall. "The flowers look amazing, Max," Lou said. "I took so many photos to add to the wedding brochure. I think it's going to be a great collaboration."

MaineStems provided all the flower arrangements for the inn, complimentary as long as Lou let me put a plaque next to the vases with a QR code to our site so guests can order their own flowers on demand. That was the premise of my business. Flowers delivered when you needed them for men who forgot birthdays and anniversaries and Mother's Day.

Like this, said a small voice in the back of my mind,

my gaze dipping to the bouquet in my hand. *For men like Todd.*

"Thanks, Lou," I replied as she moved aside, only for Harper to block the doorway next.

"Harp, where are you—"

"Frankie just texted that the candles are all packed up and ready, so I'm going to go help her and Chandler."

"Okay..."

She beelined right around me like she couldn't leave the room fast enough.

And then it was just Daisy and me.

My breath bled through my lips as I looked over the woman sitting on the edge of the bed. Jeweled combs gently pulled her loose waves of sunlight back from her face, spilling them over her shoulders and down her back. Her dress was a pristine white, the lace sleeves reaching to her elbow and then fanning over the fullness of her breasts. With the high waist, it obscured the growing swell of her stomach. She had the fabric pulled up to her knees, her bare feet dangling off the edge. *They still didn't touch the ground.*

"Hi, Max." Her makeup highlighted those big, hopeful brown eyes as they stared at me and reddened every inch of her full lips while they teased out my name.

Hi. The response stuck in my throat. She was too damn beautiful...forever a pixie goddess who decided to dip her toes onto Earth.

Say something. My jaw worked overtime to let some sort of sound out as I approached, but there was nothing. Or maybe there was everything. Four years of everything I'd ever wanted to say to this woman, to tell her, to confess to her, it barreled up my throat like a runaway train, crashing into my lips and leaving only an inarticulate catastrophe for my tongue to sort through.

Her gaze followed me closely as I kneeled in front of her, like I was her knight rather than the fool who'd fallen for my best friend's fiancée.

"Most beautiful," I finally managed words, completely forgetting about the flowers in my hand.

Daisy's eyes snapped to mine, and the smile she gave me was that full-bloom beauty. The knife in my chest made a hard twist.

"Thank you, Max." Her smile dwindled into a cautious one. She wore the cautious one far too many times lately, and no matter how many times I prodded Todd, he never seemed to pick up the difference. *Because people only changed when they wanted to.*

"What is it?" I caught my knuckle under her chin, lifting it. She tried to shake her head, to look away so I wouldn't see the tears stringing like twinkle lights along her lashes. "Tell me, Daze," I pleaded, using the nickname I only ever pulled out when Todd wasn't around.

"I don't know. Something doesn't feel right, but it's probably just my hormones." She quickly swiped her eyes, but one tear snuck free.

I went to cup her cheek and catch it with my thumb, but she tensed back. I immediately dropped my hand, frustration pummeling my chest. *Dammit, Max.* It wasn't my place to be drying the tears of my best friend's fiancée, even if she was my friend too. Even if sometimes it felt like we'd spent more time together over the last four years than she and Todd did.

Frustration churned like an engine in my chest as I

offered her the bouquet like some kind of segue away from my misstep.

"Most beautiful," she echoed and brought them up to her face, a shield drawn between us. Her cheeks flushed pink, like the brush of the peony petals stained her skin.

Suddenly, I couldn't bear the thought of it ending like this. For four years, I buried how I felt about her. For the next four seconds, I had to let it live.

"Does Todd make you happy, Daze?" I needed to know. I needed to hear her answer, *just once,* so I'd never regret not telling her that my best friend wasn't the only one who'd fallen in love with her.

Slowly, her lashes peeled open, and I waited, my breath under lock and key in my chest. "Max..." Just as she started to speak, something changed. Her brow furrowed. Her head tipped. *Something caught her attention.* "What's this?"

She reached between the flowers and pulled out an envelope.

My jaw went slack. "I...don't know." I certainly hadn't put it there.

"It's from Todd," she murmured, flashing me the front that read *Daisy* in his unmistakable scrawl.

"I didn't realize he put a note in there," I said, the fist around my throat gripping tighter as she opened the envelope and slid out the folded paper inside.

I'd missed my shot. The moment I'd had to finally tell Daisy the truth—*just once*—was gone. Stolen by the man who was going to marry her. And I took it as a sign that she'd found the buried note when she did.

"I should get going. I don't want to make your groom late," I said roughly, and went to the door.

I couldn't wait—couldn't watch as she read his letter. I needed to get the hell out of here and get my shit together.

"Max..." My hand stilled on the knob. "Max, what is this?" Her voice was hollowed out by panic, a gossamer shell of what it normally was.

I spun, and my heart dropped into my stomach with all the casualty of a bomb. Daisy stood beside the bed, the note in her hand, but she shook so badly, it flapped like a bird about to take flight.

"I-I don't understand." Daisy looked at me, her tears in free fall, but that wasn't even the worst of it. The worst was the flash of betrayal in her eyes. "Did you know, Max?" She charged at me, the paper flapping in my direction. "Did you know he was going to do this?"

It took me two tries to take it from her fingers. "What are you talking about?" I growled and scanned the card.

Daisy,

I'm not good with words, just like I haven't been good with you over the last few months. This isn't the right way to do this, but it's the only way I know how. I can't marry you. This isn't...who I am. I'm sorry.

Todd

"Did you know he was going to run?"
All I knew was that I was going to kill him.

CHAPTER 3
DAISY

My fiancé was leaving me at the altar.

The thud of my heart pounded against my chest. It wanted to escape. I wanted to escape.

I was a cliché. *A pregnant cliché.*

My mind whirred. *No. No. No.*

More than my mind whirred.

"Whoa, Daze." Firm hands gripped my arms, his steadiness making me aware that I'd started to sway. "Breathe," Max ordered, and my lungs inflated. "That's it. Now, let it out." Oxygen sped through my lips, following the coarse rumble of his voice. He sounded different. Thicker and more commanding than normal as he continued to instruct me, "Deep breath in." The whirring started to settle. "And out."

Why didn't he sound normal? *Why did it make me feel good?*

I shuddered and forced my tear-clogged vision to focus. First on his chest. His dark gray suit jacket. Then the buttons on his shirt. *He'd forgotten the top one, I* vaguely noticed as my gaze moved higher, finally settling on Max's handsome face.

"Did you know?" I demanded again in a harsh whisper.

How could he not know? He always knew.

"I know a lot about the things I care about."

I'd never forgotten those first minutes when I'd known Max Hamilton before I'd learned who he was to Todd. I'd never forgotten the things he'd said or the way he'd looked at me, no matter how hard I tried.

"Sit. Please." Max's firm hands didn't give me much of a choice, guiding me onto the edge of the bed before letting me go.

My head swayed, the whirring starting up again. Max cared about both of us. Todd and me. He'd just left Todd—spoke to him not even thirty minutes ago. *How could he not know? Not sense something was wrong?*

"I have to call him," I blurted out, frantically feeling over the bed for my phone. "I have to talk to Todd. I can't—he can't—"

"It's already ringing." Max held up his phone, Todd's name lit on the screen.

"Let me—" I reached for it.

"Daze—" Max pursed his lips, a growl-like sound caged inside his chest as I wrenched his phone from him.

No wonder he was trying to hang on to it. I shook so badly, it took two hands to hold it with only marginal success to my ear.

As it rang and rang, Max's stare bored into mine. Burrowed straight down to where I was sure he could see how all the caution tape wrapped around my heart was starting to fray and tear with every unanswered second. I tried to look away, but the room was too small or he was too big—there was no *not* looking at him.

Tall and broad. Strong but not overly muscular. Thick hair that looked like warmed whiskey and green eyes like grass after a fresh rain. Even frustrated, Max Hamilton was gorgeous.

The thought wasn't unfamiliar to me. Max had been frustrated a lot over the last five months, and always with Todd. In four years, I'd never seen Max angry. I'd never heard him raise his voice or lose his cool. While Todd was easily irritable, especially if he'd had a drink...or a few...Max was always his steadying hand.

And now, he was having to be mine.

"Daze," Max pleaded with me for his phone, but I couldn't. It felt like a lifeline—a life raft I held to my face. If I could just talk to Todd, it would be okay. He would be okay. We would be okay.

The line rang and rang, each chime sounding less like a pleasant tone and more like the sequential firing of a machine gun straight to the center of my chest.

How could this be happening? How had I not seen this coming?

"Hi, you've reached Todd McCormick. I'm unavailable at the moment..."

The phone slid from my hands, thudding onto the carpeted floor as my arms collapsed around my middle. "I don't understand."

I knew Todd was struggling. He had been struggling before the pregnancy. His parents' expectations of him—and of the woman he was dating—created a giant wedge in our relationship. And then we'd found out about the baby.

It wasn't planned—she wasn't planned. But I was determined to give my baby girl the kind of family I never had, and I thought Todd would feel the same. Maybe for her, he'd start caring less about his parents, who only saw their son as one more piece to fit into their ever-growing political puzzle.

My hope never gained any steam.

The baby...the wedding...it made his parents more demanding and drove Todd in the opposite direction, no matter what I did or said. No matter what Max did or said.

Hate was a strong word, but after four years of watching how Todd and Mary McCormick emotionally manipulated their son, I lost my qualms when saying I hated them. Todd was a good person. He had a good heart. But he was raised with a silver spoon—a silver spoon that dug him into a hole, into a lifestyle that he didn't know how to climb out of.

"I'm going to go back over there. God, I was just there. How—" Max caught himself. "I'm going to find him, Daze. I'm going to find out what's going on."

I stared out the window, frozen in place like if I didn't move, the nightmare couldn't continue. Everything inside me was held hostage. Tortured by the knowledge that I'd just become my worst fear: *dependent.*

"You see what your asshole father left us with? You never depend on a man, ever. They're all rotten at the core. You hear me, Daisy?" My mother was a broken record, a heartbroken record that repeated the same song every day for the span of my childhood. When she died, I swore I wouldn't end up like her—bitter because she'd trusted the wrong man and resentful of

her own daughter because I reminded her of her mistake.

"Daisy." Again, that unfamiliar deep tenor bled into his voice, drawing my gaze back to his.

His stare raked over my face, drawing goosebumps to my skin because, for a second, it was the only thing that felt warm.

"I had no idea," he continued in that low, unbroken tone. "I swear to you, Daisy. I had no idea he was going to do this."

I saw the pain that ravaged his face, a mirror for the wreckage in my chest. Maybe he hadn't known, but then why had he been so absent the last five months? Ever since Todd had told him about the baby, about getting married, Max had been distant.

"Hold on," Max growled. I wasn't sure I'd ever heard that sound from him before. Releasing me, he yanked open the door and called into the hall. "Lou!"

I rose and went to the window, like I could see where Todd had gone, like I could spot him on the horizon and direct someone to go get him. My runaway groom.

The whirring brought a wave of nausea this time. This couldn't be happening. We were going to have a baby. I'd pulled out of school. Moved out of my apartment a week ago. Moved my stuff into a house Todd's parents had gifted us. We were going to work through this. We were going to get married and figure everything out. We were—

"Hey, what's up?"

I turned to the gentle-eyed innkeeper, who'd graciously allowed us to plan a wedding here that was now falling apart.

"I'm going back to get Todd. Can you stay—"

"Todd's gone." There was no hiding it, no point in hiding it.

"What? Where?" Lou pushed up her glasses and looked to Max. "Why?"

"Todd...he sent Daisy a note saying he wasn't coming," Max replied gruffly. "I'm sure it's just cold feet. He wasn't feeling well this morning. I just...I need to talk to him."

He wasn't feeling well? I didn't know whether I wanted to laugh or scream. I was the one who was pregnant. I was the one who'd tried to be gentle with Todd since we found out about the baby. I was the one who'd given him plenty of outs when his drinking seemed to get worse, when he was the one more likely to be found nauseous in the morning than I was. He was the one who insisted he wanted this—wanted marriage. Who wanted me to drop out of my program. To move into one of his parents' numerous homes.

At every turn, I asked if this was what he wanted or what his parents wanted. Maybe I was to blame for believing his answer. Now, I felt like a fool for not seeing what was right in front of me. The drinking. The distance. Spending so much time with his friends. With Max. With Scott.

"Don't you ever depend on a man, Daisy. Ever."

As intensely as devastation had come over me, anger swept through and took its place.

"I'm coming with you."

Max's eyes bulged. "Daze—"

"He's my fiancé. I'm not—" I let out a weak laugh. "I'm not letting you go alone, Max." My hands went to my stomach. This wasn't about the wedding. I didn't care about the wedding. I cared about our daughter. "It's not just me he's choosing to walk away from."

Max's mouth drew firm, turmoil charring his irises from green to mossy gold. "All right."

I moved between them into the hallway, my eyes averted. I needed to get outside. I needed fresh air.

"Daze," Max called after me, but I kept moving, the vise around my throat so tight I felt like I was being held underwater.

I made it to the front walkway, gulping in the warm, sea salt air, when Max finally caught up.

"Daisy."

I spun, finding Max right in front of me. He was gorgeous when he was frustrated and now sexy when his expression was stern. After four years, I already knew there was no emotion that didn't look good on this man. *This was just the first time I'd let myself admit it.*

"You need shoes."

I looked down, my bare toes peeking out from under my dress...and my stomach. In a few more weeks, I wouldn't be able to see them at all.

"Oh." I shook my head, thinking if Cinderella were missing her prince, that glass slipper would be the least of her problems too. "My sandals—"

Max lifted up my pair of purple slides in one hand. "Lou pointed me in the right direction."

"Thank you." This time it wasn't my voice that raised an octave, but my heart as Max went down on one knee in front of me.

For a single moment, time didn't just stop. It rewound back five and a half months.

"Well, I guess we're going to get married." There

was no proposal. No knee. And the ring had only come later. An heirloom provided by Mrs. McCormick.

I blinked, returning to the present and Max as he gently lifted one of my feet, brushed the dirt off the bottom, and then placed it in my sandal. By the time he repeated the motion with my other foot, I managed to coax my tongue into working again.

"Thank you," I said, and Max looked up, our eyes locking.

"I don't think there's anything my brother wouldn't do for you." Harper's words hadn't struck me as much earlier, but now, I felt them carry a whole different kind of weight.

"Of course." Max straightened and brushed the dust from his knee. "Now we can go," he said, leading me to his truck and holding open the passenger side door for me.

We rode in silence to Stonebar Harbor, and the only thought I had on the drive was, *had Todd planned on doing this all along?* Was that why he wanted to stay at a hotel here rather than the Lamplight Inn? Was the whole "it's bad luck to see the bride the night before the wedding" a lie? An excuse?

"Daze." I flinched at the gentle touch to my elbow, knowing later I'd feel guilty for recoiling from the man who was only trying to help me.

"Sorry," I murmured, blinking several times to focus.

One minute, I was in the passenger seat of Max's truck. The next, I was here, at the door to Todd's hotel room. Somehow, my brain had stopped processing everything between the truck and here.

"I'm going to step outside and call his parents," Max said, unable to mask his lack of optimism.

I nodded, listening for the sound of the door as it closed. My eyes swept through the room again.

Todd wasn't here. What was worse, it looked like he'd never been here at all.

The bed was still made like he hadn't slept in it. There were no clothes in the closet. No sign of his suit. No shoes. No bag. No toiletries. Everything was in its place.

The only trace he'd left was the contents in the bathroom trash can. The empty little bottles of alcohol.

"No answer," Max announced when he returned.

"Maybe he went back to their house?" I suggested, as though that wasn't the last place he would go. As though it wasn't because of them that Todd had insisted on getting married when, deep down, it truly wasn't what he wanted.

I might be angry and upset, but his parents...they would proverbially want his head for this. *For causing this scandal.*

Max shook his head. "I called there. Mrs. Abagail said Todd's not there, but she'll let me know if he shows up."

Mrs. Abagail had been their housekeeper from the time Todd was a toddler. She saw his struggles like the rest of us. I trusted that she was telling the truth.

"He was never going to come," I said softly, brushing my fingers along the comforter.

Max exhaled roughly. I could tell he wanted to agree, but was too much of a gentleman—too loyal a friend to throw Todd under the bus.

"Daze..."

"He didn't leave in a hurry. He didn't get cold feet and run." I motioned weakly to the room. "He never planned on staying."

When I turned back to Max, the crease in his brow deepened. He couldn't argue. He knew I was right.

"Let me take you back to the inn. Maybe he'll be there when we get back. Maybe he just needed a little more time."

I closed my eyes and let my sigh bleed through my lips. "We both know he didn't." I stroked my fingers over my stomach, all of my worries settling on the tiny, growing human in my stomach.

How could he do this to her? Even if she wasn't planned, even if he was more anxious than excited, how could he walk away from his responsibility to her?

"I'm going to find him, Daze. I'm going to fix this," Max promised low as I did one last sweep of the room like I expected to find my groom hiding under the bed or behind the shower curtain.

I shuddered at the soft command of his words, feeling my heart stumble as it slowed down.

Shaking my head, my eyes closed, and I felt the first unwelcome tear slide free.

"You can't fix this, Max. You can't fix him," I said thickly, feeling a ripple of my anger reach in his direction.

Max grunted, and then I heard it—the buzz of his phone.

Hope squeezed my chest as he swiped and answered, "Hello?"

Breathe. *Just breathe.*

"Shit."

I sucked in a painful breath, and Max glanced at me, saying, "I'll call you back in ten."

"Who was it? Did they find Todd?"

"No, Daze. It was my operations manager, Erica. One of my drivers no-showed today, and we've got a full schedule of deliveries…" He grimaced as he trailed off. "Sorry, it's not your problem. I'll figure it out once we get back to the inn."

Not Todd. Not about Todd.

Todd was gone.

Once more, time seemed to hop and skip forward like it didn't want to land too long on any moment of this traumatic day. Max helped me into his truck, and then a few blinks later, we were pulling to a stop by the lampposts out front of the historic inn.

Lou came outside as Max parked, looking hopeful until she realized it was still only the two of us.

The knot in my throat turned raw from all my attempts to swallow.

"I'll be in in a minute," Max said. "I just have to touch base with Erica and figure out what we're going to do about the local deliveries for today."

"Do you need to take them?"

His head snapped up, and he quickly answered, "No," but I knew if it weren't for me, for Todd and our wedding, he would. Max was one of those business owners where there was no task that was beneath him. "I'll find someone to handle it. I should've known Tucker was going to flake," he grunted. "He's missed four days in the last three weeks, and I kept covering…"

He kept giving him the benefit of the doubt. Enabling him. Just like he'd done for Todd.

I looked back at the inn and Lou waiting in the doorway, her pity both understandable and suffocating.

Suddenly, the inn was the last place I wanted to be. Not with the decorations. The flowers. The dress. The plans. *And now my almost in-laws*.

A familiar BMW with tinted windows pulled up behind Max's truck.

"Can you handle it?" I asked, desperation clawing at my voice.

"What?" Max's brow creased.

"Can you tell her you'll deliver them?"

Max used to do all the deliveries back when Maine-Stems was just getting off the ground. I would ride along in his passenger seat, just like I was now, except I'd be studying between Max's stops. Driving helped me think. Helped me process. That was why I'd go along for the ride.

Todd never did deliveries. He'd say it was because his job was to schmooze his parents' rich friends for investment money, which it was, but the deliveries usually started early. If Todd had been out the night before, he never wanted to wake up.

It was actually Todd's suggestion that I ride along with Max. *Ironically*. Not because he remembered how much I enjoyed going for drives, but because it obscured how many mornings he woke up hungover. That was before it became impossible to hide.

"I could, but I'm not going to. I'm not leaving you. Not until—"

"I want to go with you," I blurted out. "I want to take the deliveries with you."

He stared at me like I'd grown a second—well, technically, third head. And in turn, my stare darted back to the darkly dressed couple getting out of the grossly expensive car, who stuck out like stuck-up thumbs in this small town.

"I can't go back in there right now, Max." Honesty was brutal but necessary. "Everything's set up for the wedding—a wedding that obviously isn't going to happen. And I can't...I won't just sit in there hoping my fiancé decides to change his mind and come back for me and his child, all the while being judged by his parents because I'm sure, in their mind, this is somehow my fault."

"What did you do? What did you say to him? How could you let this happen?"

"You're carrying his baby. Of course, if he left, it has to be something you did."

I could hear them now because I'd heard them countless times before. The way they treated Todd when something didn't go right. The things they said about me, even when they knew I could hear them.

They wanted us to get married because of the baby, but that was about all they wanted from me.

They didn't like the idea of their son's fiancée, the mother of their grandchild, working as a bartender at a local restaurant in Portland or going to school at night for my master's in chemistry. They didn't like the *appearance* of my keeping an apartment by the school, as though Todd's home—their property—wasn't good enough for me.

It was all a twisted game of smoke and mirrors, and I hated that doing what was best for my baby and our future could be so easily conflated with acqui-escing to the wants of people who were so heartless. People who only cared about money and image and power, and who sought to control their son's life at every turn.

Anger sank its hooks into the hollows of my sadness, and it was the only thing that kept me from caving in on myself.

"Daze, I don't think that's a good idea," Max rumbled, his knuckles white on the steering wheel.

"Please." I hated to beg, but I hated it less than the thought of walking back into the place where I was supposed to be getting married right now. "I can't just sit here and wait for Todd to decide to show up and have his parents blame all of this on me." A tear dripped onto my tightly locked hands. "Please get me away from here."

When I looked at Max again, he wasn't staring at the steering wheel in turmoil or even looking at me with concern. His gaze was trained on the single splatter of wet on my hand. He looked like he would willing amputate a limb to make the tear disappear.

"All right," he agreed roughly. "Let me just talk to them, tell them what happened, and tell Lou where you'll be so no one sends out a second search party."

Max got out, and before he could talk to Lou, he was accosted by Todd's parents. I assumed he must've left them a voicemail when he called them at the hotel, so they had an idea of what was going on. They started arguing. Not loudly. Never loudly. But I knew what their presentable arguments looked like—like snakes hissing and snapping at one another. Deadly but not loud. After a few minutes, and with no one else to levy the blame, they both returned to their car, cell phones pinned to their ears. I wouldn't be surprised if the NSA was searching for Todd by the end of the day.

Max's conversation with Lou was much shorter and contained a small intermission when she darted inside, returning not even a minute later with a small, white paper bag that she gave to Max before waving to me.

"Pastries," Max said, handing me the bag as he climbed back into his truck. "In case you get hungry."

What about you? I wanted to ask, but I already knew the answer. There wouldn't be a single moment of this day when Max Hamilton stopped to think about himself or what he needed, only me.

As he pulled away from the curb, I lacked the strength to fight off the irony that the only man who'd gone down on his knees for me, who took care of me, and who put me first on my wedding day was my fiancé's best friend.

CHAPTER 4
MAX

"Let them know I'm on my way and that we're going to refund them 50 percent of their order as well as extend a 50 percent discount on their next order with us," I said, practically able to hear Erica's frown through the line.

Erica O'Connell was my right-hand woman. Once MaineStems was funded and could start hiring some support staff, Erica had been one of the first to join the company. She'd gone from customer sales and service to order and fulfillment manager and finally, after I bought Todd out, to my operations manager. We were still a start-up, small by many standards, but one day, when we were big enough, she'd become my COO.

Erica made sure my big ideas were grounded in what was reasonable and feasible. She was thinking right now that a 50 percent discount meant we wouldn't break even on these orders. She didn't say anything because she knew I didn't care. It was the right thing to do, considering three of the ten deliveries in the

Stonebar area were going to be over two hours late getting to their destinations.

"All right," she answered. "I'll send you the delivery list."

"Great. I'm just picking up the van now."

"You sure you remember how to do this?" she joked.

"Driving? Or unpacking flowers?" I grunted, my eyes darting to the passenger seat. *Or spending an extended period of time alone with Daisy and not giving away how much I wanted her?*

"All of the above."

I gritted my teeth. "I think I've got it covered."

"All right, boss. Let me know if there's anything else you need."

"Thanks," I said low, feeling like the word wasn't enough.

If I'd asked her to, Erica would've gone out and done the deliveries herself, and that was my plan. My only option. Until the woman next to me, littering croissant crumbs all over her wedding dress, begged me to get her away from her wedding.

I turned onto the drive to the warehouse. The large packing and shipping buildings sat at the very front of the property I'd purchased from Lou's mom, my Aunt Ailene, just over a year ago. This part of her farm abutted my dad's land, and both had been supplying her jam business for many years until they outgrew the parcel and bought more acreage inland. She'd sold a chunk of it to me at a substantial discount, though she'd never admit to it.

"Wow," Daisy murmured when the buildings came into view.

Behind the distribution warehouses were three

large greenhouses, and behind those, but not visible from the drive, were acres of flower fields. It wasn't quite the tulip fields of Holland, but damn if it wasn't close.

"I didn't realize you had...that MaineStems had all this." Her wide eyes roamed over the buildings again, and a shot of pride went through me. She hadn't seen this expansion. Todd was long out of the business by then, so there was no reason. *No reason other than a purely selfish one.* "I remember the days when you'd haggle with local growers to buy all the different blooms."

"Yeah."

I'd haggle for a bulk price, and when it came time to pick up the product, only half of what I'd purchased looked good enough to be considered deliverable to customers. One time, Daisy was riding with me, and she jumped in and had it out with one of the worst offenders. Almost three-quarters of the flowers I'd picked up were wilted, and all he was going to offer me was a credit for a future purchase. I wasn't going to argue—or burn bridges. Daisy had a different idea.

"I still can't believe you went in and threw that guy under the bus with his mom," I made a low sound, my head shaking unconsciously at the memory.

That particular seller was second generation in the family flower farm, and his mom just happened to be at their shop that day. Daisy had grabbed handfuls of the crushed flowers and found the older woman inside.

"Are these the kind of flowers you'd want your son to bring you? These sad, wilted wallflowers? Because this is what your son sold us. What he's telling us is acceptable to give to someone you love."

By the time we left, he'd replaced all the flowers with fresh, crisp ones and still gave me a credit for a future purchase.

The smallest smile poked at her lips. "He deserved it."

Those days felt like eons ago, though it had to be only two or three years ago.

I pulled up to the closest warehouse and parked. The mid-morning sun skipped over the aluminum siding as I went around and opened Daisy's door, offering her my hand. My truck wasn't lifted, but it was the largest Ford you could get, and just a little too high for someone as short as Daze.

I gritted my teeth as her small fingers slid into mine, a familiar rush of ache flooding my veins, then chased away by the cold course of anger. *What the hell were you thinking, Todd?*

And how did I not see it coming?

For every ounce of fury I felt toward him, it was a hundredfold toward myself. I'd been there this morning. I'd seen the state he was in, heard how torn up he sounded, and still, never in a million years had I thought he wouldn't show up to the wedding. Never had it crossed my mind that he was so low he'd abandon Daisy and his daughter.

Countless times, I'd saved his ass when his parents' money and position weren't enough. Countless times, I'd helped him make up for the stupid shit he'd put Daisy through. Countless times, I'd done it because she loved him, and I wanted him to be better for her.

And then he went and did this. Disappeared on their wedding day.

All the excuses I wanted to make for him—for what

he was going through—were nothing compared to the way I wanted to strangle him for the pain he'd caused. For the future he'd decimated with this incredible woman and their child.

"Thanks," Daisy looked up at me and smiled.

It wasn't that full-bloom smile. I didn't expect that. But it was an honest one. A grateful one. And one that had a tiny dab of chocolate attached to the corner of her mouth from the croissant she'd been nibbling on.

"Hold on," I murmured when she turned her head away.

I cupped her cheek, watching her lips part on a swift inhale. "Max—"

"You have some chocolate," I explained as I wiped my thumb over the spot. It got some but not all of it, and without thinking, I brought my thumb, along with the Daisy-infused chocolate, to my tongue.

Later, I'd tell myself she had time to stop it—to stop me. Time to pull away and clean it herself. But she didn't. She froze, pink blushing in her cheeks as I dabbed the rest of the chocolate away.

This was all I'd ever had with Daisy. These moments that I stole for myself from my best friend's fiancée.

I dropped my hand to my side like that would change the consequence of touching her. For the rest of the day, my fingers would burn from the touch of her skin.

"They packed the van up last night, so it should be ready to go," I said tightly and led the way into the building.

"It's still crazy to me that you used to do this in your truck," Daisy said as I navigated the Maine-Stems delivery van onto the road.

She didn't have to say it. I could tell she didn't want to talk about Todd or the wedding or anything about today. She wanted to escape, and I didn't blame her.

Hell, if I were her, I'd have gone to the nearest liquor store and purchased the largest bottle of alcohol I could find and escaped right into it. Obviously, pregnancy took that option off the table for her, though I doubted she would've chosen it even if there was no baby. Daisy had never been a big drinker. Sometimes, I wondered if she was always like that or if Todd's relationship with alcohol made her that way. God knew it certainly had shaped me.

The last time—the only time—I had the urge to drink was the night Todd told me Daisy was pregnant. He'd already drunk half the bottle of Tito's by the time he made it to my apartment in Stonebar. He'd been spiraling. Pacing and panicking that he wasn't ready to be a father. That his parents hadn't approved of Daisy. That they were going to kill him for knocking her up.

As I stood there and listened, all I wanted to do was knock him out for being such a damn idiot. For not seeing how fucking lucky he was to have Daisy by his side. To know that she wanted to have a baby, a family with him. *For not seeing that his nightmare was my dream.*

Before I did something stupid, I forced two bottles of water into him and told him in no uncertain terms that he needed to grow up. He needed to stop taking Daisy for granted because she was the very best person in his life and would do far more for him than his parents ever would. And then I drove him back to Portland, told him to make this right, and kicked him out of my car.

It was a good thing I'd dumped out the rest of the vodka before we left. Otherwise, I would've finished my friend's bottle.

"You and me both," I admitted. "I think when I saw those first two vans right after we had them wrapped, that was when it finally hit me that this was real. That my business—my dream—was real."

I felt Daisy look at me, but my eyes kept to the road.

"It was real before that."

My mouth kicked up on one side. "I guess it didn't feel that way when I was delivering flowers out of one of my dad's old farm trucks."

"I think when you want something for so long, it's easier to pretend it's not real than it is to accept you have something to lose."

My foot hit the brake just a little too hard for the approaching stop sign, and I mumbled an apology, sliding my gaze to her. She stared out the window, her bottom lip pulled between her teeth, the pink skin blanched white.

My hand locked on the wheel. "Daze—"

"Where's our first stop?" she asked with a hitch in her voice.

I hesitated for a second, but now wasn't the time to probe. Not with what she was going through. *Fucking hell, Todd.* I roughly grabbed my phone from the cupholder and scanned the directions on the screen. "Beach house just north of Stonebar." I hit my blinker, phone still in hand.

"Here. Let me." Daisy made a *gimme* motion with her fingers. "I can give you directions."

The phone could speak them to me too, I thought, but quickly realized she wanted the task—a distraction from the day that had thrown her life into chaos.

"All right. Where to?"

"Turn left here, and then in four miles, make another left onto Pine Road."

CHAPTER 5
MAX

"Wow." Daisy's eyes bugged at the cedar-planked mansion perched at the end of the long drive.

The house—with its sprawling grounds, tennis court, and separate six-car garage—overlooked a particularly scenic part of the coastal bluff. On a clear day like today, not only could you see the harbor in town, but also the wink of the lighthouse in Friendship.

"Yeah," I murmured, holding back that Todd's parents' seaside home further toward Portland was at least twice the size. If the owners of this house were even half as stuck up as the McCormicks, I was about to get my ass reamed out for this delivery being over three hours late.

I parked the van next to the line of three Mercedes sedans sitting out front and unclipped my seat belt. "I'll be right back."

"I'll come with you."

My hand froze on the doorknob. "You don't have to do that, Daze. I'll just be—"

"It'll be harder for them to give a pregnant woman a hard time about a late delivery."

My eyes narrowed. *She had a point.* "Okay."

Once more, I rounded the front of the vehicle to open her door and help her out. It was the third time this morning I'd held her hand, and while I'd long been branded by the bolt of heat from her touch, there was no preparing for the ache that slammed into the center of my chest every time I had to let her go.

I didn't know what was worse—not wanting to let go or knowing I shouldn't be touching her, however briefly, in the first place. She was technically still my best friend's fiancée. However, technically, reasonably, rationally, literally, figuratively...whichever way you cut it, Daisy Turner was never mine.

I released her fingers and rubbed my own on the fabric of my suit pants. At this rate, by the end of the day, I was certain that amputation would be the only way to forget the soft feel of Daisy's fingers on mine.

"Just give me a minute," I said, walking quickly to the back of the van before she could insist on carrying some of the boxes for me. *Like hell I'd agree to letting her do that.*

I wrenched open the back of the van, the packages organized in order of delivery in case someone had to fill in who wasn't a regular driver—*a lifesaver right now*. Three massive boxes, the largest for our custom bouquets, were marked for *Shelton*. I stretched for the first and immediately heard the firecracker pop of a seam splitting open.

Shit.

I yanked my arms out of my suit jacket, completely forgetting I was in formal wear. The jacket sailed over the stacks of boxes and landed deep in the van while I made fast work of removing my tie, and then unbuttoning my collar and rolling up my sleeves. My shirt still protested when I attempted to pick up the large, heavy box again. *On second thought, maybe I should've comped the entire order.* There was a decent chance I was going to rip through or sweat through this shirt and be delivering bouquets bare-chested before the day was through. While there might be a market for that kind of flower delivery service, it wasn't the market I was catering to.

"*Mistakes don't break you, Max. They give you room to build.*"

My grandmother had a way with words, though Gigi was usually more known for her uncanny fortune-telling rather than her good advice. Her *premonition preserves*, as they were known to our family, were infamous for revealing a clue to a future love and delivered by way of a scribbled label on a Stonebar Farms jam jar.

At least, that was what had happened for all four of my cousins—Lou, her twin sister, Frankie, and their two older brothers, Jamie and Kit.

I was going to be the one to break Gigi's matchmaking streak. She'd given me a premonition jar years ago, and I knew with absolute certainty it wasn't going to lead to love. How? Because it had already led me to heartbreak.

Gravel skidded under my feet, my train of thought derailing when I reached the side of the van. *Where was Daisy?* I spun in both directions, searching. I was halfway to calling her name when I spotted her.

Daisy stood at the home's front door, speaking to a

woman who was, based on her attire, the owner of the home.

I charged toward them, my pulse thudding wildly. If this woman was rude to Daisy—if she gave her a hard time because of my employee's fuck up—forget a discount. I'd comp this order and then never service this woman again.

I hardly felt the cumbersome weight of the box in my arms as I ate up the distance separating me from them.

"Oh, my. I can't believe you came all the way out here. This is—" The woman stopped when she saw me approach, her heavily mascaraed lashes widening.

I could only spare her a glance before all of my attention locked on Daisy. Did she look distressed? Flushed? Upset? After everything this morning, if someone so much as looked at her wrong—

"Max, this is Mrs. Shelton. Mrs. Shelton, this is Max Hamilton, the CEO of MaineStems," Daisy murmured, flashing an apologetic smile at me for not waiting.

"Mr. Hamilton."

I looked back at the middle-aged woman, who was manicured as nicely as her lawn. "Mrs. Shelton, I want to personally apologize for the delay this morning. I take full responsibility for the mishap, and I greatly appreciate your patience."

Her gaze raked me up and down.

Thankfully, I'd been friends with Todd long enough to have grown calloused to the scrutiny of the kind of people who ran in his family's circles. Todd wasn't like that. He was a lot of things—a lot of unfortunate things—but he wasn't a snob. Maybe it was because we were friends, or maybe it was just a miracle, but somehow he managed to be cocooned in an elitist world but not molt into that persona.

"Well, I can't say I'm not severely displeased by the delay. However, given that you've postponed your own nuptials to personally ensure my flowers still arrived in time for my dinner party, I'm inclined to look past it."

Postponed...my own...

"Please, you can place them in here." Her heels clicked off into the distance as I turned and stared at Daisy.

Her eyes weren't as wide as mine.

She let her think...

"Daze," I hissed under my breath.

"It doesn't matter right now, Max. Just go along with it," she muttered back and strode inside.

Go along with pretending this was our wedding day.

Goddammit.

Biting hard into the side of my tongue, I hefted the box higher, buried my protest deeper, and followed Daisy. Mrs. Shelton directed me to her dining room, the table long enough to easily seat twenty, though I didn't count the exact number of chairs.

Carefully depositing the box on the floor, I peeled off the tape and unpackaged her arrangement, unable to hold back a smile of pride when I saw the bright, full blooms. All healthy. All perfect. All grown in our greenhouses.

"On the table?" I confirmed, waiting for her nod before lifting the flowers by their vase.

This wasn't your average arrangement. Our largest option was close to twenty-five pounds of a dozen varieties of flowers, prearranged in a thirty-inch crystal vase that required two hands to hold. It wasn't to suggest a sentiment but to make a statement, and damn, did it do exactly that in the middle of her dining table.

I stepped back to admire the final product when Mrs. Shelton's voice bounced off the room's high ceilings.

"So when are you due, dear?"

"Just after Thanksgiving."

"Oh, lovely. What a wonderful time to welcome in a new addition. You and Mr. Hamilton must be so excited."

Like magnets colliding, my stare crashed into Daisy's, and all my muscles tensed. I wondered what she was thinking, if she was imagining how I would've reacted to news about her pregnancy if we were married—if her baby were mine. Maybe that would explain the bright red splotching her cheeks.

Or maybe it was simply embarrassment that she'd encouraged Mrs. Shelton's assumption to go this far and couldn't turn back now. That would better explain why her head jerked away.

"Yes, we are," she answered and turned her back to me.

I was sorely tempted to interrupt and claim I needed Daze's help at the van, but what kind of man needed help from a pregnant woman on her wedding day?

Locking my jaw, I gathered up the garbage and headed back outside. The best thing I could do for Daisy right now was get this delivery over with as quickly as possible.

By the time we walked out of the house, sweat sheened my brow, and my chest heaved. For anyone considering working out in formal wear, zero out of ten, do not recommend.

Somehow, miraculously, Daisy had steered the conversation toward Mrs. Shelton's dinner party plans, and the woman, like most people in her position, was only too happy to talk about herself. I'd like to think I was happy to have saved the customer relationship since, as we were leaving, Mrs. Shelton swore she was going to be ordering more arrangements this coming week, but the relief was heavily mitigated by what the delivery had cost me.

"I'm sorry," I said as soon as I started the van and cranked on the AC. Ridiculous since it was fall, but cool wasn't cold enough right now.

"Don't apologize. I asked to go with you. I went up to the door first."

And you let her think it was our wedding day, but I kept that to myself as I started to pull down the drive.

"I know, but I should've thought..." That her pregnancy wasn't the only thing one would notice about Daisy today.

"It's really fine," Daisy said, though her flushed cheeks told a different story. "When she saw you coming over, she just assumed that you...that we..."

Were getting married.

"Yeah." My voice cracked, the thought burning

through my chest like it had dipped my broken heart in vinegar. Clearing my throat, I continued, "You were right, though. It was better not to correct her given the circumstances."

"It was nice, you know. To have a fiancé for a few minutes who hadn't jilted me on our wedding day."

"Still no word?" I asked because nothing else I had to say about her real fiancé would've helped the situation.

She checked her phone, and what killed me wasn't the blank screen but how she desperately tried to hide the ripple of pain it sent through her. Like every time she checked, it ripped the wound back open.

Goddammit, Todd. Where are you? What the hell are you doing?

"I'm going to fix this, Daze."

"It's not yours to fix," she said. "You're not responsible for him, Max."

But I was. I was responsible when it came to her. I should've seen the signs. I never should've left him alone in the hotel this morning.

If you hadn't, you would've resigned Daisy to marrying a man who wanted to abandon her, a small voice in the darkest corner of my mind whispered.

I shifted in my seat, torn between two equally unwelcome outcomes: Daisy, alone and heartbroken, or Daisy, tied to a man who didn't deserve her.

"Can I tell you something?" she asked after a few minutes of silence.

My hand braced on the steering wheel. "Anything."

"I promise I'm not crazy, but when I woke up this morning, I just...knew I wasn't getting married today." She stared out the window as she spoke. "I don't know what it was, but I woke up, pulled open the curtains, saw the bright red sunrise on the horizon, and I just knew."

The poignant calm in her voice gutted me, like deep down, she wasn't fucking shocked at all to have been abandoned.

It made me want to rip out my own beating but arguably broken heart and give it to her. It made me want to confess with every fiber of my being that I was in love with her. That I'd been in love with her for years. That I thought she was smart and incredible and *most beautiful*, and deserving of someone so much better than Todd. I didn't even care if that man wasn't me. I just cared that whoever he was realized just how fucking lucky he was to have the opportunity to make her happy. To make her smile.

"Daze..."

"It reminded me of that saying your sister mentioned at one of Todd's parents' garden parties. Red sky at night, sailor's delight. Red sky in the morning, sailor's warning," she repeated the phrase Harper picked up from Kit, who lived—who *used to* live—in the keep of the Friendship lighthouse.

My teeth clenched, locking my foolish confession behind my lips and leaving me with, "You're not crazy."

"No, just hormonal," she returned with a sigh. "Where to next?"

"I thought you were my navigation?" I nodded to my phone. "Erica texted me a list of the delivery addresses."

Eager to return to her task, she grabbed my cell from the cupholder. "Got it." A few taps on the screen and she had the directions up. "Looks like the next address is closer to Portland, so at the end of the driveway, turn right."

When we reached the road, I caught Daisy slipping her feet out of her sandals and pulling her legs up onto the seat. Her dress bunched up her legs, but before I could look away, I saw her shiver.

"Sorry. We can turn the AC down." Her hand on mine stopped me from adjusting the thermostat. Unfortunately, the delivery van wasn't as electronically sophisticated as my truck, which allowed for dual temperature settings.

"No, I'm fine. You're the one getting a workout in today," she insisted, and I had to be imagining the slide of her gaze along my forearm. "Where did you put your jacket?"

"In..." My voice splintered. *What if I hadn't been imagining it?* "In the back."

She looked over her shoulder and found my discarded suit jacket a moment later. Even pregnant, when she wrapped it around her shoulders, it swallowed her whole. *And the sight undid me.*

The thing with fantasies was that as soon as you gave them an inch, they took a mile. I saw Daisy wearing my jacket, but I imagined her covered with me. My fingerprints. My mouth. My tongue. My cum.

"There. All better."

Maybe for her. My cock, on the other hand, couldn't be any more uncomfortable than if she'd stripped naked rather than covered herself with another layer.

I moved in my seat, adjusting myself twice before the pressure on my dick was bearable.

"How long?" I croaked.

"You're on this for about thirteen miles," she

confirmed and then clicked off my phone, replacing it in the cupholder and reaching for the bag of pastries.

"We can stop and pick up some lunch in Portland," I suggested, watching her pull out one of Ella's famous *nazooks* from the depths of the bag Lou had sent with us. Nazooks were a rolled Armenian pastry and a customer favorite at Ella's pastry shop in Stonebar Harbor, The Pastry Queen.

"No, I'd rather just eat these." Daisy licked her lips, and my dick jolted.

"Are you sure?" I ground out. She shouldn't survive all afternoon on sweets.

"They're good for the soul."

Well, the noises she made eating them while wearing my jacket were definitely very bad for mine. At this rate, the flowers left in the back of the van could be laid on my grave because the chance of my surviving a whole day like this *with her* was less than the chance of her runaway groom returning.

IT WASN'T UNTIL ALMOST SEVEN BY THE TIME I pulled the van back into the warehouse.

We'd finished the remaining dozen deliveries with no further confusion or conversation about who Daisy was getting married to—or who she should've been getting married to today. Instead, I let Daisy guide any conversation, which invariably ended on MaineStems and me and my family—anything that wasn't about Todd—and it seemed to help. Or had until now.

We were back in my truck, and I'd glanced over to confirm her seatbelt was on before driving away, and I watched her whole demeanor change. She looked just like she had on the way to the hotel this morning, an expression of quiet panic paling her face.

"You okay?"

"Yeah." She tried to smile, and that made the lie even worse.

For the last six hours, Daisy had been able to avoid the reality I was returning her to. And as I drove toward the inn, I couldn't help but feel like I was bringing her back to the scene of a crime. One still covered in blood and laced up with caution tape. One where she was supposed to get married, but instead had been betrayed by the man she planned on spending forever with.

But what choice did I have? Take her home with me?

No. I almost laughed out loud at the stupidity of that thought. *Not a chance.*

Not a fucking option.

We rode in silence for the next fifteen minutes. Even though we were squarely in the beginning of the fall months, the longer daylight of summer still clung to the edges of the sky, dipping them in a bright orange-red. *Red sky at night is a sailor's delight.* I glanced at Daisy, wondering if she was thinking how wrong the proverb was this time.

"What happens tomorrow?" she asked, her voice sounding just as she looked—impossibly small in a shroud of darkness.

Tomorrow, I would upturn every stone looking for Todd.

"I mean for the deliveries," she clarified, and my sudden anger drained.

"Not sure yet," I answered honestly. "I'm going to touch base with Erica after I drop you off and see what we can figure out."

It might involve me driving another day or two until we could split up the deliveries to other routes or until we found a replacement, but if that's what it took, then I'd do it. My business was my baby. There was no position or job in it that I hadn't done myself and wouldn't do again if needed.

"Todd's not coming back," she said softly when we crossed into Friendship, the old-world lampposts welcoming with their nostalgic glow.

She was so sure when she said it, my knuckles whitened on the steering wheel. "He will, Daisy. He'd never...completely leave you. The both of you," I said, like I could make it true, like I would make it true.

He would come back. Eventually. And when he did, I would make sure he made this right, no matter what it cost—no matter what bridges it burned.

Daisy's head dipped, and then her eyes closed, and she yawned, covering her mouth with the back of her hand bundled in my sleeve.

"I just want to go to sleep and forget this day ever happened."

I pressed gently on the brake, wanting to slow these last moments until I could find the right words to say.

"Let's just give it a few days. You know how he is. Sometimes, he just needs a little time to get his head right," I said hoarsely. "I already talked to Lou. The room at the inn is still yours for the week."

Whether she agreed or was too drained to argue, I

couldn't tell, but she curled deeper into the seat, almost disappearing underneath my jacket.

The candles in the front windows of the inn flickered as I parked out front, and Daisy was half asleep by the time I opened the passenger door. Still, as soon as she got out, she surprised me by starting to take off my jacket.

"Keep it," I ordered roughly. To have it back...to have the memory of her in it...*No, it was hers now*.

Inside, the inn was quiet. Lou had blocked off all the rooms for the wedding. Now, the privacy felt more like the solitude of a grave.

Hearing us enter, Lou appeared from the kitchen in the back, her smile tentative and her eyes luminous with empathy. Harper trailed behind her, probably covering the overnight shift at the reception desk. Before opening her apiary, Harper worked odd jobs for our whole family. Now, she helped out at the inn every once in a while for some extra money and just on the overnight shift, so she didn't lose any time on her farm during the day.

"Lou..." Daisy stopped and slowly looked around.

All the flowers and decor were taken down, leaving no trace of the wedding that was supposed to happen earlier today. *Just like I'd asked her to do earlier*.

"Hi, Daisy," Harper greeted Daisy with a hug.

"Hey, Harp."

My sister didn't say anything else. She didn't need to. There were no words for this kind of situation, especially something as insufficient as *I'm sorry*.

"Lou...all the flowers..." Daisy looked to the living room where the ceremony was planned to be, now bearing no trace of the wedding that should've happened there.

"I didn't want you to come back to that," my cousin replied softly, taking Daisy's hand and squeezing it. "Don't worry. We spent the day repurposing them all over the inn, so they weren't...wasted."

Daisy's head bobbed, her throat taking a few tries before it worked out the word, "Good."

"Are you hungry? I have some pot pie warmed that I can bring up to your room if you want," Lou offered and glanced to me. "You too, Max."

"I'm fine. I should get going, but we didn't stop for food on the way back, so Daisy should probably eat something."

Daisy's shoulders slumped, but she nodded. "Thank you."

Lou went to get the food, and Harper lingered for an extra minute, looking at me strangely before following her out.

"I'll check in with you tomorrow," I said once they were out of earshot.

"Can I come with you?" Daisy blurted. "If you're going on deliveries again, I mean."

My jaw went slack. *No. Not a good idea.*

But the words wouldn't come out.

My mouth opened and then shut. It wouldn't refuse her. I couldn't refuse her. Not when the same panic from earlier fringed her stare. *Not when I felt my own guilt like acid in my lungs.*

Todd was Todd. He'd always been shit at responsibility and reckless with his selfishness, but I'd been the one to prop him up like some kind of straw man for years because I'd wanted him to be better for Daisy. If

I'd just let him crash and burn that first night...if I hadn't sobered him up and told him what to say and how to apologize and make it right. If I hadn't helped him so fucking much, Daisy wouldn't be living this nightmare right now.

If I hadn't tried to make him better, it wouldn't have made his betrayal so much worse.

"Okay," I heard my guilt agree. *My dark, selfish desire to be around her, cheering me on.*

"The driving, it..." she trailed off, her brow knotting.

"Calms the mind," I finished, because she'd told me a dozen times how it settled her, helped her think straight.

Daisy nodded and hugged herself, panic subsiding from her profile. I should've left then, but I couldn't take my eyes off her. So much so, it felt like time stopped for a second just to let me stare.

My best friend's fiancée stood in her wedding dress, pregnant with his baby, but wearing my suit jacket. *A sign that I would take care of her no matter who she thought she belonged to.*

And I would take care of her. Whether Todd came back or not, Daisy would know there was one man who would never turn his back on her, even if her heart belonged to another.

"I'll call you in the morning."

"Max." Daisy reached for my arm, her touch a thousand times worse now that her hand was warm on my bare skin.

My eyes settled on her face, and just for a second, I let them linger. The waves of her hair had softened over the course of the day, wisping gently against her skin. Her makeup was all but scrubbed off, leaving only her natural flush to her cheeks. Even after everything that happened, even in the middle of heartbreak, she still looked heart-stoppingly beautiful. She always would to me.

"Thank you. For everything today," she said, and the blade of guilt shoved deeper in my chest.

"Don't thank me, Daze," I said roughly, and before I could stop it, a fragment of the truth slipped out. "You know there's nothing I wouldn't do for you." *A truth she already knew*.

Something dark pooled in the depths of her pupils. Something I was tempted to describe as longing, though that couldn't be right.

No, I was losing it. All day with her—wanting to take care of her, to treat her how she deserved, *wanting her*—I needed some fucking distance.

With a muttered good night, I turned and left before I did something even more awkward. More foolish. *More unrequited*.

She might know what I'd do for her as a friend, as Todd's best friend. What she didn't know was just how deep that promise went...and how much pain I'd cause my own heart to keep it.

CHAPTER 6
DAISY

I was right. Todd wasn't coming back.

I lowered my arm and let the curtain flutter closed. For the last four days, I stood at the window morning and night. In the morning, until Max pulled up in his truck to pick me up, and at night as he left the inn and drove off. I didn't stop believing that Todd would magically appear on his knees, begging my forgiveness, on the front lawn. I never started.

The moment I read that note, I knew it was over. I knew he was gone. The following four days without any message from Todd or his parents only buried the betrayal deeper. Four days of absorbing the looks—the well-intentioned pity from Lou and Wade, from Harper, from Lou's other siblings, Frankie, Kit, and Jamie, who'd all stopped by the Lamplight Inn at one point or another to offer their help.

Four days of coming to terms with my deepest, darkest secret—the only pain I felt from Todd's disappearance, the only heartbreak I feared, was for our daughter.

Absentmindedly, I rested my hand on my stomach like I could shield her from ever knowing her father had turned his back on her. I wondered if this was how my mom felt about me. I was two when my father left us, too young to remember anything, but not too young for the trauma to root itself deep inside me and shape how I'd grown.

Things hadn't been good between Todd and me for some time. Before the baby happened, I didn't think we would...it didn't matter what I thought. I got pregnant, and suddenly she was the only thing that mattered.

I looked down at my tote bag sitting on the desk chair in the room, my white dress carelessly stuffed into it and billowing out like tissue paper from the top. I didn't even know why I was taking it with me. No, I did know why. Because I didn't want to forget my mistake. The one I'd sworn I was too smart, too careful to make. I'd let myself become reliant on a man who'd left me. Just like my mom had warned me would happen.

There was a time when I'd imagined getting married and having kids with Todd. A time when I enjoyed his easy, carefree lifestyle. When we'd met, I'd never experienced that kind of life before. The whirlwind of it all. Being raised by a single mom, all I knew was how to pull my own weight and make sure I never relied on anyone to do it for me.

But eventually the shine of Todd's appeal wore off, leaving only his kind but spoiled core. I liked him. I cared about him. But if we hadn't gotten pregnant, I wouldn't have stayed with him, let alone wanted to marry him.

Part of me thought even my mom knew it was a mistake. She only knew him briefly before she passed, but her reaction to our relationship was guarded. More guarded than usual. Maybe it was a blessing that she hadn't lived to see what happened. The pregnancy. The engagement. *The betrayal.*

I could hear her now. *"You do what you have to do to survive without the help of anyone. You hear me, Daisy?"*

I bit my lip hard, strangling back the urge to break down and cry. It wouldn't do any good. I couldn't afford to be broken right now.

Picking up the mason jar from the small desk, I uncapped the lid and let a whiff of the scent stretch its fingers to my nose.

Peony.

Lou looked at me like I'd lost my mind, in addition to my groom, when I came downstairs that first morning and asked her for a bottle of the strongest vodka they had and a mason jar. *Not to drink,* I spelled out, *but for the flowers.*

It was a good idea, a thoughtful idea for her to put the peonies from my bouquet in a vase in my room, but I couldn't stand their reminder. Todd had left, and I was a fool. A fool who'd given up so much for a man I wasn't even truly sad to lose. I didn't need any more reminders, but neither did I want to throw the beautiful flowers away. So I started a small chemistry project to transform them...and to pass the time.

Fresh flower petals in high-alcohol-content vodka extracted their scent and produced perfume. So I filled the mason jar with vodka and plucked the stems clean, drowning every petaled reminder—*he loved me not*—into the liquid.

I'd started with one jar until Lou and then Harper

learned what I was doing, and brought me half a dozen more.

I blew out a slow breath and capped the jar again. It would be at least another week before the perfume was ready to be strained. That part was easy. I could tell Lou how to do it. I wasn't thinking when I started this that I wouldn't be able to take them with me.

Every night after I closed the curtain, while I showered and got ready for bed, I planned my next steps. I had to. I knew Todd wasn't coming back.

I couldn't stay here, no matter how kindly Lou offered. It was already too much that she'd let me stay this whole week *and* had loaned me some of her twin sister's maternity clothes. All of my things, except the handful of outfits I'd brought to the inn for our honeymoon week we were supposed to spend here, were in barely unpacked boxes at the house outside of Portland that Todd's parents had given us to move into. I couldn't go back there. Even if they'd wanted their grandchild there, I didn't want to be there. I didn't want to be around them.

Pulling out my phone, I opened up Uber and typed in my old address in Portland.

I needed my own space to get my life onto some kind of track. I had enough money saved for one month's rent if my old landlord would give me my apartment back. That was my Plan A. It had only been two weeks since I'd moved out, and he hadn't found a new renter, last I knew. Hopefully, that was still the case when I showed up there today.

My phone vibrated, the app matching me with a car. *Arriving in ten minutes.*

I gave another glance out the window, looking for

Max's truck. I didn't know why. Max wasn't coming here today.

I'd told him last night I wanted to skip going out on deliveries today. That I didn't feel up to it. It wasn't a complete lie. I didn't feel up to arguing with him—with his chivalry, to be exact. Just like I knew Todd wasn't coming back, I also knew Max wouldn't hear of me trying to get my old apartment in Portland back.

I picked up my soft duffel bag and tote and headed downstairs.

By now, he would be pulling away from The Pastry Queen in Stonebar and driving us to the warehouse. I'd be devouring one of Ella's blueberry scones while examining the list of deliveries we would make and planning out our driving route.

My chest squeezed like a pricked balloon trying to hold on to all its air. I couldn't hide in the comfort of Max's world forever. I had to face the reality of my own, and the sooner I did that, the better.

"Morning, Daisy," Harper greeted me with a smile, her blonde hair braided back as she sat with the largest cup of coffee known to man at the reception desk.

I quickly covered my grimace with a smile. "Hey, Harp."

Max's younger sister was my only hurdle. She'd been working overnight at the reception desk all week, so I expected to see her this morning. As long as I navigated the conversation carefully, maybe she wouldn't alert Max to my plans.

"How are you feeling? Max said you were staying back today?" She spun her stool and tucked her hands into the pockets of her oversized denim dress.

Not just today. My throat tightened, but I nodded.

"Harper? Oh! There she is." An old woman with bright purple hair poked her head out from the kitchen, and seeing me, moseyed her hunched form over to us.

She moved slowly, giving me a chance to take in the whole picture of her. Over her clothes, she wore a polka-dot apron that looked to have more stains on it than patterned dots. Dark purple. Bright red. They covered the front like a piece of abstract art.

"Gigi, this is Daisy. Daisy, this is my grandmother, Gigi." It was only a matter of time before I met the Hamilton-Kinkade family matriarch. She was as much of a staple in Friendship as the historic inn, the towering lighthouse, and Stonebar Farms.

"Daisy." Gigi stuck out her hand, her knuckles knobby and her skin soft. Even with thick glasses, she still squinted at me. "Wonderful to finally meet you."

"Nice to meet you, too."

"I've heard a lot about you." She smiled, adding another set of well-worn wrinkles to her face.

"Oh." I flushed. The last thing I wanted to do was talk about my runaway husband with someone I hardly knew.

"You've been helping out my grandson this week." Her head tipped as relief swept through me. Relief that quickly deflated when I detected pity in her next words. "You should come by the house for family dinner and bring Max with you. That boy works too much."

If there was one envy Todd and I both shared, it was the way Max's family was knitted together in a kind of unbroken seam. No matter how it stretched or strained, they were always there for one another, always held fast to family. Something neither Todd nor I had ever experienced. Something I foolishly thought we could build together.

"I'll tell him," was all I could offer. I wouldn't be around to do anything more. Even if I were, I wouldn't go. The best way to not want something you couldn't have was to not put it right in front of you.

Gigi grinned, her eyes almost comically large behind her glasses. "I'll see you soon," she declared and hugged me without hesitation before returning to the kitchen.

"She's making up some jars of Stonebar Farms jam as small welcome gifts for guests," Harper started to explain her presence—and fruit-stained apron—when her eyes snagged on my bag. "Wait. Where are you going?"

I looked up and realized Harper had just noticed my bag. "Back to Portland. I can't live at the inn forever," I said, aiming for a breezy tone to my voice, but not sure it quite made it.

"But Portland?" She wasn't buying it. "Does Max know?"

"He knows I can't stay at the inn forever." My phone vibrated in my hand. My driver was two minutes away. "My ride is almost here. Please tell Lou thank you for everything, and I'll send back the clothes as soon as I get new ones."

I backed toward the door as I spoke and then slipped through it as soon as I was done. Having a place to stay was first on the list. Getting some clothes would be next.

"Daisy?"

Crap.

"Hey, Lou," I said, watching her wide eyes scan over me.

"Where are you going?"

Apparently, I couldn't even get jilted without having to do a walk of shame.

"I just told Harper...I'm heading back to Portland for right now until I figure things out." I hiked my bag higher on my shoulder.

Her warm eyes rounded. "I told Max you were welcome to stay here as long as you need—"

"I don't need a place to stay, Lou," I insisted, softening my tone when I saw how my outburst hurt her. I didn't mean to be harsh, but I needed to be firm. "I'm so grateful you've let me stay this week to...let the storm pass, but I can't just live at your inn, as wonderful as it is. I need to figure out what I'm going to do and find something long-term for me and the baby."

Leaving the inn wasn't just for practical reasons. It was for emotional survival. Somewhere over the last few days, this place had come to symbolize everything I'd hoped—a wedding, a family, a man who would keep his promise to support me. And staying was like clinging to an inner tube in the middle of a hurricane. There was no hope left for that life. I needed to start on a new one, and in order to do that, I needed to leave.

Lou swallowed hard. "If you're sure."

If it were Frankie I was speaking to, she would've protested. But Lou didn't like to push, especially someone who was trying to strike out on her own. While we were planning the wedding, she'd shared with me how she'd pursued her dream to own the inn and every hurdle she'd overcome to make it happen on her own.

"I need to figure this out on my own," I said, the words as much of a benefit to myself as they were for her.

I couldn't rely on anyone. I knew that—*I'd known that.* I'd forgotten it for a blip when the baby was involved, and I decided to give Todd a chance, to give him the benefit of my doubt for every effort he'd put into the wedding. But it was a mistake. Now, I couldn't think of all the hurdles I had to sort out. I had to take this one day—one problem—at a time.

First, a place to live.

My phone buzzed twice just as a dark blue Toyota pulled up to the curb. "Oh, I think my ride is here." I pulled her in for a hug. "Thank you for everything, Lou."

"If there's anything you need..." She didn't need to say the rest. I knew. I knew I could count on her the same way I knew I could count on Max, and that was the exact reason I refused to. I was grateful for everything they'd already done. I wouldn't ask for more.

"Daisy?" The driver confirmed when I opened the door.

"Yes, thank you." Tires screeched, and I jerked my head up to see Max's white truck veer in front of the car, effectively blocking it in the spot.

What—

A door slammed, and then I saw him. He looked furious but ruggedly gorgeous in a pair of worn jeans and a soft flannel, stalking around his truck toward me. This was the Max I was used to seeing. The one I'd ride shotgun with in the early days of MaineStems. The one who let Todd deal with suits and stuck-up investors, and opted instead for the cozy gentleman who just wanted to bring people flowers.

"Hey, man—"

"Daze, what are you doing?" Max ignored the Uber driver and came over to me, stopping just on the other side of the open car door.

Me? What was he doing? How did he—I caught Harper in my periphery as she appeared at the entrance to the inn, phone in hand. *That was how.*

I lifted my chin. "I'm going back to my apartment in the city."

Letting Max Hamilton play my knight in steadfast armor these last four days was my second-worst mistake after agreeing to marry Todd McCormick. Max had an insatiable need to help everyone around him, just like I had an insatiable need not to be helped.

"You don't have the lease anymore."

"I'm going to get it back."

His jaw flexed like the muscles were laying down roots. "You can't."

"Of course, I can. I'm sure Mike didn't rent it again so soon—"

"I meant you can't go back and stay in the city by yourself."

"You mean like I used to?" I demanded, irritation clawing at the edges of my voice.

"Excuse me, do you need the ride—"

"Yes—"

"*No!*"

Max grabbed the edge of the door, looking like he might rip it from its hinges the way one would tear a Band-Aid off skin.

"You can't go back to Portland alone, Daze. Not now. Not with the baby."

"What am I supposed to do? Live here at your cousin's inn and twiddle my thumbs until either the baby comes or her father does?" I choked out a laugh of disbelief. At this moment, I wasn't sure I'd ever let Todd back into her life. Not until she was old enough to fully understand what she risked losing by doing so. "That's not me, Max. You know that. I can take care of myself. I will take care of myself and the baby. I'll get my apartment back. My old job back."

"Bartending? On your feet all day?" He rounded the door like a lion stalking his prey.

Max was rarely this...intense. This demanding. Even when people tried to take advantage of him, of his business, he was still placating. The only time I saw him like this...was this week. *Protecting me.*

I stepped back, the thought more of an assault than his closeness or his earthy-mint scent that buried into my nostrils.

"It's not forever. It's for right now. For survival," I argued. "It's doing what I have to do to get by—"

"Look, I can't wait around—" The driver's interruption was truncated when Max shut the car door. I hadn't even noticed I'd moved far enough for him to be able to do so.

"Then go," Max snarled.

The driver didn't need to be told twice. A second later, the engine revved, and he started K-turning his way out of the spot.

"Max," I pleaded, hating the weakness in my voice, hating how my reserves of strength had been so depleted.

Why was he even here right now? He shouldn't be. He shouldn't be worried about me. I wasn't his responsibility. *But if I were...*Goosebumps trickled through my veins.

He moved closer. "You need a job? Fine. You can work at MaineStems," Max said, his low voice rumbling as he towered over me. For some reason, it didn't feel imposing but instead like a shelter from the storm.

"Doing what? Delivering flowers?" I shook my head. *How was I even considering this?* "I can't. I won't take a handout. I don't need one."

"It's not a handout," he insisted harshly. "You know I need a driver. You've been riding with me all week. I'm not making up the fact that I'm short-staffed."

I bit into my cheek. *Well, that much was true.* And the driving was easy, and it settled my mind. And Max was a good boss. Working for him would be a better situation than bartending into all hours of the night. I gripped my bag tighter. Was I really going to consider this?

It wasn't just the job I needed.

"No," I heard myself say. "My apartment is in Portland—"

"There's an apartment above the MaineStems storefront in Stonebar. You can live there. It's safe. Convenient. And I'll take the rent from your pay." He added that last for my benefit, knowing I'd refuse a handout.

My brows pinched, arming myself with skepticism. "Who lives there now?"

"No one," he answered smoothly. "I've rented it to several employees before who needed time to get their bearings. It's why I have it."

I stared at him, lost myself for several seconds in the

warm moss of his eyes. There was something about his offer that pricked at me, like a thorn on the stem of a rose. There was something he wasn't telling me, but at this point, how much of a difference would it make? I had to rely on someone's charity right now, whether it was Max's or my old landlord or last boss to take me back, knowing I'd be going out on maternity leave in a few months.

I rolled my bottom lip through my teeth, considering. *Rationalizing.* It was a steady job. A place to live. Even if it was temporary. Everything about my life was temporary right now. I just needed something temporarily stable, and this...this was so tempting, I thought as my gaze slid down the pulsing cords of his neck to the stretch of his broad shoulders and the hard planes of his chest.

The offer wasn't the only thing that was tempting, my hormones whispered, like some kind of little devil on my shoulder.

Swallowing, I ducked my head to the side and then turned my steady, attraction-absent gaze up to his. "It's just temporary."

Every angle of his body sharpened. I hadn't even technically agreed to his offer, but he saw I was going to, and somehow that made my acceptance feel that much more vulnerable.

Max lowered his chin, saying nothing.

"And as soon as I figure out where the baby and I are going to go, you'll have to find someone else."

"Understood," he said, already removing my bag from my shoulder. I stood a little taller without the weight, thinking there was a metaphor somewhere in there to unpack.

"One last thing," I said, waiting for Max to stop and meet my eyes. "I need you to tell me you're not doing this because you feel responsible."

Beggars couldn't be choosers, but I needed to hear the words. His help, a handout—I could manage my resentment toward either of those things. What I couldn't handle was being Max's guilt trip.

My ex-fiancé's best friend dropped his head for a second before looking up at me with pure anguish. "I'm not doing this for Todd or because of Todd, Daze." His lips tightened. "I'm not thinking about Todd at all right now."

Suddenly, I felt the soft weight of a blush on my cheeks and a strange, warm buzz trickle through my veins.

"Okay," I murmured. "Then I accept your offer."

Just temporarily.

A temporary job. A temporary home. A temporary connection to the man who stayed when the boy I was going to marry fled. And then I would move on, independent and alone and without the forbidden attraction I'd harbored for Max Hamilton from the very first day we met. Before I knew he was my boyfriend's best friend...and then in spite of it.

It wasn't ideal, but I was no longer a girl with options. I was a pregnant woman whose only concern was her baby. So I broke my own rule of not putting myself in front of temptation and followed Max Hamilton back to his truck. He was the best thing for my daughter's future, in spite of what he risked for mine.

CHAPTER 7
MAX

Her duffel suitcase didn't feel very heavy as I pulled it from the backseat. I guess I must've missed the lightness of it against the heavy weight of my anger, realizing Daisy was planning on leaving. On going back to Portland. Without telling me.

My hand tightened on the bag's handle.

I hadn't thought twice when she'd asked for a day off from deliveries. She had ridden shotgun every day, including and since her wedding day. At some point, reality was going to catch up to her. At some point, she was going to grieve Todd's leaving.

Meanwhile, I was long past grieving. I was steeping steadily in fury at the man I'd considered one of my best friends. One of my childhood friends. At one point, my business partner.

I switched her suitcase into my other hand and then grabbed her tote, the remains of her wedding dress wilting from the top of the bag.

"When did you open this again?" Daisy asked softly.

Nudging my truck door shut, I turned and caught her staring at the floral facade of the MaineStems store in the heart of Stonebar Harbor. Its forest green exterior is broken by a bright yellow door smashed between the two front windows, their displays whimsically filled with our summer bouquet options.

"A year ago?" I said, trying to recall exactly when. I'd bought it, but the old colonial-aged building needed a lot of work, so by the time the storefront actually opened...I'd bought it before Todd told me Daisy was pregnant. Everything after was somewhat of a blur.

She nodded slowly, walking up to one of the windows. "I remember Todd mentioning something..." Her attention settled on the displays.

Our flower arrangements changed with the season, and periodically throughout the season, depending on what was available or if there was a holiday we created limited editions for. It was one of our selling points. *Not your same old, ordinary bouquet of roses.*

Every arrangement was handcrafted, every flower chosen for color and quality. I wanted to give customers something intentional, not easy. Something remarkable, not just acceptable for the last minute.

That was all MaineStems started as. Exclusive floral arrangements, on demand. But like most things that are watered well, the business grew. It grew from an idea and my dad's truck to the farm and my house, to a warehouse and shipping building, to a storefront in town, to an expansion down to Boston.

"Do you need—do you want me to go up to the house and get more of your clothes?" I offered, reaching for the door.

They'd moved all of Daisy's things from her apartment to one of Todd's family's homes two weeks ago. I knew because it was the excuse Todd gave for why he couldn't go wedding cake tasting and asked me to go for him—one more thing he'd left to the very last minute because nothing was last minute when you could pay enough to make it happen. But because it was last minute, Daisy had doctor's appointments that day, and Todd was moving her things, I was the only option left.

So he said.

Except Todd hadn't been moving shit. He'd hired movers and then spent the day out golfing with Scott—his reluctant confession coming when I noticed his sunburn the next day.

"What's the big deal, Max? It's just cake. Chocolate, vanilla, who cares?"

His fiancée did. Daisy didn't like chocolate, and vanilla made her nauseous, so I'd picked the blueberries and cream. I wanted to be angry with him then, too, but all I could think was Daisy would've been worse off if he had been the one to go. If he had picked vanilla without caring and resigned her to puking all over her wedding cake.

Daisy came over as I opened the door to the shop. "No," she said, breathing deep the floral wave of scent that ebbed free. "There's nothing that will fit me there."

Sure, she could be talking about her clothes. Even in just the span of a few days, I'd seen the slight changes continuing to shape her body. But I could tell that wasn't the only thing on her mind.

"Are you sure? It's easy for me to go." There was no reason for her to face a future that no longer existed. To walk into the house, missing the husband who it belonged to.

"No, it's fine. I'll be fine." *Wrong answer.*

She tried to take her tote from my shoulder, but I angled myself, keeping it away from her grasping hands.

"Do you want to go out and get some clothes?"

Her head snapped up. "No, it's fine. What I have—"

My gaze narrowed on her, now recognizing the boldly colored outfit as belonging to my cousin. "Then why are you wearing some of Frankie's maternity clothes?"

Her throat bobbed, working up an answer. "Because Lou brought them over, and I didn't want to seem ungrateful for not wearing them."

Not the whole truth, but it was all I was going to get, as Daisy walked through the honey-yellow door.

Inside, the shop was designed to look like a bookstore. Display tables filled the room, the walls lined with rising shelves. Every surface was covered in flowers. Bouquets. Single blooms. Books on various species. Framed photographs of our previous arrangements. It was all Erica. Well, not all of it, but most of it, and I was happy to give credit where credit was due.

"Oh, Max." The brunette rose from behind the desk at the very back of the room. "Is everything okay? I didn't realize you were coming in..." She trailed off when she saw Daisy. My head was immediately visible above some of her taller arrangements, but Daisy was too short to be seen until she was close. "Daisy, hi."

Of course, Erica knew what had happened with Todd, with the wedding. I had to explain how I could suddenly cover for our missing delivery driver on the day my best friend was supposed to tie the knot. We didn't talk much about it besides the basic facts. Erica knew when it came to Daisy, there were certain questions that were off-limits.

"Hey, Erica."

The women embraced.

"It's really good to see you again. You look great. How are you feeling?"

"Mostly good. Still getting some nausea in the mornings, but driving...doing the deliveries with Max has been helping," Daisy said, her palms absentmindedly rubbing the sides of her growing stomach.

Between my cousins, there were enough new babies in the Hamilton-Kinkade clan for me to know that every pregnancy was different. As Frankie said, "Some bellies were early poppers, and some were late." *Early* and *late* didn't mean much to me, but what I did see was Daisy changing every day. Her stomach rounding out. Her clothes—or whoever's clothes—pulling tighter across her chest. The glow of her skin. Even the little things seemed fuller. The swells of her cheeks. The deepness of her breaths. I noticed everything about her. *Always had*.

Which was what made it so fucking painful to watch her choose Todd when he noticed nothing.

"Oh, that's great. When are you due again?"

"December 12th."

"Oh, a winter baby. That's so exciting. I'm so happy for you," Erica gushed with so much excitement, it was almost easy to forget the *you* she was happy for was singular. That Daisy was now treading down the path of single parenthood. "Max mentioned you know you're having a girl. Do you have a name picked out yet?"

Erica was great at conversation, at making people feel comfortable and getting them to open up, and at reading between the lines when they didn't. As her boss, that skill was a double-edged sword. It worked just as well on customers as it did on me. She was about the only person who knew that it wasn't for work-related reasons I'd kept my distance from Daisy over the last six months. There was no business, let alone rational reason, that I was too busy to go up to Portland and visit the happy couple, yet I'd had time in my schedule to pick up the slack on their wedding planning.

"You were the one who suggested the inn. Who suggested a show. Daisy said she was fine with the court-house." That was what our conversations always devolved to—Todd blaming my being involved on myself. Because I'd insisted that the mother of his child deserved better.

The real reason I couldn't complain? I'd buried the knife in my own chest and then chose to keep twisting it. By helping him. By making excuses for him. *By making up for him.* I wanted Daisy to be happy more than I wanted her to not be with Todd.

"Not yet," Daisy replied, her smile falling.

"My parents already have names picked out. What's the point in talking about other ones?"

Another argument. Another disappointment. Another hour spent trying to draw him out of his...resig-nation...when it came to his parents. To the baby. It was the same fruitless discussion when he didn't understand why she wanted to look at things for the nursery.

"It's so far away. Why look at stuff now? She hasn't even been to the house yet. How does she know what can fit in the room?"

How did I explain to someone for whom there was no negative concept of last minute why some people liked to plan ahead—why Daisy, the child of a single mom who worked multiple jobs to support them, who had to work as soon as she was old enough, who had to allot every penny, every second, and every emotion of her life because she couldn't afford otherwise, would take comfort in being prepared for the birth of their daughter.

"Her name is McCormick. That's all that matters, right?"

I cleared my throat and unclenched my fists before one of them realized.

"Daisy's going to be helping us out for a little while with deliveries, so I'm having her stay in the apartment," I said firmly, not having had the chance to warn Erica about the change of plans.

"The apartment? But aren't you—" At my sharp stare, Erica snapped her mouth shut and quickly recovered. "That's perfect." She carefully—purposely—avoided my gaze now. "Well, then I guess I'll be seeing you around more often."

"Yeah."

I went around Daisy and led the way to the bookcase in the back corner of the room, shifting all her bags to one hand.

"Where are we—" Daisy stopped as soon as I pulled the bookcase off the wall, the Murphy door opening to a staircase leading to the second floor. "Did you really...a hidden door?" she asked, an almost childlike expression of excitement on her face as I moved aside so she could go up first.

When I'd asked my cousin, Jamie, to put in the hidden door for me, I told him it was because I thought it would be cool, and I always wanted one. It wasn't the whole truth. I wanted one since the day I'd met Daisy at the Bean Bar. When I'd approached her, the book she was reading was *The Lion, the Witch, and the Wardrobe*.

"It's not a wardrobe, but welcome to Narnia."

OKAY, IT WASN'T NARNIA UP HERE, BUT IT WAS A nice apartment.

The main floor was open with a galley-style kitchen at the back, the only full bath tucked off to the side, and a dining table and cozy living space settled against the tall front windows that overlooked Stonebar Harbor. It was to the windows that Daisy went first.

My gut clenched. There were reasons I hadn't brought her to the shop—reasons I protected this space as my own—and they were all wholly selfish. The fewer parts of my life Daisy touched, the better. The easier it would be for me to finally forget her.

So much for that. My plan was eviscerated by the gorgeous woman standing at my front windows, where anyone walking by would think she was mine. *She and her baby*. But they weren't. The only thing that was mine was the pain of wishing it were true.

"I'll clean up some of this stuff over the next couple of days. I've been using it...as a workspace," I said when her attention finally shifted back to the apartment.

There were papers, folders, my laptop, photographs, and magazines spread all over the couch and coffee table. Along the wall, boxes of my stuff sat unpacked from my house.

"Bedroom's up here," I said just when her brows started to pull together, questions starting to string between them. *What were the boxes for? Where did they come from? Was I sure no one was staying here?*

Her gaze followed me as I climbed the spiral staircase up to the lofted bedroom, the wrought-iron stretching into a metal railing that overlooked the main floor. The metal trembled under my footsteps and then Daisy's as she followed me to the loft. I held my teeth locked, hoping she would've stayed downstairs and waited to explore until I left.

"Bathroom was the door straight ahead when we walked in," I said, trying to keep my back to her when she reached the loft.

The space was small, only fitting a queen bed, a nightstand, and a five-drawer dresser for clothes.

I guessed there was a silver lining to my sleeping on the couch these last couple of nights. The bedding was clean and freshly made, hopefully adding to the impression I wanted her to have: that no one was staying here.

I set her bags on top of the navy-blue duvet, again bothered by their weight and the conversation from earlier.

"Are you sure you have enough clothes? That you don't want to go out and get anything?" I asked again.

"Yes." She turned and gripped the railing.

"Don't lie to me, Daze," I charged, my voice low. "Because this feels pretty light, and I just want to make sure you have everything you need."

"No, Max," she said and whipped toward me, anger shimmering in her sudden tears. "I don't have everything I need. I don't have anything I need. I don't have a fiancé. I don't have a home. I don't have—" She broke off, her full pink lips turning down in a bitter laugh as she came over and stopped next to me. "You want the truth? The truth is that I packed mostly lingerie because I was supposed to be on a honey-baby moon right now." With an angry yank, she ripped open the zipper and dumped the contents of the duffel onto the bed. Whites and pale pinks and purples tumbled onto the duvet, the satin and lace pooling like hydrangea petals on the dark cover.

A jolt of anger went through me, and then it was suffocated by a blanket of lust.

My mouth felt like a cave of sand, everything suddenly painfully dry as I stared at the pile of delicate fabrics, imagining them against the pale of her skin. Stretched over the fullness of her breasts. Puckered at her hard nipples. Soft over her growing stomach.

There was no stopping the tension stringing through my muscles. The uptick of my pulse. The hardening of my cock. Reality was dipping its toes dangerously close to the deep end of my fantasies, and I wasn't adequately—hell, I wasn't even *in*adequately prepared.

"I'm sorry, Max." She reached for my arm, jarring me, and not in a good way, from my thoughts. Her left hand rested on my biceps. She was close to me now. Too close. "It's not you. You've been...so amazing." *Then why did she make it sound like that was a bad thing?* "I'm just overwhelmed, and I need time. Time to figure out everything all over again." Her big, luminous eyes melted into mine. "And I need you to stop treating me like I'm glass," she murmured. "I can't afford to be broken right now."

"You're not broken, Daze," I said, my voice tangled between lust and loathing.

Shaking her head, I felt her pull her hand away, but it didn't draw my attention until she placed it on her stomach. Then I saw it—her engagement ring still anchored around her finger like a giant beacon of hope. She said she knew Todd wasn't coming back, but she still wore his ring. She still...*belonged*...to him.

"I'll let you get settled," I said and stepped back, my skin still burning under my shirt from her touch. "I'm going to give Erica a rundown of what you'll be doing, and then when you're ready, she can go over the details with you as far as routes for the upcoming days."

"I can start—"

"Tomorrow," I finished firmly. "You'll start tomorrow. Today is...orientation." I defined this single day off in a way she'd be able to accept it.

"Okay." Her head lowered, and her shoulders slumped. She looked like she just wanted to sag against something—against someone—and let them take all the weight from her for just a few minutes.

I wanted to be that someone.

I almost reached for her. Almost drew her to my chest, the words, *"It's going to be all right, I promise,"* perched at the tip of my tongue, along with all the other ones I'd buried for years.

He never deserved you.

You're the most beautiful woman I've ever seen.

You're not broken.

You're going to be an incredible mother.

You're so strong.

I've been in love with you all this time.

But then she folded her arms. It wasn't the subtle

barrier that made me step back, but the glare of the cool fall sun reflecting off her engagement ring that spurred my retreat.

Idiot.

Guilt hammered in my gut.

Daisy was having the worst week of her life. Her fiancé had left her basically at the altar, pregnant with his child, with no explanation. No place to live. No... nothing. And all I could think about was wanting to have her in my arms and if she'd accept my comfort. If she'd want it. If she'd feel even a little of what I felt for her.

I cleared the knot of selfishness from my throat and walked back to the spiral steps. "If you need anything, just text or call me. If not, I'll see you tomorrow."

Forty minutes later, I was sitting at the counter in Dad's kitchen, taking a can of cold seltzer from his hand.

"So what brings you out here?"

I popped the cap. "I was wondering if I could stay here for a little while?"

His brows rose, an audible response in the case of George Hamilton, but when I didn't reply right away, he spelled out what I already knew was going through his mind.

"You have a house, an apartment, and you want to stay here?" He set his can down. "You know you're always welcome, but can't say I'm not confused."

I took a deep breath. There was no point in hiding the situation from him. He'd find out sooner or later. "I still have the house up for sale, so I don't want to interfere with the showings or whatever Aria has planned, and the apartment...Daisy is staying at the apartment. Temporarily."

"Daisy? Harp said she was staying at the inn."

"She was." I took a swig of the prickly water. "But she doesn't want to impose...and I don't want her going back to that apartment in Portland. Not with the baby..."

I trailed off as bare footsteps slapped on the wood floor. My younger brother, Nox, appeared from the hall.

"Well, look who finally woke up," Dad drawled with a chuckle as Nox dragged a hand through the mess of his sandy-brown hair and then stopped when he saw me.

"What are you doing here?"

"Nice to see you too." I shook my head and gulped down another mouthful of water, wishing it were something a little stronger.

"Apparently, your brother is moving back in with us," Dad declared, making Nox stop again on his way to the coffee machine.

"Seriously?" Nox blinked twice, probably wondering if he was still dreaming.

I hadn't lived at home since I left for college a dozen years ago. It wasn't that I didn't love Dad's house or being around my siblings, but I'd always wanted my own space. To me, it was part of becoming the person I wanted to be. The guy with the big ideas. The entrepreneur. I was the weird kid who was thinking about the legacy I'd leave behind when I was eighteen.

It was that part of me that admired Daisy so much because I got the same sense of determination from her. On the one hand, it made me wonder what drew her to Todd in the first place, but that was the pot calling the kettle black because I was drawn to Todd too, for probably similar reasons. He was fun. Personable. He didn't worry about the future because he'd never had to. He was the kind of person you just felt like you could let go with, and it would all be okay. And it would be...until it wasn't. His kind of life was really attractive and shiny at first. It drew you in, thinking it was some kind of gem. Only once you were in the thick of it did you realize it was nothing more than a spotlight in a hall of mirrors.

"Seriously." I nodded.

"What happened to the apartment?"

My hand tightened on the can. "Daisy is staying there." Period. End of story.

Nox's brows rose. "*Daisy* Daisy?"

My chin lowered again, feeling his question like a noose around my neck.

"Well, all right then, *old sport*," he said, shaking his head, and I caught the distinct bump of his shoulders in amused disbelief as he continued toward the coffee machine. "Welcome back to West Egg."

Old sport. West Egg. I didn't miss his allusions to Fitzgerald's famous Jay Gatsby...another self-made man whose greatness was rooted in his unrequited pursuit of a woman. *Another Daisy.*

"Don't you have to go blow something?" I grumbled at my brother's back, hearing the coffee machine wake back up.

Only two years younger than me, Nox and I couldn't have been more opposite. I was an early bird, he a night owl. I was reserved. He was outgoing. I was type A. He was type fly-by-the-seat-of-your-pants. While I'd always known I wanted to start some kind of business on my own, Nox had been content to work with Dad and Aunt Ailene at Stonebar Farms or help Jamie deliver his custom furniture or pick up other manual labor jobs in town. Until a year ago, when he suddenly decided he wanted to learn glassblowing and make his own glassware.

Even for someone flying by the seat of his pants, the decision seemed a little out of left field. Especially because he decided he was going to learn glassmaking from the famed artisans in Murano, an island just off the coast of Venice. He had his ticket, and by the end of the week, he was on a plane.

"Looks like the next couple of weeks are going to be fun with the two of you here," Dad drawled, crunching his empty can in his fist. "Maybe I should see if Harp will let me sleep on her couch."

Dad's property originally belonged to two farmers. He purchased one parcel and then the second a few years later, when he and Aunt Ailene needed more growing capacity. Because the pieces used to be separate, there were two residences on the combined grounds—this house, and a much smaller cottage that Harp commandeered when her hobbyist beehives turned into a full-fledged apiary. The cottage was older and nestled well into the fifty-acre property, but she enjoyed the solitude. She got her social fix helping Lou out at the inn.

"I don't know about you, but I'll crash in the barn if Max gets too lovesick and weepy," Nox said.

Nox worked out of one of the barns nearby. The building used to be used for the manufacturing and preservation process for Stonebar's jams, but when they outgrew this property and moved to a much newer plant on several thousand acres inland, the barns—and the fields—sat empty. I'd commandeered the fields, and Nox had taken one to transform into his glassmaking shop.

I flipped him the bird, muttering, "Dick," as he took his coffee and walked out of the kitchen.

"You sure this is a good idea, Max?" Dad asked, drawing my attention back to him. Unlike my brother, there was only concern in his voice.

"No, but I don't have another one."

"Well, you're always welcome here as long as you want," he said, patting my shoulder. "Have you heard anything from him?"

I shook my head. "No." *Nothing*.

In spite of my anger, it hadn't stopped me from reaching out to him every day. Multiple times during the day. But there was no response. No trace. I checked with his parents—torn between hiring a private investigator to find him and not wanting word to get out that their son had done something shameful.

Dad let out a heavy sigh and muttered, "Never ends well."

"What does?"

"When you hide how you feel."

Somehow, I knew he wasn't just talking about Todd.

My favorite book was *The Lion, the Witch, and the Wardrobe*. I must've checked out *The Chronicles of Narnia* a dozen times, if not more, during high school. I guessed it was what you'd call my comfort read. My escape.

I couldn't remember if I'd ever told Max that, but of course, he knew. *Or remembered.* He was the kind of person who heard my offhand comment about liking sparkling water more than still, so he always made sure there was a bottle of sparkling in his truck every morning. The kind of person who noticed how I'd go for drives before big exams to steady my mind, and offered for me to ride along on deliveries with him because it was safer than driving around alone. Or saw me carry a book one time—mentioned it was a favorite one time—and welcomed me into my temporary home with the reference because he knew it would make it easier.

Max didn't just notice the little things. He noticed and never forgot them.

"When I like something, I want to learn everything about it."

Unlike Todd. Maybe it wasn't all that terrible to wish Todd had been more like Max, but it probably was a little terrible to wish that more than once over the last four years.

"Do you do weddings?"

I looked over my shoulder, finding Erica first and then the customer who'd asked her the question.

"Not officially yet, but soon. If you're subscribed to our newsletter, you'll get the announcement," came her reply.

"That would be wonderful. My daughter's wedding is next year, and your arrangements are always so exquisite. I know you'd do an excellent job for her."

Weddings. Arrangements. Pain blanched my chest, and I quickly moved farther along the wall. My gaze leapfrogged over the titles of vintage books on flower species and an encyclopedia on botany until I reached the display windows at the front of the store, where I couldn't hear them.

After I'd stuffed all my lingerie *back* into my duffel and explored the apartment, I not so casually waited until I saw Max's truck pull away from the curb before returning downstairs to the flower shop to chat with Erica.

Sure enough, she was prepared for me at Max's instruction and had started reviewing delivery protocols with me when that customer walked in. Apologizing, she'd gone to speak to them and take their order— summer bouquets to be delivered to their condo every Sunday for the rest of the month. It was being rented as a VRBO, and they wanted fresh flowers for the arrival of new guests. *And now something about weddings.*

I pressed my nose into a cotton candy-colored bouquet of garden roses and mini carnations, drowning my riot of emotions in their scent. *It would make a perfect perfume.* I wondered if there was a liquor store close by. *And how would that look, Daisy? A pregnant woman buying a bottle of vodka?* That was a surefire way to go from homeless to incarcerated.

But I wasn't homeless. Not anymore.

Guilt washed over me for the way I'd lashed out at Max. I knew I should cut myself some slack because of Todd...and hormones, but I didn't like it when the cracks in my composure showed, when the edges of those cracks started to cut people who were only trying to help. People I cared about.

"You're not broken, Daze." Even the memory of his words felt like a warm blanket.

Why couldn't I graciously accept Max's help right now? Why did I have to be a jerk about it? If there was ever a time that allowing help was understandable, it was right now, while I was pregnant, fiancé-less, everything-less—except Max.

I wasn't without Max.

And maybe that was the problem. It wasn't about accepting help. It was about accepting help from him when I harbored a deep, dark guilty attraction for my ex-fiancé's best friend.

Never in a million years would I have cheated on Todd, no matter how bad things got between us, but neither could I deny the pull I felt toward his best friend. That I'd always felt toward his best friend.

Now, I was afraid to rely on Max because there was

a part of me that always wanted more. A part of me that would readily sink into the space of, *what if you hadn't picked Todd?* and *Max never would've left you like this.* A part of me that would've been instantly and completely broken if the man who'd left me at the altar had been Max.

I stopped, my gaze catching on a small framed photograph tucked into the corner on the end, and my heart pinched. I picked it up and stared at the image of Max and Todd standing in front of Max's old farm truck, each holding a bouquet like it was a sword and pretending to duel.

I remembered when the photo was taken because I was the one who'd taken it. And right after, Max had let Todd land a winning blow, falling to his knees in mock defeat. *He always let Todd win.*

He always put everyone else first.

I put the frame down just as Erica returned to my side. "Sorry about that."

"Oh, don't apologize. I'm on your schedule today."

"Do you have any questions so far?" she asked as we walked back to the desk.

Closing the catalogs she'd opened for the customer, she moved them aside and pulled back out the delivery schedule for the week.

"I don't think so. It's pretty straightforward, just making sure everything is delivered to the desired location, that the bouquets are signed for, and that all the flowers are inspected for quality before leaving," I ran through the gist of it. "I think I have a pretty good sense of how everything flows after riding along with Max these last few days, so I should be okay on my own."

"Oh." Erica looked at me and then back to the

schedule. "Well, you won't be on your own for the next week, maybe two. Max will still be going with you."

"Why?" I blurted out the question. "Sorry, I don't mean...He doesn't need to come with me. I can handle the deliveries on my own."

"Oh, no." She waved her hands. "He usually does at least a week of training with all the drivers...with every position, really."

"He does?" I wasn't sure why I was surprised. It sounded exactly like something Max would do.

"Oh yeah," she said and flipped her hair over her shoulder. "He's very hands-on, especially when it comes to the teams that are interfacing directly with customers, since a lot of our orders come through the app or online. Wants to make sure everyone is giving their best."

I nodded but found it hard to speak. *Of course Max would do that.*

"There are also a bunch of our largest arrangements on the schedule, so you'll need a second person with you for those anyway."

"I don't need help. I can carry them, especially if there's a dolly in the truck. I don't have any lifting restrictions." *Yet.*

"Daisy." Erica placed her hand on mine, stopping me. "This isn't because of you. Or the baby. This is our standard protocol for the safety of all our employees."

Heat flushed my cheeks. "Oh."

"Our customers are paying a lot of money for our largest displays. Max wants them to feel like they aren't just getting a beautiful product, but also top-tier service."

"Of course." My exhale blew through my lips. My

paranoia over appearing helpless was showing. "I'm sorry."

"Don't apologize." Her hand moved to my shoulder and squeezed. "How about this? I'll tell you when Max is creating some kind of exception for you, and then you can take it up with him. How does that sound?"

"Sounds perfect," I said, the tension easing out of me. "He's already doing too much. I don't want any more handouts."

"I get it, but to be fair, in the dictionary under chivalry, there is only a picture of Max Hamilton. I've checked," she said with a droll smile.

I chuckled, ignoring the flutter in my stomach as I neither agreed with nor denied her sentiment. Reaching for the closest catalog, I thumbed through it, not wanting to linger on one of the many reasons I was attracted to a man I shouldn't want and couldn't have. *For God's sake, Daisy, you were going to marry his best friend not even a week ago.*

"Oh, this would be amazing," I murmured, my attention snagging on one of their fall specials, the *Harvest Moon* bouquet.

"I can get you one for upstairs if you want," Erica offered, her eyes flicking to her phone for a second when it buzzed.

"Oh, no." I shook my head. "I mean, that would be great, but I was just thinking these—the roses and hypericum—with a little bit of cinnamon would make a perfect perfume."

Erica tipped her head. "Perfume?"

"I've been...distracting myself with making home-made perfumes over the last few days with all the left-over flowers from my—from the inn."

Erica blinked and said nothing.

I closed the catalog, feeling silly. "I'm sorry. Please continue—"

"No, don't apologize. I'm just fascinated. You made perfume? With our flowers?"

"I started. Vodka and peony petals, but it takes a few weeks to pull all the aroma out."

She opened the catalog back to the harvest special. "What would you use from this?"

"Well, the rose and the hypericum leaves—they have an amber-like aroma. I don't think...does anything else have a scent?"

She scanned the list of flowers included in the bouquet. "Pincushions. Safari sunset...No, I don't think anything else in there is going to add much."

"Those with a dash of cinnamon..."

"I'll get you whatever you need," she said eagerly, grabbing a notepad and writing as she spoke. "Roses, hypericum, cinnamon, vodka."

"You don't have to. It's just a hobby."

"I want a bottle," she said and pointed to the bouquet in the catalog. "This was one of the arrangements I designed, so I'd love a matching scent."

"I could make a matching scent for any of them," I said without thinking...and then thought, *what if I did?*

Erica blinked. "That is...a great idea, actually." She grabbed a notepad and a pen. "I keep telling Max we should do more add-ons. We're going to start doing custom vases once Nox gets his production up and running, and I'd suggested scented candles. But perfume...I never thought of perfume."

My brows lifted, and I looked between her and the catalog.

"Oh, I don't mean that you would have to do them all," she quickly assured me with a pat on the arm. "I know you're not...that you've got other things—" She broke off and then started over with a smile. "It's just a great idea."

"Thanks," I said softly, staring at the image again. *What if I didn't have other things? What if I started making custom perfumes for Max? For everything he was doing for me?* "I'd love to give it a shot. Make a few samples for you and Max to test and see what you think."

"That would be amazing," she gushed just as the bell at the door sounded again. I went to stand, ready to step back and let her handle the customer who'd walked in when she stopped me. "Oh, no. Sit. It's not a customer."

She took her phone and went to greet the young guy holding a brown paper bag. I glanced at the clock, realizing we were well into lunchtime. Maybe I could walk along the main road here and find something for lunch. I doubted I'd find a place that had a—

"Meatball parm." She pulled a sub out of the bag and set it on the desk in front of me.

The delicious scent would've knocked me off my feet if I hadn't already been sitting. "How—" *Dumb question.*

"Max ordered lunch for us," she said, and quickly added, almost as though she'd been instructed to say it, "Since we're doing your orientation, he wanted to provide lunch."

He wanted to make it look more official so I wouldn't see it for what it was: Max taking care of me.

But I let it slide because I had a feeling I knew how I was going to pay him back.

"Well, it smells delicious." My stomach rumbled in agreement as I took the sandwich and started to peel off the paper.

"Usually we do something from the deli a few doors down, but Max insisted we order from this Italian restaurant like an hour north of here."

"Ferrulli's?"

Erica nodded. "Yeah, that's it. Have you had it before?"

"It's a favorite of mine." *Another one.*

Back when Todd worked with Max, they did a lot of boots-on-the-ground marketing for the start-up and a lot of working dinners with investors. Todd always invited me, but if I had to stay back to study, he'd send one of these sandwiches to my apartment. But that was a long time ago. He hadn't done that since he'd left MaineStems. He hadn't done a lot of things like he used to before leaving MaineStems.

"Wow, that is...obscenely excellent." Erica's dramatized groan of enjoyment broke my derailing thoughts.

"An excellent exception?" I lifted a brow. Max could justify buying lunch, but could he justify ordering it all the way from Ferrulli's?

"Whatever it is, if you're the reason for it, then I'm going to need you to never give Max that apartment back."

I froze. "Back?"

Erica made a bunch of unintelligible sounds before waving her hand like she didn't mean it the way I took it. "Back to the empty space that didn't bring these meatball sandwiches."

I believed her even though I had the feeling I knew better.

CHAPTER 9
DAISY

MAX

Can I come up?

I stood from the couch and scanned the apartment, forgetting for a moment that it was his apartment, along with almost everything in it.

Of course.

I winced as my response went through. *Of course* made it sound like he was welcome to just enter at whim. Like it didn't matter if I was in the shower or walking around without clothes on.

For a second, I lingered in the thought, wondering just what Max would do if he walked in on me naked. Would he be the gentleman? *Would he...not be?*

"Hello?" he called from the stairwell.

"Yeah. Hi." I set my phone on the coffee table and began to tidy all the MaineStems catalogs I'd brought up with me at the end of the day. I wanted to familiarize myself with their current arrangements and pick out which flowers I would need from each to create a complementary perfume.

"I wasn't thinking...expecting to see you again today," I said when I heard him enter the apartment, my hands moving to close the binders I'd stacked open one on top of another.

"I just wanted to check in after your first day," he grunted.

"Do you do that for all your employees?" I asked, grateful that I wasn't looking at him because I might not have had the courage otherwise.

His steps approached me slowly, inversely to the increasing beat of my heart. "Workday is over, Daze. I'm checking on a friend."

Don't. Don't. Don't. My heart pumped the word— the warning rather than a beat.

"Is that okay?" His low voice rumbled.

I grimaced and closed the final binder, stacking it neatly on top of the others. *Get over yourself, Daisy. Max is helping you. He's your friend, and he's helping you.* I needed to stop pushing Max away. I hated that I was doing it, but I couldn't stop. It felt like instinct. Like self-preservation. Like I didn't know how I'd recover if he abandoned me too.

"Of course, it is," I said as I finally straightened and turned, my chest pinching when I saw him.

Gone were his business casual clothes from earlier, replaced now with a pair of jeans that fit him just right and a plain gray tee that made it clear Max worked just as much on his physique as he did on his business.

My mouth slowly dried, my eyes roaming like they

were my hands, down the column of his neck, along the stretch of his shoulders, over the muscled swells of his pecs. Ache pooled in my stomach—unreasonable, second-trimester hormonal ache. He was so close I could touch him. So close I could reach for him and pull him to me. So close I could search for the look that was in his gaze earlier when he saw all my lingerie spilled on the bed.

I wonder how that look would change if he saw the lingerie on me.

I was about to apologize again when his warm gaze sank into mine, the weight of it like a stone rippling through everything I wanted to say.

"How are you? Was your day okay?"

"Yeah." I found my voice. "It was good. Erica was great." I folded my arms over myself, and his stare sank to my chest.

Without warning, my nipples pebbled, heat spilling into my veins. My breath caught. Did he know...could Max see how attracted I was to him? Would he think this was why Todd left me? My heart started to pound. Did he know—*had Todd remembered?*

No. My chin lowered, and I realized what had caught his attention. I had on a large MaineStems tee that I'd found.

"It was sitting on top of that box," I explained, pointing to the cardboard box that was half open and filled with T-shirts. "I hope it's okay I borrowed it. I got some marinara on the shirt Frankie loaned me," I said, not the least bit embarrassed for making a mess at lunch because the sandwich had been so good. Thankfully, the maternity leggings had been spared.

"You're welcome to anything up here, Daze. It's all yours."

It was when he said these things that I started to shut down—to shut him out. "Max—"

"I also got you these," he interrupted, extending his hand, a large Target bag suspended from his fingers.

I stared at the bag for so long, Max gave up waiting for me to take it and instead set it on the ground. I didn't need to look to know what was inside. While I'd been *orienting*, he'd gone out and bought me clothes this afternoon, even though I'd insisted...*What? That I had lingerie that I could wear?*

"Why?" I croaked, finally bringing my eyes to his.

"You have no clothes here, Daze. It's just a few things, and if you really want, I'll take it out of your first paycheck."

He wouldn't. I already knew it. He'd tell me he did, or he'd tell me he forgot, but the very last thing Max would do was ever take money from me for the things he'd just purchased.

"And if I ask you to take them back?" I wasn't going to, but I wanted to know, on principle, just how far he was willing to take this.

The angle of his jaw tightened. "I'd ask if you plan on doing the deliveries in your lingerie."

My brow arched. "Why? Would you plan on charging more?"

"No." His voice lowered, his eyes piercing. "I'd need to plan on who is going to bail me out of jail for blinding customers."

Air sealed into my lungs, hot and buzzing inside my chest. I'd never had someone be protective of me like this before. *Or was it possessive?* My heart lurched.

Whatever it was, I craved the dark heat of it wrapping over my skin. I craved this look in his eyes that settled low in my stomach and sent ripples of longing out over my skin.

Todd was never the jealous type. Maybe it was because he knew I wasn't that kind of person, but also, he wasn't that kind of person. He liked it when other guys looked at me. When his friends or his parents' friends' eyes lingered just a little too long, he liked knowing they wanted something that was his.

I didn't. I liked this. I craved this, even though it felt reckless and unreasonable for someone whose relationship—whose planned future—turned to ashes a week ago.

For someone who was pregnant with another man's baby.

The tension stretching between us snapped like a hot rubber band, making me flinch. *What was I thinking, looking at him like that? Thinking of him...*My gaze sank to the bag of new clothes.

"Do you want me to take them back?" He asked roughly. "Because I will if you really want."

My breath fired through my lips, guilt clawing at my throat. At my chest. In my stomach. Somehow, I'd managed to make him feel like an asshole. For the second time today.

"No. I'm sorry. I—thank you," I said, my voice cracking under the weight of it all. *Don't fall apart, Daisy,* I coached. Not now. Not in front of him. *Pull yourself together.* That time, it was Mom's voice in my mind, her calloused thumbs quickly wiping away my tears so no one else would see. *Head tall. Let the tears drain back where no one will see.*

When I was little, I imagined the tears running back and dripping down the inside of my spine, filling me up from the inside. I remembered wondering just how full of tears Mom was. How full I would be when I was her age.

"You really didn't have to do this, Max, but I'm grateful," I said slowly and drew the bag closer.

I couldn't bring myself to look at him. If he were Todd, that would be a different story. Todd struggled to notice a tear unless it stained his shirt.

Reaching inside, I started pulling out the clothes. Maybe they wouldn't even be the right size, and I'd have to return them. *Who was I kidding?* Anything in the vicinity of large worked right now when my body felt completely different every morning.

I pulled out whatever sat on top—a lavender shirt—and held it up in front of me. Most people would've been blocked from view, but not Max. He was too tall. Those warm eyes found mine over the edge of the fabric. Protective and penetrating.

A row of flowers rose up from the bottom of the shirt, the words "Little sprout coming soon" scripted in the center.

The words felt like a punch to the inside of my chest. Unexpected, and knocking the wind, and everything else, right out of me.

"I thought since you're helping with deliveries, it was fitting—"

My sob cut off whatever he was about to say. A sudden, ugly sob that fired from the hollow in my chest. My little sprout was coming soon, and we had no home. No nursery. And currently, no father. A whole week I'd gone without crying, and then a silly garden pun was all it took to send me careening over the edge.

I didn't even know what I did or said or sobbed. All I knew next was Max.

"Shit, Daze," he muttered. His curse reached me as he did, his big arms pulling me tight to his chest. I didn't have the strength to stop him. *Nor the desire.*

All week, I thought I'd been paddling myself to shore. Bringing myself to something stable and steady and out of the storm. As it turned out, I was only bailing water from my sinking heart, and tonight, it got to be too much.

"I'm sorry," Max said against the top of my head, and I only sobbed harder.

He shouldn't be sorry. This wasn't his fault. None of this was. Not even my tears. And yet he took it all—took them all. They soaked his shirt. They soaked his palm where it cupped my cheek. I couldn't stop them.

"It's all right, Daze. I've got you," Max murmured over and over again, holding me, rocking me in the middle of the living room.

It wasn't all right, though. Nothing was all right. I was alone and pregnant with only temporary solutions. *Where were we going to go? What was I going to do? How was I going to do this by myself?* Suddenly, all the insecurities I'd fended off for a week attacked with full force, feeding off my hormones, off my stress, off my fears. And I would've collapsed in on myself if it weren't for him.

Max didn't just hold me. The harder I sobbed, the closer he clutched me. Protected me. One arm snaked around my back, the other bent along my arm, his hand cupping the back of my neck as his fingers gently massaged the base of my scalp.

His presence rose like a wall, shielding me from the rest of the world. In this apartment. In this job. In his arms. He was giving me the space to be vulnerable and the decency to pretend he didn't see it. With every sob, I breathed him in. Flowers and mint. With every shake, I felt the strength of his arms support me. He'd never let me shatter. With every cry, I felt the pain dissolve against the heat of his hard chest.

"It's all going to be okay, Daze. I've got you," Max repeated, his lips against the top of my head. How many times had he said those words? I'd lost count. They'd become a melody in the background, a comforting chant that steadily pushed my worries back at bay. "I'm sorry—"

"No." I shook my head against him, slowly tipping back. "I'm sorry, Max," I said through a bout of hiccups. "I shouldn't have...I didn't mean for this." I sniffled, looking down at the T-shirt, the flowers on it now watered with tears.

"It's okay, Daze. I'm always here for you. Always."

I felt my armor crawl back over my skin like icicles. All I wanted was his warmth. All I wanted was his arms around me all night, even if it was to hold me like that and nothing more. *All I wanted was to confess the weight on my chest.* I wasn't sad that Todd had disappeared.

I wasn't sad that I wasn't married to him. I was sad because, for my daughter's sake, I felt like I should be. It was for her sake that I'd said yes when, weeks before, I'd considered finally ending things with Todd. It was for her sake I muddled through Todd's doubts and drinking and distance. And now, I didn't know which version of me was worse: not being sad that her father had abandoned us or accepting so little from a man just so she'd have more of a father than I had.

Or was it this version? The version who'd always harbored a fantasy about being with Max Hamilton? But even that had its chinks. *Even Max had left me.*

"Are you?" I looked up at him and asked, my voice still clogged.

Pain lanced his eyes. "Of course. How could you think—"

"Because you disappeared too, Max. For the last almost six months," I charged. "As soon as Todd told you about the baby, about our wedding, you got so busy that we never saw you. That you never saw him. He needed you—I needed you. Was it because—" I flinched and stepped back, shocked at how easily I'd almost brought up that night. He couldn't know. And if by some unbelievable chance he did, he was too much of a gentleman to say anything. "I'm sorry. I shouldn't be...It doesn't matter. Todd was going to do this no matter what anyone did."

"I am sorry, Daisy." It wasn't his words as much as it was his expression that ripped a new tear in my heart— *like I'd just driven a knife through his.*

"No, I shouldn't have said that," I said, pressing my hand to my forehead and then holding it protectively over my stomach. "This is just a lot for me right now, and all I can think about is the baby. I have to figure this out for her. I will figure this out for her," I said, my voice quieting. "I appreciate everything, Max. I truly, truly do. I just..."

"I understand," he said so I didn't have to finish.

My throat swelled tight. How many times had I called Max in the past? Todd and I would argue, and I'd get in my car and drive, and then call him. No matter how many ways I explained it, Todd didn't understand why I wanted certain things. Why I clung to my independence. And when I couldn't get through to him, I told everything to Max. I used to think it was because I'd hoped he could get through to Todd. Now, I had to wonder if it was simply because I knew Max would understand.

"Thank you for the clothes. And the apartment. And the job." I needed to accept that I needed help right now. It wouldn't be forever. It wouldn't be my undoing. *I was going to be okay*.

When he didn't say anything for a beat, I turned to him, my breath catching at the intensity of his gaze.

"Max..."

He closed the space between us, his knuckles instantly propping under my chin and lifting my face to his. *Kiss me*. The thought sprang unbidden from the insane corner of my mind, and I quickly shoved it aside.

"There's nothing I wouldn't do for you, Daisy," he murmured with a rough voice, his stare impossible to break. "*Nothing*."

His eyes dropped to my parted lips, and for a second, I thought he'd heard my insanity, that he'd heard my ache to kiss him, but then his arm fell to his side, and he backpedaled several paces. He speared his fingers through his hair, gripping the strands hard before releasing them. For a blip of a second, I imagined my own fingers clenching his hair.

"I'll...umm...see you in the morning."

"Yeah." I swallowed down the urge to ask him to stay and nodded. "Goodnight, Max."

"Goodnight, Daisy."

I watched him leave, feeling my heart beat into the front wall of my chest a little harder, like it wanted to go after him. Just to have him hold me again. But I couldn't.

I could accept his generosity, but I couldn't afford to want more. No matter what he said, the way he'd put an ocean of distance between us when I got pregnant spoke volumes. I couldn't afford to want one more person it would kill me to lose.

"Y**ou have to try my blueberry honey." A mini scone slathered in dark blue goo appeared in front of me, Harper's smiling eyes begging me to take it.

"I shouldn't..." I groaned, feeling my mouth water from the scent. I'd already tried two other toasts layered with some of Stonebar Farms' famous jams, and I'd only been in their flagship Friendship store for ten minutes.

"You definitely should," Harper insisted, winking when I took the treat. "It was Max's idea."

I didn't think I had pregnancy cravings. With the morning sickness that no one mentioned could extend beyond the first trimester, it was sometimes hard to believe I could even crave food at all. But lately, all I wanted was berries. Blueberries in particular.

"Oh my god, Harper," I moaned, licking every last sticky drop from my lips as she took my now-empty hand and placed a plain glass jar of dark honey into it.

"From the first batch."

"It's delicious. So delicious." And all I could think

about was mixing this into a nice big bowl of yogurt with some fresh blueberries later.

At least half of the nights over the last two weeks, my dinner consisted of a bowl of yogurt with fresh berries and granola. The other half of the nights, Max managed some excuse to be responsible for feeding me, whether it was the deliveries ran late, or "there's this great Italian place," or he was feeling really hungry and asked if I would mind just getting dinner on our way back to the warehouse...

They were obvious excuses to buy me dinner, but not obvious enough where I couldn't pretend to go along with them. It was just easier. Max just made things easier. And as much as I didn't want to take advantage of it or rely on him, the reprieve was too tempting—*and temporary*—I reminded myself every time I gave in.

"Well, I'm glad you like it because I made it just for you."

"What? Me?" If I hadn't already completely devoured the scone, I would've choked. "Why?" I gave a small laugh.

"Because you made me peony perfume that I'm obsessed with," she said, having spent the first five minutes gushing about how much she loved the scent that had finally matured from those first few mason jars I'd steeped my wedding bouquet in.

The bell chimed, and warmth fizzled along my spine. *Speak of the devil.*

"Why am I not surprised?" Max drawled, and I only partly angled my head so he fit into my periphery.

"What did you expect us to do, Max? Not feed her?" Ailene charged, coming out from the stockroom with a smile on her face. "And what about you? You look like you could use a snack."

She rounded the counter with the same tray of toasts she'd offered to me, pointing to the three different ones she wanted him to eat.

"After this, I'm going to have to walk back to Stonebar, Aunt Ailene," he teased, but didn't turn her down. It was pretty impossible to turn down Ailene Kinkade.

From the moment you met her, Ailene made you feel like she'd take on the world to take care of you. Maybe it was only striking to me because it was so different from when I'd met Mrs. McCormick. *Never call her Mary,* Todd instructed me. Maybe he was thinking, hoping she'd tell me to call her Mom now that we were going to be married. She never did. The only thing *Mrs. McCormick* made me feel was that no matter how hard I tried, I'd never fit into her world.

"What's that?" Max nodded to the jar in my hand.

"Harper's new honey." I handed him the jar, our fingers brushing like sparks on kindling.

Two weeks I'd spent almost every day by Max's side while we did the MaineStems deliveries. It reminded me of the early days of his business and our relationship —*our friendship.* Except there wasn't Todd between us now. Not like he was then.

"Here, give me your hand," Harp demanded, sinking her knife back into the open jar and pulling out a dab.

Max only pretended to look wary as he extended a single finger. The reality was that there was nothing Max wouldn't do for his family, but especially for his younger sister.

"What is it?" he asked as she smeared the honey on his index finger.

"Blueberry honey," I answered, catching the way his eyes darted to his sister. *And was that a blush?*

"It took a few tries to get the blend perfect, but I'd like to see Eastwood try to claim I copied this," Harper said it with bravado, but I heard the pain buried in her chest.

Yesterday, after our normal deliveries, Max said he needed to drop off some pallets to Harper and asked if I minded coming along. On the way, he revealed Harper was embroiled in a legal battle with another local beekeeper, Adam Eastwood, who claimed she was infringing on his branding because she had a bee in her logo, and so did he.

It didn't matter that hundreds of honey brands used bee icons in their logos. He was jealous of her product and decided villainizing her was the best way to bully her out of the market. He targeted her online, got his customers to review-bomb her business, but Max worried it was more than that. Harper refused to ask Wade for legal help. She continued to weather the damage to Harper's Honey's reputation in silence.

"Harper, could you put those jars up front for me?" Ailene asked, drawing Harper away and leaving Max and me to ourselves for a second.

One second for time to taste the treat. And for me to lose my mind.

Max dragged his tongue up his finger, electrifying every nerve in my body. And then when his lips closed around the tip, everything shorted. My mouth dried. My heart stumbled. My core clenched. All of me was an open fuse that wanted that mouth to ground me.

That wanted his tongue gliding over my skin. Into my mouth. That wanted his lips sucking on my sensitive nipples and then lower, between my thighs—

"Daisy?"

I flinched, blinking rapidly back to the present. Harped looked at me with worry, completely ignorant of what her brother's mouth was doing to my mind. *Or maybe not.*

"Are you okay?" Her head tipped. "You look a little flushed."

They were wrong about the morning sickness, but they weren't wrong about the hormones. They swept in like a hurricane. One minute, I was fine. The next, I was aching and horny and salivating...and only for Max.

"Yeah, I'm fine."

"Aunt Ailene, do you have some sparkling water in the fridge?" Max interrupted, now scrutinizing me as well.

"Of course." His aunt disappeared to the back again.

I almost protested, but decided having them think I was overheated was better than revealing I was just horny.

"Thank you," I said when she returned with a fresh bottle. I didn't know what fizzy magic it was, but there was something so quenching about the tiny bubbles gliding back along my tongue.

"Better?" Max checked after I'd taken three large sips.

"Cooler. Thank you." *But not better.* To be better, I'd need a different kind of *tall drink of water.*

Satisfied, Max's shoulders relaxed a little, and he spoke to his sister, "That was really good, Harp."

"Maybe I'll call it *the Daisy*," she said, and I watched the color drain into Max's face.

"Harp—"

"Why wouldn't I? She's the reason I made it in the first place—" she went on blindly.

"Harper—"

"Well, technically, you're the reason because you were the one who told me about her craving and asked—"

"*Harper.*"

Finally, she heard her brother's tone and stopped. "What?" She cocked her head to one side.

Meanwhile, all of me felt off-kilter. *My craving.* The familiar band around my chest tightened. Of course he noticed, but it went beyond that. He'd asked her to make this honey specifically for me. One of these days, I'd figure out if the way his thoughtfulness stole my breath was comforting or threatening, or maybe I'd accept it was both.

"Never mind." Max's jaw flexed. "We should probably get going. We've still got one more stop to make."

"Okay," Harper said, letting the word drag as it came out, almost as slowly as her eyes moved between her brother and me.

"Thank you for the honey," I said and reached out to hug her.

After a warm goodbye to his aunt, who repeated her invitation from last week to dinner on Sunday, we walked out of the Stonebar store and headed for the delivery van.

The silence between us lasted until we drove beyond the border of Friendship.

"I'm sorry about Harper. I didn't think—"

"Don't apologize," I cut in. "I didn't know...didn't realize you knew—"

"That you've been getting a blueberry smoothie every morning we stop at the Maine Squeeze or two blueberry muffins if we go to The Pastry Queen instead?" His gaze quickly flicked over to me and then back to the road, like he'd give away too much if he looked at me too long. "Or that the only groceries in your fridge are yogurt and blueberries?"

I swallowed. "I guess it was pretty obvious." *And something Todd never would've noticed.* "Max—"

He grimaced when he saw the screen, like he didn't want to answer but had to. "Sorry, I have to take this."

"It's okay."

He tucked his phone to his left ear. "Hey, Aria, what's up?"

I glanced over. *Who was Aria?* I caught myself and pinned my attention to the window. Unfortunately, there was nothing I could do not to listen.

"On Sunday? Yeah, that works for me," Max said, and now, all I wanted to know was who Aria was and what was Sunday? "Can't wait." And then, "You too, bye."

He dumped his cell back into the cupholder, giving no explanation of the conversation. But he didn't need to because it wasn't my business, I argued with myself. Max wasn't my business. But he was a friend...and sometimes a fantasy.

"Is everything okay?" I heard myself ask, testing the waters.

His hand tightened on the steering wheel as he replied, "Yeah." I almost thought that was all I was going to get out of him, but after a beat, he continued, "I'm selling my house. Aria is my realtor. Aria St. George. Her twin brother, Andre, is good friends with Nox."

"Oh." I swallowed down the information, wishing it satiated my curiosity.

I remembered now that Max had purchased a house down here. I wasn't sure exactly where, but I knew it was close to his dad's. He'd bought his house around the time things were getting really bad between me and Todd, so we'd never come to visit. I'd only ever been to Max's apartment in Portland.

That whole time felt like a blur now. I'd felt so... distant from Todd, but I didn't want to quit on the relationship. I wanted to give it one more honest try. *I didn't want to face the idea that I'd made a mistake.* So I'd gone with Todd to his family's beach house for his dad's sixty-third birthday party. And one more honest try turned into two pink lines.

"You're selling it already? You've only had it—"

"A year."

"What happened?"

Max stared ahead, his extra second of pause telling me there was more to the story than I was going to get.

"Wasn't what I thought it would be."

My chest pinched, and I rested my hand on my stomach. "I know how that feels."

I heard the sharp pull of his breath, and I bit my cheek, annoyed at myself for saying too much. We were doing so well, not talking about Todd. About my runaway fiancé. *About my disaster.*

"Daze—"

"Did you just put it on the market?" I interrupted, wanting desperately to continue this conversation over the alternative.

"A few months back."

Months? So right around the time he'd disappeared from my and Todd's lives. *Right after that birthday party.* I tried not to think about the coincidence, but it was impossible.

I tried not to think how, even after all the time we'd spent together, even over the last two weeks, our conversations spanning *almost* every topic under the sun, it was things like this that made me feel like I didn't know much about Max's life at all.

Meanwhile, he knew everything from my favorite childhood books to my pregnancy cravings.

"I'm surprised there's no interest in this market," I said, a glutton for punishment as I tried to keep the conversation afloat.

Max grunted. "Aria thinks the price is too high, but I know what the property is worth, so I'll wait it out."

That sounded...exactly like Max.

Now, it was my turn to be distracted by my phone. Every time it buzzed, I expected it to be Todd, and at the same time, hoped it wasn't. It was a strange and terrifying place to be. A limbo I'd lived in for two weeks. Two weeks of no contact. Not a call. Not a message. Not an Instagram post. Not even a carrier pigeon. And nothing to Max or his parents either.

Todd was just...gone.

Of course, part of me worried if he was actually okay, but even that started to wane. If something terrible had happened, we would've heard by now.

Even the authorities weren't inclined to spend resources looking for him, no matter what kind of political weight Mr. McCormick threw around. The last Max heard, the McCormicks had finally settled on hiring a private investigator to look for their son.

Whether they found him or he came back, I knew exactly what to expect when I saw Todd next. His usual childlike repentant self, replete with apologies and gifts and begging forgiveness. To give me a thousand reasons —many of which blamed his parents—for how he acted. And I didn't want to hear it.

No, I didn't want to have to face the decision it came with: walk away because I deserved better, or stay because my daughter deserved to have her father? There was a middle path, but I imagined it was narrow to the point of invisible when squeezed by the expectations of Todd's parents.

"Daze?"

I blinked, the number on the screen swimming into focus. It wasn't Todd. It also wasn't a call I wanted to answer right now.

"Who is it?"

"Not Todd." I clicked to silence the call. They would leave a voicemail.

Max's eyes narrowed. "Is everything okay?"

"Yeah. Fine," I said, irritation firing in an undeserved direction. *It wasn't Max's fault I was dodging calls from my OB's office.* "Let's finish up here. I don't want to be late."

WHILE THE WOMAN TOOK MAX AROUND HER house, asking his opinion on how many and which bouquets she should order for her daughter's baby shower, I stepped back outside. Fishing my phone from my pocket, I tapped to listen to the voicemail from earlier.

"Hello, this is Jackie from Portland Birthing Center. I'm just calling to confirm your appointment for tomorrow morning with Dr. Barrett. Please note we do have a $150 late cancelation or no-show fee."

Great. Not only could I not afford to go to my twenty-four-week check-up, but I couldn't even afford the late fee they would charge me to cancel right now.

The urge to cry hit me like a freight train, and I quickly bit into my bottom lip to stifle it. *Damn you, Todd.* It was he—his parents—who'd insisted that I go to this fancy private birthing center. Private rooms. Water baths. A husband suite. A chef on staff. *Translation: expensive.*

It didn't matter if I wanted the luxuries. I couldn't afford them now.

I tapped on the number to call them back. Swallowing my pride was almost enough to make me want to gag, but I wasn't just not going to show up.

"Hello, thank you for calling the Portland Birthing Center. This is Dolly speaking. How can I help you?"

"Hi, Dolly. This is Daisy Turner. I have an appointment tomorrow morning, and unfortunately, I'm going to have to cancel it."

"When would you like to reschedule for?"

"I'll have to call back, I'm sorry."

She paused, and I braced for what I knew was coming. "Are you aware of our cancelation policy? This is considered less than twenty-four hours' notice."

"Yes, I know. I'm sorry. I was...on my honeymoon, and I completely forgot."

"Unfortunately, I can't make an exception for you."

If that wasn't the story of my relationship with Todd's...world, I didn't know what was.

"I understand."

"Are you sure you don't want to reschedule? It would spare you the fee, and the twenty-four-week ultrasound is a very important checkpoint for development. You shouldn't put this off."

"I know," I snapped, unable to handle a single shred more of judgment on my shoulders. Tears sprouted in the corners of my eyes. "I know this appointment is important. Every appointment for her is important, but unfortunately, I can't make this one right now—"

"I'm going to have to charge you the late fee—"

"I'm sure Senator McCormick can afford it. I believe his card is on file," I said and hung up before she decided to scold me further.

The only thing I hated more than hanging up on the woman was using my ex-almost-father-in-law's name to get me out of this jam. Not once since meeting them did I feel a sense of shame for anything they judged me for. My looks. My upbringing. My work ethic. My missing social connections. But I felt ashamed now. Not for being unable to afford the birthing center without them, but for using their name to get me out of a tight spot. I didn't want to rely on them—I never had—but dropping the McCormick name was the only hope I had for dissuading the center from actually charging the card Todd put on our account.

"Daisy?" Max appeared next to the open door.

Gasping, I stood quickly from the bed of the van, my phone clattering to the ground as I bumped it from my hand. If he heard me...if he knew...My heart stammered in an unsteady beat.

"What's up? Are you finished?" I asked, wiping my tears on the soft sleeve of my tee as I bent to pick up my cell.

Max's expression was drawn tight when I looked at him, my lungs holding my breath hostage until he spoke, "Yeah, I'm done. We can head out."

I thought I nodded, I hoped I did, and then I spun for the passenger door, which Max still beat me to hold open. "Thanks."

Unlike Todd's parents, who the thought of relying on them made me physically nauseous, Max was the opposite. Relying on Max didn't make me sick with shame, but ache with undeserved longing.

"Everything okay?" he asked once he joined me in the van and started the engine.

No, but it would be soon, I thought, and rested my hand on my stomach as he started to drive. Almost instantly, I felt the churn of worry start to settle. *It would be soon, little sprout.* As soon as I started saving. As soon as I got on MaineStems's insurance policy. As soon as I stopped needing to rely on the man next to me so much.

"Yeah." I smiled through my guilt.

Max offered health insurance to his employees. I knew because Todd had been on it until he left the business, and his parents bought him a private plan that I was supposed to go on.

Health insurance wasn't the first thing to cross my mind when I realized Todd had jilted me. It wasn't even the second or third thing when I was managing hurdles like where I was going to live and where I was going to have to work to afford to live. But now that I was settled into the apartment, I was starting to face all the other consequences of Todd's abandonment, like having no car of my own to even get to my job.

"You can't continue to drive that rust bucket, Daisy. It's not safe for the baby."

My 2003 VW bug wasn't completely full of rust, but that wasn't the point. Todd wanted me in a Mercedes like his, like his parents drove. And he knew just how to get me to agree to it. *"After the wedding, we'll go and you can pick out a nice, safe SUV in whichever color you want."*

Without a car, I'd relied on Max to give me a ride to the warehouse every morning, both of us pretending it was just part of the job.

Health insurance was a different story. I needed it *ASAP*. I hadn't broached the subject yet because I was still in training this week, but come Monday, I'd ask. I'd have to.

I hated to feel like I was asking more from them, from Max, when he'd already done—was doing—so much, but I didn't have a choice. I wasn't getting any less pregnant. Even with insurance, I couldn't afford the birthing center in Portland, which meant I'd have to find a new doctor, a new hospital. There was one just outside of Stonebar, but I had no idea what their facility was like.

"Why are you canceling doctors' appointments, Daze?" Max growled after a single strained minute.

Every muscle I had tensed. *He'd heard.*

"Why are you listening to other people's phone calls?" I countered, trying to keep my voice light and teasing. Maybe if I made it seem like no big deal, he'd drop it.

"I'm serious, Daze. If it's because it would interfere with work, please tell me. I can have someone cover—"

"No." I tried to protest. He was getting the wrong idea, and I couldn't stop him.

"After everything, after all this time, if you think I wouldn't let you take time off to go to a doctor's appointment for the baby..." He trailed off, and I looked over at him, shocked by the hurt on his face. "Is that really what you think of me?"

"No," I blurted out, my chest feeling like it was splitting in two. Why was it every time I tried to protect myself from embarrassment, from vulnerability, it was at the expense of the one man who'd done more for me than anyone, especially over the last few weeks?

Max stared at me, his warm eyes screaming for an explanation.

"Of course, that's not what I think of you, Max. It's just..." I said, my tongue slowly untangling the vulnerability knotted on its tip. "I don't have insurance yet. That's why I canceled the appointment. Well, that and it was at this fancy birthing center in Portland that I couldn't afford anyway."

"What do you mean you don't have insurance?"

My throat worked for a second. "I mean, Todd was going to put me on his as soon as we were...married." It was strange how the idea sounded so implausible now. Only two weeks after he'd disappeared. "It's fine. I'll just wait until I go on your...on MaineStems insurance. It's just a few weeks, right? I'm assuming after orientation and..." I trailed off as all the color started to drain from his face. "Max?"

"Three months."

"W-What?" I didn't, couldn't have heard—

His voice was hollow. "The waiting period for insurance as an employee is three months."

Three...

I'd have a baby by then.

"Can you pull over?"

He swung the van off to the side of the road, hardly coming to a complete stop before he threw it in park and tried to get to the passenger door. He didn't make it in time.

I pushed open the door, my head barely clearing the doorframe before my blueberry smoothie from earlier, along with the jam and crackers, made an encore appearance onto the ground.

"Shit, Daze."

"I'm fine," I said, though I was anything but. I wanted to shrug off his hand, but if I was being honest, it might've been the only thing holding me together.

"You're not fine." His hand rubbed slow circles on my back, the other gently gathering my hair back in case I threw up again.

I would be fine. I had to be fine. *I had to get health insurance.*

Clutching my stomach, I straightened and looked at

him. There was no shame. Not anymore. Not when it came to my baby. "Can you make an exception?"

From his expression, you'd think my question had been a hot poker driven through his gut.

"I can't, Daze. If I could...if there were any way—" He broke off with a ragged breath. "It's against the law for me to make an exception for you. Benefits have to be equal for every employee."

It took a second to process what he'd said. The weight of what I'd unknowingly asked him to do and the reality of why he couldn't.

"It's okay," I said quickly and pulled away. "I'm sorry. I didn't realize...didn't know there were rules. I didn't mean to ask you to break them."

"Daze—"

"I'll figure something out," I insisted, knowing if I let him continue, he'd do exactly what he said he couldn't. He'd break every rule to be my knight in shining armor, and I couldn't let him. He'd already done so much. I drew the line at him breaking the law to save me. "Don't worry about it, Max. Please, let's just finish our deliveries."

I started to go into trauma response mode again, just like when I read Todd's letter. I didn't want to think about this moment—about the implications of what I'd just learned. I wanted to get back in the passenger seat and ride. I wanted to finish our job and find some success in today. And somehow find a way to face all my failures tomorrow.

CHAPTER 11
MAX

It was getting easier to hate my best friend the longer he wasn't here to defend himself.

Who was I kidding? There was no defense for what he'd done to Daisy. Not when there were a million other ways to battle his demons. People he could've asked for help. Conversations he could've had. There was no defense for running. *For leaving her to pick up every piece, pregnant and alone.*

She wasn't alone, but she might as well be for how hard she pushed back against every offer of help. I understood because I knew her, because I'd been the one who'd listened to the stories and comments and pain that shaped her past, but that didn't make it any easier for me to get through that barrier.

"One Blue Moon and one house Pinot." The waitress doled out the drinks from her tray—the beer for me, the wine for my brother. "Know what you want to order?"

I motioned to Nox to go first.

"Lobster roll."

"Same," I said because I didn't want to think about it.

As she walked away, I pulled the beer to my lips, turning away from Nox as I took a long drink.

I wasn't much of a drinker, especially after dealing with Todd's entry-level alcoholism over the last couple of years. A social glass of wine with investors or a beer with my brother or cousins was the extent of my enjoyment.

"Rough day?" Nox broached the silence, swirling the wine, and for a second seemed more interested in the wine glass than the dark contents. But only for a second before taking a sip.

It was almost comical to see him drink wine. Old Nox had never been a wine drinker. Always whiskey and cocktails. But that all changed when he got back from Murano. *And it wasn't the only thing.*

"Something like that," I muttered, taking another swig as I stared out the salt-stained window at the Rusty Scupper, the glass just as clouded as my thoughts had been since I'd dropped Daisy off an hour ago.

We'd finished the afternoon deliveries, just like she'd wanted, and I didn't bring up a damn thing about what had happened. I wanted to respect her space, but I also wanted to help her figure out a solution. She'd kill me for thinking it was my fault, but it was. All I'd been focused on was getting her a safe place to stay and something to do where I could keep an eye on her and make sure she was okay.

I hadn't thought about fucking insurance. But now I was.

Now, I couldn't stop thinking about it—how she was canceling doctor's appointments. Her desolate expression outside the van was burned into the backs of my eyelids, the sound of her chest heaving like she wanted to vomit again but wouldn't let herself on repeated in my ears, and her eyes glazed like they'd been dammed up, prevented from crying for days. Like she hadn't let herself cry again since the night I'd brought her the bag of maternity clothes.

After our last stop, I'd suggested burgers and fries at this pub in Stonebar. It was nice and quiet, right on the way back and on the water. I figured we could talk there about what she was going to do and how I could help.

But she said no. She said she was tired and wanted to go back to the apartment. It was bullshit. A lie. She was reeling, and she didn't want to let me in.

"Because you disappeared too, Max. For the last almost six months."

That was the worst of it. It wasn't watching her break down that killed me. Don't get me wrong. It hurt like hell, but it was this—it was hearing those words that was the fucking worst. When she looked at me like Atlas with the world on her shoulders, the weight of everything bringing her to her knees, she still didn't feel safe enough to offload any of it.

"Because you disappeared too, Max."

I hadn't disappeared. I'd been fucking dying. Propping up their relationship from the shadows, knowing I was digging my own grave. But I couldn't tell her that. I couldn't confess I'd been there the whole damn time. I had to be okay with letting her think that because to call her out would mean calling attention to the lies I'd told her. And the four years of secrets I wanted to keep.

So I dropped her off and texted Nox, someone who was as crotchety and acerbic as I felt right now, and asked if he wanted to meet for dinner and a drink. We settled on the Rusty Scupper because it was a local watering hole far enough on the outskirts of Stonebar that the tourist crowd didn't venture to it, and it was about halfway between town and Dad's.

"What happened?" Nox asked, looking at me like I'd been staring off into space for some time now.

I took another swig of my beer, deciding whether I wanted to answer him or not. The *or not* won out. "Nothing," I grumbled and chugged another sip.

Nox swirled the red wine in his glass and heaved a sigh. "Okay, let me try this again. What happened with Daisy that's got your balls in a bunch?"

My bottle clanked on the table. "Nothing happened." I'd asked him here to get minorly intoxicated, not be interrogated. "How's the workshop coming along?"

He blatantly ignored me. "So you're telling me this silent, snappy version of you is just the standard progression of your world record?"

"My what?"

"Your Guinness Book of World Records' longest stretch of blue balls known to man."

If I were holding a can, I might've tossed it at his head for being rude—and being right. The only reason I didn't throw the glass bottle was because it wasn't empty...and I doubted it would make a dent in that hard head of his anyway.

Two weeks of eight-to-ten-hour stretches spent one-on-one with Daisy, and I wondered what version of idiot I had to be to think that would be anything other than torture. Like a movie trailer for the life I could've had if things had been different. If I'd spoken up for myself rather than falling in line behind Todd. If I'd let him flounder and fail rather than swooping in and counseling him to be better for her. *If I'd just been the better man for her*.

Fuck.

"I'm starting to think I liked you better when you were in Italy," I returned with only a fake shred of sincerity and a flat stare.

"Yeah, I bet." My brother's lopsided grin appeared for a brief second. "So you going to tell me, or do I have to start guessing?"

"No—"

"Is it the daily torture of spending all your time with your dream girl?"

Dammit.

"Nox—"

"Or is it the fact she's staying in your apartment?"

"Enough—"

"Maybe it's the pregnancy hormones. I've heard the second trimester can make them want to bang anything—"

"Health insurance," I choked out furiously and then coughed to keep him quiet when the waitress returned to take my empty bottle. I shook my head so she wouldn't bring me another. "Christ, Nox."

He shrugged, not giving a shit what he said or who heard. "Health insurance?"

"Daisy doesn't have it, and she obviously needs it." My hands flexed into fists in my lap. "And I can't give it to her through the business because she hasn't been working for me long enough."

"She could buy it for herself, right?"

My jaw flexed. "She could."

But that was expensive, and even with the few hundred bucks I was taking out of her paycheck for rent, the job she was doing wasn't paying that much. I couldn't give her a raise or even a cost-of-living adjustment without doing the same for the rest of my team. And to just give her the money or offer to pay for it...I'd already played out that losing argument in my head.

"If she won't accept your help, you can't beat yourself up over it, Max. You've already done a ton for her—and a ton she has no idea about it." Nox drained another sip of wine, letting what sounded like an accusation settle in my gut. "Just let her figure it out. Plus, you never know. Todd could show up with his tail between his legs tomorrow and marry her, and voilà, problem solved."

My stomach hollowed. *Problem solved.*

"That's a shit reason to marry the man who left her and their baby at the altar."

"Well, it's better than marrying some rando for the same result."

I stilled, his flippant comment like a hard slap across my face. Todd wasn't the only man who could marry her and put her on his health insurance plan.

No.

NO.

"I'll figure something out," I said gruffly, leaping off that train of thought before I crashed somewhere I didn't belong. "So what about you? Still looking for a place of your own?"

"I'm not buying your house, if that's what you're trying to get at." He chuckled.

"No, it's not." We paused then as the waitress delivered our dinners. This place had the best lobster rolls on the coast, and I'd bet every local in Stonebar would be willing to fight for that claim. "So...are you?" I pressed as Nox dove into his sandwich.

"Thinking about it," he replied once he finished his bite. "It's easy living at home right now. Plus, I'm at the barn most of the day, so I doubt I'm too much of an inconvenience to Dad. Maybe in the next few months, once I get things up and running."

We ate for a few minutes in silence, the last of the tables in the restaurant filling with customers.

"Are you going to call Aria?"

Nox looked at me. "No," he answered quickly.

"Why not?"

I couldn't tell if he hesitated or not. "Because I don't need a realtor to find an apartment," he said, shrugging off the question.

"I know, but she's just getting started, and she's Andre's sister. It would be good experience for her."

Nox shoved the last bite of his sandwich in his mouth and then licked his fingers clean. "I'll think about it," he finally said begrudgingly, like we were talking about a stranger and not his good friend's little sister.

"All right, boys." The waitress returned then, taking away our empty plates. "Thoughts on dessert? We've got some blueberry cobbler made with blueberries from your dad's farm."

Shit.

"How can we say no to that?" Nox grinned at her. "Two, please."

"And one to go," I added before she walked away.

Nox stared at me for a long second before giving his head a slow shake and uttering a low laugh. I didn't need to ask why he was laughing. Just like he didn't need to ask who the third piece of cobbler was for.

"And you wonder why I don't feel bad for you, *old sport*," he finally spoke again after dessert was brought to our table. "Beating on, boat against the current, borne back ceaselessly into the past."

"You have the whole book memorized?" I muttered and stabbed my fork into the cobbler.

"You forget how the story ends?" he countered.

I took a bite and then replied, "I'm not Gatsby, and this isn't a tragedy." Though I was already imagining the sounds Daisy would make when she tasted this. *And how uncomfortable my pants would be.* I was already hard from the fantasy.

Nox scoffed, but without malice. "What else do you call wanting something that you can't have?"

Problem solved.

I stared at the takeaway container in my hands. I shouldn't have ordered it. I should just take it back to the house for Dad. Or Harper. Hell, I should just throw it away and forget the six bucks and the whole idea. Instead, I watched myself tap on Daisy's name on my phone.

I didn't like how we left things earlier. How all she wanted to do was get back to work and pretend like she wasn't worried and hurting, and how I'd gone along with it. I wanted to find a way to fix it—needed to find a way, really. And this blueberry cobbler was my ticket in the door.

"Hi, you've reached Daisy Turner. I'm sorry I missed your call..."

I pulled my phone back and looked at the screen. Why did it go straight to voicemail? Weird. Probably a fluke. I ended the call and then tapped on her name again.

"Hi, you've reached Daisy Turner—"

"What the hell..." My jaw locked as I opened up our text thread and tapped out a message.

> Hey, are you okay?

Sending...Sending...*Message cannot be delivered.*

Ice-cold dread dripped into my veins. Something was wrong. Not answering was one thing, but not even ringing? Unable to deliver the message?

I hit the gas and ignored every speed limit to get back to Stonebar—to get back to her.

What if something happened?

If she fell?

What if Todd came back and was drunk—No. Todd might be a spoiled, thoughtless sap, but he wasn't violent. He wouldn't hurt her. But what if someone else...

My mind raced through scenario after scenario, chewing up the miles to the apartment and not even bothering to check my rear view for flashing lights. Thankfully, Aria's brother was on the Stonebar police force, so if one of them did pull me over, he'd be able to get me out of the ticket. Not that it mattered. I'd happily take a suspended license if it meant making sure Daisy was safe.

My truck tires screeched to a stop outside the shop. It looked just as locked up as I'd left it a few hours earlier, and I wished that did something to ease my chest that felt ready to split open.

"Daisy?" I called even before I'd reached the Murphy door to the apartment. I took the stairs two at a time and then pounded on the door. "Daisy?"

Later, I'd realized it was the blood thundering in my ears that prevented me from hearing her.

I punched in the code for the lock and shoved through the door. "Daisy? Are you—"

"Max?"

I stopped at the sight of her standing at the bottom of the spiral steps, whole and healthy. *And her eyes red-rimmed from crying.*

"Max, what's going on? Is everything okay?" She sniffled and pretended to look out the window with the hope I wouldn't see her lift the back of her hand to her cheek to wipe her tears.

My jaw clamped tight, and my eyes did a pass over the whole of her, needing to double—triple—confirm she was okay.

One swipe of my stare down her body, and I knew she was fine. I, on the other hand, was not.

She had on another one of my tees from one of the open boxes. It was big enough to be a dress and would've fallen to the tops of her knees if not for her belly. It didn't lift the hem much, but it was enough. Enough to make my lungs seize and my dick harden. Enough to swallow up the guilt I should feel for being glad she was here. For being glad Todd left her. *For wanting her like she and her baby were mine.*

I made the mistake of telling her they were just some extra shirts that had ended up here by accident. I didn't want her to feel bad for wearing them, and the fib worked too well. She didn't feel guilty for wearing them, but I did. I felt guilty for lying to her. *And for thinking that nothing had ever looked more right than Daisy wearing one of my shirts.*

"Max?" Her tremulous voice snapped me from my trance as she came to stand right in front of me. Right where I could see the fabric rise and dip over her breasts. Her nipples. Where it bowed out over her stomach and fluttered in front of her thighs.

I balled my fist to hide how my fingers itched to reach for the hem and explained, "Your phone went straight to voicemail, and my message wouldn't go through...I was worried."

Her lips rounded, and my cock twitched. She pressed the back of her hand to her mouth and nodded, reaching for the bowl of rice I just noticed on the counter.

She took two steps closer and extended her arm. Inside the bowl of rice was her cell phone.

"I dropped it in the bathtub," she murmured, a strained laugh pushing from her chest. She set it back on the counter and added, "Part of me hopes it doesn't make it."

"Daze—"

"What were you calling about?" She bundled her arms over her chest, the stance highlighting the growing swell of her stomach...and lifting the shirt higher on her thighs.

Lust bolted into my veins...from a bared inch of her leg. God, I should've spent the last six months dating instead of wallowing.

"Dessert," I choked out. "I'll be right back." In the span of minutes, I went back to my truck, grabbed the takeout container from the front seat, and returned to the apartment. "Figured you might like some blueberry cobbler," I offered her the treat.

To my surprise, she just stared at the container but made no move to take it.

"Daze?" I rasped.

She spun and walked to the window, her head swaying slowly in the low light.

"Daisy." I slid the container onto the kitchen counter and went to her. I wanted to pull her into my arms again like the other night, but I stopped myself, instead placing my hand gently on her arm. "What is it? What's wrong?"

Her shoulders shook with a restrained sob, but she didn't pull away from my touch.

"I'm fine," came her hollow defense.

"Tell me you're fine one more time, and your nose will be long enough to poke me in the chest, Pinocchio."

That earned me a weak smile and finally, a white flag of surrender. "Everything's wrong, Max," she said defeatedly. "Everything but you."

My heart rocketed into my ribs. "What?"

"I'm sorry. I know you're just trying to help, and I keep being horrible about it."

"Daisy," I groaned, the sound coming straight from my heart, cracking. I tried to turn her toward me, but she refused to budge. "You're not being horrible." She shot me a sideways stare. "All right, maybe just a little stubborn."

She blew out a shaky breath, but it didn't seem to lessen any of the tension in her body.

"What's going on, Daze?" I asked, keeping my voice soft and low. "Is this about the insurance? Because we'll figure it out..." I trailed off when she started to shake her head, her balled fist resting in front of her mouth. "Then what is it?" Tightening my grip, I tried to turn her again, and this time she let me. "You can talk to me."

I wasn't going to let her get away with pushing me away again. I let it happen earlier, and it clearly hadn't helped.

"Can I?" she murmured, her eyes welling up with tears again.

"Of course you can—"

"Do you think I trapped Todd into marrying me?" She blurted out.

"What? What are you talking about?" I couldn't decide if I was more shocked or hurt or angry at her question. "Why the hell would you think—"

"Because you've been MIA for the past six months, and Todd said it was because of work, but I can't help but think it was because you knew we were having problems, and then I got pregnant, and you thought it was to force Todd to stay with me, which I never would've done—"

"*Daisy*," I growled and stepped closer, holding her arms with both hands now. Her bottom lip trembled as she tipped her head to look at me. I groaned, the urge to kiss her hitting me like a freight train. "I don't think you trapped Todd into marrying you."

I think you were trapped into marrying him was what I wanted to say—was what I felt.

"Promise?" Her lashes fluttered, but not quickly enough to catch every tear.

"I promise," I murmured and lifted my hand to swipe away the droplet with my thumb, a trail of pink dusting her skin in its wake. Her gaze dipped like she had a hard time believing me, and I realized this had to be coming from somewhere else. "Why would I think that, Daze? Why would anyone think that?"

Her throat bobbed, but when she tried to look away, I wouldn't let her.

"Because apparently that's what Todd's parents think."

"What?" I demanded with enough of a snarl to make her eyes widen. "Did you talk to them?"

"No, but Mrs. McCormick left me a voicemail." She shuddered. "I was running the bath when I realized I'd missed her call. I thought maybe she'd heard from Todd, but when I listened..."

Now all the pieces clicked together. The broken phone. Her crying eyes. The root of her question.

"She called to accuse you of trapping Todd into marriage?" *Why now?* Todd had been gone for two weeks. *Why wait to be a heartless bitch?*

"She called to yell at me for canceling the doctor's appointment, saying I was trying to bully Todd to come back by harming his baby and that this was just what she should've expected from me since I trapped her son into marriage."

A kind of fury I'd never felt before knifed through me. I'd never been disrespectful to Todd's mom before. Not when she'd leave Todd depressed after every phone call and visit while we were in college. Not when she gave him so much shit for starting Maine-Stems with me. And not even when she spoke to me with the chill of arrogance in her tone, her displeasure seeming to increase with my success. *Like she'd wanted me to fail to prove to Todd that I hadn't been worth his time.* Not even then did I break and insult her.

But this...

"She's wrong, Daze. She couldn't be more wrong," I managed to say steadily. "In fact, the only thing she knows how to be is a giant, cold-hearted bitch."

Her blue eyes turned to saucers, and her mouth opened and then shut. "I don't think I've ever heard you call someone a bitch before, Max."

"Because I've never seen someone hurt you like this before." The reply was out before I could stop it, along with the hoarse ache in my tone.

The flush in Daisy's cheeks deepened, and I swore I felt her body sway toward mine, quaking the invisible wall between us.

"Todd always made excuses for her. For the way she acted. Treated him. Treated me."

Of course, he did. He was the same way with me. *'That's just how she is, Max. You just have to learn to ignore it like I do.'* He ignored it because that was what he was raised to do, how he was raised to think. No matter how hard I tried to break him from that mold.

"That's how they are, Daze. Do whatever they want, and then when the consequences come up, it's 'oh, that has nothing to do with me.' It's the Boston Brahmin mentality."

I remembered the first time I'd heard the term. Scott and Todd were arguing about something—something that had happened at a party the night before. I never knew what. Scott told him, *"Why would you want anything different? You're a Boston Brahmin. You don't get a choice."* Whatever it was, they got over it. Meanwhile, I looked up the term that explained a lot.

The Boston Brahmin was coined by Oliver Wendell Holmes Sr. to signify members of New England's elite. Those of the highest echelon of society who held themselves to a decaying level of aristocratic virtues.

"The only person she cares about is the version of herself society sees," I went on quietly. "And that version isn't looking so good with a son who left his pregnant bride at the altar. You can't listen to her."

She sighed, her shoulders going limp in my hands. "It's not listening to her that worries me."

"What do you mean?"

Her throat worked for a beat to get the words out. "She threatened me."

Threat—

"What?" The word cracked with deadly harshness from my lips.

I had a long fuse. Arguably, all I ever had was an almost endless fuse. The only other time I'd reached the bomb was the night Todd came to me when Daisy told him she was pregnant. That night and now.

"What did she say?"

"She said that I needed to fix this. That I needed to go back to the house, and I don't know, I guess wait there for Todd to come back since I'm to blame for him leaving?" She wasn't the only one struggling to understand Mrs. McCormick's logic. "She said if I didn't...if I didn't keep the doctor's appointments and make excuses for Todd, that she was going to contact their lawyer and get custody of the baby. She said she was going to take my baby—"

"No. Not a damn chance," I growled and pulled her to me. The swell of her stomach pressed to my waist, and the thought of Mary McCormick, world's worst mom, taking the baby growing inside it made me furious and sick at the same time. "Over my dead body."

Neither Daisy nor her baby was mine, but so help me, I would protect them as if they were.

"I don't understand," she cried against me. "I don't understand what she thinks I'm supposed to do—why she thinks this is my fault. I'm n-not just going to go to the appointments and put the bill on Todd's card. God, if I did that, she'd probably still accuse me of taking advantage of him, of using his money without his knowledge. Or stealing. I can't—" She broke off, starting to hyperventilate. "I can't...she can't take...she can't take my baby."

My palms slid to her face, holding it firmly to mine. "She's not going to take your baby, Daisy. You hear me? She's not. She can't. *She won't.*"

"Max..." Her head swayed, fighting herself, wanting to believe me.

"I'm going to fix this, okay?"

"How?" she whispered, and all I could think was, at least she wasn't trying to push me away again.

Problem solved. Nox's words came back to haunt me, and I shuddered.

"Well, the first step is...blueberry cobbler." I turned her toward the kitchen before she could protest. "No problems get solved on an empty stomach."

"I'm not hungry," she murmured when we reached the counter.

I gave her a flat stare and then crouched in front of her, addressing her stomach. "And what about you, baby? Are you hungry for some blueberry cobbler?"

At her soft whimper, my head snapped up, thinking something was wrong, that I'd done something wrong. Maybe I had. Daisy looked on the verge of tears again, and I cursed myself for treading over some invisible boundary I hadn't seen. Maybe I shouldn't be talking to her baby. Maybe it was weird.

"Sorry," I murmured and straightened.

She reached for my arm, a partially bloomed smile on her lips. "You're right. We do want some cobbler."

I stared at her for another second, letting the heat of her touch melt into my skin, and then moved away. Grabbing a fork from the drawer, I went to set it and the takeout container on the counter, and saw she'd taken a seat on one of the stools, one hand cupped under her stomach, *and the hem of my shirt riding higher on her thighs*.

The plastic crinkled in my grip, my fingers—my mouth—hungering for a different kind of dessert. One that lived underneath that shirt and between her thighs.

I wanted to taste her. I wanted to give her a taste of pleasure that I knew Todd hadn't. I wanted to give her new memories of a man who wanted nothing more than her pleasure, and then slowly wipe away all the ones of the man who'd only been concerned with his own. *And effectively erase the friendship we'd formed, the trust I'd earned from her over these last four years*.

"All yours." As soon as my hands were free, I shoved them into my pockets, dragging my gaze anywhere but her.

That was when I noticed the line of mason jars

running the length of the counter, each filled with... *water and flower petals?*

"What are all these?" I bent and squinted.

"Oh." She paused, having just popped open the box. "I'm just...it's an experiment."

Looking at her, I lifted an eyebrow.

"I'm making perfume." She licked her lips. "It's vodka and different flowers. The alcohol pulls out the scent. It takes a few weeks, but then I'll strain them, and it'll be perfume."

I picked up the closest one, turning it as she dug into the dessert like it was the first meal she'd had all day. And there it was. The throaty moan, the flutter shut of her eyes, and the sultry tip of her head as she savored that first bite. "Oh my god, Max, this is so good," she purred, and the sound burrowed straight to my dick.

Gritting my teeth, I shifted my weight, trying to ease the strain of the fabric over my groin. The last thing I needed was for her to notice how her enjoyment affected my cock. That definitely wouldn't help the situation right now.

"I thought you'd like it," I said and roughly cleared my throat, staring into the jar like the alcohol could wipe the sound from my brain too. Rose petals. *And was that hypericum?* I tipped the glass. "Daisy, these flowers...they're all from one of our fall arrangements."

A few seconds passed without an answer, and when I looked at her, she gulped and then sent her tongue darting out over her lips.

"Yes." A blush rose to her cheeks. "I was talking to Erica, telling her how I made peony perfume using my bouquet and that the blend of the fall flowers would smell nice. If it comes out good, she said it would be a great add-on offer for your customers. Small batch perfume."

Flowers and perfume.

I stared at her, the idea exploding in my mind. Why hadn't I thought of it before? We'd done so many other options—chocolate, Frankie's candles, for spring last year, we even did some jams. But perfume...custom blended to match the arrangements...

"You don't have to if you don't want—"

"No." I shook my head roughly, replacing the mason jar back into its position. "No, it's a great idea, Daze. You're incredible...your idea is incredible." I fumbled over the words. Her idea was brilliant, but hearing—seeing—how she'd thought of me and my business when her world was crumbling at the seams. Damn, if that wasn't enough to bring me to my knees...

Problem solved.

I sucked in a breath. Dammit, Nox.

"I'm glad to be able to do something for you after everything you've done for me," she said, her flush deepening, and I couldn't hold back my groan.

There were a few other things she could do for me —*take off my shirt, spread her legs, let me eat my own dessert*—but nothing business-related.

From the outside world, I imagined how this must look. Daisy in my apartment, working with me, bouncing ideas off me for my business. Wearing my shirt. Eating the dessert I brought her. Pregnant. *Mine.* From the outside world, it would look like she was mine.

Problem solved.

I shook off the thought and forced myself to figure

out a way to be helpful. Unfortunately, that meant asking questions that would lower the slight lift to her spirits. I didn't want to bring it up again—god, it was the last thing I wanted to do—but I had to.

"Daisy, did his mom say she'd heard from him?"

Daisy paused mid-chew, looked at me, and then finished her bite with a slow swallow. "No. I mean, not that she mentioned. Though I can't say I heard the very end of the voicemail, because when she mentioned lawyers and...all that...I dropped my phone into the tub."

"Got it."

"He's not coming back, Max."

My heart crashed against my ribs. "If he did...if he knew what his mom was saying—"

Her cornflower-blue stare found mine. "Even if he did and even if he knew, I wouldn't...I couldn't marry him now."

I stilled, the words like an audible unicorn.

"As horrible as this is right now, Max, as scared as I am, I won't go back to that. To him. Not even for health insurance."

Problem solved.

The seed Nox planted burned in my chest. The fantasy I'd plucked continued to sprout higher and higher, fervently clawing up the column of my throat.

"It's not your fault," she trudged on. "It's my fault for not asking before I took the position, and it's okay. You don't have to do this. I'll figure something out. I just need a little time to process. To think. To figure out a way to protect my baby—"

"Marry me."

Daisy jerked, her eyes flung open at me like the offer was a freight train speeding toward her.

She waited for me to take it back. For me to tell her she hadn't heard what she thought she did. But I wouldn't—couldn't. I knew her problems weren't my fault, but that didn't change that I wanted to be their solution. I wanted to be *her* solution.

Problem solved.

For a single, stunning second, the world stopped spinning, waiting for her answer like I did.

"You're joking," she said weakly, her voice knocked right out of her.

"I've never been more serious."

The fork slipped from her hand, clattering to the floor. Without thinking, I dropped to my knee in front of her to pick it up.

All the people around her ever did was leave. I didn't want to be one of them. I wouldn't be. Looking up, I extended the blueberry dessert-covered fork back to her and repeated more firmly, "Marry me, Daisy."

CHAPTER 12
DAISY

"*Marry me, Daisy.*"

I really thought I was hallucinating until Max went down on one knee and proposed again with a blueberry-covered fork.

Why was he doing this? *Why was it making my chest ache?*

"Max, what are you doing? Please get up." My thick tongue fumbled over the words.

I needed him up. Standing. Talking. Handing me the fork. Telling me everything was going to be okay, that he has some magic solution to stop Todd's parents from taking my baby.

A magic solution that wasn't marriage.

"I'm asking you to—"

"Don't." I choked out. "Don't say it again."

"Marry me."

I shivered. Marry him. *Marry my ex-fiancé's best friend.* It was crazy. "You're not making sense."

"If we get married, you won't have to worry about

health insurance," he said, his voice like fine gravel, filling in all the cracks in my protest.

Marry Max for his insurance. I wanted to laugh. The idea should've been so ridiculous. Why was I even considering this? Why was I letting him string up this web, my mind settling in like a fly in a trap? A strangled sound wrenched from my lips, and I turned away.

It wasn't ridiculous, was it? I wasn't in a good spot. There was no denying it. If it were just me, if it were only my life affected, it would be different. But it wasn't.

Little sprout chose then to flutter her kicks into my stomach as though weighing in on the offer.

Say yes. Kick kick. *Say yes.* Kick kick.

No. There had to be another way.

"Max, I can't. I'll figure out something...something else," I said, scrambling to pull together more reasons why it was a bad idea. "I don't need you to—"

"If we get married, you'll be safe from Todd's parents."

I inhaled swiftly.

"They won't be able to pressure or force you to move or see their doctors or do anything—"

"They could still get lawyers involved."

"And I can afford just as good ones."

"Can you? From running a flower business?" I didn't mean to sound harsh, but the McCormicks were private-jet wealthy, and the way Todd spoke about Max's absence made it seem like MaineStems needed the extra push, and that was why Max was working so hard.

"Daisy, all the work I've been doing...it was for huge contracts. A huge hotel contract in Boston. I have money. Maybe not quite generational wealth, but... enough to fight back," he said, and I tipped my head, my gaze zeroing in on his face. Was Max blushing?

"How wealthy are you?" I asked, not because I cared about his money, but because suddenly I was learning about pieces of Max that I didn't know.

His gaze dropped, and he turned sheepish for a second. "Millions, Daze."

Millions. Max Hamilton was a millionaire who'd spent the last two weeks riding around in a delivery van with me.

A millionaire who was asking me to marry him.

The money didn't matter. It had never mattered to me. Not that Todd had it, and certainly not how rich Max was. What mattered was that I didn't know. We'd been so close when Todd was working with him, and now...Now, I didn't have any idea that MaineStems had become so successful.

"Daisy?" Max said, but it wasn't until his finger brushed my shoulder that I broke from my trance.

"Sorry, I just...I had no idea. Todd said—" I broke off, feeling stupid. By now, I should know there wasn't any reason to trust anything Todd had told me. "I just had no idea."

And then his fingers were under my chin. "Do you trust me less now?"

"No, of course not."

His gaze darkened. "Then marry me."

Marry him.

Marry Max.

Get health insurance.

Get the McCormicks off my back.

Protect my baby.

Marry Max.

"God, Max," I whispered, catching his big body ripple with the words. Was I really considering this? Marrying him for insurance? For safety. For stability.

Was it any less ridiculous than marrying Todd because I was pregnant with his baby? Any less ridiculous that I tried to convince myself it was for something more?

My stomach twisted and twisted, but Max's soft and steady stare kept any knot from forming. This gorgeous, kind man was on one knee for me. To ask me to marry him. *For purely practical reasons,* I reminded myself, though that look in his eyes...it was the one he'd tried to hide and the one I'd tried to ignore for the last four years.

"You know, Todd never got down on one knee," I murmured, detouring to that less-than-fairy tale moment because it felt safer than this one.

That was just the icing on the disastrous cake. He'd panicked when I told him about the baby, went out for a few hours, came back apologetic but reeking of alcohol, and then just...decided. It wasn't a proposal. It was a declaration. Not of love or happiness or anything I would've hoped, but a declaration of duty. I could practically hear his parents screaming at him inside his head.

"A baby outside of marriage, Todd? What were you thinking? How could you be so careless?"

"Because he's always been careless, Mary. He was careless when he started with her, careless with his whole damn life, after everything we've done..."

I'd heard the way they spoke to him. The comments they'd make, even when I was standing right there. It was tragic the way they treated him. A justification for how he acted, but not an excuse.

"Daisy..."

I blinked, Max's tortured face swimming back into focus.

He was still down on one knee, for me and my baby.

The perfect gentleman who deserved better than this—than his happy ever after becoming nothing more than an answer to a friend's cry for help. Because that was all I was. A friend. A friend who was pregnant with another man's baby.

"Max, I can't ask you to do this." I shook my head.

"You're not asking, Daze. I'm asking you."

"And what about you?" I blurted out and took the fork. It wasn't an agreement. It was the safest time to take it without him thinking I was saying yes.

"What about me?" Max answered and slowly rose. Somehow, his standing only made things worse.

What about him? What about the man who towered over me, all heat and presence and perfection? What about the man who stepped in without asking? The man who gave without thinking? The man who thought—who was always thoughtful before acting?

The man who asked to marry me with a look in his eyes that felt like anything, everything, but charity? *A look that felt like he wanted me.*

No.

Wanting to help me. There was a difference. *A very big difference.*

"I mean you. Your life. Your...love life." There were a hundred reasons my voice cracked at the end. A hundred I could and would list off before I'd ever admit to the kernel of expected jealousy that sprouted in my chest.

A shadow passed over his expression like a summer cloud. There and then gone. "I don't have a love life, Daze."

"Okay, maybe not now," I acceded, burying the unwelcome kernel of happiness I felt knowing he wasn't seeing anyone, and instead focusing on my guilt. "But... but you will. You'll want to..."

"This doesn't have to be forever." That perfect curve of his jaw flexed.

Was anything? I caught myself before I spoke, my hand pressing a little tighter to my stomach. *You are, little sprout. I will love you forever.*

But this solution with Max came with an expiration date. It had to. Of course, it had to. *Why would I think he meant our marriage to be forever?*

"Just, you know, until the baby is here and—"

"Five months," I plucked the date out of the fugue in my mind and then swallowed. "Then I'll be back from maternity leave and be able to get insurance as an employee." Or figure out another plan.

"Five months," Max repeated, his agreement bringing goosebumps to my arms.

A warning that I was starting down this path. *Five months.* How different things would be then. I would have a baby. Be a mom. *Be married to Max.*

"Why are you doing this?" I asked quietly. This was already more than he should ever have to do, and more I wanted to accept. "You aren't responsible for Todd or for—"

"Because I want to," he said so fiercely, the words sent a shock wave of sincerity through the air, stopping me from speaking and clipping the thought right where it rooted in my brain. "I want to do this, Daze."

Max's fingers slid around mine, the fork still miraculously gripped in my palm as my heart turned and turned like a child spinning in circles.

"I want to marry you."

"I guess we're going to have to get married."

Two proposals. Both because of the baby. But they couldn't have been more different. *Felt* more different. Todd's proposal was a postcard of what could be. A picture to look at and hope for. Max's was a heady promise of everything I'd ever wanted.

"Daisy." His voice broke through the fugue. And then his golden eyes. And his warm, strong fingers. "Marry me."

I pressed my hand to my mouth, just barely able to hold back my heart from climbing out of my throat.

When I looked at Max, there was no reluctance, no regret, no hesitation in his offer, when that was all Todd made me feel. With Max, it wasn't logic or responsibility that hardened his jaw or clouded his stare. It was something hotter. Heavier. Something that made my chest tighten and my core clench.

Something I shouldn't have felt for him before, and something I definitely couldn't afford to feel for him now.

"For five months." My throat bobbed, the words floating like a buoy of defense at the top of my throat. "Only five months." Setting the fork down, I extended my hand.

Max looked at it and then back up to me, the heat in his eyes turning to smoke.

"Five months," he acknowledged and slowly

wrapped his big hand around mine, swallowing it whole.

Countless times, he'd touched or held my hand over the last two weeks. Helping me in and out of the truck. Showing me how to unpackage the flowers and arrange them. So many times I'd felt the electric slide of his skin on mine, but never like this. Never like this was the first spark that created the universe.

Our hands shook, and for a second, I imagined him using it to pull me to him. Into his arms. Against his chest. My face up to his. *No.*

I tugged my hand free and buried it in the oversized T-shirt. "I'll still stay here," I blurted awkwardly.

"Of course." Max pushed his hand back into his pocket. "Nothing else will change. Just the paperwork."

For health insurance. "When…"

"Monday morning, we'll go to the courthouse, and then I'll call our health insurance rep and get you on my plan so you can reschedule your doctor's appointment."

"Okay." I nodded slowly again. "Thank you, Max," I said, the gratitude like lead on my tongue. I didn't like the feeling of being grateful for something I could never repay, and how could I ever repay him for this?

Worse, I hated knowing that buried far underneath that gratitude was the ache for something more.

I want to marry you.

Even worse, why did I keep hearing those words as real rather than a remedy?

Did a bride wear white to her fake wedding?

I stared at myself in the mirror on the back of the bathroom door, my wedding dress only marginally less rumpled for the half hour it hung in the steam-filled room while I showered. It didn't look the same as it had a little over two weeks ago. Not the way it fit over my changing body, nor the way I saw it after my change in circumstances.

Reaching up, I undid the braids in my hair, running my fingers through the resulting full waves. White was meant for pure and innocent, which I certainly wasn't. It also signified a new beginning, and that wasn't this either. This was...a means to an end. Biting my lip, I slid my hands to the zipper on the side. I shouldn't be wearing white, not when this marriage was a lie. Not a complete lie, but a white lie.

My fingers stilled. *A white lie.* My arms lowered, feeling a kind of comfort in the thought. That was why I could, should wear white, because this marriage wasn't a lie. It was true I needed Max's help, and true that he wanted to help me, and this served both of those things. The omission was that our marriage was for any other reason.

The omission was that we weren't getting married for love.

I closed my eyes and saw Max's face when he proposed, staring up at me from his knee on the floor. *Wanting to marry me.* My breath caught, and I sprang my gaze open. White dress. *White lie.* I went and walked to the window at the front of the apartment, glancing out the glass just as Max stepped out of his truck below.

He looked up, and I quickly moved away from the window before he saw me watching...waiting.

Was I really going to do this?

My heart beat against the front of my chest, wanting a front-row seat to my decision. My baby kicked, and I steadied myself in my decision, splaying my hands on my stomach.

I know, little sprout. I haven't even met you yet, but I would do anything for you.

Anything, including marrying my ex-fiancé's best friend.

I heard Max's footsteps on the stairs. By now, their sound was synonymous with the beat of my own pulse in my ears.

"Come in," I called at his knock, looking down at myself once more.

The wrinkled white fabric stretched over my stomach, which seemed to have popped overnight. The hem of the dress now hit my shins rather than below my ankles. I couldn't even wear the little matching jacket because my boobs were too big, barely fitting zipped into the bust of the dress, my chest spilling over the neckline. It looked ridiculous. Why didn't I see it before? I looked ridiculous, like a sausage stuffed into too tight a casing.

"Daze."

I jerked my head up, and Max's eyes captured mine. Not just his eyes, the intensity in his stare as it roamed over me. *The hunger.* "You look beautiful."

Heat dammed in my cheeks. *How did he know?*

How did he know what to say? When to say it?

"You've seen me in this dress before," I said, like it would pop the bubble the butterflies in my stomach were fluttering in. It didn't. In fact, it seemed to have the opposite effect.

"Not like this," he murmured, his stare leaving a path of fire over my skin.

"Like what?" More pregnant? More belly?

Or about to be his?

And in that moment, I let my own eyes wander over my soon-to-be groom.

Unlike me, Max had on a different suit than my last attempt to get married. Deep navy instead of dark gray. It favored his dark caramel hair and warm skin. It also highlighted his wide shoulders and trim waist. And somehow, I'm sure, the perfect proportions of his face.

His gaze snapped back to mine, and I watched him rein whatever had come over him back in. "Ready?"

I nodded, suddenly too overwhelmed to speak. A condition that plagued me as we went down to his truck and through the entire drive all the way to the courthouse.

Was I ready? Why was I acting like this was some huge change? It was signatures on a piece of paper. A document as a means to health insurance and safety, stability for me and my baby. Nothing more.

So what was I afraid of? That it would turn into something more?

Or that it wouldn't?

CHAPTER 13
MAX

"I want to marry you," I said and handed Daisy the bouquet of lavender and peonies I'd made especially for her this morning and then hid on the floor behind my seat in the truck.

Courthouse or not, marriage of convenience or not, I wasn't going to walk through those doors and swear to cherish her without showing her that first, even if it was only as friends.

Daisy balked, staring at the flowers with more surprise than when I'd dropped to one knee.

"Daze?"

"Sorry, I..." She blew out an exhale and carefully reached for them, her hand brushing mine. "Thank you for these." As she pulled them to her, I just managed to catch my wince. Todd's engagement ring still glinted on her finger—giant and flawless and wholly unlike the man who'd given it to her.

The words burned on the tip of my tongue to ask why she still wore it, but I swallowed them down, letting them scorch the air from my lungs.

It doesn't matter. It couldn't matter to me.

I lifted my hand to my neck, hooking my finger into my collar and giving it a tug. I shouldn't have been surprised when it didn't help the tightness in my chest.

"You didn't have to do this," she murmured even as she pulled the bouquet to her nose. Her appreciative moan destroyed me.

"I know I'm not Todd and that this isn't the wedding you imagined, but I care about you, Daisy. About what you deserve. And you deserve to have flowers on your wedding day."

She deserved more than fucking flowers. She deserved a husband in more than name, and a ring that didn't belong to a man who never deserved her. And that was why I'd driven up to Portland yesterday to visit a jewelry store. It made sense—going far enough away where people didn't know my family and the rumors wouldn't spread back to them. It made sense right up until I made it home with the simple, elegant gold band in my possession.

Daisy wouldn't want my ring. She didn't want anyone to know we were even married. It wasn't a marriage for show but a business arrangement. A contract for benefits. And I didn't give rings to anyone else I'd ever signed a contract with.

"Thank you, Max," she said, but just kept staring at the flowers.

"Are you sure you want to do this?" I asked, my throat thick. I was sure. I'd never been surer.

It took a second for her to nod and finally look at me. "Yes."

I managed that smile I'd perfected over the years. The friendly one that hid how I'd always felt about her.

"After you," I murmured and held open the door to the courthouse.

It was a few minutes past eight. I'd hoped by going first thing, we wouldn't have to wait long or run into too many people who might ask questions. I wasn't wrong.

The ceremony took twenty minutes. The clerk sat in a chair in the corner of the room as our witness. Judge MacDonald tried to look excited as he repeated the script he'd said hundreds of times. I didn't realize how much I'd expected Daisy to change her mind right up until the moment she said, "I do."

When it came to the end of the vows, and he declared I could kiss my bride, I reached for Daisy, cupped her face, and then just before my lips reached hers, I veered them to the side and kissed just next to her mouth. Close enough to feel the swift catch of her breath like she'd just dodged a bullet.

Because I wasn't the one she wanted. Not really.

I embraced the pain that slammed through my chest, expecting it to be my constant companion until our arrangement came to an end. It was a safety measure, the airbag that went off to save me from making a mistake that would irreversibly injure my heart.

The second I started blurring the lines of this convenient marriage was the moment I sealed my own downfall. I couldn't blur the lines but keep the emotional boundaries clear. If I kissed Daisy, I wouldn't be able to let her go. It would be like jumping off a cliff and expecting to fly. I wasn't the exception to gravity. And I wasn't the exception to falling for Daisy when her heart wasn't ever—had never been mine.

"What now?" she asked when we climbed back into

the truck, her face as white as the marriage certificate in her lap.

"We'll stop for breakfast, and I'll call my health insurance rep, and then we'll do our route for the day."

I'd thought about dividing up the deliveries to the other drivers to give us the day off, but I stopped myself. This marriage wasn't real, not to her, so the only thing that mattered was making good on my vow to take care of her. In order of priority, that was feeding her, getting the ball rolling on getting her on my insurance, and then driving. Lots of driving.

"Do we have a lot of stops?" She curled deeper into the seat, her fingers playing with the fabric of her dress on her stomach.

"Yeah." I pulled my printout from the driver's door and passed it to her.

She scanned over the list, and her shoulders slumped. "Perfect."

My grip on the wheel tightened, another blow of pain hitting my chest. I should be grateful for the distraction too.

"MEATBALL PARM SUBS." I SET THE DELIVERY BAG on the counter.

Daisy's eyes widened eagerly and then snapped to the second bag in my hand. "What's that?"

"Blueberry honey ice cream." I stuffed the dessert into the freezer and then pulled two plates from the kitchen cabinet in the apartment. When I turned back, she was staring at me cautiously. "Harper collaborated with Cool Beans on a special batch with her honey. She asked me to swing by and pick up a pint for you."

All true. It was also true that while we'd spent the better part of the day pretending things were the same, the reality was everything had changed. *We were married.* Even if it was only a temporary arrangement, only out of convenience, the longer we avoided mentioning the elephant, the bigger it would become.

"We got married this morning, Daze. Figured a little dessert wasn't a bad way to end the night."

Her gaze dropped, guilt flushing her cheeks. "Yeah." She offered a weak smile. "You're right."

I started to unpack the bag with the sandwiches, unwrapping each and placing them on plates. There were a dozen things I wanted to say, but I could tell there was something on her mind, and I didn't want to be the reason she never spoke it.

"Did you tell her...tell Harper?"

I stopped. "That we got married?"

Daisy nodded.

"No." I handed her a plate.

"Are you going to?"

"Judge MacDonald plays Canasta with Gigi and Frankie every week. They're going to find out whether I tell them or not," I admitted. I'd hoped it was a different judge who would be in this morning, but of course, it wasn't.

"They should hear it from you," she said and took a bite.

I watched her for a minute, devouring the dance of enjoyment over her features. I could survive on the sight of her, like a flower under the rays of the sun.

"Max?" Daisy's voice made me jerk. "Is everything okay?"

Shit. "Yeah." I shoved my sandwich into my mouth.

"You were staring at me. Is something wrong?" I felt her looking at me a little too closely. "Is there food on my face? Sauce?" She proceeded to drag her delicate pink tongue over the full curves of her lips, and desire settled straight and heavy into my dick.

"No," I said through gritted teeth.

"Is it something I said? Do you not want—"

"It's not anything you said or did, Daze," I said, frustration leaking into my voice. "It's just...you. I'm just staring at you."

She didn't respond right away. Instead, she stared back for a long second before averting her gaze back to her dinner. "I'm okay, Max. Really," she finally said with a soft, weak laugh.

Of course, she assumed I was worried about her. She wasn't wrong, but she wasn't right either. I was worried about her, but that wasn't why I stared. I stared because I couldn't stop myself. I stared because, from the moment I'd met her, if she was in the room, I couldn't keep my eyes off her.

I didn't trust myself to say anything else. Better that I didn't veer any closer to secrets I couldn't afford to share. The minutes filled with ravenous silence, both of us eating in a quiet orbit of all the things that were between us.

"When are you going to tell them?"

I picked up a napkin and slowly wiped my mouth.

"Your family, I mean," she clarified when I didn't reply quickly enough.

"Not sure yet." Until this morning, the only thing I

could think about was whether Daisy was going to say I do this morning or not.

"What if we go to dinner at your aunt's house this week?"

My muscles stiffened. "You want to be there?"

"I thought it would be easier." Daisy slid off the chair, intending to wash her plate, but I got to it before she could. "I don't want you to tell them yourself. You did this because of me—for me. I should be there. I should be the one to explain."

"They're not going to be mad, Daze," I tried to placate her. "They'll understand."

"Please, just let me do this."

I gritted my teeth. She thought she was helping me —to be there to weather the storm. Only she was preparing for a hurricane rather than an earthquake. It was the wrong catastrophe, believing they'd be upset that I'd married Daisy to help her. The real disaster was that I'd married the woman I wanted for four years, and she'd never know.

Abandoning both our plates in the sink, I went to the freezer, welcoming the blast of arctic cold to my face, hoping it could freeze my expression from revealing too much.

"Okay," I agreed, pulling out the ice cream. "We can tell them together."

And hopefully, Nox could keep his sarcastic mouth shut.

I popped the lid on the ice cream and turned to grab bowls. When I spun back, Daisy already had her spoon in the container, scooping out her first bite. She met my gaze. "I'm okay eating from the container if you are."

"Sure." I swallowed hard and replaced the bowls as she ate. "What's the verdict?"

"Delicious," she garbled, her mouth full of ice cream.

Fuck.

A drip of ice cream leaked from the corner of her lips. In any other scenario, I would've praised the speed of my reflexes, the way my hand went out and caught the droplet as it reached the edge of her jaw. Unfortunately, in this scenario, as I slid my knuckle up the soft patch of skin between her chin and lower lip, the only thing I could think was that I'd acted without thinking. I'd reached—touched—without considering the consequences.

A drop of ice cream on the floor or on her leggings was a small casualty compared to the torture of touching her. Infinitesimal compared to the torture of what happened next—Daisy's tongue collided with my finger, both sent to do the same job. And it was like gunpowder to a flame.

Was it not enough for me to be married to the woman of my dreams?

I yanked my hand back with such force I was surprised my entire body didn't ricochet with it.

"Sorry," she stammered, grabbing a napkin and wiping her whole mouth. It had to be the white of the paper that made her cheeks look redder. "You should have some before I eat the whole thing."

I too wiped my finger clean as I said, "It's all yours if you want it."

"I do," she paused and swallowed. "But I don't want to do something I'll regret." My eyes snapped to hers, the blue in them looking clear enough to fall into.

Was she talking about more than the ice cream? Daisy pushed the carton in my direction. No, of course not.

"Plus, I'm sure your sister wants you to try it too," she added when I reluctantly took the container and dug my spoon into the pale purple treat.

"Yeah." I took a big mouthful, welcoming the freeze on my brain.

More like she wanted to give me one more reason to be around Daisy, and that was the problem. My family knew but ignored—some better than others—my...obsession with my best friend's girlfriend-turned-fiancée. It was fine when *friends* were all that we were. When there was a propriety in not crossing the line and stating the obvious. But that line was gone. Todd was gone. And now Daisy and I were married.

That was why I didn't want her with me when I told my family. I doubted they'd be so bold as to say something, but there'd be no hiding their concern for the condition of my heart and the jeopardy I'd put it in. All for the sake of helping her. For being a friend. *For being a gentleman.*

I looked up and caught Daisy staring down at her engagement ring, spinning it around her finger.

The blows kept coming.

"I'm sorry," I said, hoping she attributed the crackling of my voice to the cold.

Her head leveled, pain tightening her features. "Please don't pity me, Max. I can accept anything from you but that."

I handed her the ice cream carton, knowing I should have kept silent. Or changed the subject. Anything but what I did.

"I don't pity you, Daze. I just mean I'm sorry that I'm not Todd," I said, not in the dramatic *I'm-not-as-good-as-him* way, but in the *he-should-be-your-husband-because-that-was-the-plan* way.

Her hand stilled, a spoonful of ice cream on its way to her mouth. Her clear blue eyes now cut like glass. "Don't ever be sorry for that."

My jaw clenched, and I went to the sink. "Just let me be sorry," I begged, flipping on the faucet and washing my hands so they'd stop themselves from reaching for her. "You should be married to him, and you're not, and I'm sorry for that. I'm sorry because this isn't what you wanted. You wanted him." *The father of your baby.*

After several seconds steeped only with the sound of rushing water, I set the last plate on the rack to dry and looked at Daisy. She was staring into the ice cream like it had frozen her from the inside out. I turned off the sink and gripped the edge of the counter, cursing myself for saying anything at all.

"Daze..." Her eyes slowly lifted, their surface watery. *Shit.* "Daisy—"

"I didn't want Todd," she said, and I swore those four words punctured every lobe in my lungs. "I didn't want to be with him. Not anymore. Things weren't good between us, Max. You know...had to have known. I was trying. In some ways, I know he was trying, but it just wasn't enough against what his parents wanted." She let out a bitter laugh, her eyes closing and severing the first curtain of tears. They fell right into the blue-berry ice cream, adding a whole new shade of *blue* to the container.

I tightened my hold on the sink, refusing to reach out and touch her.

"I used to think I was this independent person, that because of my mom, I'd never put myself in a position to rely on someone else. But somehow, I did. When I realized about the baby, protecting her was the only thing I could think. Giving her a family was the only thing I wanted."

My knuckles were so white I was surprised I wasn't cracking the base of the sink. I wanted to tell her that wasn't anything to be ashamed of. That she was doing what any good mother would do. But I knew she didn't want to hear that now.

"I cared enough about Todd to make myself think it would be better—that a baby would make things better, even after he responded like he did. Even after he continued to pull farther and farther away..." Her eyes closed again, sending another shower of tears dripping down her cheeks and an injection of ice into my veins. Dangerous, frigid guilt. "It just didn't make sense. He'd insist he wanted to get married. You know how he could be, sweet in that lost puppy dog kind of way. He'd hug me and promise me he wanted to get married, buy me gifts, or bring me flowers, and then a few days later, he'd drink and disappear into himself or somewhere else." She paused and swallowed. "It was like being in a boat floating near the shore. He'd pull me closer and closer only for a current to come in and rip me back out to sea."

I fought to keep my breathing steady. To not let my expression betray my emotions.

I was responsible for this. For telling him what flowers and gifts to get. I was the one instructing Todd on what to do and say, how to make amends for the things he kept fucking up because his spiraling kept worsening. I was the one who kept him afloat from underneath the surface because I believed Daisy wanted him. And to hear that she didn't...that I'd only prolonged this inevitable failure...

Air hissed from the pressure-locked chamber in my chest. Todd had royally fucked this up on his own, but to explain his actions...I couldn't tell her that. If I did, I'd have to confess my own role in them, and for that, I wasn't sure Daisy would ever forgive me.

"I'm sorry, Max. I know he's your friend. I shouldn't be telling you—"

"No," I croaked, my vocal cords grinding out the words. "You should be telling me, Daze, because you're my friend too." I swallowed hard, holding back that she didn't have to tell me because I already knew. "You're my only priority now." I went to stand in front of her, taking the empty carton and setting it on the counter so I could take her hands in mine. "You and this baby. You're the only things that matter."

She fought the urge to shiver, like a tree steeling itself against the wind. She didn't need me to take care of her. I knew that. What I needed her to know was that I was going to do it anyway.

CHAPTER 14
DAISY

"You're nervous," I said when Max opened the passenger door.

"What?" He smiled and shook his head like the idea was ridiculous. "What would I be nervous about, Daze? I told you, my family isn't going to be upset or angry at you. They know you and me. They're going to understand why we did this."

And he'd spent the past half hour reiterating it to me as we drove from Stonebar to his aunt's house.

"Then why is the top button of your shirt undone?"

Max stiffened and reached for his collar. Just like I'd suspected, he hadn't realized he'd left the top button undone. He never did.

"Must've missed it."

"You always miss it when you're nervous."

His head tipped, and whatever else I was going to say evaporated from my tongue as his long fingers thumbed and pressed the button into its rightful seat. It was the smallest movement—a fraction of a second—but that was all it took for my hormones to hallucinate his touch. Those fingers on my face. My skin. Thumbing my nipple. Pressing lower—harder where I ached between my thighs.

"Daisy?"

I yanked my eyes up to his, praying he couldn't see how my whole body was vibrating. "The day you and Todd met with those first investors in Portland. The day you bought Todd out of the business. At Todd's dad's birthday party. And then my wedding—" I stopped. I was about to say *my wedding day,* except it wasn't. My wedding day was actually four days ago, standing at the courthouse with this man who'd always shown up for me. *The button hadn't been undone that day.* "I mean, the day Todd left."

Max's brow furrowed slowly, and I wondered which thought made it crease—that he didn't realize he had a tell or that I did. "You fixed my collar right before Todd and I left for that meeting..."

Swallowing, I nodded, remembering that moment too. I remembered feeling like the axis of the earth tipped ever so slightly when I got close to him, when my fingers brushed the skin of his neck. It was so slight, I thought I'd imagined it. *I told myself I'd imagined it.*

"You told me not to be nervous," he murmured as I took his hand, his warm touch making me shiver.

"Yeah." I let him help me down, my sandals crunching in the dirt.

Even though it was only dinner at his family's house, I wanted to look nice. I wanted to put my best foot forward given the circumstances. That was why I'd chosen the long boho lavender dress I'd found at a thrift shop over the weekend. It fit perfectly, was comfy, and I thought it would hide my sneakers. But apparently, as of earlier today, my sneakers no longer fit my swelling feet.

I should've seen it coming. I knew this was common in the last trimester, and I should've seen the signs. Mostly, how every day this week, we'd get back from making deliveries and I'd take them off only to see their shape clearly indented into my flesh. But tonight of all nights was the first time I went to put them on and knew I wouldn't last five minutes, let alone through a whole dinner, with them on. So...weather-inappropriate sandals it was.

I hoped Max didn't notice. *No.* He would. What I really hoped was that if I didn't say anything, he wouldn't either. I couldn't take another blow to my pride this week. Maybe that made me foolish or ungrateful, or maybe it just made me hormonal, but I just couldn't accept anything else from him right now.

Max closed the door behind me and then took my hand. It was that hold that stopped him from walking away. He looked over his shoulder, our hands linked between us.

"If you know they're going to be okay with it, why are you nervous?"

A shadow passed over his face—the same one I'd seen a handful of times since Monday. "I just don't want them to get the wrong idea about us."

His answer needled into my chest. "That I forced you—"

"No, of course not, Daze." Max let out a rough breath followed by a shaky laugh. "I don't want them to think there's...something else going on between us."

That needle punctured all the air from my lungs.

Something else, like the vibrations still running through my body from that silly button.

"Oh." I gulped.

"I'm sorry. I shouldn't have said anything. I doubt they'll think that." His jaw flexed.

"Right," I agreed with a strained laugh and repeated, "Why would they?"

Like a sinking ship, my gaze drew down to where my hand was linked with his. If they knew even half the things Max had already done for me, maybe the better question was *"How could they not?"*

"HERE, LET ME TAKE THAT," AILENE SCOLDED WITH a smile, shifting the stack of plates from my hands to her own and bringing them to the sink.

"Thank you," I murmured and took a seat on one of the stools at her kitchen counter. I'd only moved from the dining room to the kitchen, helping the whole Kinkade-Hamilton clan clear the table from dinner. "The tacos were amazing. Thank you again for having me."

I couldn't have been happier to learn tonight was taco night. The twenty-odd-person table was filled end to end with taco shells, three different kinds of meat, roasted vegetables, and all the fixings. I'd thought there were a lot of people in the house, but that was nothing compared to the amount of food.

"Oh, of course, Daisy." Ailene smiled over her shoulder, her hands scrubbing away at the dishes with movements too coordinated to be anything but reflex now. "We're so happy to have you here. I keep telling them we need some fresh blood at family dinner."

"Fresh blood, Mom?" Lou laughed as she stood next to her mom and, towel in hand, took the wet plates one after one to dry them. "We've added Wade and Maeve to the headcount this year."

"You know what I want, Elouise."

Lou shot me a look and filled me in. "Mom wants to run out of room at her table."

"Run out?"

"Yup." Lou's lips popped on the *p*.

"This way she can ask Jamie to build her a newer, ever bigger one, and then complain it's not filled again," Frankie connected the last of the dots.

My heart squeezed painfully—beautifully—and my eyes took a sweep through the house under rapidly fluttering eyelids. Max's dad, George, was standing by the windows in the living room, holding a baby in each arm, Violet's daughter, and one of Aurora's twins, talking to each of them in turn. Next to him stood Nox, who held the other twin. In the dining room, Violet, Chandler, Jamie, and Wade laughed as they cleared the rest of the serving bowls from the table. And in the corner of the kitchen, Max, Kit, and Gigi crowded around the bar, working on a fresh round of drinks, Gigi ordering the two men around, giving them a light thwack with her cane on the back of their legs when they pretended not to listen.

It was easy to be jealous of this family. To be jealous of the way they welcomed people so easily into their fold. But it was even easier to take that green seed of jealousy and plant it deep, storing these memories away to water it later when I needed a reminder of the kind of family I wanted to give my daughter.

My gaze turned back to Ailene and Lou, my heart swelling a little bigger. This was the love I wanted her to feel. The love between mother and daughter, washing dishes in the sink. The love that was unquestionable. Tender but unbreakable. The kind of love I'd never known growing up.

Ailene had raised four children as a single mom, and as I watched her interaction with Lou, I knew it was something they'd done together like this for decades. Meanwhile, when I was younger, I'd washed the dishes alone. My mom was either working or telling me it was the least I could do. *The least I could do for the burden I'd caused her.*

I never wanted my daughter to feel like a burden. No matter what happened to me or in my life. I wanted her to look at me the way Lou looked at Ailene—like she admired her not for how much she'd been through, but for how much she continued to give to everyone around her.

"Ugh, I miss being pregnant." Frankie sighed and took a seat on the stool next to me, switching her son, Logan, from one arm to the other.

"You're crazy," Violet scoffed gently, striding around her sister-in-law toward the fridge to put away the container of remaining sour cream and salsa. "I was so bloated by the end, I told Jamie I thought I was going to lift off and float away."

"Good thing I found a way to tie you down," her husband, the oldest of the Kinkades, walked around her then, maneuvering his auburn head, and pressed a kiss to her neck. She laughed and turned so he could steal one more kiss, this time from her lips.

Frankie laughed, catching my attention just as she looked over to her husband, Chandler, and winked at him.

I quickly brought my glass of ice water to my mouth and took a strong gulp. I envied Max's cousins for the relationships they had. Even at a family dinner, they still found ways to make each other feel special. I never had that with Todd. With Todd, I'd always been like a trophy by his side. Something to show off but never to take a moment to admire himself. And when we were with his parents, I was a trophy that never gleamed bright enough. And the thought of how they'd treat our daughter made me physically nauseous.

When I lowered my glass, my eyes searched for somewhere safe to land—to give the couple a moment of privacy and let the tightness in my chest that I was ashamed to admit was jealousy loosen. And my gaze found Max. Every time I searched for him, he was there. *Always*.

"How are you feeling, Daisy?"

I snapped my stare back to Frankie. *How was I feeling?* Alone. Worried. Angry...*Aching.*

"You're in your third trimester now, right?" Frankie continued next to me.

Oh. She was talking about the pregnancy, not... everything else.

"Yeah. I'll be twenty-nine weeks next week."

"Oh." Frankie's eyes rounded. "I remember twenty-nine weeks." She tipped her chin in Chandler's direction. "Chandler remembers those weeks *very* well," she added with another wink to me this time.

The hormones. I knew. I didn't need a wink or a reminder. I lived with the reminder every day. The way Max's charm made my breath catch. How his touch made my skin sing. How just a glance made my stomach flutter. Being around Max fed my hormones like they'd been starved my entire life. I tried not to think that maybe they had.

"Everything okay?" Max's smooth voice rumbled next to me, but it was the brush of his fingers on my lower back that made my breath hitch.

I swore I must be sending some kind of hormonal smoke signal because Max always appeared when he sensed I needed something—even if that something was only his presence.

Turning, I nodded and started to say *yes*, but the word stuck in my throat, seeing the look in his eyes. It was now a look I recognized. A look that Jamie had for Violet, and Chandler for Frankie, and Wade for Lou, and Kit for Aurora. And then he blinked, and it was gone.

"How is everything going with FMH, Max?" Jamie asked as he packaged the leftover chicken and beef into savers.

FMH was a huge hotel management group based out of Boston. Their landmark luxury hotel sat on the rim of Copley Square, and the name only stuck out because I remembered how surprised Todd had been when Max got a meeting with the CEO. It was recent, after Todd had left MaineStems, but before we got engaged. I sensed Todd took it as some kind of personal failure that Max was still able to get meetings with big companies without him, without the connections of the McCormicks.

God, how many of Todd's insecurities had I ignored or explained away?

"Great," Max answered, his hand falling away from my back like he just realized someone else might see. "They have their annual pancreatic cancer awareness fundraising gala in three weeks, and we're doing all the flowers. Erica's been handling the bulk of the prep work, but I'm going to be in the city for that to make sure everything goes smoothly."

In Boston.

"Damn, Harp, this blueberry honey is good," Nox rumbled, swirling the drink Kit just handed him. It looked to be some whiskey and honey combination.

"Thanks," Harper beamed.

"Are you going to start selling it soon?" From what I'd gathered, she'd only made a small batch that had been given out to friends, family, and a few local businesses to use.

"It's going to be one of six special edition flavors that I'm going to reveal next spring."

"Next spring?" That seemed like forever from now. Maybe because so many things would be different in my life by spring. I'd have a baby. Max wouldn't be my husband anymore.

"I still have three more flavors to work out."

"And she's fighting off a bully."

"Gigi!" Harper shook her head with a groan, glaring at the bright purple head of hair that bobbled into the dining room. "I'm not. It's fine. Wade sent him a letter, so I think—I hope—it will stop."

Right. Lou's fiancé was a big-shot Boston lawyer. It was hard to remember that when he worked at the inn with Lou, like living in this small town and being by her side was the only thing he'd ever wanted to do.

"That's good."

"It is..."

"But?"

"Sometimes, it feels like the damage is already done. The ideas he planted...the things people say online or leave reviews for my products..."

I took her hand and squeezed. I hated the internet bully culture, especially when it was compounded by those who didn't even bother to take the time to verify the truth.

"Let them," I said softly. "Let them talk. Let them waste their time. Just keep doing you, Harper."

"Thanks, Daisy." She tipped forward and hugged me as best she could. Over her shoulder, I caught Max's arched brow. Without thought, my head jerked to the side as if to tell him I hadn't said anything to her. She drew back, and I wasn't prepared for what came next. "How are you doing? After everything..."

Her voice was quiet, wanting me to know this conversation was only between us. I didn't begrudge her for asking. I couldn't. Not when there was only an earnest concern in her tone.

"I'm..." How was I? Alone? Married? Attracted to my temporary husband? "I'm going with the flow."

"Have you...heard from Todd?"

I shook my head, my hand instinctively reaching for my stomach.

It wasn't the first time I'd been asked the question in the last few weeks, but it was the first time anyone but Max had asked it. There was an unspoken agreement between Max and me. We never asked if the other had heard anything from anyone because we knew the other would share as soon as one of us did. It spared us a conversation that neither of us wanted to have.

"No, I haven't," I said, offering her a brave smile but holding back the part of the answer I hadn't told anyone —*that I didn't want to*.

Todd made his choice, one I should've made long ago, and to talk to him now or for him to come back now —it would only complicate the life I had to rebuild for myself and our daughter. I wouldn't stop him from seeing the baby. Underneath all his mistakes, I knew Todd had a good heart. Time and space made clearer that he didn't know how to love anyone else because no one had ever made him feel safe enough to love himself.

"Blueberry cookies?" A tray of the most delicious-smelling treats appeared between me and Harper, Gigi's smiling face on the other side. "A little birdie mentioned the baby likes blueberries."

"She does," I said with a smile and went to take one.

"Oh, no. Take the big one," Gigi insisted, and I happily complied with a small laugh. The cookie was still warm.

"Ailene and I made them earlier with some of Harper's honey. If you want a little extra blueberry, I have some jam you can slather on top," she said the last and presented me a jam jar and a conspiratorial glint in her eyes.

"I think this is plenty, thank you."

"For later, then." Her grin widened, and she tucked the jar into my bag. "This one is special. Just for you."

I was too stimulated to think long on what exactly that meant, so I simply thanked her and went on wishing this family were mine. Their warmth. Their laughter. Their support. Their love. My chest pinched.

It wasn't the first time I'd had the thought in the last four years, nor probably the last. But like my marriage with Max, I would only let it be temporary. He and his family weren't meant to be mine. Not really.

"Oh, Daisy. You can *never* have too much of a good thing."

My hand froze halfway to my open mouth. *Was she...*

"I see the way my grandson looks at you."

Oh god—

"Gigi—" Harper hissed in warning.

"Harper Victoria, don't you shush me. I'm ninety-five. I'll say whatever I please, and you can blame it on dementia when I walk away," she chided, and it was a good thing I hadn't taken a bite of anything or I might've spit it out.

I glanced at Harper, who just mouthed *sorry* as Gigi went on.

"You deserve better," she said to me and set the tray of cookies on the kitchen island. "I'm not sorry for saying it now, just like I'm not sorry for saying it twenty-four years ago to my own daughter. Ailene deserved better than Lou and Frankie's sperm donor, who only wanted her for the wrong reasons, and you deserve better than that man who never once looked at you like Max does."

"And how is that?" I shocked myself by asking. If she was going to be bold, then so was I. I wanted to know what she saw. I wanted to be able to tell myself later that she was mistaken.

I felt the others start to draw toward the kitchen, but I ignored them, only wanting her answer.

"Like you're his sunlight."

I exhaled with a whoosh. "We're just friends."

"If that's the only good thing you want..." she said, her grin widening for a second before she walked toward Nox, the young man clearly nervous to be in her sights.

"Don't mind her. She's..."

"Got dementia?" I joked with a weak laugh. There was no way Gigi had dementia. In fact, I was pretty sure she was more with it than I was at the moment, the way my pregnancy brain was working.

Harper snorted. "Something like that."

"Everything okay over here?" Max came over then, standing close enough for his arm to brush my shoulder as he reached for a cookie from the tray. He looked at me then, and I felt warmth. *Sunlight.*

"Yeah," Harper chirped.

"Good." Max cleared his throat, his eyes swinging around the now-crowded kitchen before he spoke over the buzz of everyone else's conversation. "Because I have an announcement."

The buzz quickly died, and my heart launched into my throat, pounding for escape. *Oh god.* What if he was wrong? The thought spun like a top in my head. *What if he was wrong, and they hated me for this?* All I could see was the great loves his cousins had found—the way they talked about that for him. And now they were going to learn he hadn't married for love, but out of charity.

What had I asked him to do?

My tongue pushed against the roof of my mouth.

The words were right there...to tell him to stop. To keep me his secret.

"Before any rumors get around, I wanted to tell you all that as of earlier this week, Daisy and I are married."

For a family who hadn't been quiet since the moment we walked into the house earlier, their stunned silence hit like a freight train. Harper's jaw looked like it hit the floor. Jamie and Kit shared a look.

"Married?" George was the first to speak as he looked at his son.

Max met his dad's pained gaze and nodded slowly. "After what happened a few weeks ago, Todd's parents have been...threatening toward Daisy, so we decided it was best for her and the baby if we were married until after the baby arrives."

A collection of gasps and whimpers echoed around the kitchen, but it was hard to tell exactly who they came from.

"Threatening?" Ailene stepped forward, a protective thread of steel stitched to her voice, and my throat tightened. I wasn't part of her family, yet with a single word, she made me feel like one of her own.

My whirring mind braked hard and reversed back through what Max had said—and what he hadn't. He hadn't mentioned anything about needing health insurance. That he'd left what I needed from him out of the equation. *That he'd spared me from any negative assumptions that might come my way.*

"We have everything under control," Max assured her with that easy calm of his, but only I could see the crumbs that fell from the cookie onto the counter as he held it a little tighter. "But I wanted to tell you before you heard it from anyone else."

"When?" George's salty-gray eyebrows furrowed together.

"At the courthouse on Monday," Max answered his dad, whose head ducked in response.

He was disappointed, if not angry. I could feel it. The shift in his demeanor was like a chill through the room, and Max felt it too because his hand moved to rest on my back.

"I'm so sorry you're going through this, Daisy," Aurora said, tears welling in her eyes as she came over, the first to envelop me in a hug, but not the last.

Over the course of minutes, there was a soft flurry of conversation between Max and his family while Frankie, Lou, Violet, Ailene, and Gigi all came over to hug me in turn.

"I'll be okay. It's just for a few months until everything settles down," I assured them, tugging a quick smile to my cheeks, trying to ignore the growing heat there and the panic in my mind that Max's dad hated me for this.

"So does this mean you're moving back out of Dad's?" Nox chimed in.

Move out of his dad's? I turned and looked at Max, and he refused to look back at me. *What was Nox talking about?*

"Nox." Max's voice lowered to a tenor I wasn't quite sure I'd ever heard before. It was hard. Commanding.

Nox just arched his eyebrows, and suddenly it seemed like the entire conversation hinged on the answer to his question.

After a long glare, Max ground out his monosyllabic answer, "No."

His brother's mouth wilted, and then with a shake of his head, he muttered something along the lines of, "Good luck with that," and then headed for the door to the back porch, drink in hand.

"Let him go," George said in a low voice, echoing the sentiment I'd told Harper earlier.

"What can we do? What can I do?" Wade chimed in, a distraction for everyone except the hamster in my brain that latched onto what just happened with Nox and ran in circles with it.

Does this mean you're moving back out of Dad's? Back out. Like he wasn't living there, but now he is again. And there's only one most likely reason for that. Me.

"Nothing right now," Max answered as the pit in my stomach yawned wider. "I'll let you know if that changes."

The next twenty minutes passed in a blur of more questions and condolences and tender support. The untempered beat of my pulse strengthened when Max's dad came over to him, and they talked in hushed voices that I couldn't hear, not when Ailene and Gigi were talking next to me. And then George stepped away from his son and finally moved to talk to me.

When he stopped in front of me, I felt the words *I'm sorry* collect on my tongue, but before I could work them out, he reached out and hugged me.

"I'm so sorry, Daisy," he said gently, and I wanted to cry with relief. "If there is anything we can do..."

"Your son has done more than enough—more than I can ever thank him for." My throat clogged.

George tipped forward then, surprising me by muttering low, "Take care of him, Daisy. Please."

Take care of Max? Did he not hear any of this conversation? Max was the one taking care of me...

CHAPTER 15
DAISY

The last forty minutes blurred into a fog until Max helped me into his truck. A haze of sad looks, understanding hugs, and offers of support—all of which I was grateful for, but nothing that surmounted the brief but memorable exchange Max had with his brother.

"What did Nox mean?" I asked as we drove down the long drive, the light rain tapping the windshield like sharp fingernails on the top of a desk, waiting for his answer too.

Max didn't tense. He *was* tense since the moment he'd started the engine. He knew this was coming. He knew I wouldn't just let it go.

"Don't worry about him. He's just dealing with some stuff that happened before he went to Italy, and he projects onto others," Max offered, and while it explained some, it didn't answer my question.

"I meant, why did he ask if you were moving back out of your dad's? Is that where you're living?" *Was it really any of my business?* Last week, I would've convinced myself no, but now...now, he was my husband. Whatever the reason and for however long, we'd sworn for better or for worse, and if there was a way I could be there for him in even a fraction of the way he'd been there for me over the last month, I was going to take it.

"Daisy—"

"I won't judge you, Max. How can I judge you? My life is in shambles. I was stood up on my wedding day, my first one, and now I'm living out of your apartment—"

"Yes, it's where I'm living right now," he interrupted, and I cut off my self-deprecating ramble because he was answering me. "And no, I'm not worried about you judging me, Daze."

"Why didn't you just stay at your house until it sells?" Something wasn't adding up, but when I looked to Max, the only thing I could see was the catch of the moonlight on the hard planes of his profile.

"It was easier," he grunted. "House stays nice for showings. Honestly, I thought it would sell faster, so it seemed easier to move out when I had the opportunity and not have to worry about it later."

I let those words sink into my head. Maybe I should let them be the end of the conversation. I had my answer. I had an answer I was comfortable with. But I knew Max well enough to know when he was giving me enough of the truth to satisfy me yet spare me at the same time.

"So you left your own home to move back in with your dad?" When he didn't answer right away, I continued, "Why is Nox upset about that?"

"He's not. He just wants to give me a hard time."

"Because of me," I finished what I knew he wouldn't say. "Because you're helping me."

"No, that's not—"

"Then tell me what it is, if it's not that, because that's the only thing that makes sense." His knuckles were white on the steering wheel as he turned onto the highway toward Stonebar. "He's upset you're helping me...upset you married me to help me. It's okay."

"Dammit, Daze. That's not the reason." Max huffed and pried one hand off the steering wheel to run through his hair.

"Then tell me what it is. Stop treating me like I'm too fragile to handle the truth."

"Fine," he growled. "Nox is giving me a hard time because I was staying in the apartment before moving back in with Dad."

His answer hit like a wrecking ball.

"The apartment...you mean the apartment you're renting to me? The one you told me no one was using?" Shock and anger surged inside me like fire and ice.

"Well, I wasn't really using it. I was only there temporarily." Max slowed the truck and cranked the wipers up to full blast, but I wasn't seeing the storm.

I was seeing the boxes of clothes. All his things he'd cleaned out the following day, insisting he'd been using the space as an office. *How had I not realized?*

Because no matter how deep Max planted himself in my life, there were whole chunks of his that he kept hidden from me.

I lifted my hand to my throat, feeling the drum of my pulse along my fingers and the way it matched the incessant batter of the rain on the windshield.

"Max, you were *living* in it. I think that's the definition of using it," I said, my voice strangled between the urge to laugh and the overwhelming tide to cry.

Max didn't move back home because he was selling his house. He moved back home in order to give me the apartment. And if that wasn't enough, he'd gone and married me so I could have good health insurance. *No wonder Nox was annoyed.*

"Fine, I was using it, and when you needed a place, I decided I didn't need to use it anymore." He shrugged it off like he'd loaned me a pen and not his own living space.

The rain lightened again like we were reaching the edge of the cloud, and my back pressed into the seat as Max picked up a little speed again.

"No." I shook my head. "You don't get to do that. I asked you—"

"And if I told you the truth, you never would've accepted it, no matter how not big of a deal it was."

Not big of a deal...

"I wouldn't have accepted it because it wouldn't have been the right thing to do—to kick you out of your own place so I wouldn't have to deal with my reality," I fired at him, the air in the truck cab suddenly charged as though all the nerves that had built all day, worried about how his family might react, now caught like gunpowder set on fire by the realization that..."You lied to me, Max."

"No, I didn't—"

"You didn't tell me the whole truth. It's the same thing."

"Dammit, Daze—*Shit!*" Max shouted, his arm swinging in front of me as he slammed on the brakes.

The tires screeched, his truck sliding on the freshly

slicked fallen leaves on the road. I cried out when the back tires swung off the edge of the asphalt, bouncing the whole vehicle as they landed on the gravel shoulder, and we finally came to a halt.

My chest heaved, my arms locked around my middle. I stared out the front windshield at the doe and her baby, who'd darted into the road in front of Max.

They were the reason he'd slammed on the brakes.

"Daisy?"

I heard him, but it was at a distance. As though I were frozen in a block of ice and Max was calling to me outside it.

"Daisy, are you all right?"

Slowly, my gaze lowered, taking stock of myself. I willed my arms to move, but they wouldn't. They refused to let go of the baby even though we were safe.

I started to shake, the surge of adrenaline now flooding my system.

"Shit." I wanted to look at him, but I couldn't. I couldn't take my eyes off the doe in the middle of the wet, leaf-covered road, standing like the proverbial *deer in headlights*.

She'd run into the road after her fawn. To protect it. She'd run right in front of the charging truck and now was just as paralyzed as I was.

You're okay, I wanted to tell her. *He'd never hurt you.*

The passenger door opened, and the movement spurred the deer out of her trance.

"Daisy." Max's voice was on the other side of me now, and the deer jerked her gaze to him, and then bounded off the side of the road and into the woods, her baby close behind her.

"Daisy..." Max took my shoulder in his hand and rested the other on top of mine, where it lay over my stomach. I let out the exhale that had gone stale from sitting held in my lungs and slowly turned to him.

Rain dripped onto him, stringing my gaze along with each droplet. From the wet waves of his hair to the hard crease of his brow to the ridge of his cheekbones, I let myself look at him in the way I'd only stolen glances of before. I let myself linger on the warm amber of his eyes, the taut curve of his jaw, and the tight bow of his mouth...

I could only imagine what that mouth would do to a woman. *I could only imagine what that mouth would do to me.*

"Are you okay?"

Physically or psychologically? Physically, I was fine. But the way I wanted to kiss him right now...psychologically, that didn't bode well.

"I think so..." The words were hardly out before my seatbelt was unclipped and strong hands shaped my waist, somehow making me feel small as he spun me like a doll in the seat.

If Max heard my gasp, he didn't register it. Meanwhile, all I could register was how his characteristically calm face had turned to granite. His warm eyes were now the gradient of hot metal, cool and dark in the center and hot and glowing on the edges.

"Are you sure?" His molten gaze, and then his big hands, roamed over me. Well, not over the parts that ached for him. *Unfortunately.* But over my arms and shoulders. He framed my chin in the V between his thumb and forefinger, turning my head side to side. "The baby?"

"She's fine." My fingers grazed low on my stomach, feeling her move. "We're fine. I promise."

He clenched his jaw, fighting to accept it for a second. "I'm sorry. The deer came out of nowhere."

"Don't apologize, Max," I rushed to stop him. "It's not your fault. She was just worried about her baby..."

As I trailed off into silence, our eyes remained tangled, his searching for danger, and mine, a space to ask for forgiveness.

He'd never hurt you. The thought I'd had for the momma deer now circled back for me.

No, Max hadn't told me the whole truth, but he was right. If he had, I wouldn't have taken the apartment. I would've gone back to the city, to my crappy apartment, which would've exponentially increased the stress of the situation and of my future.

Maybe he should've told me the whole truth, but maybe I needed to stop pushing help away on principle.

He'd never hurt you.

Max would never hurt me. *Never.*

"I'm sorry," I said, my deep exhale dragging my head down between my shoulders. "You're right, I wouldn't have listened if I knew you were living there. I'm not good at...being helped."

I'd been hurt enough times—and warned about being hurt just as many—that I'd poured tar into the cracks of my heart and then dipped the whole thing in steel, determined not to let anyone close enough to break it. But Max didn't give me a choice. He was just there with everything I wanted. Everything I needed. Eroding all my defenses.

"I will always be there for you, Daisy," he rasped, and as my gaze lifted to his face, I caught the violent quake of his chest, the rain having molded the fabric to his muscles. "Not because of what Todd did. Not because you were his fiancée. But simply for you. For your baby. I will always be there for you. Always. And if that means a white lie to make sure you've got a roof over your head or a temporary marriage to make sure you're safe, then so be it."

My lip trembled. How could someone be this good?

"I know—"

"No, I don't think you do." Max skated his hands to the sides of my face, holding me to his stare. "I'm sorry your mom didn't show up for you when you were young, Daze. I'm sorry she warned you no one else would either. And I'm sure as shit sorry that Todd proved her right. But I won't. Just because none of them showed up for you doesn't mean I won't. I'm not repeating this cycle, Daze. I'm breaking it. I want better for you. For her. And I'm going to do everything in my power to give it to you."

Was my jaw on the ground?

I'm not repeating this cycle, Daze. I'm breaking it.

Did I even want to pick it back up?

My eyes sank to his lips, and I breathed in deep. Fresh rain. Charged oxygen. Mint and raw male. *I want better for you.* His promise turned over and over in my mind until it turned completely into a question. *Who wanted better for him?*

Max was always giving. Always doing for others. *Who took care of him? Gave for him? Sought to please him?* I couldn't remember the last time I saw him with a woman, let alone the last time Todd mentioned he was dating anyone. I knew he was busy—knew he carried the weight of his business's success and the livelihoods of the people he employed solely on his shoulders. But even then—especially then—how could he not have anyone to take care of him? *To be there for him?*

And I wasn't talking about his family.

He might be able to hide behind a busy schedule to them, but I saw how he was selling his house because it was *too big,* rather than searching for someone to share it with. I saw how he made time to get dinner with me most nights of the week. I saw every effort he made to be thoughtful for me, whether it was buying me clothes or bringing me back blueberry cobbler for dessert. It wasn't a lack of time or effort that stopped him from finding someone to be with, so what was it?

Me.

The answer clawed from somewhere deep inside my chest. *Because I was his wife.*

"Max..." I reached out and spread my palm on the wet fabric on his chest, feeling the hard thump of his heart, like it wanted to punch right through his ribs and put itself in my hand. A grenade with its pin pulled, waiting to let loose everything I'd watched him contain for years.

Wanting. Aching. Longing. *I wanted better for me too.* And Gigi was right. There was no man better than Max Hamilton. Not for me.

"What about you?" I asked, my tongue slipping out and over my lips, trying to calm the quell of my nerves. "What if I want better for you?"

Better than a fake wife. Better than having to care for his best friend's ex and unborn baby.

The warm ebb of his breath turned ragged, and I realized something changed then. *Now.* The way he looked at me, the way we looked at each other...there was something there we'd tried to keep hidden before, but there was no hiding it anymore.

His head inched closer, and I realized how little space separated us, how my legs had drifted apart to make room for him.

"Daisy," he drawled, his voice hardly above a whisper as his thumb skated along the edge of my bottom lip. "There is nothing better for me than you."

My eyes, which were almost shut, snapped open wide and up to his. *I couldn't have heard...He couldn't mean...*

I've had years of moments spent with Max. Public moments. Private moments. Sad moments. Happy moments. But no moment ever felt like this. No moment had ever felt both intimate and combustible at the same time, like a seam about to burst.

"Max..." His name wasn't a sound, but the hum of longing in my chest.

His lips tightened like he was trying to rein them in, trying to keep them from kissing me. But god, all I wanted was for him to kiss me. All I wanted was to taste every promise he'd made me on the edge of his tongue. All I wanted was to give something to the man who gave everything.

"I'm sorry..."

I reached up and grabbed his wrists. "Don't" was all I could manage. My tongue was too thick to say more, my lungs too clogged with lust.

I didn't want him to pull away now. I wanted him closer. I wanted those lips on mine. I wanted even more from this man who'd already given me too much.

His muscles tensed as I slid my hands up his arms, his gaze tracking them like they were snakes—predators

—and he wasn't sure if it was safer to shake me off or stay perfectly still. In the end, he didn't move until my fingers found the side of his face, and his whole body released a shudder.

For a second, I thought the sound I heard was thunder, but it wasn't. It was the groan that quaked from his chest, the one that sounded an awful lot like restraint breaking under the weight of longing.

"Max," I whispered, the tip of his nose bumping mine. We were so close now, not even the rain had space to fall between us. Instead, it splattered on my cheeks as I tipped out of the protection of the truck.

All my life, I'd been so focused on protecting myself from everyone who could hurt me or let me down. But not now. I didn't want to be protected from him.

He would never hurt me.

"Kiss me." The plea spilled from my parted lips.

"Dammit, Daze," he groaned. "What are you doing to me?" *I had no idea, but it felt like the same thing he was doing to me.* My eyes fluttered shut as his head dipped. The warmth of his breath greeted my lips, and he moved his hand on top of my left one, where I held his cheek.

"*Shit.*"

My eyes flung open. His tone changed. *Everything* changed. The longing in his gaze was now soaked with pain, and instead of kissing me like he'd been about to—*like I begged him to*—he turned his head away and pressed his lips to my palm, his eyes squeezing shut like the taste of my skin was his very last meal.

"You're getting soaked," he said, releasing my hand and stepping away from me. "Let's get you home."

My tongue was too thick to protest. I *was* getting

soaked, but it had nothing to do with the rain and everything to do with him. Everything to do with the fact that the barriers that we'd stacked between us for years felt like they'd finally come down. Until he pulled away.

To protect me.

I knew Max, and it was the only reason I could think of as he bundled me back into my seat and carefully closed the door.

How did I convince him that holding back wasn't protecting me? That he wasn't taking advantage of me by kissing me?

I'D NEVER FELT A SILENCE SO THICK AND HEAVY AS the one that filled Max's truck on the remainder of the drive back to the apartment. It was almost as though...

I turned to him. "Max—"

"Let's get inside before it starts up again," was all he said before he let himself out of the truck, making it to my side just as I slid my feet back into my sandals.

He helped me down, used his jacket over me to protect me from the drizzle, and held the door for me to enter first. It was like he wanted it to be like nothing had changed. Except it had.

He'd almost kissed me. *And I'd wanted him to.*

"Why did you stop?" I asked quietly when I reached the top of the steps, positioning myself in front of the door so he couldn't reach it.

Here in the stairwell, he only had two choices: answer my question or turn around and leave.

Max's jaw tightened. "Daisy—"

"I wanted you to kiss me, and you didn't. Tell me why," I said, lacking all bandwidth to be anything other than demanding. Anything less, and my reservations would be too overpowering. My fears that it wasn't right or fair or the right time would drown out the one thing I wanted for myself. *Him.* "The whole truth, Max, or say goodnight."

The choice warred inside him for a split second, and then he gave me what I asked for. I shouldn't have been surprised when it shattered me.

"I won't kiss a woman who's wearing another man's ring."

My gasp echoed his retreating footsteps, my eyes sinking to my left hand. *The hand his closed over when we were outside.* He'd felt the engagement ring, and that's why he'd stopped. *Why he'd changed.*

Even though Todd wasn't here. Even though we were technically married. *Even though I'd begged him to kiss me.*

Max wouldn't settle for just a piece of me, and I wasn't sure if I was brave enough to give him anything more.

CHAPTER 16
MAX

I'd almost kissed my temporary wife, and there was no worse mistake I could've made.

It wasn't the shadow of that almost-kiss that followed me around, but its ghost. The look in her eyes, the feel of her hands drawing my face to hers, the plea from her lips to kiss her...I was haunted by that moment more than any other I'd collected in the last four years.

Being around Daisy all the time was like being an asteroid in her orbit, destined to hurtle myself toward her in spite of the gravity of my reservations and the destruction promised by the way it made me burn. But there was nothing I could do. I was hers. Pulled to her by something that was as out of my control as it was unlikely to have a good outcome.

My hand tightened on the steering wheel as Daisy came out of the store onto the sidewalk. She had on a long dress and the new sneakers I'd bought her. I didn't miss how she'd worn sandals to my aunt's for dinner, but when she wore them again the following Monday for our deliveries—*when it was employee protocol to wear closed-toe shoes*—I knew there was a problem. The next morning, I left a solution—a new, larger pair of sneakers—on her steps.

Daisy waved over her shoulder to Erica, and the breeze caught her dress, flapping it around her ankles. She'd only been wearing long, loose dresses for the last week and a half. I didn't miss how every inch of her was filling out. Rounding. The dresses were a practical, comfortable choice, but the only thing on my mind was how easy they would be to lift. To remove.

Like she heard my thought, Daisy turned to me, her cheeks instantly staining a perfect shade of pink. They'd done that every time she looked at me—caught me looking at her—over the last several days. Then her nipples peaked like they did now, begging to be touched, and next her eyes strayed to my mouth just before—*gone*. Her gaze turned elsewhere, and the moment vanished like a fever dream, leaving me in a sweat.

I noticed every slight change because I had a problem. I'd always had a problem keeping my eyes off my best friend's girl, but now that she was my wife, my obsession revolted for its right to survive.

"Sorry, I had to pee again," she said, reluctantly taking my hand and climbing into the truck.

"It's fine. We've got plenty of time." I closed the door behind her and went to the driver's side.

Daisy was quieter since that night, and when we did talk, it was all about work or the logistics for her doctor's appointment this afternoon, and never about what happened on the side of the road. Never about our almost-kiss.

Daisy buckled and bundled her arms over her

middle. Instantly, the memory of her holding her stomach, her face blanched white, and her stare a fugue of static as she looked at the doe and her fawn. I'd never felt so worried. Never felt my stomach drop like it did in those moments. And the only thing that unfroze me was needing to know Daisy was okay.

"Max?"

"Yeah." I sucked in a breath, pulling away from the curb when her scent hit me. "Wow, you smell good." I couldn't stop the words from coming out, even if I wanted to.

Hello, blush.

"It's peony and lavender." Her eyes darted to mine. "From the bouquet you made me."

For our wedding.

"It's...good." More than good. She smelled fucking edible, but *good* would have to suffice.

"Thanks," she murmured, reaching up to tuck her hair behind her ear, my eyes snagging on her fingers. *On her ring.*

Every muscle in my body tightened.

As many times as I went back to that moment, to the soft-spoken plea for me to kiss her, I was equally ripped back to reality by the giant diamond glittering on her finger. I'd told her I wouldn't kiss a woman who wore another man's ring, and even though she'd asked me to—even though she'd wanted me to—she still hadn't taken Todd's engagement ring off.

And that was why I'd had to accept that night as a fluke. An unlikely combustion of anxiety, panic, and then the relief that everything was okay. It had created a moment of ache and vulnerability that suspended all reality—all reservations for those few minutes—until I felt the ring she still wore on her left hand.

"How was the glucose drink?" I changed topics.

"Not blueberry flavored, but not bad at all compared to how I've heard the normal one tastes." She smiled and tucked a strand of hair behind her ear. "You really didn't have to get me a special one. I could've stomached through the yucky one."

"I know you could've, but I didn't want you to."

Even I'd heard about the infamous glucose test and how bad the drink tasted from my cousins, and that was how I knew about the alternative: The Sweet Stuff. Frankie found the powder for her second pregnancy and told me where to order it online. I'd overnighted it on Tuesday so it would arrive in plenty of time for today. All Daisy had to do was mix the powder with some cold water and drink it an hour before her appointment.

"Well, thank you," she said, adjusting her dress over her legs. "How'd everything go in Boston this morning?"

"Good." My chin dipped, and I turned onto the local highway that led to the hospital. "Really good. It's been a few months since I've been to the hotel to see all of our displays. It's always a little surreal to walk in and see my flower arrangements everywhere."

The Copley Place Hotel was an icon in the city, and a huge win for MaineStems when I'd secured a three-year contract last year to provide the hotel with fresh flowers every week. When they asked me to curate the floral arrangements for the annual pancreatic cancer foundation fundraiser, I knew they were happy with my product, and I was happy to offer my services at a nominal fee for such a good cause. Not to mention, it was a huge visibility opportunity for my business.

I'd already divvied up the deliveries to other drivers for today because of Daisy's doctor appointment, so I figured it would be a good morning to head into the city and review the final arrangements with the hotel manager.

"Maybe it wouldn't hurt you to slow down and savor everything you've already accomplished."

"One dinner and you're already starting to sound like the rest of my family," I said before I could stop myself. At the brief mention of that night, the way Daisy tensed sent a shockwave through the confined space. Quickly, I admitted another half-truth. "I'm not sure I know how to slow down."

The other half of the truth I kept close to my chest: if I stopped and slowed down, all I would see was how everything I'd accomplished wasn't enough to make her mine.

The irony was, right now, Daisy was both more mine and the least mine than she'd ever been. She was my wife, but not mine to love.

"Sure you do." Daisy's head tipped, and a small smile toyed with her lips. "Of all people, you should know how to stop and smell the roses, right?"

I chuckled and painfully admitted, "Honestly, I can't remember the last time I walked through the flower fields on the farm and actually *smelled the roses*."

"Well, soon you won't have to go very far. I gave Erica the first batch of the fall perfume this morning. She was just dousing the whole shop with it when I walked out."

"Perfect."

"She...also gave me samples last week of the flowers you're using for the fundraiser. I thought you could spray it at the event, but then your sister suggested putting the perfume in those little sample vials they give out at beauty stores and using them as favors. I know they usually give out little thank-you bags at these things..."

I gritted my teeth. "Daze, you really don't have to—"

"I want to help," she insisted and then admitted, "It's not just a distraction anymore. I'm really enjoying making the scents. Matching them to your arrangements. It makes it feel special."

And how was it going to feel when she was gone?

"If you're sure," I grunted, ever a glutton for punishment when it came to the woman beside me. "When did you see Harper?"

"Yesterday. She dropped off the last jar of blueberry honey," Daisy replied.

So that was why my sister had popped in...or at least the excuse she gave. I was sure part of the reason was to poke around my relationship with my new wife, and I was sure our brother put her up to it.

"She's excited to go to the gala with you," Daisy added.

"Oh, yeah?" Harper had asked to be my date months ago, almost right after I told her about the contract. "I'm glad she's excited, but I'm not convinced it's the fundraiser she's excited for."

Daisy's brow creased, the effort wrinkling her nose. "What do you mean?"

"Wade's brother is going to be one of the speakers at the event." It had been hard to miss when Blaze's face was on almost every marketing poster they had ready to display.

"His brother?"

"Blaze Stevens," I filled in the blanks. "Movie star. Former Hollywood Casanova. Harper's high school crush."

Daisy mouthed an O that made my dick tighten. I quickly cleared my throat and continued to speak so she wouldn't notice how I adjusted my seat. "Pretty sure I'm low man on the totem pole compared to Blaze."

I pulled into the lot for the Stonebar Ridge hospital and followed the signs to the other side of the building for the OB wing. For the middle of the afternoon, the parking lot seemed relatively quiet.

"I don't think you could be the low man on anyone's totem pole," Daisy said, her light laugh stifled when she realized how it sounded. "I had no idea she had a crush on Blaze. She never said anything..."

"She's tried to bury it real deep now that Lou is married to Wade," I said and pulled into a spot close to the entrance.

"Yeah, I guess that could be awkward."

"And painful." I turned off the ignition and said something I shouldn't have said. *Again.* "Wanting someone you can't have is like having a thorn in your chest, stabbing your heart with every beat."

I froze. She froze. And then Daisy fumbled to unbuckle her seatbelt with the hand still wearing my best friend's ring.

"We're going to be right in here today." The nurse, Teddy, stepped aside so Daisy and I could enter the examination room.

For being a smaller, coastal town, the hospital had pretty exceptional ratings for its delivery unit and OBGYN doctors. I'd given Daisy a short list of other options I'd found in the area, including a smaller regional hospital closer to Portland and a midwife based a little south of Friendship, but Stonebar had good ratings and the first available appointment, so Daisy took it.

I'd asked if she wanted to see the hospital before making a decision, but she declined. So now, her eyes darted along the hallways, lingered on the faces of the nurses and doctors we passed, wondering which one was going to be hers, and once inside the room, scanned every corner searching for a red flag. And so did mine.

Maybe Daisy didn't feel like she had time for any other choice, but I wasn't going to let her settle. Thankfully, when my gaze found its way back to hers, she gave me a small smile. She felt comfortable here, and so did I.

"Have a seat, Mama, and we'll take your blood first and then do your ultrasound." Teddy patted the big chair in the center of the pastel-painted room. "And, Dad, you're welcome to have a seat over there..."

Dad. Shit. "Oh, I'm—"

"Can he stand by me?" Daisy cut in, her wide eyes swinging to mine. "I'm not good with needles."

Wordlessly and without waiting for the nurse's reply, my feet brought me right to her side.

"If you could just roll up your sleeve for me, Mama," Teddy asked and began to unload vials and needles and syringes from the tub on the counter.

Settling onto the edge of the chair, Daisy managed to undo the first button on the cuff of her dress's long sleeve, but the moment she saw Teddy prepping the needle about to go into her arm, her face turned white and her fingers stopped coordinating.

"Let me." I stepped in front of her, using the excuse to help her as a reason to block off her line of sight.

As I worked free the second button, the color in her cheeks started to return, her focus now on me. On my fingers brushing over her skin. Now I fought to not fumble as I carefully rolled the cuff once, twice, and a third time, giving just enough tension to the fabric that it stayed when I pushed it above her elbow.

"I hate needles," she whispered after I'd finished but before I stepped out of the way.

"Have you ever met a person who loves them?" I countered and lifted my brow.

"Good point." She pushed out a deep exhale and then nervously tried to look over my shoulder. "Will you hold my hand?"

"I'd let them take my blood instead of yours if it worked that way," I murmured, reaching for her right hand.

"If only." Her fingers squeezed tight to mine.

"So how have you been feeling? Do you have any concerns you want me to note for Dr. MacDonald?" Teddy asked as she rolled over her tray. I noticed how she positioned it just far enough back from the seat that it was pretty much impossible for Daisy to see what was on it just by turning her head.

"I've been feeling pretty okay overall. No nausea or extreme fatigue. My feet have started to swell more consistently now."

"That's the worst, isn't it?" Teddy empathized with a shake of her head. "Thank God both my girls were born in the middle of summer. I was going around barefoot the last four weeks because none of my shoes fit, and when I did have to go out, I ended up buying those horrible-looking toe socks, you know the ones?"

Daisy nodded, her eyes sinking to the needle in Teddy's hand.

"I got the ones with rubber on the bottom so I could wear them out of the house, but I looked ridiculous. Toe socks in the middle of summer." She laughed and shook her head, noticing then that her attempt to distract Daisy was fading, so she doubled down. "And don't get me started on the cravings. All my youngest wanted from the womb was ketchup sandwiches. No burger or hot dog or chicken or veggies. Only ketchup and bread. My husband looked at me like I'd lost my mind every time I asked for one." She laughed at the memory. "Make a fist for me, Mama."

Daisy balled her hand, the one the nurse wanted, and the other one locked with mine. I squeezed her fingers back. *I'm here. I will always be here.*

"How about you? Any big cravings?" She was trying, I'd give her that. But the second Teddy uncapped the needle, Daisy was gone. Her focus was solely on the needle that you'd think, after decades or centuries of drawing blood, could be a little smaller than it currently was.

She tried to wait for Daisy to answer, but I wasn't sure Daisy had even heard her question. Maybe that was the reason I spoke instead. *Or maybe not.*

"Ours only wants blueberries," I answered, my voice a low rumble.

Ours.

Not hers.

Not Todd's.

Not theirs.

Ours.

Later, I'd tell Daisy it was only because the nurse thought I was the father, and I didn't feel like explaining while Daisy looked as white as a sheet.

"Sounds much better than a ketchup sandwich," Teddy said with a laugh, and then finally gave up on the tried-and-true distraction technique. "All right, Mama, why don't you look at your handsome dad for a minute here for me, okay?"

Dad. This time, it was only Daisy's gaze that cut me off. Afraid. Borderline panicked. I no longer gave a shit about correcting the nurse. All I cared about was caring for Daisy.

"You're good, Daze. You're doing real good."

Pink seeped back into her cheeks like sunshine breaking through the clouds, and in the corner of my eye, I saw the nurse tie a band around her arm and then clean her skin with an alcohol swab. Daisy's fingers tightened on mine.

"That's it. Nice deep breaths," I said, my voice suddenly morphing into a different beast. A lower, huskier beast. And I couldn't control it. Not the way she was looking at me. *Not the way she obeyed my command.*

Her lips parted, their color a shade of hungry red as she let out a slow exhale.

The moment the needle punctured her skin, she whimpered and tensed, a wash of moisture coating her eyes.

"That's it. It's almost done. You're almost there," I kept talking, watching her visibly relax to the cadence of my voice. "Almost done, Daze. You're doing so good. Just keep breathing for me."

Air loosened from her lips.

"There you go. Deep breath in," I cooed, watching her nostrils flare as they pulled in oxygen. "Deep breath out."

*God, she obeyed so well...*and it simultaneously stiffened my dick and absolutely gutted me.

There was another reason I didn't date a lot. I had...preferences. Ones that took time and consideration for a partner to understand who wasn't already exposed to that brand of intimacy. I wasn't a *red-room-of-pain* Dom, but I liked to give orders. I liked to be in control. And it felt very different from the kind of man I was outside of the bedroom. *Chivalrous in the streets, commanding in the sheets.* It was easier to find like-minded partners at a kink club or website than it was to date and hope it wouldn't turn the woman off.

It was also easier to have that be the reason than to admit the only woman I wanted to date in the last four years was already dating my best friend.

"All done," Teddy announced cheerfully, the needle and vial clanking back on the tray, and a piece of gauze pressed to the crook of Daisy's elbow. "You did great, Daisy, and so did you, Dad."

My eyes still locked with Daisy's, and neither of us attempted to correct her.

"Just give me one minute to get this going, and then we'll do your ultrasound."

It wasn't until the door clicked shut that Daisy stirred and untangled her fingers from mine, knotting them back in her lap. "Sorry if I hurt you."

I shifted my stance a little wider to accommodate my cock. She hurt me all right, just not my hand.

"No hurt at all."

For the rest of the appointment, both Nurse Teddy and Dr. MacDonald referred to me as the baby's father.

For the rest of the appointment, neither Daisy nor I corrected them.

"Here, let me—"

"I got it." I shifted the takeout bags to my left hand, my right one colliding with Daisy's as we both reached to open the Murphy door. "I got it, Daze."

She sighed and pulled her hand back. Whether it was because she really wanted to let me open it or because she didn't want to prolong our contact, I wasn't sure. As soon as it opened, a knock rapped on the shop door.

"I'll get it."

"It's after hours, Daisy. They can call—"

"After hours by only fifteen minutes. Let me just see if there is anything I can help them with," she insisted, already waddling toward the door.

I bit back the threat to tie her down to stop her from working because that threat was more dangerous to me than it was to her. Quickly setting the bags on the step, I strode after her. Five seconds or fifteen minutes didn't change that I didn't want her opening the door alone. Sure, Stonebar was safe, and this was a flower shop, but I wasn't rational when it came to protecting Daisy or our baby...*her* baby.

"Mrs. McCormick?"

My blood turned to ice hearing Daisy's shock.

"Miss Turner—"

"What are you doing here?"

Red fringed my vision as I homed in on Daisy standing wedged in the opening of the doorway, facing her almost mother-in-law on her own.

"I'm here because you never returned my voicemail and aren't answering my calls."

"Because I don't want to talk to you," Daisy blurted out, her voice choked with disbelief.

I reached for the doorknob, my hand settling over Daisy's letting her know I was here. The last thing I wanted was to scare her when I unceremoniously ripped the door open to tell Mary McCormick to go fuck herself. Politely, of course.

As soon as Daisy felt my fingers, she lifted her hand and pushed, and then waved me away. Her message was clear. *She was handling this.*

"Don't be a child, Miss Turner. You're carrying my granddaughter. You canceled your last doctor's appointment. You're living above a...shop. You don't have a choice not to talk to me. I have a right to ensure you aren't harming the welfare of the child because of Todd's decision."

There were few things that angered me to the point of rage like Mary's words did in that moment. After everything she and her son had put Daisy through, to come here and insinuate Daisy wasn't taking care of her child...I'd never felt the urge to physically harm someone until that moment.

How fucking dare she?

"You don't have a right to anything," Daisy charged right back, and as much as I wanted to step in and *save* the day, it was surprisingly even more satisfying to hear Daisy put Mary McCormick in her place. "This is my baby, and I'm taking care of her—taking care of us, which is more than I can say for your son."

"My son will be back to handle his responsibilities and his legacy. He knows this isn't acceptable, no matter how extenuating the circumstances. He played right into your hand, and now he has to accept the consequences. He's always been childish—foolish— when it came to sticking to this path, but eventually he will heel," she rattled like her son was nothing more than a poorly trained pet. "He knows he's expected to come back and marry you and secure our legacy. He knows there's no other option for him."

Daisy went stiff. "*For him—*"

"In the meantime, Miss Turner, we would like to make sure his daughter is being properly taken care of—"

"Have you talked to Todd?"

The shock in her voice was as heavy as the kind that sat in my chest. He wouldn't have...

Mary paused and then scoffed. "Of course Todd called me. I'm his mother. When I tell him to call me, he listens."

Goddammit, Todd.

I went to reach for Daisy again, but stopped myself, my fingers curling instead into a fist and falling like a hammer to my side. I wished I could at least see her face, look at her eyes. Then I would know what she was feeling right now. Was it more betrayal? Was it anger? Was it heartbreak?

Maybe it was better I couldn't see. The fact that she still wore his ring told me enough.

"Now, let me inside, Miss Turner, so we can discuss this like adults. I will not stand on this...stoop while I lay out how my granddaughter's future is going to proceed."

Jarred into action, Daisy lifted her head. "No. And I'd like you to leave."

"You don't get to tell me *no*," sneered the other woman's voice, and I caught the door drifting in like she'd pushed on it. Instantly, I flattened my hand to the back. *Like hell I was letting her in here.* "Let me in, or I'll call the police. Is that what you want? To not only destroy my son and granddaughter's lives, but also your friend, Max? I'm sure he'll regret helping you..."

Oh, hell no.

There was nothing and no one that could've stopped me from opening the door then. Wide. So fucking wide because all I wanted her to see was me. And she did.

Her perfectly manicured face fractured as I filled the doorway, easily wedging myself slightly in front of Daisy so there was no mistaking my position here.

"I'm sorry, Mary. Did you say my name?" I dared her to repeat herself to my face.

"Max." Her pointed nose wrinkled like she could

smell a traitor. "Good to see you. I'm glad you're here," she said with a tight smile, and already I knew where she was going with this. "I know you think you've been helping Todd by allowing Daisy to stay...here." Her barely controlled disdain was almost comical. She wanted me to side with her, but even that couldn't stop her from insulting me. "However, that's just not the case. Daisy needs to return to the house we set up for her and Todd and continue to go to her doctor appointments at the birthing center we chose. This is Todd's baby she's carrying. She can't just—"

"I'm pretty sure it's her own baby she's carrying, Mary."

The look on her face was part fury and another part disgust. Ironically, she had the same look the first time Daisy had gone to their house for dinner. Todd had asked me to come along too, and Daisy had used her dinner fork for her salad by accident.

"She can't stay here, Max. It's...unseemly," she hissed and then stamped her foot. "And if you can't see that, if you want to betray your best friend in this way, then so be it. I'm not here to talk to you about your misguided choices, so if you can't help, then please excuse yourself so I can speak to the woman carrying my grandchild in private."

My teeth locked down. Not Daisy. Not the *mother* of her grandchild. *The woman.* Like Daisy was nothing more than a vessel for the precious McCormick genes. I didn't care what she said about me. I didn't care that she insulted my decades-long friendship with her only son —a friendship that had saved his ass far more than it had ever benefited mine. The only thing I cared about was Daisy.

"How dare you?" Daisy put her hand on my arm. "This is my child, Mrs. McCormick. You have no right to any of my decisions regarding my baby or my body, and you have no right to be here."

"I have a right to ensure the welfare of my grand-child, and if you refuse, I will have our lawyers step in to protect it. I can't imagine CPS will look too kindly on you living in a flower shop."

"I'm going to have to stop you there—"

"This has nothing to do with you, Mr. Hamilton," she was now shrieking. "This is between me and the woman carrying my grandchild."

And there was that fury again. *That brutal rage.*

"It has everything to do with me, Mary, because the woman you are *threatening* is my wife." It wasn't until the words boomed from my chest that I realized I'd barricaded my hands on either side of the doorframe, putting myself directly between the two women like a wild bull, nostrils flaring and ready to charge.

"Threat—*your wife?*" She spat the word with almost as much vitriol as she had when Todd told them he and Daisy were getting married.

"And the property you are standing on is mine, so I'm going to have to politely ask you to leave."

"What do you mean, *she's your wife?*" Mary's head whipped back and forth like a windshield wiper trying to clear up her confusion.

"What I mean is that this conversation is over, and my polite request is about to become not so polite."

"Absolutely not. I will not leave until you explain this very minute what you are talking about."

I stepped through the doorway now, forcing her to take a step back. It finally hit her then that she wasn't in control. Her money and power and my relationship with her son had no bearing on what I was willing to do to keep her away from Daisy.

"Either you're going to leave or I'm going to call the police, and unlike in Portland, Mary, the police here are *my* friends. So unless *trespassing* is what you want your next call to your lawyer to be about, I suggest you get back in your car, and you don't come back here to my business or to our home because you won't get this warning a second time."

She huffed several times like she didn't know how to breathe in a world where someone didn't instantly bend to her will. Or worse, where someone stood up to her.

"I'll be in touch." She levied us with her final words, but they rang as hollow as her heels on the sidewalk as she charged back to her waiting car.

Pushing away from the door, I followed her to her glistening black Mercedes, not taking my eyes from her as she climbed into the back seat and slammed the door. And then I stood at the curb until the driver pulled away, watching the car and memorizing the license plate until it disappeared from sight.

Only then did I turn back to Daisy, prepared to face whatever it was she felt for my intervention. *And for revealing we were married to probably the last people on earth she wanted to know.*

CHAPTER 17
DAISY

"Daisy?" His hands on my shoulders were like a palm over a spinning coin, flattening all my whirling thoughts to the man standing in front of me.

My husband.

And now the world would know it.

"Are you okay?"

I nodded first and then said, "Yeah," as my nod turned into a slow shake of disbelief. "I can't believe she came here..."

I couldn't believe a lot of things right now. That Mrs. McCormick physically showed up to threaten me. That Todd had called *her* to check on the baby, not me. Not Max. *Her.*

"She's not coming back, Daze. I won't let her near—"

"What did you mean 'our home'?" I interrupted him, my focus playing Whack-A-Mole in my mind.

Max stared at me, his jaw flexing. *Hard.*

"I don't think you should stay here anymore," he

said, his voice sinking into that warm grit that coated it back at the hospital when he'd coached me through my blood draw. "I don't want you staying here alone."

I knew what he was going to say because I felt the same way. I didn't want to. I wanted to feel like it would be fine and that Todd's mom got the message to leave me alone. But people with power rarely understood a message they didn't agree with, and even less so complied with it. And even though I was pretty confident that I wasn't in any physical danger, that almost seemed like less of a concern than the other ways the McCormicks could harm me.

Blinking, Max's stare collected back into focus. "What did you mean 'our home'?" I repeated because he'd answered the part of the question I hadn't asked.

Releasing my shoulders, he reached for his collar and popped the top button. I wondered if he even realized he'd done it.

"I mean, I think we should stay at my house for the time being."

"The one you're trying to sell."

"I'll take it off the market until we don't need it anymore. It's not like the offers were rolling in anyway," he added, trying to play down what he was offering— what he was doing. *For me.*

"And we'll stay there...together." I couldn't tell if I was asking him or telling him.

It wasn't bad enough I spent almost every day with the man I was inappropriately attracted to. It wasn't bad enough that I'd *married* him for access to good health insurance for my baby. It wasn't bad enough he'd come with me to my doctor's appointment earlier, and every time they'd referred to him as the father, I didn't correct them because I wished it were true.

Apparently, no, it wasn't bad enough because now I was going to live in the same house as him—*sleep* in the same house as him.

"I don't want you staying there alone, Daze," he replied, even though I hadn't meant it as a question.

"I know." I wrapped my arms over my stomach and admitted, "I don't want to stay there alone either. It's just..." *I'm afraid to be alone with you.*

Max pressed his finger under my chin, and suddenly, he was closer. In that space where we were near enough to feel our breaths ricochet.

"Just what?"

There was a different kind of danger that came with sharing a house with Max Hamilton, but what choice did I have? What *good* choice did I really have?

I swallowed hard. "I just can't believe this is happening. First, you had to marry me. Now you have to move me into your house—"

"Don't," he cut me off. "I don't have to do any of those things, Daze. I want to. Please," he pleaded, his thumb pressing on my chin and a different kind of anger darkening his gaze. "Stop thinking of me the way Todd made you think of him."

Air speared from my lips. He was right. And I hadn't even realized I was doing it—treating him as though everything I needed from him was an inconvenience. *As though I were an inconvenience.*

"I'm not him, Daze," he murmured, and I felt like a jerk. Max and Todd couldn't be more different. Not in who they were, not in how they made me feel.

Max moved closer, his face lowering to mine, and

then we were back in that moment—the one where he stood outside the truck in the rain, ready to kiss me.

"I know," I murmured, my lips parting and my head tipping just a little farther into the path of his.

His eyes scoured my face. Every lash and every line. Every freckle and blush of color. All of it confessing how much I wanted to kiss him right now. And then he was gone.

My shoulders felt the empty chill first when his hands slid free, and then my lungs unspooled the energy crackling inside them. "The house has four bedrooms, Daze. So I'll just be there...in case. Nothing else needs to change."

Needs to...but what if I wanted it to?

"With my luck, there's going to be a bogeyman under three of those beds," I said with a weak laugh that wilted into nothing when his stare pinned mine, dark with flashes of desire like lightning behind storm clouds.

"You don't need luck or a bogeyman if you don't want to sleep alone."

My heart slammed into my rib cage, and I clutched my hands tight, my ring—Todd's ring—digging into my palm. *Why was I still wearing it?*

"Let's eat, and then we'll pack your things and head to my house," Max instructed, locking the shop door behind us and heading for the apartment stairs.

I followed him, spinning the band with my thumb the entire way.

"Do you think he really called her?" I wasn't upset. Maybe I should've been, but I wasn't. Honestly, I was surprised when she said it, but deep down, I wasn't even that either.

I wasn't surprised or upset that Todd had chosen to step back into reality by calling his mother rather than calling me.

"I don't know," Max answered honestly. "I wouldn't be shocked if he did, but I also wouldn't put it past her to lie to get what she wants. Can't imagine after the choice he made that Mary would be his first call..."

I made a soft sound in response, letting his words sink into my mind as we drove, the truck somehow full of a stupefying amount of clothing and personal items of mine that had collected at the apartment over the last couple of weeks.

The coast of Maine stretched its craggy peninsulas like knobby fingers out into the sea. It was so peaceful here. So majestic. I'd buried the memories of the times Todd had taken me on long weekends to his parents' house on the coast, one because they were steeped in his parents' judgment. And two, because every time I mentioned how much I loved it out here, Todd's response was that it was a nice short getaway, but that I'd get bored after a couple of days.

Translation: *He* would get bored after a couple of days.

He wanted to be back in the city. With all the

things to do. With his friends. *With the bars.* How many times had I curbed the things I wanted to fit into his world? Little things, like individual grains of sand. Hardly noticeable until I stepped out of his orbit and saw just how much of my world he'd eroded.

"He never came to a single doctor's appointment with me," I blurted out, unsure why now was the moment I wanted to confess this.

"What?" I wasn't sure if it was intentional or not, but a heavy brake accompanied Max's question as he turned onto a small private drive.

A few feet later, he stopped completely in front of a wooden gate. "Hold on," he grunted and put the truck in park.

I watched him walk from the truck over to the locked side of the gate and open it. Before coming back to the truck, he walked to the For Sale sign stuck in the yard. It was a nice one. White wood. Brass accents. Not one of those cheap plastic signs held up by metal twigs.

With one yank, he wrenched it from the ground.

My chest squeezed. I hadn't been able to bury the feeling of being an imposition on him, but now, I felt like a downright intruder. I wasn't sure why. It wasn't like he was even living or let alone wanted to keep this house, but for some reason, as he opened the gate and stared down the moonlit drive, I saw a weight on his shoulders that hadn't been there before. And I knew it had to be because of me.

I forced my gaze back to the driveway, but in my periphery, I caught Max walk to the back of his truck. I heard the clunk of the sign being deposited in the truck bed, and then Max was back in the driver's seat, a taut expression creasing his face.

"What do you mean, Todd never went to the doctor with you?"

Maybe I shouldn't have said anything.

"He always...had a reason," I said, keeping my gaze fixed out the window, the deep blue sea sparkling between the tall pines. "One time, he sent his mom instead." I grimaced at the memory. I don't think I managed to speak a single word during that appointment. Mrs. McCormick had just taken over, and I was so exhausted and...shocked that Todd hadn't shown up, I didn't do anything to stop her. "After that, I stopped telling him about the appointments until afterward, and he...never asked."

And, fool that I was, I somehow fitted that into my world like it bolstered my independence. Like it was some kind of proof that I could still stand on my own rather than seeing it for what it was: evidence that I'd settled for a man who wasn't worthy of being by my side.

When Max didn't reply, I looked over and found his knuckles ghostly white where they gripped the steering wheel.

"Max..."

"I told him...he told me—" he broke off with something that was nothing short of a predatory growl, the veins running down his forearm looking like they were about to burst.

Without thinking, I reached out and put my hand on his arm. "I'm not upset, Max."

"That makes one of us." His eyes whipped to mine and then back to the drive. Ahead, the low flicker of exterior lights speckled the blanket of dark trees.

"It's hard to miss something you never had," I tried

to explain the feeling as the truck pulled from the dirt driveway onto a cobbled clearing at the end of the jutting peninsula, Max's house clutched on the bluff.

"No, Daisy, it's not," he said, his eyes boring into mine. "It's hard to miss something you never wanted." And then he shut off the engine, stopping my heart for a beat along with it.

Maybe it was the clear, starry night, but the house looked like something straight out of a dream.

The two-story home was wrapped in serene blue-gray siding, its dark metal roof so clean and reflective it made the house look like it was topped with a blanket of stars. I was still taking in the size of the home and the two-car garage when Max opened my door.

"You okay?"

"Did you build this?" I asked as he helped me down, wishing I could hold on to the warmth of his fingers for a little longer.

"No," Max said with a shake of his head, following me as I walked along the covered pathway between the garage and house that led to the back—and the view. "It was new construction when I bought it. I was casually looking in the area because the store was opening up, and we'd just opened a main hub in Portland, and as soon as I saw this..."

The path led to an expansive deck along the back of both structures with a view open to the ocean, the dark water lulling against the shoreline somewhere in the near distance.

To sit here as the sun came up every morning...I blinked, and in that fraction of a second, I saw myself exactly where I stood, but watching my daughter play in the yard in front of me.

"It's perfect." Too perfect, just like everything else about him. *My husband.*

"Yeah."

I turned quickly at his strained voice, catching his equally strained expression as he stared at me. *Not the view.*

"Come on." He cocked his head back toward the truck. "Let's go inside."

For the next ten minutes, my dream man led me on a tour of my dream home. The inside of the house was a modern open floor plan. Rustic beams. A state-of-the-art kitchen. And windows. I hadn't even noticed them when I was outside, too overwhelmed with the view—a view that could overwhelm me from the inside too.

"This house is amazing, Max," I repeated, though it was pointless. *He was selling it.*

"Make yourself at home," came his muffled reply as he turned back down the hallway toward the front door to grab my bags from the truck.

At home. *God, if this were my home...*

Even if I thought Max would let me help him unload my stuff, I found myself wanting a few secluded moments to explore this space. *His space.*

He'd left me at the invisible joint between the dining room and the kitchen, so I turned to the kitchen first, trailing my fingers along the island countertop as I went through it, half-expecting the whole building to vanish the second I didn't have a hold on it.

From there, I moved into the living room, the sofas in front of the fireplace suddenly registering that the house seemed completely furnished.

"Daisy?"

I looked up and saw Max standing at the end of the island, holding two huge duffels I'd filled with my things.

"The furniture...is it here to stage the house for buyers?" I asked, making my way to him.

"Yeah." He loosely swung one arm toward the staircase. "Let me take you to your room."

My attention lingered over the rich leather couches and then moved to the craftsman table and chairs. I slowed on the steps, staring at the dining chairs. They looked familiar.

I turned to ask if Jamie had made them, but he was too far ahead of me now to hear.

Cresting the stairs, I followed the hall to the only open door ahead of me, which led into the room I quickly assumed was the master bedroom. The rustic wood four-poster bed dominated the space, but in a way that made it feel safe rather than imposing. The windows overlooked the same view of the coast from downstairs, and there was also a sliding door that opened out to a small deck.

Max set the bags on the bench abutting the foot of the bed. "Bathroom is through there. Closet through there," he pointed to the two other doors in the room. "Unpack everything." That command was a little harsher, but instead of feeling abrasive, I only shivered with warmth.

Since when did I enjoy taking orders? I wondered, running my fingers along the comforter. Since Max Hamilton started giving them to me.

"This is all your furniture?"

His jaw flexed. "Yeah," he said and shrugged. "Nowhere to move it to, and Aria said it would help sell the house. I told her if the potential buyers are interested, I'm willing to sell the furniture with the house too. Everything but the dining set and my...this bed."

"Jamie made them."

"How'd you know?"

"The chairs look like the ones at your aunt's house." Max smiled then, making it even clearer how much tension he was holding. *Because of me. Because I was here.* "Max, you don't have to give me your room—"

"Hasn't been my room for months, Daisy. Now it's yours."

I had no will to argue. Not when this bed was looking more and more amazing by the second. "Which room will you take?"

His throat worked to swallow. "There's a fourth bedroom off the kitchen downstairs."

Downstairs. It made sense. Of course, it did. It was closer to any and all entrances and exits to the house... and it was as far away as possible from me. Safer from every angle. *So why was the only thing I felt disappointment?*

"Okay." I nodded.

"These should be your clothes." He patted each duffel. "I'm going to bring the rest of the bags inside and then hop in the shower. Do you need anything?"

My jaw slackened. *Yes.* I needed to not be left with the mental image of my naked husband showering on the floor below. Or the memory of my almost mother-in-law tracking me down and threatening me and my baby.

"No, thanks. You...I'm good," I managed to choke out, walking to the window and staring blankly out at the invisible horizon.

I felt the tears welling. The sadness. The anger. I hated when it happened like this, the way a tsunami pulled the ocean away from the shore before unleashing devastation. I hated how my emotions retreated after Max sent Mrs. McCormick packing. How we'd eaten and packed up my things, and the whole time, I'd felt fine. *I'd thought I was handling it fine.* Now, I saw the cresting devastation as it hurtled toward me.

So I closed my eyes and braced for the onslaught, but instead of the cold desolation I'd been expecting, it was a wave of heat that hit me first.

It was the scent of him, floral and spice, flooding my nostrils. The proximity of his size and the way it set my body on edge. Threatening, but in a way that made me ache for it. For him. And I tried to tamp it down. *For how long had I tried to tamp it down?*

I didn't need to open my eyes to see where he stood, and for too many seconds to count, all he did was stand behind me. Maybe he was waiting for me to look at him, to say something. *But what was there to say?*

"Daze." His hand curled over my shoulder, and then the tsunami hit.

Tears coursed down my cheeks, overflowing through closed eyelids like the watery drops were made solely of what-ifs and what-could-have-beens. I wished I could stop them. I wished I could have held them back until Max had gone.

There were no what-ifs when it came to Todd. Not anymore. The moment I read his note the morning we were supposed to be married, I realized I'd been clinging to what-ifs with Todd for four years. *What if he didn't mean it? What if he wanted to change? What if he was really changing this time? What if he truly loved me, and that was why he hadn't given up on us yet, even though he never seemed happy?* There was no wondering what if he'd shown up to our wedding. I didn't wonder. I didn't hope. I didn't want.

And I wasn't crying over what had happened with him or his mother. I was overwhelmed by what was happening with Max and everything that could've happened differently if only one thing had changed.

What if it hadn't been Todd I'd left the coffee shop with four years ago, but Max?

"Daisy..." The ragged texture of Max's voice made the first sob break free. With a deep rumble, I felt myself being spun and clutched to Max's solid chest, swallowed up in the fortress of his protection.

His possession.

And then the sobs broke free. Heavy rolling waves of sadness. Not for Todd or because of his mom, but for me. Because I was too stubborn, believing I was too smart and too cautious to end up in a bad relationship. So stubborn, how, at every sign, I sacrificed accepting what was true in pursuit of proving I was right. I wanted to be right about Todd. I didn't want to accept that my first serious relationship was a failure. *I didn't want my daughter to grow up without both parents.*

When my breaths started to hiccup, Max tightened his hold, one hand on the back of my head, the other on my low back. "It's going to be okay," Max said, his fingers lightly rubbing my scalp, the prickle of sensation reaching all the way down to my toes.

I didn't open my eyes. Couldn't. For some reason, I could face him the day my fiancé had left me at the altar, but this...this was different. That day I'd been a victim, but tonight, I was vulnerable. My raw, obstinate, and pitiable heart was laid bare in front of the man I'd always wanted. The man who'd given me in a matter of weeks what Todd hadn't been able to manage in four years. The what-if I should've chosen.

And that was what made this worse. Anger shook through me, giving more force to my cries. Anger at myself because I knew better. Because I could've chosen better. *Because I had a better choice and I didn't take it.*

Max slid his hand to my cheek and tried to tip my head, but I pressed deeper into his chest, drowning in his scent. "Daze, look at me."

This time, I obeyed because the authority in his voice gave me no choice. Like a magnet to its opposing pole, my gaze lifted, and I blinked rapidly, clearing the murk from my eyes just as they collided with his. Instantly, I was brought back to that night in the storm, Max standing at the passenger door as I begged him to kiss me.

His irises were molten with gold. Liquefied by the same hunger from that night, they traced my face. My red-rimmed eyes. Flushed cheeks. Parted mouth. Heartbeats spilled into my veins, wild and unsteady and wanton.

"Tell me what I can do, Daze," Max ordered, more hoarsely this time, as remnants of the persona that had erupted in front of Todd's mom bled through his handsome face.

Instantly, my hormones swung me in a completely different direction. One where I wasn't breaking down against his chest but bucking in his arms. Where he wasn't ordering me to look at him but to scream his name. The change was so swift, it whiplashed a shiver through my body.

My tremulous breath caught and slowed as my gaze sank to his mouth. Hard and perfect and somehow, I knew without *knowing* that those lips would take care of me in a way no man had ever done before. That he'd take care of me in that way, the same as he'd done in every other, *like I was the only thing that mattered.*

His gaze probed mine, so deep and intimate I felt the caress between my thighs. *What if I told him to kiss me again?*

The thought rippled through my mind and then sank like a stone—*like a diamond,* to be exact. The one still sitting around my ring finger, a reminder I couldn't ask for more.

Like he heard my thought, Max stiffened and slowly disentangled himself from around me. "It's been a long day, Daze. There's nothing else to do...nothing else to worry about tonight. Just relax, and we can unpack in the morning."

I nodded because what else was I going to do? *Ask him to kiss you,* a voice begged, and I quickly shut it down.

"Thank you."

He lowered his chin and let himself out.

It was only when the door closed that I let my eyes

drop to my hand, to Todd's engagement ring. I knew what Max thought. I saw it like a billboard across his broken stare when he kept himself away from me. He thought I still wanted Todd. That in spite of everything, I still pined for the man who'd left me, pregnant, at the altar.

He couldn't be more wrong.

It was true. I still wore the ring for a man, but that man wasn't Todd. I wore it for Max. To remind myself that Max deserved better. I'd made the wrong choice four years ago. I'd told myself I was too smart and too cautious to end up in a bad relationship, and then I did everything I could to prove that was true instead of accepting that Todd was a mistake.

They say when you find yourself in a hole, to stop digging. I hadn't stopped. I'd dug in deeper.

I kept the ring on, not because I wanted Todd back in my life, but as a reminder. I hadn't chosen Max the first time, and no matter how I wanted him, he deserved someone who'd chosen him first. He deserved someone who wasn't pregnant with another man's baby.

"IT'S GOING TO BE OKAY," I SAID SOFTLY, CRADLING my hands under my stomach as I sank onto the edge of the bed. A groan bubbled from my lips. It was so comfortable. Beyond comfortable. *It was heavenly*. Yet despite his instruction, my mind couldn't rest.

Like a rubber band stretched too tight, I was exhausted but couldn't relax. And neither could my little sprout, who kicked up a storm as I wandered around the room for a few minutes, exploring the massive, marble-tiled bathroom with its huge walk-in shower that had a soaking tub sitting inside it. I was definitely going to take advantage of that tub, but not tonight.

Maybe if I put on some music, it would relax me.

Where was my phone?

I went back into the bedroom and looked around, under the bags and over by the window. Nothing. Had I left it downstairs? *Had I even brought it inside?*

"Shoot." I was pretty positive I left it in the truck.

Barefoot, I padded downstairs and headed for the front door. As soon as I went to flip the lock, I stopped. Max would've locked the truck too. And was there an alarm system? Probably. I looked around like I had the code to disarm it if there were one.

Retreating, I went to the kitchen. Sure enough, on the far end of the room was a small hallway with a single door. Max's room...his new room. Maybe I could catch him before he got in the shower. All I needed were the keys and the alarm code.

I knocked on the door. *No response.*

Crap.

"Max?" I called, but that felt like it did even less than knocking. Swallowing, I stared at the handle. If I went in, I could knock on the bathroom door. Then he'd hear me.

But what if the bathroom door was open?

Okay, well, I didn't have to go inside the bathroom. I could just call to him through the open door. I reasoned with myself through various scenarios, none of which included simply waiting for him to finish and come out of his room. Later, I could figure out why that was, because right now, my hand was on the knob, and I was opening the door.

My eyes traveled quickly through the room, confirming that Max was definitely in the bathroom, in the shower. Only then did it strike me how distinct Max's stamp was on the master bedroom. By comparison, this room was...nice. Pale, soothing blue walls and a navy bedspread. It was peaceful. Not that the master wasn't, but there was just something else about it. Maybe the size of the bed?

Whatever it was, I'd think on it later because my gaze snagged on Max's shirt on the floor, and my throat tightened, too tight to swallow the saliva pooling in my mouth. A few feet to the right of it, I saw his pants and boxers.

Heat rushed my head, and I gripped the doorframe. This was a bad idea. I didn't need my phone. I didn't need music. I needed a bed and to be as far away from the man who'd inhabit my dreams.

A low groan tumbled through the crack in the bathroom door. My head snapped toward it.

Was that—

"Daisy." The rough shreds of my name stretched their ragged fingers through the opening and wrapped around my throat.

Max had heard me. He knew I was here.

CHAPTER 18
DAISY

Oh no. My heart thundered in my chest, the beats pounding regret into my veins. *Oh no. Oh no. Oh no.*

Max had heard me come in, which meant I couldn't turn around now and leave. *Oh my god, Daisy. What were you thinking?* The heat of embarrassment suffocated my senses. If I didn't answer him, he'd think something was wrong, so I had to say something. My feet carried me to the bathroom door, instructing myself, *Just apologize and tell him you'll talk to him when he's done.*

Just apologize and leave.

"Max—"

"*Fuck.*" The pained curse derailed my words—derailed my thoughts—derailed me.

Not only did syllables collide in my throat, but for a split second, I forgot about the extra inches of *baby belly* sticking out my front. I moved too close, and my stomach bumped into the door, sending it swinging open.

"Oh no!" I scrambled to catch it. "I'm so sorry, Max. I—"

One single step into the bathroom was plenty far enough to reach the knob to pull the door closed again. Except when I reached for it, I saw him.

Max's muscled shoulders cowed against the warm spray beating his back. His one hand was splayed, his long fingers flat to the shower wall at his side. The other flexed tight around his cock.

He stopped mid-pump, his ruddy flesh bulging from his grip, and his head lifted to me.

That gaze...it might as well have been the barrel of a gun I stared down the way Max had me in his sights.

Water dripped from the dark ends of his hair onto the angles of his face, making all of him glisten. I'd always thought he'd looked fit before, but he dressed well, and sometimes, clothing concealed the details of what was underneath. Now, I saw every delicious detail right down to the devastating size of his cock. *Good lord, how were there not women lined up around the block to spend a night with him?*

"What are you doing here, Daisy?" Max forced the question through locked teeth, maintaining a surprising veneer of calm.

Like I hadn't walked in on him jacking off.

Like I hadn't walked in on him jacking off and thinking of me.

The thought hit me like an avalanche. *Daisy.* He'd said my name. Not because he'd heard me come into his room, but because he was fantasizing about me. Because he was masturbating to the thought of me.

My core clenched, flooding the lower part of me with the ache I thought I'd stifled earlier. It wasn't that I didn't know he desired me. I knew. But there was a difference between knowing it and having a front-row seat to the show.

"I-I'm sorry. I didn't mean—I should go," I stammered, surprised by the fresh husk to my voice. Surprised even more when I didn't move, when I didn't even budge.

Somehow, I stayed rooted right to that spot, my eyes roaming over his well-proportioned body where the water jittered on the surface of his skin like the whole of him was electrified.

"Daisy," Max growled, a hard exhale blowing droplets of water from his lips.

My eyes snapped to his, finding a different glint in them than I'd ever seen before. Something wicked. Something predatory. He dropped his hand from the wall and straightened, but instead of dropping his other hand from...*that*, Max instead started to roll his wrist again. His forearm flexed, water coursing through the valleys cut between muscles and veins, and he pumped his cock at a leisurely pace. *Daring me to keep watching.*

I tried to swallow but couldn't, my throat like a valve sealed tight. I tried to look away but couldn't. He was so beautiful. So perfect. *So hot.*

"I should go," I repeated, like it would spur my legs to move. *It didn't.*

"Then go," Max dared me out loud, his jaw pulsing with a hard beat like he might just lunge out of the shower and make me stay if I didn't run.

My heart thrashed in my chest, wild and wanton. I said I was going to leave. He told me to. And all I did was stand there, eyes wide and mouth parted, like I was on some kind of life support, staring at him.

What do you want? What can I do? His questions and my own chose that moment to haunt me. To hit me at my weakest when there was nothing I could do except admit that I didn't really want to leave. I wanted to stay. *I wanted to watch him.*

"Daisy, look at me." Max's command was even harsher than earlier, and though it made my head lift, it also made my knees go weak.

I didn't just want to watch him. I wanted to touch him. My fingers curled into my dress, wanting to replace his hand with my own. *And wanting to place his hands on me.*

We stood, eyes locked for a long second. Long enough for his fist to drag a hard pump down his cock. *Long enough for me to confirm that my underwear was soaked.*

"Either you leave right now or you close that door behind you and obey everything I say."

Pump.

Max was giving me a choice. I could still walk away from this. From him. I could still retreat behind the ring on my finger and tell myself it was because Max deserved better. It was the truth. But as I stood faced with the man who looked like a horny Poseidon ready to drag me into his deep, I couldn't deny it was only part of the truth. The other part? I was afraid to want more.

I was afraid to want more and lose it all.

But for the first time, my mind couldn't overrule my body. Couldn't overrule my heart. I'd lived out of fear for so long, and look where it had gotten me. Pregnant and abandoned by a fiancé I didn't really love. I was tired of being afraid. For tonight, I wanted to be free.

Pump.

My fingers tightened on the doorknob, and then with deliberate slowness, I pulled the door toward me, at the last second, moving to the side so it could shut behind me.

Max's nostrils flared when it clicked closed. *Pump.* He milked his cock as I released the knob and stepped toward him.

"Stop," he ordered, and I stilled, worried I'd done something wrong. Sure of it when he peeled his hand off his length. *Was this some kind of test? Had I made the wrong choice?*

"Do you have underwear on, Daze?"

My uncertain thoughts scattered like dandelion seeds on a breeze. "Yes."

"Take them off."

It was only my breath that was unsteady as I gathered my dress in my hands at my sides, lifting it high enough to reach underneath and shimmy my thong over my hips. My heart pounded as the fabric fell to my ankles.

"Kick them over to me."

My eyes snapped to Max, seeing that he'd stepped farther out of the water and planted his palms on either side of the glass door.

Part of me couldn't believe what I was doing right now, stepping one foot out of my underwear and using my other foot to toss the sliver of fabric toward the door.

The other part couldn't wait to hear what he'd make me do next.

As soon as my thong landed just on the other side of the glass, his gaze snapped to it like a red flag in front of a bull. Slowly, those sparkling eyes rose to mine.

"Those are some wet panties, Daze," he drawled slowly. "Tell me why they're so wet."

My cheeks might've been the shade of a fire hydrant, but there was no embarrassment blocking my reply from coming out in a throaty, seductive tone. "Because of you."

A feral sound escaped through Max's tight lips. "Because you caught me jacking off in the shower?"

I nodded, like my staring wasn't answer enough.

"Is this what you stayed for?" He ground out, dragging his hand back to his length, giving his cock a hard pump up and down as I watched. "To watch me come all over my hand?"

My breath caught. *No*, I wanted to say. I stayed because I wanted to do more than just watch him. I watched to touch and taste and feel and be consumed by him.

"You want to see what you do to me, don't you?" He pressed, a gravelly edge to his voice. "You want to watch how I lose my fucking mind when I fantasize about you."

I shifted my weight, feeling the slickness that now coated my thighs. There was nothing that could've torn my gaze from him at that moment. No sudden catastrophe. No ghostly apparition. A dragon could've burst through the bathroom door that very second, breathing fire at me, and I wouldn't have even noticed over his brazenness that scorched me from the inside out.

I thought I'd loved the thoughtful gentleman Max. I'd fantasized about him as an equally thoughtful and patient lover. Never in my wildest dreams had I pictured how that gentleman became a delicious caveman behind closed doors. How his deference could morph into dominance. *And never could I have imagined just how much it would turn me on.*

"Lift your dress and sit your sweet bare ass on the counter." Max jerked his chin to the empty section of the vanity next to me.

My heart pounded in my ears, clamored for more of this electric desire, shocking and powerful. I turned and reeled the fabric of my dress into my fists again. Even though the room was filled with warm steam, it still felt cool when it hit the heat pooled between my thighs. I swayed back, my *sweet bare ass* colliding with the edge of the counter. Grabbing it, I worked myself up carefully onto the edge, my legs naturally drifting apart and my hand sliding to my stomach.

Max's eyes flashed, and he jerked himself harder. Faster. The wet slaps of flesh on flesh ricocheted around the small room, and all I could do was stare. *Admire.* The symphony of his muscles inhaled and exhaled the tension of pleasure, their tautness defining every line from his forearms to his shoulders and then down to his chest, the bricks of his abs, and then the V at his hips that pointed my gaze lower.

For four years, I never let myself look too long at my boyfriend's best friend. I'd felt the tingles, the pull when I did, so I stopped letting myself. I'd had a good reason for always looking away...I didn't have a good reason anymore.

I settled on the grip of his fist and the thick rod of flesh wedged in his grip. My lips fell apart as I took him in. The dusting of dark hair at the root. The veins that distend around his thick girth. The blunt, purple tip protruding from his hand, a bead of creamy wet pooling at the slit there.

"Show me how wet this makes you."

My eyes snapped up like they'd been caught in a cookie jar. *Or a cock stare.*

Had he—

"Put your feet up on the edge of the counter and spread them wide."

I hadn't misheard him.

My fingers unclenched from where they held my dress. I drew my right leg up first and then my left, feeling the fabric of my dress slide down my legs, but my stomach kept it pooled between them, obscuring his view.

Max looked feral, his gaze incinerating every inch of skin it raked over. "Move your dress, Daisy. Show me how wet you are."

Swallowing over the balloon in my throat, I kept my eyes on his expression as I pressed my hands below my stomach and slowly peeled my dress up, baring myself to his hungry stare.

I shivered, feeling the damp air on my bare, slick sex. I was so exposed, so vulnerable, but I didn't feel that way when I looked at him. When I saw the way Max looked at me, the only thing I truly felt was powerful.

He pushed open the shower door slowly as though any swift movement would shatter the fragile armor of control he clung to. His nostrils flared at the clear sight he had of me spread wide in front of him.

"Fuck, that's a pretty pussy, Daze, all pink and puffy and wet because of me." Max's low voice felt like warm sugar on my skin, but the way he stared...it was like pure fire injected into my veins.

He gripped one side of the shower opening. Maybe

it was the water, but it looked like his fingers dented where they pressed into the glass.

My breathing marched without care or rhythm into my lungs, my breasts straining against the fabric of my chest, my nipples aching to be exposed to his gaze too. My hands slid from my stomach to grip my knees, and my head tipped back against the wall, a restlessness starting to claim me. I didn't just want to watch. I wanted him. I wanted him to make this ache—this craving I had for him—go away.

"Talk to me, Daisy," he commanded, his irises staked to me like shards of steel. And the way he fisted himself was nothing short of suffocating as he began pumping his cock again. Harder. Faster. "Tell me what you want."

"You," I breathed. "I want you, Max. Please."

Something between a snarl and a growl steamed from the shower.

"Touch your clit, Daisy. Show me what you want me to be doing to you."

I was too hormonal—too horny—to be embarrassed by the speed with which my right hand dropped between my legs, my middle finger centering on the tight bundle of nerves that screamed for attention.

The first stroke rained fireworks over my skin. I'd been desperate for this relief for weeks, but never seemed to find it on my own. No matter how much I ached. No matter how many dreams I had about Max. I could never relax enough to orgasm, as though my mind was stuck in fight or flight, too stressed to be vulnerable even to self-pleasure.

"That's it, baby. Rub that needy clit hard. You're so swollen and wet. So fucking needy."

I shook my head, shallow breaths shuttling in and out of my lungs, as my body chased its pleasure. No, not chased. Followed Max's lead, knowing he'd take care of me. *Trusting him to take care of me.*

"Stop."

My eyes snapped wide, oxygen glugging through my lips. *Stop?* I didn't want to stop. I didn't think I could stop.

"Stop biting your lip, Daze," Max clarified huskily. "I want to hear every needy moan. Every messy sound."

A whimper broke from my throat in relief, and my fingers redoubled their efforts on my clit.

"Good girl." A sound of raw appreciation filtered through the bathroom as I continued to pleasure myself. "God, I could watch you do this all day. Touching yourself to my command. Do you like to obey, Daisy?" His voice sounded cut from stone.

My throat worked. "I...I don't know."

I liked this—whatever it was. But before this—before him—I wouldn't have answered yes.

"Do you like to obey me?"

I sucked in a breath.

"Because your pussy sure looks like you do," he continued with a dark chuckle. "I wish you could see what you look like right now. Like a drenched fucking flower that all I want to do is bury my face in."

"Max," I panted, my back arching into his words that at this point felt like a physical caress. "Please."

"Please, what?"

My brain was mush. A muddy, murky mess of pleasure and ache, and the only thing that was clear was the low tenor of his voice. My gaze ebbed back to him, taking a moment to settle firmly on his gorgeous face.

"More," I begged breathlessly.

"Use your other hand and push a finger inside your cunt," he commanded, so cool and confident despite his own desire tearing him apart at the seams even as he tried to ignore it.

My left hand slid down my inner thigh, my feet inching wider to make space for both my arms and my stomach. I moaned when I felt how wet I was, my finger dipping easily into my entrance.

"Wait."

I stilled.

"Not that finger," he clipped, his voice etched in stone. "The one with his ring."

My jaw dropped open further. I had no idea where this was going, but god, did I want to go there. I wanted to go wherever that possessive look in his eyes promised to take me.

And so I curled my index finger back and teased my opening with the tip of my ring finger.

"Push the whole finger inside your pussy. I want his ring buried in your cunt when you scream my name," Max growled, his hands so tense on the glass, I was shocked it hadn't shattered. Maybe it was bulletproof.

My head tipped back against the vanity mirror, my eyes instantly growing hooded as I flicked over the swollen bundle of nerves, every single one aching to come.

My gasp turned into a choked breath as my finger pushed through my tight, begging muscles.

I was so wet, so soaked already, my finger slid in easily, Todd's ring included. It should feel wrong, the hard stone in my core. *I* should feel wrong, obeying my ex-fiancé's best friend as he instructed me toward an orgasm and desecrated my former engagement ring. But wrong was the farthest thing from what I felt as my body clenched and trembled. Wrong was the farthest thing I felt when I obeyed *my husband's* orders.

"Fuck yes," Max growled. "I hate seeing his ring on you, especially now, but even then."

Even then. He meant before Todd abandoned me. Before he had a good reason to hate it. *Before, he simply coveted his best friend's girl.*

I forced my eyes open. Forced them to focus on the man barking salacious orders at me from the cell of his shower. Now, Max was no longer as still as a statue. His eyes were locked on my pussy. On my finger, pumping in and out, coating Todd's ring in my desire for him. *For Max.* But his hands were no longer on the glass.

In the moments when my eyes had shut in pleasure, he'd grabbed my thong from the floor and wrapped it around his cock. Now, he wasn't pumping into his hand, but into my drenched underwear.

My core clenched wildly on my finger, and I knew my desire was dripping onto the counter.

"That's it, Daze. Don't stop working that clit," he encouraged roughly, his own movements slowing as all his focus went to me. "Show me how beautiful you are when you come."

"I can't," I whimpered breathlessly, my head thrashing to the side.

"You can," he growled, both palms on the glass now, his cock bobbing heavy and frustratingly forgotten in front of him. "Show me how bad you want it. How bad you want me, baby."

Need spiraled through me and erupted in my core. I wanted to obey him. The more he talked, the more I wanted to obey. His words made me more aroused, and I felt desire gush against my finger and run onto the counter.

"Fuck yourself with that finger like it's my cock inside you. Like I haven't been the only one imagining fucking you all these years."

"Max..." An emotion stronger than pleasure tore through my chest. A longing I'd buried for years, hoping it would die, and a hope I never thought to harbor, hearing he'd felt the same.

My fingers swirled and shunted in a faster rhythm, chasing my release. Chasing my pleasure. *Chasing his commands.*

"Show me that I'm not the only one who'd wished it wasn't Todd next to you in bed every night. Touching you. Tasting you. Filling up that perfect pussy and making you beg for more."

My ragged breaths crashed to a halt.

"Oh god." A cry exploded from my chest, along with every deep, dark fantasy I'd buried inside me. Never would I have admitted those thoughts out loud. Even now, I wasn't sure I'd be able to form the confession through my lips that I'd wished it more times than I could count. But he didn't ask me to say it. He knew I couldn't. Just like he knew my body would willingly show him.

"Yes, Max. Yes," I chanted as I careened straight toward the edge of release, my hips lifting off the counter to meet my hand, the collision making a wet, slapping noise against my core.

"Look at me, Daze," Max growled one last command, and his glittering gaze was suddenly the only thing I could see as the periphery of my vision turned fuzzy. "Come all over that ring and show me who you really belong to."

His possession should've shocked me. Worried me at the very least. But with my head cleared of everything except how I wanted him, I could only admit that I did belong to him. *And had wanted to for a long time now.*

The out-of-reach ache suddenly hit me head-on and catapulted me over the edge. "Yes. Oh god. Yes—Max!"

I screamed as my orgasm ripped through me. Darkness stole my vision as my body bucked with wild release. My core squeezed and gushed around my finger. Weeks of pent-up want, years of buried longing overloaded my senses until I was sure the intense rush of pleasure had fried every nerve ending, rewiring each one with only my need for him.

"That's it, baby." His low praise filtered back in through the fugue. "You did so good. You were so beautiful."

I blinked until my vision sharpened, until what was clear was that Max had brought me my release but had held back his own.

Carefully, I slid my hands away from my core and let my legs drape over the edge of the counter one at a time. He watched me, and I wondered what he was waiting for—why he was torturing himself?

Was he not going to let me see him? Was he going to make me leave before he finished?

My racing heart stumbled to its knees in my chest. "Max—"

"Come here," he interrupted. He sounded like a piece of metal about to snap, all twisted and strained, too brittle to bend.

I lowered my feet to the floor. My palms clung to the edge of the counter, feeling how badly my legs trembled. I wanted to sink into a puddle, but I needed to go to him. Needed to obey. *Needed to know.* And if I couldn't walk, then I'd crawl.

Miraculously, I could walk. One unsteady step in front of the other for the short few paces it took to put me right in front of him.

Pump. Pump. Pump.

My eyes flicked down, watching beads of creamy moisture pool from the tip of his cock and then run down the blunt head to be caught in my bunched underwear. The close-up made my body sizzle with ache all over again.

"Put your finger in my mouth."

My gaze snapped to his with a sharp breath. I didn't need to ask which finger he was talking about.

"Let me taste how sweet you are," he growled. "Let me taste how much you want me."

I lifted my left hand, my eyes never leaving his as I pressed the tip of my ring finger to his hard lips. With a deep, chest-breaking groan, his mouth parted and drew my finger inside. His tongue coaxed it deeper and licked it clean at the same time. As much as I wanted to stare at the beautiful etch of pleasure over his face, I couldn't help the way my head lowered to his cock.

He jerked it fast now. Rough and hard and unrelenting. I watched the flesh thicken and the veins swell. The drips of pre-cum spilled faster, and then Max's lips coasted over my ring, and his teeth clamped down firmly on the flesh on the other side.

I gasped, pain and pleasure spiraling straight to my core. Max sucked hard, and his hips jerked violently. A strangled sound erupted against my digit as he pumped himself one last time, dragging my thong over the head of his cock as he came into the fabric.

All I could do was stare as the fabric filled and filled and filled with his release before spilling cum onto the shower floor.

Never had I experienced anything this hot. *And Max hadn't even touched me.* Not until the very end.

His teeth released my finger, and it slipped languidly back through his lips, which gave one final tug on the tip before freeing my hand.

"So fucking sweet, Daze," he rumbled, dark irises fringed with something painful. "You taste like blueberries to me."

My heart stumbled over each one of its next several beats. Max didn't mean literal blueberries. He meant a craving he couldn't quench. *A craving he'd been starved of until now.*

I went to reach for him, too overwhelmed from... everything to be able to speak, but he stepped back. All the way back to the other side of the water spray, and my heart plummeted into my stomach.

"You should go to bed, Daze," Max rasped, dragging his free hand roughly through his wet hair.

Was that regret in his voice? My throat tightened. "Max—"

"It's late. We'll talk tomorrow," he insisted, and I was too overwhelmed, too wrung out to press.

"Okay. Good night," I murmured and walked out of the bathroom.

He'd just confessed to wanting me for years, and I... I had done the same. The admission started a war inside me. Longing fighting guilt. Desire fighting self-preservation. We were married. I wanted him. My husband. *Desperately*. I was also having another man's baby.

The convoluted web of my life was hard enough to process on a good day, and utterly impossible to untangle when I could hardly even stand straight.

How long had he felt this way? The questions started to pump into my mind like the slow and steady pound of my pulse. *How long had he wanted me?*

How would all of this have been different had he just told me sooner?

What had I done?

I dragged in a deep breath and flipped the bacon in the pan, grateful for my dad for dropping off the breakfast essentials—eggs, bacon, toast—at the crack of dawn this morning without asking any questions. At least, no verbal ones. His curious stare was easier to answer with a short rundown of what happened with Mrs. McCormick at the store yesterday. If it had been Nox or Harper, they wouldn't have left it at that—the simple facts, not the complicated feelings.

I'd spent half the night tossing and turning, feeling like an ass for the way I sent Daisy away, but I was so fucked in the head after what had happened in the bathroom, I didn't trust myself to make any decisions, let alone the right ones.

Grease sizzled and sprayed from the pan, catching the back of my hand holding the tongs, but I didn't even flinch. There was nothing that burned me nearly as much as the memory of Daisy's legs spread on that counter, her bedroom eyes soaked with lust and moaning my name as she pleasured herself to my command—came to my command—with his damn ring buried in her perfect cunt.

I tapped an egg on the counter to crack the shell. Too hard, apparently, because it split before I could get it over the bowl.

"Shit." I grabbed a paper towel and wiped up the soppy mess, tossing it in the trash.

A metaphor for what happened last night. I'd been weak, a fragile shell of frustration in that shower, and as soon as she'd walked through the door and saw me, I shattered. The way I wanted her, the way I'd always wanted her, spilling into messy, mind-numbing domination.

I groaned and rinsed my hands.

What had I done? Guilt whispered.

What she wanted, a whisper talked back.

My second attempt to shell the eggs went better, six of them sliding smoothly into the bowl. I turned on another burner, cut a slice of butter into a second pan, and fished out four slices of bread from the bag.

The sound of my—Daisy's—bedroom door opening tumbled all the way down into the kitchen. I gritted my teeth and grabbed a fork from the drawer.

There was no going back after last night. I'd crossed a line, a double-yellow one, that I couldn't come back from. All that was left was to see just how completely I'd mangled not only our friendship, but our fake marriage.

Her footsteps started to make their way downstairs. She didn't try to quiet her approach, maybe a warning for the both of us to prepare for the conversation that was about to happen.

What if she wanted to leave?

What if she wanted to walk away from me? From my help? My protection?

I smashed the fork through the eggs so hard you'd think I was trying to hand-crank an engine to start, not scramble soft eggs.

What if after the way I treated her, she never wanted to see me again?

"Max."

Shit. The fork stopped, my heart stopping right along with it.

Daisy stood at the base of the stairs wearing one of my MaineStems tees over a pair of leggings. I couldn't help the quick detour of my gaze, raking over those legs that had been spread wide for me last night, before I braced myself for the worst and lifted my eyes to hers.

She could put on a front like the very best showgirl, but her eyes would always tell me what she was really thinking, how she was feeling. I met her stare, and my gut clenched. I'd prepared all morning—and all night— for what I'd see when she looked at me, but somehow, I hadn't prepared for this. And I wasn't sure if that was worse.

Instead of finding regret or embarrassment or anger, Daisy looked at me with the same expression she wore when she slid her cum-soaked finger into my mouth— the one that told me she wanted more.

Fire chewed through the marrow of my bones. She wanted more.

And then her hand came to rest on top of her stomach, pulling the shirt taut to her fuller breasts. Instantly, my cock thickened, having a memory instead of a fantasy to feed it. And then I saw it. The ring still on her finger.

An arctic chill seared through me, making me feel as brittle as a bomb.

She looked at me like she wanted more of me, more of us, yet she still wore another man's ring, knowing it would stop me every single time.

"Good morning." I couldn't hide the shredded tone of my voice.

"Morning." She came into the kitchen but stuck to the far side of the island, her eyes roaming over the food. "It smells amazing down here. Where did the food come from?"

Turning away from her, I whipped the eggs roughly with the fork, the most paltry vent for my pent-up frustration. "My dad dropped it off earlier. I texted him and asked if he could bring over some food."

She let out a small hum, the sound sinking straight to my groin. *Christ.* I gritted my teeth. Would I ever not be turned on by even the smallest of things about her? Probably not, came the whisper again. Hell, I hadn't even been turned off by the ring on her finger, let alone the biggest of things when she'd been my best friend's fiancée.

"Do you want some orange juice?" I asked, dumping the eggs into the hot pan.

"He brought orange juice?"

I looked for her because she didn't sound close anymore. I was right. She stood at the window on the other side of the living room, staring at the ocean.

She turned, and our eyes collided, a pop and crack echoing through the room. It came from the bacon grease erupting in the pan, but it felt like it happened between us, because of this tension combusting between us, heating dangerously close to igniting.

"He brought everything," I grunted and returned to the stove. "Is that a yes?"

"Please."

My family—and extended family—didn't do anything in half-measures. Maybe that was where I got it from. A blessing and a curse. I traded the egg carton—because Dad had brought over a whole dozen —for the orange juice from the fridge and poured Daisy a glass, setting it on the counter for her as she came over.

"This...your house is incredible."

I stiffened. I didn't want to talk about my house, but there were other topics hanging between us that I wanted to avoid more.

"Thanks." I turned the eggs over in the pan and then staggered the bread into the toaster.

"I can't believe you're selling it. I'd never want to leave if I lived here."

"I know," the reply came unbidden, and I swallowed down a curse. Maybe she hadn't—

"What do you mean *you know*?" She'd heard. When I didn't answer right away, her bare feet padded closer. "Max..."

"'I don't know how anyone could have a house next to the ocean and not want to spend every waking moment here. Not even something big or fancy.'" I cranked off all the burners, the food finished cooking. I shouldn't say anything else, but I couldn't stop myself. "Something peaceful. Big windows to watch the waves. A back porch to sit on and watch the sunrise. A yard to lie in and count the stars. Somewhere...to stop and just be."

I grabbed the frying pan and turned to split the eggs between the two plates on the counter. In my periphery, Daisy's brows pulled together, the words tugging at something buried in her mind.

Her words.

"I told you that," she finally breathed out.

Like watching a train wreck about to happen, I knew devastation was coming, and I was powerless to stop it.

"The night of Mr. McCormick's birthday party," I revealed roughly, plating the bacon next before grabbing the toast from the toaster oven.

I wasn't surprised it took her a beat to remember. Daisy was a lightweight. Even before Todd's drinking became a problem, she never indulged in more than a glass of wine here and there.

That night, she'd had two glasses of champagne to bolster herself against Todd's parents by the time I'd found her sitting on the railing of the grand mansion's back patio, her hands propped on the edge, her head tipped to the sky.

"I remember...on the deck..." Like a Jenga tower being built in reverse, I watched her piece together the memory. "I was avoiding Todd and his parents," she murmured with a strained laugh.

"You told them how much you loved the house, and how if you lived there, you'd never want to go into the city..." I offered up another piece along with her plate of food.

Her eyes flicked wide. "Mrs. McCormick said, of course I'd think that because I hadn't grown up with multiple residences. Something about how society doesn't stay in one place, and as Todd's girlfriend, I should know that."

I nodded, vividly recalling what she'd told me about why she was hiding out on the deck, and exactly how furious it made me.

Taking her fork, Daisy stuck it into her eggs, irritated by the memory. Only when she had a mouthful of food did I start to pick at my own.

We ate for several minutes in silence, and I could practically hear her mind turning through everything I'd just told her. A Rubik's cube turning the facts round and round until the only explanation that lined up was that I'd bought the house because of her.

Her fork clanked on her plate, drawing my attention straight to hers.

"I remember..." she began. "I remember you asked me if I really wanted a house on the coast. A place out here to start fresh."

My body stiffened like my veins were being pumped with steel. "Are you finished?" I asked, though I could see she wasn't.

"No," she said with an edge, pulling her plate toward her. "You asked me if I wanted a house on the coast, and I said yes, and you...you asked me what I would do if you bought me one."

"Daisy—"

"No, Max, you asked what I would do if you bought me one, and I said I doubted Todd would ever agree to live in it. And you..." She paused, her breath catching. "You asked me if it was really Todd I saw myself living with..."

She'd finished the Jenga tower, and now I wanted to knock it all down.

I never should've said any of those things that night. I knew I was overstepping. I knew I was busting through a barrier I'd obeyed for years. But she was so damn beautiful out there under the stars, and Todd was too busy drinking himself away and avoiding his parents, hanging with Scott and me, to even notice his girlfriend was upset. *Just like he'd been too distracted to realize that Daisy never liked daisies.*

But I noticed.

My hand curled around my napkin. "It was a hypothetical."

"No." Her head swayed. "It wasn't."

"Daisy—"

"Was last night a hypothetical too?"

My hand released, the crumbled napkin falling like a paper grenade onto the counter.

"Tell me the truth," she begged.

I gritted my teeth. It was one thing to torture myself all these years, unable to stop myself from wanting her. It was another thing to dig my own goddamn grave and confess what a fool I'd been.

"How long, Max?" I could practically hear the lump in her throat. "How long have you felt this way?"

There was no avoiding this, I reminded myself. She literally caught you with your dick in your hands and her name on your lips.

"Since the beginning." I felt the force of her exhale from the other side of the counter.

"What?"

"I've wanted you since that morning in the coffee

shop, Daze," I forced the words out, freeing them from the prison they'd been locked in for years.

Her head swayed. "But you were meeting—"

"I was meeting Todd there, but I had no idea about you. Todd told me he was seeing someone, but he wouldn't give me details—didn't give me details. Not even when he arranged a surprise meeting for us." Pain stabbed my chest like a thorn buried deep between my ribs. "I thought he was introducing me to a potential investor, the way he was excited. I had no idea he...no idea you..."

No idea I was about to be introduced to the woman of my dreams as my best friend's girlfriend.

"All this time, Max..." Daisy's head kept twisting in disbelief, like if she shook it enough, my answer would turn into something different. *Would mean something less.* "Why did you never say something?"

I couldn't tell if it was pain or anger that roughened her voice, and the glaze that came over her eyes made them too murky now to read.

"What was I supposed to say?" I bit out, scraping my plate clean and setting it in the sink. "Todd was my best friend. I'd never put that between us—put that between the two of you."

"And what about me?" Her brow furrowed deeply. "Was I nothing compared to that?"

"Christ." I drove my hand through my hair, the level of my voice rising. "You were everything, Daze. Every fucking thing to me. The reason I don't date. The reason I don't have a girlfriend. The reason I bought this house." My arms fell to my sides, all the fight going out of me in a single sentence. "And you wanted him."

Her breath came out of her in a single burst. Like a balloon popping on the point of a needle.

"And every time I thought about ending things with Todd? Every time I came to you about his drinking? About how he never seemed to care? Never seemed to have any dreams or goals except those of his parents?"

My jaw erupted, the muscle firing like grenades had been daisy-chained together.

"You chose him, Daze. You wanted him, and even when you came to me, you came wanting to figure out a way to work through it. The right thing for me to do was to be there for the two of you," I rasped. "Not exploit a moment of weakness to try to steal you from my best friend."

"So you're saying you were too much of a gentleman to tell me the truth? To be brave enough to tell me how you felt?"

"Dammit, Daze." I swallowed, feeling like acid had been dumped down my throat, hollowing out every idea of honor I'd held onto. "I won't apologize for it. I care about him—about you. I wanted the two of you to be happy if that was what you wanted, and it never seemed like it wasn't. So yeah, I did everything I could to make things work for you and Todd, to fix things, to help him, to make everything perfect for you because it was the right thing to do."

I'd thought her anger was bad. Her silence was worse.

"What are you talking about?"

I winced. *Shit.*

No. *Fuck.*

"Daisy—"

"What did you do, Max?"

"I talked to you. Talked to him." I reached out and gripped the edge of the counter. "Little things...nothing, really. The peonies. I would send the peonies from him. He would always send daisies no matter how many times I told him they weren't your favorite."

The first tear that fell felt like a bullet to my chest.

"What else?" She was resolute, knowing that wasn't the end of it. "You don't do little things, Max. Not for me. You moved out of your apartment so I could stay there. You married me so the baby and I could have insurance. Nothing you've ever done for me has been little."

I held my ground like a bull pawing at the ground. *What was I trying to preserve?* I'd already—thoroughly —wrecked the veneer of a friendship I'd spent years propping up.

"Tell me the truth," she charged, the red flag waved.

"The notes. I helped him write them. The dates he'd take you on, I'd tell him about the Monet exhibit you wanted to see because you saw the billboard one time while we were out on deliveries and said you'd love to go see it. The Titanic experience. The Albanian restaurant you kept saying you wanted to try..."

Her cheeks were soaked now, but she stared at me like she hadn't even noticed. "What else?"

I ground my teeth together. "The wedding. He was going to agree to do it at the courthouse. I was the one who asked Lou to use the inn. Set everything up. I went to the cake tasting. It wasn't a big deal—"

"Not a big deal?" She chuffed, her tears burned away by the flames in her cheeks. "Every time I gave Todd another chance, it was because you were turning him into someone he wasn't. You made me think I was remembering why I fell in love with him, when really I was falling—when really it was you."

Her fingers chased the tears on her cheeks, and mine dug into the counter, furious to be standing on the sidelines.

"I regret it, Daze," I said, my voice breaking all over the place. "I regret being honorable. I regret being considerate. I regret not being a shitty best friend and swooping in on his girlfriend every single chance I got because you deserved so much better, and I wanted to be the man to give it to you."

"So why are you holding back now?"

"Because I don't want you to regret being with me."

"I regret these years of not being with you, Max. Why would I ever think that?"

"You know, for days...weeks, I've thought Todd was an asshole. A coward for what he did...how he left me—"

"He is—"

"Well, then, he's a brave coward." She pushed back from the counter and stood. "At least when he felt too much, he acted on it. Maybe in the worst, most painful, most horrible timing way, but at least he acted on what he wanted—or didn't want—instead of continuing down a path that wasn't right."

I recoiled like a bomb had just gone off.

Todd...brave for leaving her. I wanted to call her crazy for thinking it, that the man who'd left her pregnant and waiting at the altar was any shade of brave, but I couldn't get her point out of my mind long enough to protest.

His choice was horrible. The way he went about it, callous and cruel. But with all of that stripped away, was Todd brave for walking away from something he knew wasn't right?

Was he brave for acting on what he felt?

Had I been a coward for not?

"Daisy..." I was in front of her in two steps flat.

"No." Her head shook, and she stepped back like a caged animal, angry and afraid.

"Please."

A knock sounded loudly on the door a second before Harper's voice yelled, "Hello? Anybody home?"

Shit. Perfect fucking timing...

"Yeah," I clipped and moved away from Daisy, hearing my sister approach.

"Is everyone clothed?"

"Harp—"

"Kidding," she gushed as she strode into the kitchen, stopping when she saw Daisy and me. Her gaze swung between us.

"Do you need something?"

"Yeah," she returned, staunchly folding her arms. "Daisy."

My head cocked.

"I went to the shop to pick her up this morning because I told her I would give her a tour of my apiary, and imagine my surprise when she wasn't there."

Daisy let out a whimper. "I'm so sorry, Harper."

"I called both of you," she continued, at which point both Daisy and I looked around sheepishly for cell phones that weren't in sight. "And then finally got a hold of Dad, who told me you were here...and why." She went to Daisy and pulled her in for a hug. "I'm sorry." My sister squeezed her tight, and I watched as

Daisy relaxed into the embrace, hating myself even more.

I should've never let her stay in the bathroom last night, no matter what she said she wanted.

"I just wanted to come check on you and see if there was anything I could do," Harp said and released her. "We can go to the hives another day—"

"No," Daisy interrupted firmly. "I want to go this morning. Please. I could use the drive"—her eyes flicked to me—"and a distraction."

"If you're sure..."

"Just let me grab my sneakers. I'll be right back," came Daisy's answer as she went upstairs. I made a note to bring all her shoes back to the main floor.

"What did you do?"

I turned to find my sister's scowl. "What are you talking about?"

Harper stared at me, and I felt her gaze penetrating right through all the holes Daisy had left in my chest.

"You told her, didn't you?"

"Harper—"

"You told her you've been in love with her all these years?"

Love. I tensed.

"I warned you. You were being too much of a gentleman."

"You don't understand," I groaned and shook my head, not in the least bit of a mood to explain it to her.

"No, I think I understand perfectly," Harper stepped closer to me and hissed, Daisy's footsteps getting louder toward the stairs again. "Learning that Prince Charming was too chivalrous to step in when she was falling for the villain is a hard pill to swallow."

CHAPTER 20
DAISY

I fled Max's house the best a seven and a half months pregnant woman could, too upset to wonder if I looked ridiculous or not.

Harper called that she was coming right behind me, so I didn't stop. Let her talk to her brother. I couldn't... didn't have anything else to say right now.

Outside, Harper's yellow Volkswagen bug looked ridiculous next to Max's big truck. A spot of sunshine parked alongside a giant white bull. My silent prayer was answered when her car was unlocked when I reached it.

I sank into the passenger seat and closed the door.

Since the beginning.

I squeezed my eyes tight and whimpered. Even here I couldn't escape his answers...or my questions. How could he not say something...anything to me? How could he try to keep Todd and me together, given how he felt? How could he plan my wedding to his best friend *and say nothing?*

Because Todd was safe.

I swatted the thought from my mind before it took hold.

Harper appeared and jogged to the driver's side. "Sorry." She closed the door and started the engine. "Ready?"

I nodded and tried to work down the lump in my throat that kept floating like a buoy to the top.

Especially when Max stepped out the front door and stood there, watching us turn around and drive away. I was no better, staring at the side view and the man inside it until he was too small to see.

"Are you okay?" Harper asked once we turned onto the main road, drawing me back to where I was and who I was with.

Okay...what did that word even mean anymore?

Okay that my ex-almost-mother-in-law tracked me down and threatened me?

Okay that my convenient husband made me feel things last night I never thought were possible?

Or okay that my convenient husband confessed to having feelings for me for years—for the whole time I was his best friend's girlfriend?

"It's just been a...shocking twenty-four hours."

"I can't even imagine," she said, driving cautiously. "I can't believe Todd's mom showed up at the apartment like that. What a psycho."

Her appearance at the store felt like it had happened a decade ago rather than less than twenty-four hours ago. So much had happened between then and now. I couldn't even find my anger with her on my radar right now.

"Yeah," I murmured, unable to tear my eyes from the window as she stopped at the end of Max's drive.

And then I saw the holes in the ground where the For Sale sign had been.

"*Is Todd really who you see yourself living in it with?*"

Max had bought this house because of me. He was *selling* this house because of me.

Harper turned onto the road, letting me forget about that for a little while.

"How far is your farm from here?"

"Just a few minutes up the road." She pointed her finger ahead. "It's a lot closer to Max's house than Stonebar."

I responded with a wordless nod, watching the trees stagger past us, one after another after another, until they turned into a blur and my breathing started to steady. Slowly, I felt the tension start to drain from my body. Time kept marching on, and this, too, would pass.

"Do you think she'll come back?"

"I have no idea, but if she does, at least I won't be there." I sighed and then reasoned. "I don't think she will, though. Not after what Max said."

The foreign sensation of a smile tugged up one side of my mouth, remembering how Max had put her in her place...and the look on her face when he'd done it.

"What did he say?"

My smile fell as I attempted to tamp down the warmth flooding my chest when I recalled his words. *My wife.*

"That she had no right to be there, and he'd press charges if she tried to harass us—me again."

Harper snapped her eyes over and then back to the road. "Did he tell her you were married?"

My mouth opened and then shut as I opted for a

nod as an answer. Better not to say too much now that everything with Max was so...complicated.

"Finally." She turned off the road onto a gravel drive, the car rocking over the unsteady ground.

My neck swiveled. "What do you mean *finally*?"

"Oh, Daisy." Harper slowed in front of a good-sized shed, older but with a fresh coat of navy paint and the Harper's Honey logo sprayed in warm yellow on the wall.

Harper put the car in park and fanned a pained smile in my direction. "I've known for a long time how Max felt about you."

Well, that made one of us I wanted to tell her, but something stopped me. *Had she been the only one? Or had I just ignored what I didn't want to see...what I didn't want to feel?*

Harper was out of the car before I could say anything else.

"Welcome to Harper's Hives." She beamed, handing me a beekeeping suit to put on and then ducking back into the shed to grab a suit for herself.

"Are you sure this is going to fit over my stomach?" I asked, sliding one foot and then the other into the legs.

"It should. It's a men's large."

That explained why the arms and legs were too long, but at least the zipper went up easily over my front.

"Why do you have a men's large?"

"Because I'm waiting for my Prince Charming to show up in apiary armor," she quipped with a chuckle and then explained, "Sometimes my brothers or Dad help me with the hives, so I got a suit for them."

Right. I'd tack that obvious answer squarely in the pregnancy brain column.

"Hat is next." She took a wide-brimmed hat off one of the hooks and placed it on my head before carefully unrolling the fine netting that draped around the rim. "And then gloves." After plopping her own hat on her head, she handed me a pair of thick gloves. "You can wait to put those on until we get to the hives."

Wordlessly, I took the gloves as she gathered her tools and led the way.

As we walked, Harper dove right into telling me about her growing honeybee business, how it started, when she moved to this parcel of land that once belonged to her aunt's farm, how many hives she began with, how many she maintained now. I was more than happy to listen and ask questions...anything to give me a little distance from Max.

I was surprised by the path to the hives. I'd expected them to be close by the shed, and maybe they were. Maybe it just felt farther because the incline was noticeable, and I moved slower nowadays. But it wandered through a thicket of loosely packed trees, sprigs of flowers blooming along the footpath and at the base of the trunks.

If there was any real place that could've served as the inspiration for Taylor Swift's *folklore*, this little grove could've been it.

"Why aren't the hives closer to your shed?" I finally decided to ask.

"The shed was already there when I decided to put a bee farm on the property, but it's always shady here. Hives do best when they get some sun, but shade to block out the extreme heat, so the best spot for them was through the trees over there." She turned over her shoulder, and I could see her smiling under the fine black netting. "I like coming out here and having nothing in sight except me and the bees. It's...you'll see."

The thicket dissolved a few feet later, and Harper stopped a couple of steps out of the clearing, and I came to stand by her shoulder.

I did see.

Wildflowers of every pastel stretched as far as the eye could see. A sea of serene color lined on either side of us by two rows of narrow but tall box-like structures. *The hives.*

"Told you." She nudged my elbow. "All right, let's go check on my bee babies."

My hands went to my stomach, feeling my own baby buzzing under the surface.

"Jamie built me these supports for the hives." She pointed to the base that lifted the hives about a foot off the ground. "I was using wood pallets that I attached legs to, but he wanted to make me something custom. You want to keep the hives off the ground, and having an open framework is good for airflow."

"That was nice of him."

"Yeah." She smiled. "All right, gloves on."

I followed her lead, sliding on the thick elbow-length gloves.

"Yeah, Aunt Ailene let me lease this property. Jamie built these stands. Dad helps me manage and harvest when he can. Frankie uses my beeswax for some of her candles. Lou serves my honey at the inn." She turned and faced the flowers. "And Max helped me grow the field of wildflowers."

I stiffened. "How many hives did you say you had?"

If she noted my obvious change of conversation, Harper didn't let on. "Sixteen right now, but I'm going to probably add a dozen more next year. Hopefully."

"Why hopefully?"

The bubbly happiness she carried dimmed a little. "I'm just nervous to expand with everything going on."

"You have so many people supporting you, Harper. I'm sure it's going to be just fine." I buried the twinge of jealousy at just *how* many people...how much family she had supporting her.

But it wasn't just how much family support she had, was it? No, I admitted. It was *who* that family was that really made my chest tighten.

All this time...I could've been a part of this family too. If Max had just said something...

"Thanks." She reached for the top of the first hive. "Sometimes, the internet makes me feel like I need some kind of personal PR campaign to turn my reputation around."

"Not a chance," I assured her. "Unless you do end up with a Prince Charming in apiary armor. Then, I think it could be worth it."

That got her to laugh. "I'll keep that in mind."

Harper carefully lifted off the hood of the hive and propped it carefully on the ground. Immediately, she reached for the small dome-topped metal spray can she'd brought out with us.

All I could think of was that it looked like the oil can the Tin Man carried around to grease himself up in *The Wizard of Oz*.

"The smoke puts them to sleep." She sprayed on top of the slat inserts stacked in the box, like files in a filing cabinet. "The guard bees usually roam on top of the frames, so we smoke them right away. The others in the middle of the cluster rarely sting."

I watched as the small creatures started to settle and still after just a few puffs of the white smoke.

"Now we can check on the honey."

Harper set the tin down and grabbed another tool that she used to pry up the first frame inside the hive.

"Are you still harvesting?"

"No." Harper shook her head, examining the screen that was splotched with bees on top of honeycombs. "Sometimes, when it stays warm like this, the hives will continue to produce honey in September and October, but I don't like to risk taking too much from the hive so that they don't have enough stores for the winter."

Satisfied with what she saw, she slid the frame back into place and pulled out the next one, repeating her inspection.

While she worked, she explained the process of harvesting the honey during the summer months. The different kinds of bees found in the hives. How to go about finding the queen.

We made it down the entire row of eight hives and turned back toward the second stretch of tiny towers before Harper fell silent, and I knew what she was thinking about.

I knew because I was thinking about him too.

"So...any new men in your life?" I must be really desperate to avoid talking about Max.

Harper flushed, and her head fell. "I've been too busy with the business."

I was the master of crafting truth-coated excuses, so I easily recognized when I was being given one.

"Too busy? You can't be too busy to put yourself out there." It was as close as I'd come to revealing what Max had told me about her crush on Blaze Stevens.

Harper glanced around like she wanted to make sure there was no one else to hear—no one but the bees. "I think it's for the best. The heart never seems to act rationally," she said, and smoked the guard bees of the next hive like the white cloud could erase parts of her thoughts too. "So do you want to talk about what happened with Max this morning?"

Speaking of not rational.

"You don't have to," she said when I didn't reply immediately. "I just want you to know you can talk to me. You're family, Daisy, and not just because you married Max."

Without warning, tears welled to the surface of my eyes. Even with the netting covering my face, I was afraid she'd see, so I took a few steps into the wild-flowers.

Pink and purple and orange and yellow petals dotted my vision, bees flitting between the various blooms before heading back to their hives. Their homes.

Family.

Little sprout started to kick then and seemingly knocked my tears free. I bit into my cheek. God, these hormones were going to be the death of me.

In previous versions of my life, I would've kept my conversation with Max and my feelings to myself.

But now...

Now, I had the opportunity to be a part of the family I'd always been jealous of. An opportunity to be close to people who would support me no matter what.

Who would help me without question, and more importantly, without considering me helpless.

Who would I be if I didn't take it?

The old Daisy.

The independent coward.

I returned to Harper's side as she carefully replaced the lid on the first hive.

"I'm sorry, Harp. It's all just a lot right now. Todd. The baby. The wedding. Todd's parents. Max."

"Don't apologize." Setting her smoker down, she pulled me in for an awkward bee-suited hug, the attempt alone drawing a watery laugh from my chest.

"I know he's my brother, so you don't have to share—"

"He told me he's always had feelings for me," I blurted out. "Before he knew I was with Todd. While he knew I was with Todd. Now."

Meanwhile, I was so afraid to admit I'd made the wrong choice, that I'd ignored the right man standing in front of me all these years.

"For the record, I told him many times he was an idiot for not saying something," she muttered, annoyed.

"He was trying to be respectful of Todd. Of me," I found myself defending him because, in spite of my anger earlier, he was defensible.

What kind of person would he have been to drive that wedge between Todd and me? *Not the man I knew him to be, that was for sure.*

"Max is too respectful. I get not wanting to ruin a friendship or a friend's relationship, but everything he did to help Todd keep you? And on top of that, planned your wedding? Talk about beating a dead horse." She slid the top off the next hive. "You have every right to be angry at him for not saying anything. In fact, I really think you should take the opportunity to torture him with it."

"Torture?" Remnants of a laugh splintered free as I shook my head. "I can't torture him. Not after everything..."

Not after four years of torturing himself to try to make me happy.

"Well, it's still my vote. And Nox's." She pulled out the honeycomb crawling with bees. "Plus, it'll be good to get out some of the anger."

"I'm not angry with him," I admitted, catching Harper's gaze through the screens in our hoods. "I'm angry with myself."

"What?" She shoved the honeycomb back inside and closed up the hive. "What are you talking about? You didn't do anything—"

"That's it. That's why I'm upset." I gulped, guilt clawing at my throat. "I didn't do anything. I didn't do anything when things with Todd weren't right. When I saw all the signs that I should've left him." *When I couldn't stop fantasizing about his best friend.*

This was what had broken my heart into a hundred pieces earlier. Not Max. Not his holding back how he felt. Me.

Me, afraid to accept how I felt. Me, holding back that I wanted him the same.

"He was right. I went to him, to Max, when I was upset with Todd. I wasn't looking for someone to tell me to leave. I was looking for someone to give me reasons to stay, someone to give me reasons why I'd made the right choice and hadn't fallen for disappointment like all the men my mom dated."

And Max had taken my lead. *Like he always did.*

He'd given me what I'd told him I wanted: reasons to stay with Todd. He'd tried to make Todd into the man I wanted...*the man Max was.*

"You can't beat yourself up for that, Daisy. I'm not sure there's a single person who isn't guilty of trying to hang onto a relationship that wasn't right for them," she counseled, sounding far too wise for someone so young as we walked back through the thicket to her tool shed. "We're all afraid to put ourselves out there."

"It's not just that," I confessed quietly, my gaze dropping to the ground, sprigs of wildflowers shooting up between my feet.

"Then what is it?"

I met her stare. "I'm angry with myself because, deep down, I've wanted him this whole time too."

I wasn't angry at Max for keeping how he felt about me a secret. I was angry at myself for doing the same. For four years, I'd fantasized about him. Savored the time we spent together. Ached for more. But did nothing because Todd was safe. Todd was who I'd picked. *Todd was never a real threat to my heart.*

Max wasn't a coward for not speaking up. I was. I was the one who was too afraid to be wrong, even when it kept me from being with the person who felt right.

"I don't know what to do."

"What do you want to do?"

What did I want?

I wanted for this time with Max to never end. I wanted for every moment to be like those in the bathroom last night, where there was no invisible barrier between us.

"I want to be with your brother," I said and held my stomach.

"Okay. So tell him that."

The ball in my throat swelled. "I don't think the answer is as simple as that. I'm..." I motioned to my stomach. "Not as simple as that."

I was surprised Harper didn't sway with how hard she rolled her eyes, but then she lifted her arms in mock surrender.

"All right, maybe *you* aren't that simple, but my brother definitely is," she insisted. "And I'm telling you that the way he looks at you now is no different than he has for the last four years."

The way he looked at me last night from the shower was definitely different. Better. Complete. But I refrained from telling her that.

"So you think I should just waltz back into his house and tell him I feel the same way about him?"

"No." Harper's eyes twinkled.

"What?"

"Forget telling him. Just go back there and kiss him."

Something between a laugh and a choke sounded from my chest. "No, I can't just...do that."

There was so much to say. So much to apologize for. To figure out. And we hadn't even scratched the surface of what had happened last night.

"Why not?" Harper pulled off my hat, her earnestness silencing me. "He's your husband, Daisy. I think that's exactly what that means."

CHAPTER 21
DAISY

My time with Harper didn't end after the tour of her apiary.

Even though I was feeling marginally better after our conversation, I wasn't ready to go back to the house and face Max yet.

So after we left her hives, she took me over to Nox's barn-turned-glass-blowing factory. He wasn't there, but Harper walked me through his burgeoning operation and then proceeded to show me the custom beehive-shaped containers he'd fabricated to jar her honey.

We stopped at a restaurant for lunch before heading into Friendship. Harper had errands to run—a stop at Frankie's candle shop, a few minutes in the Stonebar Farms store where Ailene plied us with blue-berry scones and fresh maple butter, and then some time at Jamie's woodworking shop. Harper was coordi-nating with Violet about the specs of the new support stands for her new hives.

It was dinnertime by the time we finished, and Vi invited us to join their family for sloppy joes. Harper offered to take me back to the house then if I wanted, but I didn't.

I wasn't ready.

Somehow, the four years I'd spent concealing my feelings for Max sat like a boulder on my chest. Not crushing me, but like a weighted blanket. Somehow, it had become soothing to only want him in secret. Safer to desire him in the shadows of slumber. It buried the beats of my heart under something that was as impenetrable as it was inescapable.

I could long for Max in secret because there was no chance of getting hurt. And I could simultaneously fight to make things work with Todd because he wasn't a threat to my heart. He never had been.

Now, that boulder was gone. Lifted. My heart, freed to beat and ache and *be* with him. *And risk getting hurt.* And that was what frightened me.

So Harper and I accepted the invitation to dinner and spent a few laughter-filled hours with Jamie, Violet, and their kids before calling it a night.

By the time Harper's bug took the turn to Max's driveway, daylight was in short supply.

"Thanks for everything today, Harper," I said when we reached the end of the drive, my hope hollowing out when we pulled into an empty parking pad. Max's truck was gone.

"I think he's at the farm," Harper said, and I looked over. "He's been texting me all day—and no, I haven't responded except to provide proof of life before he sent the whole state out searching for you."

I managed a weak smile. "Thanks."

"Are you okay?"

I looked over the house rising in front of us. Max's house. *My dream house.*

"Everything I've done has been for you."

Over the course of the day, Max's words metabolized in my mind, dissolving my fears word by word, piece by piece, until the only thing left was the deep-rooted yearning in my bones.

I wanted him. I'd wanted him since the beginning.

And after last night, I couldn't hide from it any longer.

"I think I will be," I answered finally and squeezed her hand when she reached over and took mine. "Thanks again."

I worked my way out of the car, somehow feeling like an extra-wide tractor-trailer by the end of the day. Holding the rim of the door, I turned and dipped my head to her. "Good night, Harp."

"Good night, Daisy." Harper leaned over the console. "Don't forget, feel free to torture him a little. He needs to not be so much of a gentleman all the time."

I pulled my bottom lip through my teeth, the corners of my lips curling slightly into a stifled but sheepish grin.

"Don't worry, Harp. He's not."

I shut the door on her comically round eyes, chuckling to myself all the way to the front door.

Toeing off my sneakers just inside the door, I went to the kitchen for some water. Filling a glass from the sink, I gulped it down, staring at the windows over the rim until I'd drank it all.

Leaving it on the counter, I let myself out the sliding back door, filling my lungs with the crisp night air. Stepping off the back deck, my bare feet pressed into the ground.

Tonight was one of those nights that could've been ripped straight from my dream. A calm, glistening ocean. A star-studded sky. A peaceful pocket of...home.

"Daisy."

I turned. "Max." I hadn't even heard him come outside.

My gaze raked over him like I hadn't seen him in years, rather than hours. Like he was a figment that could disappear at any moment. I curled my toes into the grass, wanting to root myself here. With Max.

"I'm sorry I left earlier," I started before the pressure bubbling up from my chest flagged.

"It's okay. I know...it's a lot." He dragged his palm along the edge of his jaw, and it killed me to see him torture himself like this. "I shouldn't—"

"I wanted you too, Max," I blurted out, watching him freeze. "I *want* you too."

His stare pierced mine, his irises like twin comets of lust barreling toward me, and I...I lowered my arms and anticipated the collision.

"Daisy, you don't know...don't understand—"

"I do," I interrupted, taking my first step toward him. "I know why you never said anything. I do understand. You're a good man, Max, and an even better friend. Maybe I wished you weren't so good to Todd, but I'm not—I can't fault you for not telling me before. If anything, all the signs were there...if I'd wanted to see them."

His jaw pulsed. "It's been a long day, Daze. Why don't we—"

"Why are you still trying to walk away from me?"

He drove his hand through his hair, his gaze dropping for a split second to my hand resting on my stomach, and then growled, "Because you're still wearing his ring."

I held up my hand, staring at the diamond like it was a sparkling scarlet letter.

"Do you really think I'm wearing this because of Todd?" I asked, lifting my eyes to his. "That, after everything...I could still be hoping...wanting him to come back?" I took another step closer, a thrill running down my spine when I saw Max's reaction, like my closeness tugged on a string. Not a string...on the sole rope of restraint anchoring him to the shores of sanity. "That there's any part of me that aches for Todd...after last night?"

His sharp inhale pierced the air like a star shooting through the sky.

"Then give me a better reason."

Air shuttled to the pit of my lungs and then back up again, unearthing my deepest secrets with it.

"I wore it because I've been trying to remember it was safe to be with Todd." I reached for the ring, slowly twisting it up my finger. "That he was the devil I knew —a devil who had many faults but none that put my heart at risk. It sounds stupid considering he left me at the altar, but at least when he left, he didn't take my heart."

The band popped over my knuckle and slid into my palm.

"I wore it because it symbolized the old Daisy. The cautious, stubborn, independent Daisy. I wore it because it reminded me I was jobless, homeless, and pregnant, and the last thing I could afford to do was catch feelings for the man who kept stepping in to help me. The man who's always been there to help me...even when I didn't know it."

I took another step, feeling the cool grass flatten under my feet.

"Daze." Max hissed and held up his hand in a staying motion.

"It reminded me that I shouldn't be so selfish as to desire my convenient husband."

I held out my hand and the ring to him, an offering.

It came as no surprise when he didn't take it.

Be brave. Curling my fingers around the band, I spun and walked toward the edge of the property.

"Daisy!" Max shouted, coming after me.

I had this dramatic moment cued up in my head where I'd toss the ring over the cliffs into the ocean, but I didn't even know how far away that cliff was, let alone that I'd be able to make it there before Max caught up to me.

So I settled for the gesture. *It was the thought that counted, right?*

I heaved my arm back and slung it forward, the ring flying into the night.

"Shit, Daisy," Max swore as he grabbed my other arm and spun me. "What are you doing?"

"Removing the barrier." I flattened my palm to his chest, feeling the pounding of his heart, and then following it up the column of his throat to the angle of his jaw.

"Daisy."

"What is it, Max?" I asked, torn between begging him and beating him for what was still holding him back. When he didn't say anything, I started with the obvious. "You want me."

His groan rumbled my fingertips before it reached my ears. "I do."

"And I want you." I lifted my now ringless hand, his grip still attached to my wrist. "So what's holding you back?"

His eyes darkened. "Because, Daze..."

"Because why?" I curled my fingers into his shirt, wishing I could bury them right into his skin, so he couldn't hide from me anymore.

"Because of how I want you, the way I..." He let out a slow breath. "It's not how you've known me to be. And you deserve better."

"Better?" I whimpered. "Was 'better' Todd stuffed up with your words and actions? Was 'better' a man who was puppeting what you told him?"

"Better," he interrupted with a growl, shackling my free wrist with his other hand. "*Better* is a man who takes you inside and tells you to go take a long bath and relax after a long day."

My breath hitched. "And you?" I managed to choke out. "What do you want to tell me to do?"

His jaw beat like a war drum, fervent and furious. "Daisy, please," he clipped. "You should go relax. Get off your feet—" He broke off with a hiss when I slid my hand from his chest up to cup his face, my fingers drinking in the feel of his stubbled skin and the hard-ened planes of his cheek.

"Tell me."

"Dammit, Daze." His jaw looked about to crack.

Too respectful was right. All Max had ever done was take care of me, try to make me happy, even when it came at his own expense. I didn't know what he was so afraid to say, but maybe he needed to know I wasn't afraid. No matter what it was.

Maybe he needed to know there was nothing that could make me not want him.

"I used to think about you...about being with you when I was with Todd," I confessed in a husky voice, and I watched the instantaneous change that came over him. The dilation of his dark eyes. The flare of his nostrils. The tightening of his grip on my arms. "All those times I would go with you on deliveries, I would fantasize about you laying me down in the back of your truck—"

"Fuck, Daisy," he growled, his voice unraveling.

"When it got bad with Todd's drinking, and he'd come home and want to...I'd hide in the bathroom until I heard him snoring. And then I'd come out and turn him on his side and then check my phone."

"Daisy..."

"You'd always message me to check on him, but deep down, I knew—I know you were checking on me. And I'd...touch myself."

"*Fuck.*"

"You'd ask me what I was doing, and I'd text back *nothing*, but I'd be thinking 'if only you knew,' 'if only you could see.'"

He was heaving breaths now, like he was locked in a fight to the death rather than a spectator to my submission.

"And I'd come thinking of you, my boyfriend's best friend, while Todd was passed out next to me." I pushed through the last before I lost my nerve. "The way I wanted you felt too risky, so I fought it. Hid it.

Especially when all you did was try to keep me and Todd together. I don't want to fight it anymore."

His head turned slowly into my hand, his warm breath coating my palm. And then his mouth opened, and I gasped as his teeth sank into my skin.

"I want more of what happened last night, Max," I said in a hurried whisper. "The things you did to me, the way you made me feel, I've never felt like that before. Please...I want more."

His eyes closed, his teeth locked on my hand for one more second as he breathed in deep, and then let his exhale release. When his eyes opened, the look in them was different.

It was the way he looked at me last night.

"A gentleman would tell you it's been a long day, and we can finish this discussion tomorrow."

"And you, Max? What would you say?"

"Get on your knees."

I tried to stop myself. Tried to hold steady when she chucked a thirty-thousand-dollar diamond engagement ring into the brush. Tried to stay still when she touched me. Tried to stay sane when she begged for an answer.

And I almost succeeded.

Until I had to listen to her describe how she'd think of me when she pleasured herself while Todd was passed out drunk in the bed next to her. A man could only take so much.

A gentleman could only resist so much for so long.

My restraint snapped inside me like a rubber band pulled too tight. I've been stretching myself so damn thin all these years that when the hold finally broke, I didn't even feel the sting, only the burn—the sear of all this time I'd missed with her. Because of me. Because of her. Even if I only had one night, I wouldn't miss any more.

"Get on your knees," I ordered, my voice rough and gravelly.

Her eyes shot wide, and I fought not to retract the command. I fought to keep my expression unwavering at the slight startle that rippled through her.

She wanted to know, I reminded myself repeatedly in those handful of seconds. *She asked for this.*

And then, like a flower bud unfurling into a bloom, Daisy's surprise unfolded into petals of pink in her cheeks, her teeth biting into her bottom lip, and a jolt of lust staked through me. *She wanted this.* And because she did, she lowered herself in front of me.

Aware—*fully aware*—of her condition, I kept my grip on her wrists, holding them high to give her a counterbalance as she went to her knees. If we were inside, I would've made sure there was a pillow under her. I might be a Dom, but cruelty wasn't my kink. I only put her on her knees because I wanted her off her feet, and I knew the ground was soft from the last couple of days of rain.

"Now what?" She looked up at me and asked, her eagerness stretching my cock painfully against my jeans.

I wanted all of her, but after last night, I had to play my hand carefully. It took all of my strength to not walk across the bathroom last night and fuck her on the counter. I didn't trust what strength I had left, especially if she changed her mind when she realized...*how* I was.

Taking both her wrists in my one hand, I lowered the other to my waist, undoing my belt buckle and the flap of my jeans in rough movements.

"Max," she whimpered, her eyes glittering like open flames as I stroked myself through my boxer briefs.

Fuck, I was so hard. Painfully fucking hard. Closing

my eyes, I gave myself a few hard pumps to keep my desire at bay. *Christ, her mouth hadn't even breathed on me yet, and I was ready to burst.* When I opened my eyes again, Daisy was staring up at me with the gossamer of fear removed from her gaze, need naked underneath.

"Do you like watching me, Daisy?" I grunted, working the elastic band over my tip, letting her see the pre-cum that pooled there.

"Yes," she blurted out, her breath rushing out.

Groaning, I tugged my clothes just low enough to free my cock. Instantly, Daisy's jaw dropped, and her soft whimper rose to me.

"What is it, Daze?" My grip strangled my length, the flesh pulsing under my fingertip.

"You're so...big."

My flesh jumped at her praise. I was just as big last night, I wanted to say, but last night, she wasn't on her knees in front of my monster cock.

"Oh, yeah?" I hissed, giving myself one long stroke. *Focus.* "Are you worried I'm too big, Daze?"

"No," she blurted out and swayed forward.

Fuck.

Gripping her wrists tighter, I held her back. *Not yet.*

"Do you want to taste me, Daisy?" *Pump. Pump.*

"Yes," she panted, dragging her tongue over her lips.

God, the plans I had for that tongue.

"Open wide and stick that pretty tongue out for me, little wife." The command erupted from my chest, but it wasn't until she looked at me that I realized what had made her pause. Not the instruction. *The endearment.*

Little wife.

My little wife.

But instead of finding resistance on her face, there was only submission. Holding my stare, her jaw lowered open for me, and her tongue rolled out a perfect pink carpet for me.

"Such a good girl." I fisted my girth and angled my hips forward enough to tap my cock against her tongue, the slapping noise sending a bolt of lust straight to the base of my spine and another drop of moisture to my tip.

With her mouth open, she couldn't hide the whimper that escaped her chest, and I didn't want her to. All I wanted was to hear the way she wanted me for the rest of my life.

"Stay open," I said gruffly, every nerve pushed to the limit by the sight.

Daisy on her knees for me. Her tits stuck forward because I held her arms above her head. And her tongue splayed from her full pink lips, just begging for a fucking taste of me.

Locking my teeth, I dragged the tip of my cock along her tongue, wiping the pre-cum onto the soft velvet. The sound she made then was more intense, and I barely pulled back in time as she tried to close me in her mouth.

"Not yet." *Pump.* Her pupils found mine, their centers blown wide as she swallowed. *Pump.*

"Max..."

"Show me that pretty tongue again," I ordered, and as soon as she complied, I lifted my cock and slapped it down harder this time. The sound more lewd. She panted but didn't try anything. "*Good girl.*"

The next time, I didn't tap her. I lowered the top third of my cock to her tongue and let it rest there like she was some kind of sex shelf. "Fuck, you're so beautiful, Daze."

Maybe it was supposed to be a test for her, but in the end, it only tested me. I'd only been able to fantasize about this for years, sure that in my mind was the only world where Daisy would be mine. Except now we were here. Together. Married. *And she was begging me to dominate her*. And for all those reasons, my cock felt ready to blow.

"You know how pretty this tongue would look coated in my cum?" I growled, tightening my grip at my base and sliding myself up and down her tongue, just barely teasing the entrance to her mouth like it was a goddamn cave of wonders.

Daisy whimpered, but to her credit, didn't do more than translate her ache into sound. And then I saw it—saliva leaking from her mouth, some of it dripping from the corners of her lips, some of it draining toward my cock. *Good girl*.

"Look at you salivating for my cock," I grunted, dragging my shaft over her tongue until it glistened. "You're soaking me so good, baby." Her breath shuddered. "I bet your pussy is soaking for me too, isn't she, Daze?"

Her eyes flicked to mine, sure and begging. My heart slammed erratically in my chest. I wasn't going to last much longer. Releasing my throbbing cock, I moved to cup the side of her face.

"You can nod."

Her unbroken stare was like a current of electricity straight to my groin. As her head lowered, her top lip brushed my flesh, and I slid my hand back, threading my fingers through her hair. I buried my next breath deep in my lungs, and when her head rose, her mouth at the perfect angle to take me, I shunted my hips forward.

Her gasp seemed to suck me in deeper, even though it wasn't possible. With my palm backstopping her head, I didn't stop until I bottomed out against the back of her throat. *Until I almost died from ecstasy.*

Her whole body jerked, tense, and a strangled sound gargled out from around my cock.

"Fuck, Daisy," I ground out, working a few short pumps into her wet heat until my brain unscrambled enough to slide myself free. "Was that the *more* you were hoping for?" I demanded roughly, hearing her catch her breath. I wasn't going to sugarcoat how I liked things. Even if I wanted to, I couldn't. I needed her too damn badly to rein myself back in that way.

"Yes," she blurted out.

My cock pulsed where it hung heavy and wet between us. "Are you sure?" Because I could still stop. It might kill me in the process, but I could do it.

"Yes," she husked, more plea than answer. "Please, Max. Please..." She arched toward me again, her open mouth searching for me to fill it.

"Fuck, Daze." I groaned and let her have me. Her lips latched onto my tip, sucking me in and stroking me with her tongue. Stars erupted in my vision, every caress undoing me down to the level of DNA in my cells. "God, you're so fucking perfect."

Framing my hand to the back of her head, I thrust into her slick heat, watching her cheeks balloon and leak every time I hit the back of her throat.

"You're so perfect, Daisy," I groaned. "So fucking perfect like this." I shunted faster, chasing the wet, slurping sounds she made around me.

Pleasure pooled at the base of my spine. I'd thought to only prime her with this. To fuck her mouth until she was sloppy and panting for more. Turned out, I was the one who had no composure. Not when she whimpered and gagged every time I thrust deep. Not when saliva coated my length and ran from the corners of her mouth.

Not when, somehow, my hand holding her wrists slid higher until her fingers interlocked with mine.

"That's it. Choke on that big cock and show me how bad your pussy wants it." My palm widened on the back of her scalp, and I pumped my hips harder. Faster.

There was no chance I could hold my release back now, but I wasn't worried. I'd wanted this woman every day and every night for four goddamn years. You better believe I had more than one round in me. The pressure at the base of my spine knotted tight. And then tighter. And tighter. Daisy moaned, making herself sputter and her throat clamp around me, and it sent me right to the edge.

With a rough curse, I ripped my cock from her lips, releasing her head to catch the wet length in my fist. I jerked it hard with my fist. I was so close, but when her jaw fell open and her tongue rolled out the welcome mat for my cum, I lost it. I came with a deep groan and sprayed my release on her throat and chest. Purposely—miraculously—avoiding her mouth.

For a long minute, all I did was watch the milky-white ropes of cum streak her neck and the top of her chest and savor the perfect sight. And then I caught the slight shiver that went through her with the cool breeze. I wasn't even sure she noticed. The rest of her flushed and panting from a different source of heat, but I wouldn't risk it.

I let my cock go, the rest of my release dripping to fertilize the grass, and slowly lowered my arm, bringing Daisy's down with it.

Her hazy eyes drifted up to mine. "I thought..."

I cupped both my hands over hers and crouched down so my gaze was level with hers. Pressing her fingers to my lips, I murmured, "The first time I come inside you, Daze, you better believe it's going to be in that pussy I've been dreaming about for four goddamn years."

Her breath hiccuped into her lungs, and then, almost comically, she looked down at herself to see where my mess had landed before dragging her gaze up to me.

"Don't worry, I'll take care of it." I kissed her knuckles. "And you, *little wife*."

I wondered how long I'd have to call her that for her not to tremble. I hoped forever.

And then I released her hands, moved to the side, and scooped her up off her knees, her squeal echoing out over the ocean.

"Max!" she cried out adorably, clutching her stomach. "You can't—"

"Can't what? Carry you?" I chuckled as I did just that. Even pregnant, she weighed what I would consider nothing compared to the weight of wanting her and having to hide it that I'd carried for years.

"What are you doing?" she murmured, burying her head in my chest.

I brought us to the house, not caring that my semi-hard dick bobbed in front of me with each step. No sense in putting myself away when I was far from finished.

Sliding the door open with my foot, I used my elbow to shut it, finding Daisy's eyes once we were inside in the light.

"Carrying my bride over the threshold and up to the bath so I can clean her. Thoroughly."

"Wow."

I turned to see Daisy coming into the bathroom. I'd deposited her on the bed to relax while I went to draw her a bath. That clearly hadn't lasted for long.

She stood just inside the door, staring at herself in the large vanity mirror. Messed hair. Swollen lips. Cum-streaked skin.

Fuck, she was a dream. My dream.

And tonight, she'd finally be mine.

I dipped my hands in the bathwater, confirming the temperature was perfect. Hot but not too hot. Another minute and the tub would be full and ready for her. I'd never been more grateful for the fast-fill feature I'd paid extra to install. There was nothing more annoying than the time it took to fill the soaking tub. By the time it was full enough to get in, I no longer felt like taking a bath.

The fast-fill fixed all that.

I turned off the faucet and caught Daisy's gaze in the mirror. "Is it ready?"

My chin lowered slowly, the hum of desire buzzing stronger in my blood.

"Take your clothes off."

My semi swelled at the wide-eyed stare she gave me. Like I'd just put dessert in front of her when it hadn't been on the menu. She reached for the hem of her dress but then stopped.

"Max." She chewed on her bottom lip, and I didn't like the expression that came to her face. *I didn't like how she held her stomach as it happened.*

"You know how I was thinking of you last night?" I said with a low growl.

Swallowing, she shook her head. "Tell me."

"It wasn't you not pregnant," I rumbled low and rose to my feet, determined to cut off this shadow of self-consciousness once and for all. "I imagined you in that black lace lingerie I saw on the bed the day I brought you to the apartment."

Her mouth rounded, and if I hadn't just fucked those perfect lips, they would've been the first hole on my list.

"I imagined your full tits spilling out of the top and filling my palms. Your stomach straining against the lace." My teeth ground together, drawing up the fantasy like it was carved in stone. "I imagined you riding my cock like some fertility goddess, needing me to fill you up with cum. To keep you pregnant. To keep you full of softness and curves and sex appeal."

I knew about my soft Dom kink, but the breeding one was new. No, maybe not new. Just unique. A kink gene only expressed around her.

"Now take off your clothes."

This time, my command was met with no hesitation. She drew her loose dress up over her head and let it fall to the floor.

Fuck. A hoarse groan cracked from my throat, watching my fantasy become reality.

Her breasts strained against her thin lace bralette, her nipples hard and big and begging to be sucked. *Shit.* My fists balled, and I widened my stance, regretting my decision to put my cock away while she was in the bedroom because now, it was fucking painfully hard and trapped against my jeans.

Next, she shimmied out of her leggings, kicking them to the side and leaving her only in her matching bra and thong.

"Perfect," I praised low, and if there was the smallest shadow of self-consciousness left, I erased it with the flick of my wrist that popped my jeans open again to relieve the pressure on my cock. "See what you do to me, gorgeous?" Her jaw slackened as I palmed myself until the pain lessened. "Take off the rest."

Now, she moved with nothing short of eagerness, unclipping her bra and letting it fall to the floor.

"Fuck, Daze..." I breathed out hoarsely, watching her blush spread lower on her chest, toward her nipples that tightened under my gaze. I definitely wasn't trying to hide the way I wanted her, but now, I couldn't stop myself from stroking my cock through my jeans. She was a goddess, the way her skin glowed. The sight of her could bring me to my knees.

"Don't stop."

She hooked her fingers around her thong and drew the scrap of fabric down her legs just far enough to let it fall to the floor. She straightened, her arms wrapped over her stomach, and my heart stopped.

"So beautiful," I murmured and watched how the

compliment made her blush deepen and her thighs clamp together.

"Don't do that," I growled, and her eyebrows popped up. "I want to see how wet you are for me." I pinned my stare to her pussy. "Spread yourself for me."

A tremor ran through her, but her eyes remained locked on my face, sparkling with lust. She reached between her thighs, sliding her feet wider, and then spread herself open to my stare.

I clenched my teeth so hard, I was surprised something didn't crack, and then adjusted myself for the millionth time. To see her like this—or kneeling in the grass or spread open on my bathroom counter—was pure torture, but to know she wanted to be tortured too was nothing short of heaven.

"You're so fucking wet and perfect," I told her, knowing she couldn't see herself, and for some reason, that made it even hotter to tell her. "Feel how soaked you are for me." My chin jerked, and without hesitation, she slid a finger through her pussy. "So needy for your husband's cock."

"Max," my name trembled from her lips, and I watched her knees quake.

"That's it. Stroke that clit."

She was so swollen, it didn't take more than one swipe of her fingers to send her into a shudder, her eyes rolling back in her head.

"Stop," I clipped.

She stilled and whimpered, "But—"

"Not yet, my little wife. Tonight, you only come to my touch," I promised, my body on fire with just how turned on she was from sucking my cock. "Now, get in the tub." I stepped aside, offering her my arm to hold on to as she climbed into the steaming water.

"This is...amazing," she hummed, sinking deep into the heat, her head falling back along the edge.

I moved to crouch behind her, taking the washcloth I'd draped over the edge in my hand and murmured, "Just wait."

She inhaled sharply, trying to turn to look at me.

"Let me," I said softly, extending my arm over her shoulder so she had nowhere to turn.

I dipped the washcloth in the water and then grabbed the bottle of body wash I'd set next to the tub, squirting a good amount onto it. Reaching my arms around her, I sudsed it where she could see.

"Let's clean you up."

Starting with her neck, I gently washed the slender column and then over her collarbones, teasing lower. And lower.

"Max." She shuddered and tipped her head back against my shoulder, giving me a full view of her straining tits just under the surface.

"Don't worry. I'll take care of you."

Daisy gasped as I closed one hand over her breast.

"Perfect." I reveled in the feel of her. The soft, heavy weight as it spilled from my fingers, the tight bud of her nipple pressing into my palm. Latching my teeth to the side of her neck, I nipped and licked the patch of skin as my fingers teased her breast in tandem. Pinching and rolling, pulling and flicking. It didn't take minutes before she was arching into me, begging for more.

"Please, Max."

I've dreamed of hearing her beg for me, and I don't think I'll ever stop.

I gave her breast another squeeze and rolled the tight peak under my thumb once more, hearing the water groan as she arched into me. "Does that feel good?"

"Yes," she moaned, and so I did it again, her body arching more sharply.

"So sensitive," I muttered, shoving the knowledge—and a different fantasy—to the back of my mind to play out another day. Right now, I wasn't going to survive much longer if I didn't get inside her. "Bend your knees."

Water sloshed as she moved, her knees rising above the water. Slowly, I slid the washcloth up her thigh and then draped it over her knee.

"Good, now keep them spread to the side of the tub," I muttered, moving my head to the corner of her neck and her ear.

Sinking my free hand back into the water, I trailed along her stomach, following the darker line that ran down the center of her swollen belly all the way down to the juncture of her thighs.

I groaned roughly when I found her soft heat.

"There's that needy cunt. So puffy and ready for me." I stroked over her clit, and her arms shot off the sides of the tub and latched around mine like they were a life raft.

"Max!" she cried out.

"Relax, baby," I husked, teasing the swollen bud before dipping into her entrance, sinking into her muscles with a rough groan. "Fuck, you're tight, Daze."

I pushed one finger inside her, her muscles revolting. *Damn.* She was going to need at least one orgasm, if not two, before I even had a shot at fitting my cock in here.

"Max..." My name hitched a ride on every sigh and moan that left her mouth, and I was addicted to the sound of it. Addicted to the feel of her. *Addicted to her*.

"You feel so good, Daisy," I praised, slowly pumping my finger into her as my thumb brushed a merciless rhythm over her clit. "Better than all my dreams. So much better."

She whimpered and clenched around me.

Gritting my teeth, I worked two fingers into her. "Need you to relax for me."

She quivered, and I thumbed her clit faster.

"God, Max, that feels..." She dug her nails into my arms, her hips rising now to meet my hand.

"Tell me."

Her head swayed. "I need more. Please."

She felt fucking combustible. Shaking. Begging. Straining.

"I'm going to make you come, Daze," I growled into her ear, my other hand starting to tease her nipple again. "And then I'm going to fill this tight cunt with my big cock."

"Please," she panted, gasping not for air but for release. "Please. *Please*."

"Is that what you want?" I moved my fingers faster, feeling her clit swell against them. "You want to come for me?"

"*Yes*." Water splashed over the side of the tub as her hips bucked into my hand.

I swirled her clit harder, feeling her fingers claw into my arm. "Show me how good you can come for me.

Let me feel how good you're going to come for me, *my little wife*."

"Max!" She shattered—and sent a wave of water crashing onto the bathroom floor as her body bucked and bowed with release.

Black spots chewed at my vision as I pushed two and then three fingers through her clenching muscles, preparing them for what was coming.

"Perfect," I murmured over and over as she came back down, her breath slowing, her trembling starting to still. "You are perfect."

"Max, that was..." Slowly, her head turned, wide, glazed eyes sinking into mine. She was beautiful. *She was mine*.

"Just the beginning," I rasped, attempting a playful smile, but my cock was too damn hard for anything about me to come off as playful right now. Sliding my hand up her body, making sure I left no curve untouched, I cupped the side of her face. "You don't know what you do to me, Daisy...what hearing you scream my name does to me."

"Max..." Her lashes fluttered, her eyes suddenly searching for anywhere to land that wasn't on me.

"Daze." I framed her chin in my fingers, forcing her head up and scouring her expression. "What is it? What's wrong?"

Her lips peeled apart, and a deeper color stole over her cheeks.

"There's something I have to tell you."

CHAPTER 23
DAISY

"What is it? What's wrong?"

I couldn't bear the concerned look on his face. After that orgasm, my whole body felt like nothing more than one giant heartbeat, an angry thump caged in nervous skin.

"I need..." Air pushed from my lips. "I need to get out."

I stood, but too quickly. Blood rushed from my head, and I swayed right into Max's waiting arms and his muttered curse.

For the second time tonight, *my husband* carried me into the bedroom and laid me on the bed.

"Wait, I'm wet—"

"That's never a bad thing in this bed, Daze," he growled and kneeled in front of me, between my legs. I shivered even though there was nothing sexual about his position now, not the way concern bled from his honeyed stare. "What's wrong?"

"I have to tell you something," I repeated, hating

how it sounded like it was a bad thing. It wasn't. *Or was it?*

I didn't know up from down, right from left, real from fantasy anymore. All I knew was Max. *All I knew was that nothing had ever felt more right.*

"You can tell me anything, Daze." He reached for my hands and curled them into his big ones.

How things would've been different if he'd just told me how he'd felt...*and if I had done the same.* But what kind of different would they have been?

Would I have been ready to face that I'd made the wrong choice? Or would I have dug my heels in and stayed with Todd? Would it have ruined Todd and Max's friendship? Maybe I never would've seen Max again. Maybe we would've had everything—each other—sooner. Or maybe my stubbornness would've blown my chance to be with him, and instead of getting this dream, it all would've crumbled into disaster.

With each breath that shuttled in and out of my lungs, I accepted that *disaster* would've been the more likely scenario. Until that night at the McCormicks', I wasn't ready to admit Todd was the wrong choice. I wasn't ready to accept that Max had always been the right one.

Until that night when I was forced to.

"That night of the party...after our conversation on the deck..." I gulped. "I realized how you felt about me... what you were really trying to tell me. And I was afraid of how I wanted you too. I tried to tell myself I was wrong. That I'd imagined what you said...how you said it. I convinced myself the man I'd been dating for four years was the one I wanted to be with...not his best friend."

"Daisy..."

"When Todd found me, he was upset too. Something with his parents. I think...I think we both just reached for each other because it was safe."

God, I sounded so pitiful. Who would stay with someone when they wanted to be with someone else? Me. I did. Because I was so afraid of how Max made me feel, so afraid to be uncharacteristically vulnerable, and Todd...I was comfortable with Todd's flaws. I was safer with the devil I knew than the dashing gentleman who made my heart race.

"You thought of me the night you...got pregnant?" Max's calm voice cracked through the room, but it was the only calm thing about him. Every other inch of him, from his pupils to his fingertips, vibrated with tension and possession.

"It's not just that, Max." My heart clanged around like a train off its tracks, barreling at an unsteady pace toward him. Guilt gnawed at my throat, but something stronger clawed at my throat. *The truth.* "I didn't just think of you, Max. I...it was an accident, but I..." I swallowed. "I said your name."

My confession hung like a single strand of a spiderweb spun between us, so fragile but so full of possibility.

I blinked and let my focus settle on Max kneeling between my legs. He was so still. Not carved from stone, but sculpted from wax. Soft but immovable. Except his eyes. Pure fire churned in their depths, and I watched it melt him from the inside out.

"You said...my name," he croaked as his throat softened.

My cheeks felt like fireballs. It was the most embarrassing moment of my life. The kind of despicable act they give to playboys in movies to show how big of a dick they were. And there I was, sleeping with my boyfriend of four years, just drunk enough—*just shaken up enough*—to let the wrong name slip.

"Screamed." I paused, knowing the obvious question that came next, and vomited the answer before I lost my nerve. "Todd heard me, but he was...wasted, and he passed out almost right away. I thought in the morning he'd say something, but he didn't. I planned on saying something—how could I not?—but then I found out about the baby..."

"Daisy," he growled, his hands suddenly framing my face. The world narrowed to the radius of his eyes. Everything I wanted to know, to feel, contained in the bolts of his gaze. "You screamed my name."

"Yes," I answered before I realized it wasn't a question.

His fingers peeled from my cheeks, his eyes following their path as his hands skated down my neck, my shoulders, and then rested on my stomach.

I felt so huge, and yet, when I looked at Max's hands splayed over my bump, they made me feel small. Not just me. Max made everything else feel small. Every problem. Every worry. Every danger. Everything he took from my plate that seemed insurmountable suddenly appeared like nothing more than a mote of dust in his hands, something he could easily brush away.

"You made this baby with my name on your lips," he murmured, staring at me like it changed everything and nothing at the same time.

I drew a trembling breath, suddenly so overwhelmed with a million emotions I felt like I was going to burst. "Max—"

His mouth silenced mine, kissing me for the first time since...all of this.

It was sweet—bittersweet—for a moment. A blend of guilt and longing, regret and anger. For a moment, that kiss housed everything that four years of ignored and hidden feelings could provoke. And then it transformed, shaping into the giant, ravenous beast that grew in hibernation.

"You're mine, Daze," he growled against my lips, his voice like velvet-coated steel. "Finally mine."

With one hand anchored to my stomach, he wrapped his other hand around my throat, pinning my head to the onslaught of his mouth. His tongue lashed and stroked against mine in a fury I fought to keep up with. My prickling skin now felt like every cell burned. My lungs breathed, but only for more breaths soaked with his scent. It didn't take long for my mind to turn into a tangle of want, my body a knot of need, and Max was the only cure.

"Max," I gasped, clinging to him because I could register nothing but his large, pulsing presence as it consumed me.

"Mine," he repeated, and I couldn't tell if it sounded more like an order or a plea.

My lashes fluttered. I felt myself giving over to his storm like a boat pulled out to sea. The posts of the bed swam into focus, and I realized he'd laid me on my back at some point during that kiss.

"And now I'm going to enjoy every inch of your perfect body," he muttered, the soft press of his lips to mine reverberating like the strike of a hammer onto the head of a nail.

I sagged onto the soft mattress as his hand drifted from my throat down to my breast. A sigh seeped from my chest as he resumed the torture he'd started in the tub. Stroking and plucking, kneading and weighing. The whole time, I felt the footprints of his breath march down to my other breast. My heavy-lidded eyes forced open, focusing on his dark hair and the hard angles of his face as he stared at my nipple, watching it pebble tighter toward him. *Begging.*

And then I was begging too.

"Please," I whimpered, my back bowing just as he leaned forward. A strangled cry washed away my plea when he wrapped his lips around my nipple. His mouth...that tongue...it had been devastating the way he'd kissed me, but now it felt dangerous.

He licked and lashed, swirled his tongue and sucked hard, until I was nothing but a puddle of moans and heartbeats and a baby under the onslaught of his tongue.

"Max," I chanted his name, pleasure ebbing me in an unexpected way toward release.

Growling against my skin, his mouth moved to my other breast, stirring a fresh current of pleasure through me.

"You're so perfect, Daze," he murmured, teasing and coaxing my nipple against his tongue. "So perfect and sweet."

I whimpered as he sucked hard again and sent a ray of bright, hot sparkles shooting through me. I tried to rub my legs together, the ache between them suffocating, but Max's leg remained wedged in my way. Huffing in frustration, I tried to arch and rub my core against his jeans. Needing pressure. Needing friction. *Needing some kind of relief before I started to come apart at the seams.*

"Don't worry, baby. I'm going to give you what you want," he promised in a low voice, the rough husk caressing my skin. "Now spread those pretty legs for me, wife, and show me how wet you are."

I simultaneously wanted and didn't want his brand of torture. The way he drew me taut to the point of bursting. The way he wrung everything from me. *The way he pleasured me until he knew I could hold nothing back.*

It wasn't just about release. It was about surrender. *It was about trust.*

I felt my legs release their clamp on his, drifting wider and baring myself for him. My eyes worked open as Max moved down my body. His mouth stamped a hot path down my sternum and over my stomach, every kiss pumping more fire into my cells until I felt his big body kneel between my legs.

"That's a wet pussy, wife."

A quake of pleasure ripped through me at his praise. "Max..." My hands dug into the comforter as I tried to keep myself from combusting.

"Christ, you're so wet for me." The groan that followed signaled even more desire leaking from my core at his pleasure-wrought words.

"Max, I can't," I panted, straining toward him. "Please, I can't..."

It was as though he hadn't just turned my body to Jell-O in the tub not that long ago.

"You can," he growled. "You can and you will

because I've been dying for a taste of you, and I won't go another night without it."

His dark head bent between my legs and covered my pussy with his mouth.

Maybe it was the hormones. Maybe it was me. But I would swear on my life—whatever little I'd be left with by the time he finished with me—that if I wasn't already pregnant, that tongue of his would've impregnated me.

Every stroke, every unbelievably perfect lick, every tug on my clit, I felt every touch in the most far-flung corners of my body. It didn't make me see stars. It made me see him. His face. His smile. His stare. The hunger in his eyes. The meaning behind every word. Every lingering touch. Every stolen glance.

I cried out, clawing at the mattress and trying to arch into him, but failing. His hands caged my hips, pinning me to the bed and to the torture of his mouth— the torture of his tongue as he went from licking and strumming to pushing it inside me. Gasping, I searched for leverage as he fucked me with his tongue, and my feet, too short to reach the floor, found purchase on the broad roots of Max's thighs. I felt the rumble of his groan as I pushed against his mouth.

"Fuck, Daze," he growled, more savage than a gentleman, and then sucked hard on my clit.

I screamed.

"That's it, baby. Let me hear you." And then he sucked again.

I bucked against him. Against his lips. Against the sharp flick and soft slide of his tongue. And then he made another sound, something deep and guttural, before his hand moved from my hip and two long fingers pushed inside me.

"That's it, wife," he cooed. "Relax for me."

Relax? I whimpered as my scream knotted in my chest. How could I relax when he was doing this to me? When his finger curled against a spot no one—not even myself with a toy—had found before? When he stroked that sweet spot in sync with the draw of his lips on my clit? When he pummeled my nerves with pleasure like a famous fighter giving a one-two punch?

There was no *relaxing*. There was only submission.

And I felt it come for me the way a head rush claimed every ounce of blood from my brain, drawing it down my body and pooling it right where his mouth—

"Max!" I cried as he pulled away—his fingers, his mouth—everything. Gone. I blinked, everything slogging into focus. My body. The bed. *Him.*

Like he was waiting for me to see him, he pushed himself up slowly until he stood between my legs that dangled over the side. I felt like a limp, overstuffed, red-splotched rag doll, and he stared at me, licking his lips like I was the first dessert he was about to have in his entire life.

His jaw pulsed as he reached for his waistband. I couldn't look away, couldn't breathe as he lowered his jeans over his hips and freed his thick cock, catching it in one fist and giving himself a long stroke.

Even lying back, my jaw managed to fall open. Had he been that big earlier? Outside, in the dark? Had I fit all of *that* inside my mouth? Or last night? Had the steam from the shower obscured what I saw?

He pumped himself slowly. Again. And again. My mouth went dry when a bead of moisture pooled at the tip, my tongue wanting to lick it off.

"You love watching me, don't you, my little wife?"

he drawled, a tipped smile shadowing his mouth as his eyes dropped between my legs. "I see how wet it makes you."

"Max," I whimpered, inching one hand toward my stomach, needing to ease the ache he'd left me with.

"Don't," he warned, and my fingers stilled. "That pussy is all mine tonight."

Taking my legs, he lifted one and then the other so my feet were propped on the broad wall of his chest. I felt the pound of his heart against my right sole.

"You don't know how bad I want you, my little wife," he growled, dragging the head of his cock along my slit. "How bad I've always wanted you," he added and then tapped the thick crown against my core.

I jerked at the sudden, pleasurable sensation.

"Steady, baby." He anchored one hand to my hip and slid himself to my entrance, my desire making him slick. "Breathe."

My mouth parted, but there was no room for sound, for gasps, *for breath* as he fed himself inside me.

"That's it, Daze," he cooed, just like he had that afternoon at the doctor's, as he pushed his cock deeper. "You're doing so good. So good taking my big cock."

I clutched at the bed, my body in a tornado of sensations, simultaneously drained of tension, yet every muscle, every nerve on edge as he filled me inch after inch.

He felt bigger than he looked. Like he was stretching me in ways, in places I didn't know were possible. I felt my body struggle to fit him, and it felt amazing. The first time I'd ever felt this full—this consumed.

Max grabbed my knees, his fingers skating up and

down my thighs, his fingers pressing a sensuous path into my skin as he held my feet to his chest. My lashes fluttered, my breath catching as he worked himself deeper, his thrusts measured and steady. Always in control.

"*Fuck.*"

My eyes went to his ragged curse, seeing the sheen of sweat over his straining muscles. Like he wanted to keep going slow for me, but it was killing him. *And it was killing me.*

This was right. After all these years, this—us—*we* were right, and I wanted him to stop holding back these last pieces of himself because he was afraid they were too much for me.

Too much of Max Hamilton would never be enough for me.

"Please," I pleaded, so on edge from my other orgasms, I was ready to combust. "Stop being a gentleman."

His eyes flicked to mine, darkness charring their centers. Air hissed through his tight teeth, and I felt his cock swell inside me.

"*Please.*"

"As you wish," he growled and grabbed my ankles. He yanked my legs straight, and with one sure thrust, buried himself inside me.

Crying out, I jerked from the discomfort, but he didn't stop. He didn't even pause. Shackling my legs in his firm grip, he yanked my legs into a wide V as he fucked me, driving deep, long strokes into my core, his hips making a slapping sound as he bottomed out.

"This what you wanted, my little wife? Or is it too much?" His rhythm didn't break, didn't even falter. He kept moving like the part of him responsible for breathing was responsible for fucking me too.

"No." My breathy answer turned into a moan as pleasure swelled deep inside me.

"Good," his voice dropped as he worked himself in and out. "Because you're made for me, Daze. This tight little cunt is a perfect fit for my cock." He drove deeper, harder until he took my hips off the bed with each drive and took over all my senses.

His voice as it chanted my name. His body as it slapped wet and fast against mine. The feel of his hands imprisoning my ankles and his length finding new ways to split me wide with each drive.

"Yes, Max," I whimpered as he angled his hips and thrust deeper, hitting that spot buried inside me that only he was big enough to reach. "God, yes."

Moans, pleas struck from my chest with each hammer of my heart. The ache in my core built into a tangled knot, the pressure drawing tighter with each moment, until I was certain my body only existed for him.

Forget vulnerable, I was vacant except for the way I wanted him. Empty of everything except every look, every touch, every forbidden want, every secret fantasy I'd harbored for this man for the last four years.

I was wholly his. Irrevocably. And instead of fear, all I felt was peace.

"So perfect, my little wife," he murmured—chanted —to me, and I heard myself beg for more in return.

"Please, Max. Please," I begged, my hands clawing at the covers.

He stopped so suddenly it was almost painful, and I was left trembling, choking, and searching for an explanation. As soon as my eyes snapped to his, I had one. He wanted my stare.

"Tell me who you belong to," he demanded with that intensity I've come to crave, and started to fuck me again. Not fast and hard like I needed, but slow. Just enough to feel every ridge and vein as they pulsed inside me. Just enough to keep my orgasm on life support.

"You," I breathed out without hesitation, without effort. Wanting him was now as effortless as breathing. "You, Max," I repeated in case there was any doubt.

His eyes flared with satisfaction, and then with a feral growl, he let loose.

Dropping my ankles, he grabbed hold of my hips and drove mercilessly into me. For a second, it felt like he fucked my mind straight out of my body, hitting both my G-spot and clit with each drive, and turning me wild. I bucked and thrashed, hurdling with him toward release.

"All mine, my little wife. Always," he ground out as I came, fracturing apart on his words like dynamite on a fuse. I screamed his name, feeling him bury himself deep inside me as he came, his cock jerking as he spilled hot cum against my womb.

After that, I was nothing but a puddle of limp muscles, uneven heartbeats, and a single steady thought that this was where I was meant to be. *Where we were meant to be.*

Finally.

CHAPTER 24
MAX

"**M**ax..." The way she whimpered my name, rousing from sleep, turned my cock to stone.

Maybe I should've gotten up and made her breakfast in bed, but damn if I didn't wake from one dream into an even better one. Daisy. In my bed. *As my wife.*

To hell with being a gentleman, I'd decided, sliding my hand from its hold on her naked hip, along the seam of her belly, and then down between her thighs. I was going to wake her up as her husband. As the man who'd waited four years to have her, and who wasn't going to waste a single second more.

"Shhh," I cooed, pressing my lips to the corner of her neck just below her ear. "Just relax, my little wife." *God, I loved how she responded to that nickname.*

Daisy let out a deep sigh, settling back against me with a soft moan as I stroked her slick slit.

"That's it," I praised, sliding her leg over my hip to give me better access to her core.

As soon as I thumbed her clit, her breath caught.

"Max," and then released, "I don't...I can't..." She grabbed for my wrist, trembling as she tried to stop me from pleasuring her. Her attempt was halfhearted. By the time she held my wrist, she was pressing my hand harder rather than pulling it away.

"You can," I promised, easing my middle finger inside her slick heat. I felt her stiffen, her muscles sore from the way I'd stretched them last night. "You took me so good last night, little wife." I couldn't resist the temptation to feel her muscles flutter around me. "You deserve to be spoiled this morning."

She moaned low and throaty as I rubbed her clit. I gritted my teeth as her body started to rock into my hand—and then back against my stiff cock.

"Max." She shuddered. "I want you."

"Later. You're too sore this morning," I growled, sliding my fingers faster. Harder. "And I'm too hungry."

In one smooth movement, I slid down her body and wedged myself between her thighs, my mouth sinking onto the sweetness I'd been craving.

"*Max!*" Daisy cried out, gripping my head and bucking.

I smiled against her cunt, lapping at the sweet desire that coated my tongue before I set on her swollen clit. I could get used to waking up like this. No, I would get used to waking up like this, to enjoying every inch of my delicious wife before I shared her with the world.

"Oh god, Max. Yes..." she panted, her nails scoring my scalp when I started to suck on her clit, the bundle of nerves throbbing for more of what I wanted to give.

Her nails scraped and clawed at my head as I worked her over with my mouth. Sucking. Flicking. And biting just hard enough to turn my name into a chant. It only took minutes before her desire ran down my chin, her body trembling in its rush toward release. My cock swelled painfully, hanging heavy between my legs. I wanted to fuck her. I wanted to sink into her tight heat and never leave. But it was too soon. Too soon for it not to be more pain than pleasure.

So I'd settle for eating the sweetest pussy known to man...which wasn't settling at all.

"Max. *Max...*" Her body bowed, and I quickly supported her hips with my grip. I drew her clit between my lips again and sucked on it slowly, pulling harder and harder, bringing her higher and higher, until she shattered, and her desire flooded against my mouth.

Groaning, I lapped her pussy, savoring every drop of her sweet release until I felt the tension start to seep from her limbs, and her hands sagged from my head.

"You taste so sweet, my little wife," I murmured, pressing a gentle kiss to her slit. "I could eat you for every meal."

She let out a whimpered laugh. "I don't think I'd survive that for very long."

I lifted my head, meeting her eyes over her stomach, and grinned, "I'd make sure you did." Tipping forward, I pressed another kiss to the top of her stomach and murmured, "Time for breakfast, Daze."

She sighed softly, but as I climbed from the bed, she surprised me by grabbing my wrist. "What's wrong?"

I'd know that stubborn stare anywhere, and I watched it lower from my gaze down to my groin. "I'm not getting up until you let me take care of you," she insisted and then licked her lips.

Fuck.

I grabbed my length and blew out a hiss of pain. I

should have more control than this. I usually did. But I *usually* wasn't fucking the woman of my dreams.

"You want more of my cum?"

She nodded, so damn eager.

"So greedy for me," I ground out, pumping my length. "Hungry for more of my cock."

"Yes," she moaned, and my cock pulsed. "Please, Max."

"Eyes on me, my little wife," I growled, turning toward her and starting to pump my length. "And stick out that pretty little tongue."

She unrolled the pink velvet carpet to her mouth and held my stare until I painted it white.

"How do we tell your family?"

My eyes flicked over the console. Daisy sat with her arms around her stomach, her gaze pinned somewhere out the window.

"Tell them what?" I was pretty sure I knew what she meant, but I asked anyway.

Daisy turned, pink flushing all the way down her neck. "That we're...us."

Us.

I hit the blinker and shifted in the seat. Just hearing her call us *us* made my dick hard.

"I don't think we need to tell them, Daze."

"Oh."

I reached over and caught her hand, dragging her

knuckles to my lips and holding them there as I spoke, "I'm pretty sure they already know."

"Oh." Her expression settled. "Did Harper..."

"I forbade anyone from coming to the house all week," I admitted roughly. "If they haven't guessed why, then I'm pretty sure they've never known me."

Her lips parted. "You...forbade them?"

"You think they've just been conveniently absent?" I teased with a low chuckle.

I'd wanted this woman for four years. You better believe I forbade visitors now that I finally had her. I didn't want anything disturbing our bubble. Not work. Not my family. Not Todd's family. That was how I convinced her to let the rest of my delivery team take over our route for the week. I told her I didn't want to take the chance that Mary or one of her cronies would try to ambush her again. The truth was now that I finally had her, there was no chance I was going to share her, at least not for a couple of days.

I lowered her hand back to her lap, keeping my fingers entwined with hers as I flashed her a wicked grin. "They wanted to bring food and gifts and...I wanted you to myself."

Which was how we ended up here. On our way to Aurora's birthday party at Aunt Ailene's. Except it wasn't a birthday party at all. It was a cover for the baby shower that Harper asked to throw Daisy. And only one of the many surprises I had in store for my beautiful wife.

She was six weeks out from her due date, and after just a handful of days living with her, I could tell she wanted to nest. I watched as she unpacked her things into my closet, organizing and reorganizing almost every day. The fridge was now full, everything from milk to veggies carefully stacked and cornered into its own space. When there was nothing left to organize, she'd started on a fresh batch of perfumes for the fundraiser. Wildflowers and violets, and now the kitchen counter was covered in mason jars.

Yesterday, she'd asked to rearrange the living room furniture after we'd had dinner on the deck. I moved the couch three times before demanding she lose a piece of clothing for every piece of furniture I moved.

It didn't take long before she was naked. Or before I had her hands on the back of the couch as I fucked her from behind.

"How very caveman of you," she teased.

I gave her thigh a squeeze. "Not nearly as caveman as I'd like to be," I murmured and then slid my hand down between her legs.

"Max!" Daisy gasped and clutched my wrist with both her hands, her laugh becoming a choked sound when my fingers brushed her pussy. "We can't—"

I silenced her with a look. "Lean the seat back." I watched her throat bob, and then she slid her hand to the side of the seat. A second later, the soft hum of the motor tipped her seat back. "Lift your dress for me, little wife."

I made no secret of how much I enjoyed the baggy dresses she favored—and how easy they made things like this. And Daisy made no secret of favoring them more since I explained in great detail, with a demonstration, how much I liked them.

"Thank you," I murmured with polite irony, sliding my hand along her creamy thigh and brushing my knuckles over her sex. "What kind of husband would I be if I left you all wet and needy like this?"

"Max..." Her voice turned into a garbled moan as I stroked her.

I knew it wouldn't take much. She was so damn hypersensitive all the time now, it felt like all I had to do was look at her and she was wet for my dick. *And I couldn't get enough.*

"Perfect, Daze," I growled, hooking my finger under the edge of her underwear and tugging it to the side. A groan shredded through my lips when my fingers slid through her slick folds. "So fucking perfect."

"Max..." she whimpered, clutching my biceps, clawing at my muscles through my shirt as I worked her swollen little clit hard and fast.

"That's it, baby," I cooed, spinning the steering wheel with one hand and turning onto my aunt's driveway.

"Max!" she gasped when I stopped, her fingers curling hard into my arm. "W-what are you doing?" She panted. "We're almost there."

The house drew closer, the rest of my family's cars already parked out front.

"Just in case they had any doubt why I wanted them to stay away from the house these last few days," I rumbled and turned to her, bringing my slick fingers to my mouth and sucking them clean. "I want to make sure they don't anymore."

"No—" She grabbed for the door—not to get out, but to have something to hold on to when I reached my hand back between her legs, finding her needy clit and tugging on it.

"What was that, Daze?" I asked, pinching her clit between my fingers and then flicking it with my thumb.

She pressed into the seat, her eyes practically rolling back in her head.

"Do you want me to stop?" Not a chance. She was so fucking soaked.

Her head thrashed.

"Tell me."

"N-no," she blurted out, chugging in a deep breath as her hips started to jerk.

"Good." I stroked faster, my fingers sliding so easily over her, it was insane. "Because you're so ready to come."

"*Yes*." She clutched my arm, bucking against my hand. "Yes, Max. Yes."

With a growl, I leaned over the console and stuck my free hand around her neck, forcing her head to turn until our foreheads touched.

"That's it, Daisy. Show them who you belong to."

The first strain of her cry made it through her lips before I covered them with mine, swallowing her scream as she came all over my fingers.

"That's my good little wife." I kissed the corner of her mouth. And then her nose. Finally, her forehead before sitting back in my seat.

I moved her underwear back into place and then reached for the waist of my pants, my cock caught painfully against my leg.

I had my zipper down and my hand in my briefs when I felt her stare, all hot and horny.

"See what you do to me, Daze," I rumbled, already tugging my underwear down so she could see my thick erection. The way she stared, I couldn't stop myself from pumping my cock, swearing I could come from that stare alone. "Makes me so fucking hard to watch you come like that."

Her pupils blew wide when I took my fingers that were still wet from her orgasm and ran them up and down my length. "We should go inside." Before I lost the last of my mind and took her to the bed of my truck instead.

"But you—"

"Will be fine," I promised, tucking my dick under the waistband of my briefs and then zipping up my jeans. Looking at her, I added with a wink, "At least until later."

CHAPTER 25
DAISY

"Surprise!"

My smile evaporated into a blank stare and gaping mouth.

The *congratulations* banner framed with pink balloons shaped like flowers, blow-up rattles, and Max's entire family packed into his aunt's living room with huge smiles on their faces—and all wearing pink—could only mean one thing, and yet I struggled to believe it.

"Happy baby shower day!" Harper squealed, the first to break ranks and wrap me in a big hug.

Then it was Ailene, Lou, Violet, Gigi, Frankie, and Aurora. Even when I saw the diaper cake in the center of the kitchen island and the mountain of presents in the living room, I kept blinking, expecting it all to disappear.

Was this for real?

"Max..." I angled toward him, searching for...I wasn't even sure.

"Surprise," he husked and pressed a kiss to my forehead, his fingers drawing delicious circles on my lower back like an intentional reminder of how they'd been stroking my front just a few minutes ago.

"How..."

His eyes slid to his cousins, and Lou was the first to confess. *No surprise there.* "I had a few things I bought for you and the baby. I wanted to bring them over, but Max said no visitors."

Frankie snorted and then grinned. "Surprised that baby's still in there after a week of going at it."

My cheeks turned fire-hydrant red, and I watched Lou elbow her twin while Harper jumped in and said, "Lou told me about it, and it made me think about a baby shower. I figured with...everything going on, you didn't have anything planned. So I asked Max if we could throw you a surprise shower."

I nodded, my throat too tight to speak as tears welled behind my eyes.

A surprise baby shower.

"You didn't ask," Max corrected, folding his arms. "You informed me there was going to be a surprise baby shower and that I either agreed to produce Daisy or you'd call for a welfare check."

A laugh erupted from my chest and broke through my stupor of surprise. That sounded more like his sister —*his family*. And now, it felt like mine.

"And you were the one who said it should be garden themed," Harper countered.

I couldn't even look at Max right now, my eyes burning with unshed tears. Six weeks ago, my idea of family was making sure I was married to the man who'd fathered my baby. And when Todd left, I'd thought it was only proof that my mom had been right all along— that the only person I could count on was myself. And now...now, I hardly recognized that woman. Literally and figuratively.

Max pressed his hand to my back, drawing me closer to him like he could see straight through me, right to my overwhelmed and emotional core.

"Glad to see I've rubbed off on you, Harp." Frankie linked her arm with Harper's and smiled. Reaching for my arm, Frankie pulled me away from Max, saying, "You have to see the diaper cake Aurora made. Oh, and the food. Mom and Gigi made a blueberry cake."

My stomach growled.

"Max, do you want food?"

It wasn't until Frankie slowed that I realized Max was no longer next to me. Glancing over my shoulder, I saw he stood where we'd left him, and even though he was already in a conversation with Jamie, he was watching me with that look of possessiveness that made my blood heat.

"I'm fine for right now," he said, catching my eyes. "I had a snack before we got here."

If Frankie heard my mortified little squeak, she didn't let on, too engrossed with getting me into the kitchen to see the spread of food. Meanwhile, my wicked husband had the gall to lift his left hand and run his fingers discreetly under his nose, solidifying the naughty flutter in my stomach with a wink.

"So have you given any thought to a name?" Aurora asked, bouncing her son, Jack, on her hip.

"Don't ask Aurora for suggestions. Kit said you told him you wanted to name Jack Nutterbutter Butterfinger," Frankie teased.

"No, I told him I had a dream that we named the baby Bushybacked nudibranch," Aurora corrected, appearing more offended that her sister-in-law had gotten the Latin taxonomy wrong than that she actually believed Aurora wanted to name their baby that.

My eyes widened as I took a huge bite of the blueberry cake. Grinning, Aurora explained, "It was one of the species I was studying at the Friendship lighthouse when I met Kit, and it just happened to make it into a dream. I wasn't serious about it."

Kit walked by right then with a poignant harrumph, and everyone laughed. Aurora turned and playfully stuck her tongue out at her husband, even though her gaze held nothing but adoration. *And so did his*.

My chest squeezed. Now, I recognized the look so clearly, and it seemed almost impossible that I hadn't realized it was how Max had looked at me all these years.

"I haven't given thought to a name, to be honest," I admitted, which felt a little crazy since I had just over a month until my due date, but I knew why I hadn't.

I felt like I'd been living in a tornado since Todd disappeared, unsure which way was up or down, right or wrong. I hadn't felt safe or settled until very, *very* recently. Max was the eye of the storm. The safest, surest place to be, but that didn't mean we still weren't surrounded by uncertainty.

We'd done a lot of things over the last week—talked about a lot of things. But we hadn't talked about more than this moment. It was like we were drowning in four years of fantasies now able to come true, and we didn't want to come up for air. But we had to. At some point, and soon, we had to talk about what came next.

We were already married. *Would we just stay married?* Already living in Max's house. *But he wanted to sell it, so would we move? Before the baby? After?* It was as though life had given up on waiting for fate to bring us together and finally forced her hand, leaving us to scramble to figure out the details.

"Well, you could always go with Blueberry if nothing else strikes your fancy," Harper teased as I was in the middle of stuffing another forkful of blueberry cake into my mouth.

"That might be the winner." I covered my mouth as I spoke. "Baby Blueberry."

"What do you think, Max?"

My skin prickled when he appeared at my side, his hand coming to rest on my lower back and resuming its slow circle there. "Think about what?"

"Baby Blueberry."

His roaming fingers stilled, and the adorable look of confusion on his face made my ovaries go wild. *How many times would I wish that I had been with Max that night?*

"I don't understand."

"We're talking about baby names, and the current lead is Baby Blueberry," Harper filled him in, plucking a blueberry from off the top of the cake and tossing it in her mouth. "What do you think?"

Max slid his head to me, but I lifted my gaze hesitantly to his, suddenly bombarded with the memory of the first time I'd treaded through this conversation.

"Maybe Rose. Or Iris. Fits with Daisy, you know?"

That had been Todd's response when his mother had asked about names during our very first conversation with her after Todd told her I was pregnant. *"I think Hyacinth would be lovely,"* was Mrs. McCormick's non-suggestion.

Maybe I hadn't thought about baby names because for six months, I'd resigned myself to the idea that it wouldn't be my choice. If Mary McCormick wanted Hyacinth, that was what she would get.

Meanwhile, I loved my name, but I didn't have any strong desire to name my daughter after a flower.

"Hmm." Max's chest rumbled, but when I looked up at him, I could tell he wasn't thinking. At least, not about a baby name. He was holding himself back, like it was overstepping for him to suggest a name for another man's baby. *Or maybe he just didn't want to help.*

"You don't have to—"

"Lucy," he cut me off firmly, quashing what I was going to say. "I think her name should be Lucy."

My eyes rounded, all the oxygen suddenly vacating the room.

Lucy was one of the heroines in The Chronicles of Narnia. Brave. Sensitive. Faithful. Valiant. And he picked it because he knew it was my favorite. Because he knew it meant something to me.

"I like that," I said, my voice catching as a foot landed squarely in my ribs. Again and again. *Apparently, little sprout liked it too.*

"Where did you get Lucy from?" Harper sounded like she was at the other end of the tunnel.

"From my brain," Max teased wryly, keeping the weight of his suggestion between us.

Harper rolled her eyes. "Okay."

"Don't be jealous because my suggestion was better than yours."

"There's nothing wrong with the name Blueberry—"

He growled. "We're not naming our baby Blueberry."

Forget oxygen, gravity itself seemed to turn off for a second, and my body simply floated on the intentional slip of his tongue. *Our baby. Our. Baby.* He'd said he'd take care of me and the baby, that he wanted me and the baby. His insistence only solidified by the secret I'd kept about that night. But he'd never said it out loud to anyone but me. Now, his whole family heard him, and they heard the significance just as much as I did.

Little sprout wasn't even here yet, and Max thought of her as his. *His Lucy.* And, god, if I didn't want to think of her that way too. Imagining Max as a lover...as a husband...was one thing. As a father? Well, it was a good thing I was sitting because that was the kind of fantasy that would send my hormones into crippling capacity.

I stared at Max. Harper stared at Max. I was pretty sure everyone was staring at Max, but the only thing that mattered was how he was looking at me—*like he meant every syllable and had no plans to take it back.*

"Hey, Max, we're ready whenever you are," Jamie came over then, his interruption shattering the moment. Jamie's brow creased, realizing he'd walked into...something, but I caught Frankie quickly jerk her head to stop him from asking. "We'll be outside."

"Yeah, I'll be right there," Max answered without looking at him.

Jamie, followed by Kit, headed for the door. When

they were a few paces away, Max explained, "Sorry, Jamie just asked if I could help them move a piece from his shop into his truck. I'll be right back."

I smiled, my eyes fluttering when he pressed a kiss to the side of my head. As soon as he was gone, Harper declared, "We should do presents next. Frankie and Lou, can you get everything ready for Daisy?"

"Yeah, I'll line everything up."

"Let me organize them first," Lou chided, hurrying in front of her laughing twin to reach the living room first.

"Let's clean up the food quick, Vi." Aurora nudged her sister-in-law into the dining room to clean up the brunch spread that was sufficiently picked through.

"You okay?" Harper asked a little quieter once it was just the two of us.

I nodded, my throat too thick to speak through all the thoughts swimming in my head.

Our baby.

My lashes brushed quickly over my cheeks, the hold on my throat even tighter. *It was always him* I wanted to say, but that was what I was afraid of.

Max was giving me everything—so why was I so afraid to take it?

"Finish your cake," Harper instructed when it was clear I wasn't going to be able to respond. "We'll wait for Jamie, Max, and Kit to get back and then start presents."

The warmth of her embrace hadn't even started to cool before a smaller figure saddled up next to me and hung her cane on the back of the neighboring counter stool.

"You look happy, dear," Gigi said as she cut an

impressive piece of cake and slid it onto her plate. "Glowing and happy."

I was.

I was so happy it was frightening—and how could I not be scared? I'd never let my happiness be so dependent on another person before, and now, I felt like I was waiting for the other shoe to drop.

"Thank you." I smiled at her, hoping she couldn't see the knot of emotions tying themselves up in my chest.

My hopes fizzled as her stare pierced straight through me, surprisingly sharp considering how *googly* her thick lenses made her eyes appear. "Did you try your jam?"

Relief swept through me. "Yes, it was delicious. Thank you so much," I said, grateful that I'd found the jar in my bag earlier this week, having completely forgotten Gigi stashed it there the last time we were here.

"Did you read the label?"

My chewing faltered. I had read the label...and it didn't make any sense. I mean, it did, and it didn't.

Peony.

I swallowed, scrambling to answer her without sounding confused or rude. "I did." My head bobbed, and I licked my lips into a smile, adding, "Peonies are my favorite."

I assumed she knew, and that was why the blueberry jam came with a label that had *peony* written on it —why Gigi had told me that jar was made just for me. I convinced myself it was relief, not disappointment, I felt when I read the word. I thought it would have something to do with Max. I mean, I guess it did. His business was flowers, but still, why *peony* instead of just *flowers?*

"Of course, they are, dear." Gigi's smile broadened. "The king of flowers."

I froze. "Excuse me?"

"Peonies. They're known as the king of flowers."

My heart tripped.

I'd convinced myself the word meant nothing when it really stood for everything. For him. Max knew every flower, every bloom. The way they looked together. How their scents complemented each other. I didn't just love peonies. I loved the *king of flowers*.

I loved Max.

"Perfect timing," Harper exclaimed, coming back to the kitchen just as Max and his cousins returned. "We're ready to open presents!"

CHAPTER 26
DAISY

"What is it?" I blinked and set the delicate vase back on the table, looking over my shoulder at Max. "Hmm?"

Today was the first time I'd been back to the store since the incident with Todd's mom. Max had stopped in a few times to handle some things with Erica for the upcoming fundraiser because it was crunch time, but he always managed to coordinate those stops when I wasn't with him. I was honestly surprised when he'd told me we were going to pop in today on our way back from deliveries, but maybe he was finally convinced that the McCormicks were going to let this go—*let me go.*

With every day that passed, I grew more convinced that Mrs. McCormick was lying about having spoken to Todd. That it was just one more attempt to hang onto control of a situation that she had no control over.

"I know that look," Max said, coming closer. "What are you thinking?"

*How did he...*My stare slid back to the vase. Nox had made a handful of vases in various sizes—practice rounds for him and free decor for MaineStems.

"I was thinking this would be pretty as a perfume bottle," I paused when he stopped beside me, his look making me shiver. "Do you think Nox would make bottles for you?"

He took my hand and brought it to his face, pressing his nose right to my wrist and breathing deeply from my skin. "For your perfume."

"Yeah." I swallowed. My hobby—my distraction from the raging urge to nest—had ballooned. I knew it was a consequence, a side effect of avoiding asking Max what was going to happen with the house, with us, but I wasn't ready to give up this bubble. The one where we couldn't keep our hands off each other. The one where, when I was too exhausted to come again, he'd rub my back or my feet or my head until I was sound asleep. The one where I woke up to a home-cooked breakfast every morning. The one where we sat on the back deck every night and watched the sunset.

The one where I was wholly in love with my husband.

"If you ask him, probably."

Nox had warmed since that first dinner. There was still a general frostiness and edge to his demeanor, but he seemed satisfied that I was here to stay.

Before I got a chance to reply, Max got a message. Something about the way he checked his phone bothered me. Maybe it was how his eyes flicked to mine like he wanted to see if I was watching him. Or maybe it was how he turned his screen away from me, even though there was no way I could see it.

"Everything okay?" A tremor betrayed my worry.

"Yeah. Let's go home," Max said, brushing off the questions as he tucked his phone away and took my hand in his, my grip just a little looser as we walked back to the truck.

"Did you know peonies are the *king of flowers*?" I asked after we'd driven a few minutes in silence.

Something was wrong. Max was too quiet, too focused on something else. And I felt the familiar noose tightening around my neck—the one that whispered *I told you so* as it cut off oxygen to my heart. So I scrambled for a thread of conversation and found this one. I'd meant to ask after the shower last weekend, but I'd been so exhausted, I'd fallen asleep on the ride home, waking only when Max carried me inside.

How this man kept carrying me, like the added weight of the home stretch of this pregnancy made no difference, I had no idea.

"I did," he admitted. "They've been called that for centuries. Why?"

"The jar of jam Gigi gave me had *peony* written on the label."

"Your favorite."

I looked at him. "Because you're the king of flowers."

His eyes pierced mine, desire flaring deep in them,

and then he quickly boarded it up and looked back at the road as we turned onto the driveway.

Max parked the truck to go out and open the gate. Meanwhile, I watched him, feeling panic bubble up in my stomach, dislodging all the questions I'd been afraid to ask sooner. I needed to know—needed to get it over with.

"When are you going to put the house back up for sale?" I blurted out when he got back in the driver's seat.

He jerked. "What?"

"The house. You wanted to sell it. I know you took down the sign while we're staying here, but I just wanted to know when you're going to put it back up for sale."

"Daisy, what are you—"

"I can even go back to the apartment if you want. I think it's safe to say Mrs. McCormick isn't going to come back there."

Max stopped in front of the house and threw the shifter into park. "Is that what you want?"

No!

"I know we..." I swallowed. "We're together now, but the rest of everything happened fast, and I don't want you to feel pressured—"

"Stop," he cut me off, shaking his head.

"No, Max. We should talk about this. We should've talked about this before."

He got out of the truck with a growl, long strides bringing him to my door. "I have to show you something."

"Max, please," I begged, even as I held onto his arm

until my feet landed on the ground. "Can we just talk first?"

"Not until you see this."

I went to pull my hand away, but he wouldn't let me. Locking it in his grip, he led me inside, heading straight for the stairs. We reached the second floor and walked right by the room where I'd stored all the gifts and other things I'd bought for the baby. *For Lucy.* Another sharp pain jabbed my chest.

We walked past the master bedroom, and I grew even more confused. There was another bedroom at the end of the hall, I knew, but I hadn't gone in it since the night Max had brought me here and given me a tour.

He stopped just outside the door, staring at it for a second before stepping to the side.

"Go inside," he said, angling himself against the wall so I could pass him.

"Max," I breathed out.

"Please, Daze."

I should resist. I should get clarification of what was going to happen to us. How *us* was going to work moving forward. But I wanted just one more minute of that bubble. So I bit my tongue and grabbed the doorknob and turned.

Every inch the door swung open was another inch my jaw dropped. Gone was the staged guest room, and in its place was the most magical nursery I'd ever seen.

The dark green walls had been hand-painted with trees and flowers and forest animals, transforming the room into a magical space between a fairy forest and a secret garden. *Or even a scene straight from Narnia.* I noticed all the dark wood furniture. It was impossible not to. The large dresser. The rocking chair. I didn't have to ask. I knew Jamie had made it all. But it was the crib that drew me right to its side.

It wasn't like anything I'd ever seen before, the antique style as beautiful as it was uncommon. The way the sides were solid panels rather than fence-like. How it rested on two bows of wood so the whole crib could rock.

It was exquisite. Perfect.

It was all perfect.

"Max..." I hung my head, unable to look at him because I knew I'd simply collapse.

It was too much. *Too thoughtful.* Especially when, moments ago, I'd been mentally preparing myself to leave this house and live separately from him, convinced that, in spite of how he told me he felt, things had moved too fast. That we needed to backtrack all the steps that circumstances had forced us to skip.

"I'm not selling the house, Daze."

"I don't understand."

He cupped my face, holding it to his. "I think you do, but I'm happy to say it if that's what you need, my little wife," he rumbled, dipping his head until his eyes could find mine. "I bought this house for you, Daisy. For my dream to live here with you." He swiped a tear off my cheek. "I put it up for sale when you and Todd decided to get married because I figured that dream was off the table. But now that you're here, now that you and Lucy are mine, I have no reason to sell the house. I don't want to," he paused when I couldn't control the whimpers that blubbered from my chest. "Living here, with you, is all I've ever wanted."

"I can't believe..." I hiccuped. "I can't believe you did all this."

Max tipped a grin. "I did almost none of it," he confessed. "But I did ask for a lot of help."

"Jamie..."

He nodded. "When I went over to his shop to help him the afternoon of the shower, that was to take a look at the crib. It wasn't done yet. I hadn't asked him in time for it to be finished for the shower. But he wanted to make sure it was what I wanted."

"It's beautiful. So beautiful. And I—" I broke off, my head sinking into his hold with shame. "You did all this, and I doubted it. Doubted you."

"Daisy, honey...I don't expect you to not have doubts. Or to not worry." He tenderly brought my face back level with his. "In fact, I thoroughly enjoy proving them all wrong."

A watery laugh fluttered from my chest. "I bet you do."

The nursery. The murals. The furniture. He'd orchestrated all of it and managed to keep it a surprise for me.

I slid from his embrace, my heart feeling like it was about to burst. Walking the perimeter of the room, I stopped at the dresser, opening the drawers to find all the gifts from his family inside.

"I just told Jamie to put everything in drawers for now. Figured you'd want to unpack it all and decide where it goes."

I nodded, unable to speak. This was why he'd kept everything in the other room and brushed off my questions about putting it away somewhere earlier.

With my hand still in his, I continued walking around the room, taking a closer look at the details of the mural. "Who painted the walls?"

"Kit."

I exhaled. "Of course." I'd forgotten his cousin was a painter with his own art studio in Friendship. *Pregnancy brain.* "I can't believe I had no idea. I didn't even smell the paint."

"He's been working every day when we've been out on deliveries. He worked with the window open and put some vanilla extract out. I guess it helps soak up the paint fumes," Max said as I took a closer look at the magical murals. "He finished yesterday and said to give it a night to dry before letting Jamie deliver the furniture."

"It's beautiful." I blinked back another round of tears that hit me unexpectedly. "Perfect, really."

"It was Jamie who texted me when we were at the store. He ran late getting the furniture over here today, so that's why we stopped at the store," Max said, his voice lowering. "I was waiting for his text to tell me when he was finished and gone."

And I'd assumed the worst.

"So you don't want me to move back into the apartment?" I teased hoarsely.

"I'm not giving you a choice, my little wife." He put his hands on my waist and pulled me as close to him as my belly would allow.

"Going to chain me to your bed?"

"I just might," he husked. "But I also told Wade that his brother and his brother's daughter could stay at the apartment for a few months."

"Is everything okay?"

He gave a shrug. "I didn't pry, but I'm guessing there are some issues with the press again leaving him alone. That's usually the only time Blaze comes to Friendship, to get Paisley away from the media."

I couldn't imagine. It was bad enough when I had to imagine all the ways the McCormicks planned to show off their grandchild. The formal announcements and massive parties they wanted to hold. The way Mrs. McCormick talked about having the baby at Mr. McCormick's campaign rallies for good PR. It made me sick, thinking of how they just wanted a grandchild to augment their image. It was even worse to imagine being a target of publicity that was only in it for the money. *And to target a small child.*

"He's going to be fine, Daze," Max murmured, sensing where my thoughts had gone. "We'll make sure he gets some privacy here."

I sighed and blinked up at him, his handsome face swimming into focus. "I still can't believe you did all this."

"Everything I've done has been for you, Daze. It's been you all along."

I felt something shift inside me. Turning my mind from impossible to believe him to impossible not to.

"I know we went about things in a backward order. Marriage, then moving in together, then a baby, but I don't want anything else, Daze. And I definitely don't want to go backward, or in any direction that doesn't consist of waking up to you in my home, in my bed, every morning. Forever."

"Max..." I locked my arms around his neck, pulling myself up closer.

"I love you, Daisy. You're home for me."

My heart erupted in a flurry of beats. I wasn't

falling—I'd fallen. Hard. For my convenient husband. For the fantasy disguised for years as my friend.

Tears dotted the corners of my eyes.

"I love you too."

I pushed up on my toes, knowing Max lowered his head enough so I could kiss him. And boy, did I kiss him. I kissed him like his mouth could get me drunk, and most times, I swore it did. The depth of his kiss, the intoxicating strokes of his tongue...by the time I pulled away, my legs trembled from being up on my toes too long, the room starting to sway.

"Does this mean you're not going to talk about moving out again?"

I shivered and went to smile up at him when the lust in his eyes prompted a different response.

"Only if you'll still tie me to your bed."

His growl of appreciation coiled right between my thighs. "As you wish, my little wife," Max rumbled low, angling himself and holding out his arm toward the hall. "Go get in bed. I have one more surprise for you."

I discarded my clothes as I went, feeling the heat of his stare clawing at my naked skin the whole way.

"**A**re you sure you want to do this?" I asked through the hotel's bathroom door, an edge slipping into my voice that I'd managed to keep out for the last two days.

"Yes, I'm sure." Her breathless laugh from inside should've been comforting, but it wasn't. The mirror on the outside of the door showed just how *not-comforting* it was. My jaw was locked. My hands balled into fists in my pockets. Every inch of me tense and wishing I would've insisted she stayed at the house rather than come with me to Boston.

It was my fault.

I was the one who'd thoughtlessly mentioned to Daisy that Harper had bailed on coming to the FMH fundraiser gala with me. The remark had been more along the lines of "And *here I'd thought Blaze being the guest of honor guaranteed Harper's attendance.*"

A joke turned into Daisy offering to go with me.

I couldn't say no. God knew I'd never be able to say no to my beautiful wife. But damn, did I want to.

It wasn't that I didn't want her by my side. I wanted more than anything to show this woman off—and how much I fucking adored her. But I was under no illusions about this event. It was exactly the kind of thing that belonged in the McCormicks' world. On top of that, she was two weeks from her due date and generally uncomfortable all the time despite my best efforts to make her anything else.

"Do you not want me to go?"

I turned as Daisy came out of the bathroom, and my jaw dropped.

She looked like a Roman goddess of fertility, wearing a gold dress, the high waist drawn just under her full breasts, their curves on display in the deep V of the pleated fabric. The rest of the fabric fell all the way to the ground, shimmering in the light.

"Fuck, Daisy," I growled, bracing myself.

"You like it?" Her eyes flicked down. "I ordered it online from the site where Frankie got her wedding dress. I was a little nervous about sizing, but she said they were pretty true to size."

I hardly heard what she said. It felt like even my ears were salivating over the sight of her. "I more than like it, Daze. I don't want either of us to go now." *I wanted to spend the rest of the night fucking her in that dress instead.*

Pink brushed over her cheeks, and she smiled. "We have to go."

I grunted my reluctant agreement.

She licked over her lips, and my cock jolted, hard enough to make her eyes drop to my groin for a second before they snapped back up. "Why do you keep asking me if I'm sure?" she asked, taking a step closer to me. "Do you not want me there?"

A frustrated breath whipped from my chest. "Of course I do," I rasped, dragging my eyes over her again as I adjusted myself in my pants. "Even though it's going to torture me."

"Then why do you keep asking?"

My jaw clenched. "Because this event...it's filled with people like Todd's family. I go because I have to. Because it's good for my business. But it's not exactly fun rubbing elbows with people like that. I know how much you hated going to things like this with Todd and his parents, and I just want to spare you from it. Especially at thirty-three weeks pregnant."

Her shoulder sagged, and she came to me. "Max." Her hand landed on my chest, and my heart jumped to its home—*in her palm*. "It wasn't the parties I didn't like. Not really. It was how they treated me. How Todd treated me." She shuddered. "He'd show me off, but it wasn't because he was proud of me. He did it like...how I looked was supposed to be compensation for me not being part of that social class."

I took her wrist and pulled her hand to my mouth, kissing the center of her palm and then releasing it. "I have something for you."

Something I should've given her a long time ago.

"What?"

I went to my suitcase and dug into the bottom of the one compartment where I'd hidden the box. As soon as I turned, her eyes went to my hands and widened.

"Max..." She cupped her hands over her mouth and started to shake her head. "What...you didn't...don't have to do this. We're already married."

I reached for her left wrist and pulled it to me with a grin. "One day, you're going to accept that nothing I've done—nothing I do for you is—because I have to, Daze. It's because I love you." My voice cracked as I spoke the words. "And when the whole world looks at you tonight, I want them all to know it."

I opened the black velvet ring box, selfishly enjoying her bulging eyes and audible gasp.

I was a lot of things, but I was still a man, and you'd better be damn sure the ring I designed for her was a helluva lot bigger than the one Todd had proposed with.

"Max..." Her head swayed, her eyes darting from me back to the five-carat Miller-cut diamond, housed in a delicate yellow-gold setting. A slim gold wedding band rested beneath it. Simple, elegant, and priceless. *Just like my wife.*

I lowered onto one knee, the movement surprisingly painful because of how damn hard I was. "Daisy Hamilton..."

"We're already married," she whispered, still in disbelief, like that was justification for me *not* giving her a ring.

I smiled and pressed a quick kiss to her knuckles. "Which is why I'm not asking you to marry me, my little wife. I'm asking if you will promise me your forever?"

The sweetest whimper left her lips as she nodded almost uncontrollably. "Yes."

I pulled the rings from the cushion, sliding the band and then the diamond onto her ring finger.

"Good," I grunted and stood, reaching for the waist

of my pants. "Now, come sit on my cock and say it again."

She let out a breathless laugh as I pulled her with me to the bed. Sitting on the edge, I caught her between my legs. "You can't mess my dress."

"Don't plan on it," I murmured and pressed my face between her breasts, kissing along the edge of the dress until I could taste her goose bumps.

"Max..." She held my shoulders, swaying closer.

That sound in her voice, the ache that infused it, flipped my switch. *Every damn time.*

"Lift your dress, Daze. Show me that pretty pussy."

I leaned back on my hands, trying to alleviate the pressure on my dick as she obeyed, hiking the gold fabric up to her waist.

"Lose the underwear," I grunted. "You won't need them tonight."

"Max—"

"Lose them, or I'll ruin them."

Her thong fell to her ankles.

"Good girl." I spread my legs wider, the pressure on my cock excruciating. "Now show me that wet pussy."

Her shoulders drew back, the color in her cheeks deepening like she knew she was a goddess. *Like she knew she was my goddess, and I would worship her every damn day.*

Holding her dress high, she shivered when the air hit her bare cunt.

Pink. Swollen. And soaked.

"Perfect," I breathed out and gripped my cock through my pants, stroking myself hard. "Come give me a taste."

Inching forward, she gathered her dress into one hand and reached between her legs.

"Wait." She stilled. "Use your ring."

Her eyes flashed, but my woman—*my wife*—didn't even hesitate before swiping her massive, half-million-dollar pristine diamond ring through her slick cunt. Extending her hand to me, it wasn't the stone that glistened, but the way she wanted me.

"Perfect." I took hold of her fingers and drew them to my lips. "Now, every time someone greets you tonight, remember this. Remember who you belong to." I dragged my tongue over the diamond, slowly licking it clean. "Remember how much I fucking adore you."

Daisy whimpered, and before I could stop her, her hand slid to my cheek, and she bent down and kissed me. Hard. *Hungry.* In a second, I was back in control. I cornered her tongue, stroking it and deepening the kiss until she was melting against me again.

"Take my cock out," I ordered roughly. "Left hand," I added in case there was any question.

I swelled even thicker when her little fingers wearing my massive ring reached through the slit in my briefs and pulled my cock through the hole. A hiss blew through my lips when she started to pump me.

My little wife learned too damn quick what undid me—*and this was exactly it.*

"Enough," I clipped, watching her reluctantly let go of my cock. "Climb on my lap, my little wife."

Steadying herself on my shoulders, she put one knee and then the other onto the bed, framing my hips.

"Good girl," I crooned. "Now lift your dress a little higher. Can't have it getting dirty, can we?"

She tugged up the fabric again, breathing heavily as she tried to keep steady on her knees.

I framed her thigh with one hand. With the other, I lifted my heavy cock from my stomach and tapped it against her swollen clit.

"Max!" She gasped and let some of her dress loose.

"Dress, Daisy." I barely got the words out, my dick pulsing so damn hard to be inside her.

She recovered the fabric, and I rewarded us both by sliding the head of my cock through her seam. "Fuck, you're so ready for me, Daze." Her slickness coated me, and I let myself enjoy one torturous second of watching the fat head of my cock slide back and forth through her folds before I notched it against her entrance.

"Down you go, baby," I said, my vision swimming as the slightest pressure on her hip sent her sinking down on my cock, impaling herself on my entire length in one shot. *"Fuck..."* My curse rattled around the room with her throaty moan. The feel of her tight heat, stretched and squeezing me, was enough to make me come. "Ride me, baby. Ride my cock, and don't fucking let go of that dress."

My gorgeous goddess instantly started to bounce on my dick, panting and whimpering as she chased her orgasm.

They came quicker now, I'd noticed over the last week. The way her body changed—the way her hormones changed. She'd become so fucking sensitive. After I'd tied her to the bed and fucked her, I'd given her a second orgasm just from blowing on her tight little clit. I didn't know if it would change after she gave birth, but I wasn't going to waste the experience, and I damn sure wasn't going to waste her ability to enjoy it.

"You're so fucking beautiful when you're horny, my little wife," I growled. "Riding my cock like you need me to get you pregnant again."

"Max," she whimpered, her hips slapping wetly onto mine. "Max, please..." She stretched her fingers, her flat palm keeping her dress from falling.

"Hold it, Daze," I demanded. "Don't fucking let go."

She cried out but closed her fingers once more. As a reward, I took her hips in my hands and thrust into her.

"Is that what you needed, baby?" I demanded, driving harder into her soft cunt, angling myself to make sure I hit that sweet spot with my tip.

"*Yes!*" She panted, her chest glistening with a sheen of sweat. "Yes, Max. Oh god..."

Oh god was right. My jaw threatened to crack under the strain as Daisy started to buck, her body ricocheting with pleasure from each thrust. Darkness chewed at the fringes of my vision, making the beautiful pregnant woman glow even brighter as she fucked me.

I pumped faster, watching her eyes squeeze tight. Her flush spread down to her tits. Her swollen stomach tensed. But I felt the effect on my cock. The tightening of her muscles. The spill of heat down my length and onto my balls.

"That's it, baby. Tell me you're mine," I commanded roughly, the words stretching through locked teeth. "Tell me you're mine forever."

Air pierced her lungs, our eyes connecting before hers rolled back as she screamed, "*Yes!*"

Her release claimed her, her body going blissfully tight as I drove into her. Her pussy clenched so impossibly tight, my thrusts shortened into hard, quick drives.

Once. Twice. And then the pressure at the base of my spine erupted, my cock filling her with hot jets of cum.

"Fuck," I groaned, holding myself buried inside her for long minutes, feeling completely atomized by my release. And I wasn't the only one.

Daisy let go of her dress, her hands sliding down on top of mine, where I held her thighs. Our damp fingers linked together, and we stayed like that for long minutes until breathing felt normal again.

"We're late," Daisy was the first to speak.

I looked up at her and smiled. "Are you complaining?"

"No," she murmured and, bracing her palms in mine, lifted herself up off my cock.

"How's the dress?" I asked, sitting up and holding my wet cock away from my clothes.

Dropping the hem, she looked down and then to me. "I think it's okay from what I can see, but I can't see my feet, so..."

I grinned, checking the lower part of the fabric. "Looks good."

I slid off the edge of the bed and grabbed a handful of tissues from the nightstand, making quick work of wiping myself down and tucking myself back into my pants.

"Daisy."

She stopped mid-reach for her underwear. I took two steps toward her and then kicked them across the carpet.

"Hey!"

"I said no underwear."

"But..."

"Your dress is long," I said, sliding my hand around

the back of her neck as I murmured next to her ear. "No one will know my cum is dripping out of you all night. No one but me and you."

She made a delicious sound somewhere between a sigh and a moan. "Maybe we should go to events like this more often."

"We don't have to go to things like this for you not to wear underwear," I said with a low chuckle. "Just say the word, my little wife, and I'll be happy to rid you of every pair when we get home."

CHAPTER 28
DAISY

Home.

It had always been a place in my mind. An apartment. A house. A physical structure where I lived. It wasn't until Max brought me to his house—my dream house—and made me his, that I realized home was, in fact, *not* a place but a person.

Home was him.

His smile. His warm gaze that set my skin on fire. His touch that seemed to read my skin like a mood ring, going from gentle to supportive to possessive to dominating without me having to say a word.

"Mr. Obrien, this is my beautiful wife, Daisy," Max introduced me to the hotel manager, his hand remaining firmly on my lower back. *As though the cum running down my inner thigh wasn't possessive enough.* "Daisy, this is Mr. Obrien."

The way Max was looking at me made it hard to want to look at anyone else. To think of anyone else. *His beautiful wife.* Todd never introduced me like that. Not to people like this. *Beautiful* had been implied by the

smug look on his face. *Like I was proof of something.*
But Max...Max looked at me like I was his world. Like
we were his world.

"It's a pleasure to meet you, Daisy," Mr. Obrien
said, and I finally turned as he extended his hand.
"Congratulations."

I placed mine in his and watched as he brought my
knuckles to his mouth. Every time someone kissed the
back of my hand, I had to wonder if they could smell
me on my ring. I knew Max licked it clean, but...*But
that was the point,* the butterflies in my stomach
whispered.

"Thank you."

"I can see why you've been so busy recently," Mr.
Obrien said as he straightened.

Max's smile didn't even falter—nor did his gaze
break from me. "Family comes first," he said, slipping
me a wink as he looked back to the other man. "But it's
my beautiful wife that you have to thank for the
perfume samplers."

"Your idea?" He looked to me.

"Her idea and her talent," Max said proudly. "She
developed the blend herself."

"Yes, that was a very nice touch," he replied,
seeming more conciliatory now. "You know, Mr. Hamilton, it may be something I'm interested in using
throughout the hotel..." He trailed off, and my heart
thudded, and then something—someone—caught his
attention. "But we can talk about that later. If you'll
excuse me."

As he walked away, my breath let out in a whoosh,
and then I felt Max's head dip next to mine.

"You're incredible, do you know that?"

I let out a weak laugh and then reached for my stomach, feeling a small cramp.

"Max..." I tipped my head.

"Incredible and all mine." His mouth dropped to mine, kissing me in the middle of the crush without a care in the world.

"Max?"

We pulled apart as a very handsome and vaguely familiar face came over. In the background, a banner echoed his striking features. *Blaze Stevens*.

"Blaze," Max greeted warmly. "Good to see you again."

The Hollywood star smiled, but the expression didn't reach his eyes. "I was hoping I'd find you here..." he said as he shook Max's hand.

"Blaze, this is my wife, Daisy. Daisy, this is Wade's brother, Blaze."

Blaze gave me the same clipped smile, like a flower that had been clipped and pruned so it didn't grow too tall or too wide. Like he'd trimmed his emotions into the image the public wanted to see.

"I just wanted to thank you for letting me rent the apartment," Blaze continued, his voice lowering a notch. "It'd be different if it were just me, but with Pais, I don't trust a hotel or the strangers there to keep my privacy." There was a flash, and his head snapped to the side, though his expression remained untouched. *Like a man who smiled as he was being tortured.*

"It's not a problem. Glad I could help."

"Flowers look great, by the way. And the perfume... genius," he added, and I felt a blush of pride warm my chest. "Heard a bunch of people remarking on it."

I looked up at my husband, who just smiled calmly and said, "Wonderful."

Max's reserve carried new meaning now. New weight. A gentlemanly kind of armor he only shed when he was around me, and that made my blood heat. *Just like I shed a few things only around him and became something I never thought I'd appreciate: submissive.*

"*Blaze!*" a deep voice called from behind the famous actor. With a nod that looked more like a grimace, Blaze excused himself and disappeared into the crush.

"Everything really is beautiful, Max," I said, inching closer to him as a group of men who were drinking and talking loudly moved behind me.

He took my hand and lifted it to his mouth, pressing his lips to the back for long seconds and staring at me. "You're beautiful, Daze. Exquisite."

"Max." I sighed and shook my head.

I'd lost count of the number of times he'd complimented me tonight. In every private intermission between meeting and greeting people, Max had told me how beautiful I was. How exquisite I looked. How he couldn't stop looking at me. *How he couldn't wait to get me back to our room.*

"I'm serious, Daze." He stepped closer and cupped my face. "Everyone in here is looking at you." His voice lowered. "You're a goddess."

"You keep saying that—"

"Because it's true," he growled. "Everyone is looking at you, and all I want is to take you back upstairs and remind you that you're mine."

"Max." I shivered, my eyes fighting to stay open as his mouth found the shell of my ear.

"Do you still feel me running out of you?" he husked with a devilish grin.

My jaw went slack, my nipples pebbling hotly against my dress. I picked this one because the way the fabric pleated over my chest, I could get away without wearing a bra. *I had to get away with it.* I was too big and uncomfortable for bras anymore, and Max acted like I'd made the decision solely for him.

To him, I didn't live in oversized T-shirts and dresses because everything else was too tight or uncomfortable. I wore those things because they gave him easy access to my body. When I woke overnight, tossing and turning because there was no position comfortable enough when you were about to pop, it was just one more invitation to give me an orgasm. When I couldn't bend down to put socks on or tie my sneakers, he never wasted an opportunity to get on his knees for me—and make mine weak for him.

Every moment when I could've felt bloated and overstuffed, uncomfortable and unattractive, he turned those thoughts on their head. He made every minute of this pregnancy—every change my body endured—like I was providing him one more facet of his fantasy.

I'd never felt more attractive. More desired. More cherished. *More loved.* And I would admit to being wrong, to picking the wrong man a thousand times over, if every time it meant it would lead me to the right one. To Max Hamilton.

"A little," I murmured, my gaze hazy as I stared at the crowd around us.

"Maybe I should take you back upstairs and fill you

back up. I wouldn't want my little wife to forget who she belongs to."

I sucked in a breath and turned my head, forcing him to look at me. "You." I placed my left hand on his beating chest. "I belong to you."

"Max." Mr. Obrien clapped him on the shoulder and then took a step back, not realizing Max and I were having a moment. "Sorry to interrupt. I wanted to introduce you to some of the donors for tonight."

Max's eyes flashed possessively at me.

"Go," I murmured and smiled. "I'm going to sit for a few minutes."

Catching my chin in his fingers, he held me steady and took my mouth in a long, deep kiss. "I'll be back soon," he murmured.

As Max dipped into the crowd, I heard Mr. Obrien remark, "I can see why you keep her to yourself, my friend."

And Max wanted them to see. He wanted everyone to know I was his, and it was the sweetest feeling in the world.

I walked to the water table a few feet away and took a small glass, finding a chair at a table near the perimeter of the room and sinking into it. We'd been milling around the ballroom for over an hour, but it was only now that I was sitting that I felt the exhaustion start to creep in. That was why I told Max to go with Mr. Obrien alone. The second he realized my energy was flagging, he'd want to leave, and I knew tonight was a big night for him. I wanted him to have it.

"Mrs. Hamilton," a voice drawled from behind me, its vitriol scratching at my skin, ripping away the glossy sheen Max had put on the night.

No.

My spine stiffened into steel as I turned and looked up at my former almost-in-laws.

"Mrs. McCormick." Her dark-red lips were pulled into a severe line. "Mr. McCormick." His lips were hardly visible at all except for how they anchored his expression in a frown. "It's nice to see you."

I was polite because I was too panicked to be anything else. My arm instinctively slid over my stomach when Mrs. McCormick's gaze dropped to it, and I had to remind myself that she couldn't take my baby. Not now, when Lucy was still inside me. *Not ever.*

"If you'll excuse me—" I broke off, sinking back into the chair when Mrs. McCormick moved in front of me, bodily blocking me from standing. Suddenly, the grand ballroom felt as small as a janitor's closet.

"Absolutely not. We have some things to discuss."

My hand curled into the tablecloth as I fought to breathe. "I believe I said everything I needed to say to you weeks ago," I said, my heart thudding faster. "Now, if you could move out of my way. I have to go—"

"No."

"My husband—"

"Is here by the grace of his business," Mrs. McCormick snapped. "A business which is successful by the grace of *our* name."

Dread curled like a snake in my chest, not only suffocating me but threatening to bite.

"The clients he has, the ones he's meeting right now, Daisy, would disappear like a dandelion on a breeze with just one word from Senator McCormick. One hint that MaineStems is a *business non grata*."

I stared at her, unable to believe what I was hearing. She was threatening me. *Threatening Max*.

"That child is a McCormick, and it will be raised as one. Do you understand?" she demanded, but with a smile on her face. My eyes drifted around us, guests walking by, smiling, drinking, laughing—no one realizing this wasn't a conversation. No one realizing she was blackmailing me. "You will either hand that child over to us, or you can be responsible for Max's failure. For his business's failure."

My head started to sway. I had to get out of here—get away from her. "Leave me alone."

"If that's what you want, Daisy, but then you'll be responsible for the swift and sudden failure of your *husband's* business. His ruination," she clipped. "Then you'll not only have saddled him with a child that's not his, but no way to support it or you." She paused to smile and wave at someone in the distance she knew, as though she wasn't too busy threatening a pregnant woman to be social. "Is that what you want? I doubt it, judging by that ring." She scoffed. "Hardly missing one rich groom before landing yourself another. A veritable Jezebel, Miss Turner...or I guess I should say Mrs. Hamilton." Disdain didn't drip from her voice. It suffused it. "I wonder what all of Max's clients would think about that? What being married to a gold digger will do for his reputation?"

I wanted to scream at her. *Liar!* And then maybe strangle her. I didn't want Max for his money. I didn't want him as a backup because Todd left.

I looked at Mr. McCormick for the first time. He hadn't said anything to this point, and I wondered if there was any way that meant I could convince him to put an end to this. Whenever Todd needed something —or had done something stupid—it was always his dad he called first. But instead of a possible ally, all I saw was another victim in his gaze.

He looked nervous. Angry. Complicit. But nervous. His stare left mine and darted around the room, as though he was afraid someone was going to make a scene.

"It's your choice, Miss Turner," Mrs. McCormick continued, ripping my attention back to her as she called me that on purpose—to prove her point that what I had with Max wasn't real. "You can either give that baby over to its rightful family, or you can be responsible for the downfall of your husband's business. His *dream*." She sneered the last, like dreams were dirty. Like they were only meant for those without wealth and power.

"*Hey!*"

Max.

He shoved between Todd's parents and lowered straight onto one knee. "Daze, are you all right?" He held my face, turning and searching it for signs of distress. "Daze...you're pale," Max said low, rage brimming like a current under the calm.

"Just feeling a little lightheaded." Darkness eked around the edges of my vision, and I could feel every pump of my pulse as it climbed my neck. I pressed my hand to the top of my stomach, feeling like my little sprout had grown straight up into my ribs. "I think I need some air."

And to never see the McCormicks again.

"Let's get you out of here."

I wanted to protest. Mrs. McCormick's words

rattled around in my mind like spare Legos, but Max took the cup of water from my limp hands and set it on the table.

"Up you go. Nice and slow." He guided me onto my feet, his body a blockade against the two people who'd cornered me.

Taking my hands, he turned in front of me.

"Come near my wife and child again, in public or private, and I'll be filing a restraining order."

Todd's dad's eyes bulged. "Mary—"

"How dare you threaten—"

"You're *lucky* I'm threatening you," Max growled, cutting her off menacingly. "It's because of my friendship with your son that I'm *threatening* you. If it weren't for him, I'd be calling the police." And then he bracketed his arm around my waist and guided me out of the event.

The people, the space, everything turned into a foggy blur until we reached our hotel room.

"Max..." I didn't even sound like myself, my throat was so thick.

He came back over and cupped my neck, tilting my face up. "I know, Daze." His forehead kissed mine. "I'm packing our things, and we're going home."

Maybe it was crazy to drive home at this hour when we had a perfectly good room to stay in—one Max had paid for—but I didn't want to stay. I wanted to drive. I wanted to let the road untangle what just happened. What she'd said. *What Max risked by being with me.* And then I wanted to curl up in the safety of our bed and pretend like nothing could touch us.

At least until morning.

WE RODE IN SILENCE, MAX'S HAND NEVER LEAVING mine from the moment he'd taken it inside the ballroom until now. He was always there for me. No matter what. *No matter how it hurt him.*

"Do you really want to be responsible for ruining his career?"

That was what hit the hardest. Not the threat to me, but to Max.

Before...before I could pretend ignorance. It had been his choice not to tell me how he felt about me, just like it had been my choice to try to ignore my attraction to him. But now I knew. I knew all he'd done for me. All he was doing for me. And I couldn't—wouldn't let him do this.

Maybe I could be convinced he didn't want those things more than he wanted me, but I'd be a fool to think I took first place over his business. I wouldn't let him convince me that he'd weather whatever storm the McCormicks threw at him.

Before I knew it, the onyx carpet of freeway turned to tree-lined local roads that snaked toward the coast. Toward Max's house. *The house we'd been playing home in.* And I felt like a fool.

I thought I was safe—that we were safe. I let myself believe the warning he'd delivered to Mrs. McCormick was enough to drive the point home, but then they showed up at the fundraiser and pulled that rug—that magic carpet dream I'd been riding—right out from under me.

The only point that mattered was the baby I carried was a McCormick, and I'd no sooner be able to get rid of my ties to that family than my daughter would be able to get rid of half of her genes.

I sat frozen, seeing the familiar moon-drenched outline of the coast through the trees. What was I thinking, believing I could fit safely into Max's world? Assuming that just because he'd wanted me there for so long, there'd be no hurdles. Hoping that I could just start over—start again with the right man when I was pregnant with another man's baby.

Ironic that Todd had left me, but apparently, I wasn't allowed to leave him, his family, or their prestigious name.

"Are you okay?" Max finally asked, his voice rough like the night tide against the shore.

Shame washed over me. I almost couldn't bring myself to tell him. Why would I? Why would I want to tell the man who'd done everything and more for me—who loved me in secret for years—that what he'd sacrificed wasn't enough. That being with me would ruin his dream too.

"She wants me to give up the baby."

"She's insane." His fingers curled into mine, giving them a warm squeeze. "It's not happening, Daze. She can't touch the baby or you. Or us."

A cry untethered from my throat.

"I love you, Daze. Both of you. I won't let anything happen, do you hear me?"

Max Hamilton loved me, and I'd never been more certain of anything in my entire life. But this wasn't about loving me—or me loving him. This was...whatever it was, love wasn't enough.

"You're wrong." I covered my stomach with my hand, feeling the baby turn. "She can touch you."

"What?" He stiffened. "What did she tell you?"

"She...they can ruin you, Max." Fear reamed all steadiness from my voice. "Everyone there...all the contacts you're trying to make, the ways you're trying to grow your business—they can take it all away." I paused to catch a breath. "A few words from them and everything you've worked for will be ruined."

"Daisy, that's not—"

"You can't tell me it's not, Max," I insisted, my voice rising, my heart pounding. "I know them. I know what you and Todd went through building MaineStems. I know how many connections he made for you—all because of his family. You can't say no because I know the truth. I know what their name means. I know how—"

"Daze." He shook my hand until I stopped, realizing I wasn't stopping to think, let alone breathe. "You know I will fix this."

Tears strung up along my lashes. "You shouldn't have to."

And what would he risk to do it?

He'd loved me through every obstacle, but what if this was the one that broke him? What if loving me meant losing his business—his dream? What if he couldn't have both, and he came to resent me for it?

"I need you to trust me, baby. Please." He pulled my knuckles to his lips, tattooing them with his plea. "Please."

I did trust him. It was never a question of trusting

him. I just knew what the McCormicks were capable of, and I knew they wouldn't relent. They hadn't relented on Todd when he'd tried to do his own thing. They'd even let him barter on the family name to help MaineStems grow, but it was an insidious kind of help. The kind that grew like a blueberry bush, producing fruit even as it completely invaded its surroundings, choking out every other kind of life.

"I do trust you," I said, my lip quivering as I let out a sigh and turned to him.

The glow from the dash caught on his tousled hair and the hard profile of his face. He'd never been more handsome than in this moment. My knight in a gleaming black tuxedo, willing to fight any battle for me, even one that could mean the death of his dream.

Just knowing that made my heart swing harder at my chest with every beat, wanting to crack out of its cage and go to him. To leave me to the consequences of my situation and free him to be happy.

"I'm sorry, Max," I heard myself say, a heartbroken husk overtaking my voice.

His hand pulsed around mine. "Don't apologize, baby. None of this is your fault. None of it." He dragged my hand to his mouth again, kissing the back of it like he could infuse his confidence straight into my veins. "I'm going to handle it."

My eyes burned, but I refused to cry. I didn't want to waste whatever moments I had left to look at him like this. Like he was mine. Moments that turned out to be too few because it felt like I blinked and we were pulling down the driveway, Max parking in front of the house minutes later.

"Daisy..." He groaned and leaned over the console, cupping my cheek. "What is it?"

It wasn't fair.

It wasn't fair that he had to keep cleaning up the mess of my life. It wasn't fair that he had to keep saving me. *It wasn't fair that to keep the woman he loved, he'd have to risk the dream he chased.*

It wasn't about asking him to choose. It was about having to live with the consequences of his choice. Until Max, I never would've dreamed of Todd or any other man putting me first. None of them had, just like my mother had told me, none of them would. *Until Max.* But Max would put me first. He always had. Always would. He'd pick me time and time again and never think twice about what it could cost him.

How could I live with myself knowing the position I'd put him in? Knowing the choice he'd make? I was the reason he'd been alone for four years. I was the reason he'd given up on the idea of marriage and a family. I wouldn't now be the reason he lost his dream too.

"Let's go inside...to bed," Max rumbled, stroking my cheek like he was searching for tears to wipe away but found none. That was because they were all inside, filling the deep well I'd dug for decades.

I didn't have the strength to argue when he carried me inside, only realizing when my feet hit the floor that he'd carried me because I'd taken my shoes off at some point during the drive home. Upstairs, he unzipped the back of my dress, the material falling in a gold whoosh to the ground.

"Max." I shivered as his lips fell to my shoulder.

"I have to go back to Boston in the morning. To

finish up everything from tonight," he said, clearly sounding like he wished there were any other option. "It shouldn't take me long, but I'm going to leave first thing, so I'll be back before noon, and then we'll talk about this. About them."

I nodded, my throat too thick to speak as he ushered me into our bed. The only thing that felt better than the comfort of climbing into familiar sheets was when Max settled in next to me and drew me to him, his thigh fitting between mine like a hot pillow.

The ridge of his knuckles lifted my chin. "I love you, my little wife."

My pulse withered in my chest. We'd just said those words for the first time to each other only a few days ago. The feeling had been there for longer, but like a foundation laid beneath the surface. Still, the words felt tenuous—what we had with each other still felt fragile and uncertain. A victim of our ever-changing circumstances.

Would you still if it cost you your dream?

It was what I thought, but what I said was, "I love you too."

And I couldn't let him continue to be the one always saving me. Not because I was too independent to be saved, but because I loved him too much to let him be the one to suffer. I would figure out how to fix this. Somehow. Some way. And then I'd find my way back to him once it was safe.

But that was tomorrow's problem.

Tonight...I'd take one more night in this fantasy with him. My husband.

The king of flowers. And the king of my heart.

CHAPTER 29
DAISY

"Coming!" I called to the knock on the door, setting down the vial of rose extract I'd started earlier in the week.

A part of me instantly hoped it was Max, but logic punctured that thought like a balloon. Max wouldn't knock at his own home, and he was in Boston.

He left the bed this morning with a kiss to my forehead, almost before the dawn had risen. I knew it was because he wanted to leave so he could get back, but I didn't want him to leave at all.

I winced with every last step to the front door. I felt so achy this morning. So big. Was it the shoes from last night? They were flats but still new. Or was it the standing? We'd lapped that ballroom so many times, I'd lost count, and I hadn't been complaining. The way Max made me feel at his side was addictive. Powerful and protected.

Until that one moment shattered everything.

"Do you really want to be responsible for ruining his business?"

I peeked through the window and immediately opened the door.

"Hey, Harp." My hand set on my stomach.

"Morning, Daze. Hope I didn't wake you." She extended her arms. "But I brought blueberry muffins and honey."

I moved aside. "Max sent you, didn't he?"

A sheepish smile worked one side of her mouth. "He said you might want some company this morning."

My tongue lay heavy in my mouth as I followed her into the kitchen. I worked myself onto one of the seats at the counter, feeling like it was so much more work to move this morning than yesterday.

"Are you okay?" she asked, unpacking the basket of baked goods.

I rubbed my belly, feeling Lucy sitting low. "Yeah, just feeling really...big this morning."

"Well, you've only got, what? Two weeks until your due date?"

"Thirteen days," I answered as she set a plate with a muffin in front of me. "Thank you."

"Of course," she said and grabbed a knife for the honey. "How was the gala?"

I winced, a cramp rippling through me. *Braxton-Hicks,* Dr. MacDonald explained at our appointment last week, in depth, due to Max's probing. "What did Max tell you?"

It wasn't until I saw her eyes flare and then chin dip that I realized my tone was sharper than I'd intended, not because of her question, but because of the pain.

"He didn't tell me anything, just that you decided to come home last night. Sorry if you don't want to talk about it. We don't have to." She scooped some honey onto the knife and spread it over her muffin.

"No, I'm sorry." I shifted to alleviate another cramp. "I didn't mean...it's just been a long night."

"It's okay. I only asked..." She paused and swallowed. "I only asked because I know Blaze was at the gala."

Blaze. That's right. Now, I remembered what Max had said about being surprised that Harper had bailed on going with him to the gala—because he thought she'd want any excuse to see Blaze.

"Yeah, we talked to him for a few minutes. He thanked Max for letting him use the apartment, but that was about it."

She made a soft sound but kept eating, almost like she was trying to stop herself from asking more.

"Do you...know when he's moving in?"

I shook my head, uncertain. "He didn't say. I'm sure you'll see him around as soon as they do, though."

Her eyes dropped. "Oh, I hope not."

"No?" A crease pulled through my brows.

Harper shook her head. "I didn't mean it like that. I just...I think it's better if I don't see him. That's why I told Max I couldn't go last night."

"Why don't you want to see him?"

"Aside from the fact that my family has already made it awkward by sharing about my high school crush on him?" She laughed weakly. "I think it'll just be better for me if I don't interact with him. Help me get those girlish fantasies out of my head." She tried to play it off lightly, but there was only self-deprecation in her eyes. "Can't fight reality, right?"

I set the other half of my muffin down. What little appetite I had was gone.

Can't fight reality.

"Todd's parents were at the gala."

"What?" Food practically spilled from her mouth as it dropped. "Did they..." She trailed off when I nodded.

"I think that was the only reason they were there. To talk to me." *To threaten me.*

"What did Max do?"

"He wasn't there. Not at first." In hindsight, maybe that was a good thing. If I hadn't heard her out, who knows what they would've done—if they would've just started cutting off his business without warning.

"They want the baby," I heard myself say.

"What the hell?" Harper's hands planted on the counter, and she glared at me. In that moment, I saw the similarities between her and Max. "They can't just demand someone else's baby. This isn't the eighteenth or whatever century. I hope you told them to go f—"

"They're going to come after MaineStems if I don't," I interrupted, not wanting to hear all the ways I should've stood up to them—stood my ground and said screw it to whatever consequences Max would endure because of me.

"I don't understand."

"They're going to ruin his business. All his contacts. His contracts. All the deals he has in the works...they're going to lean on all their connections to hurt Max."

"How...can they do that?"

"What? Spread rumors? Spread lies?" I choked out, my throat burning with anger and loathing. "People can say whatever they want—write whatever they want. No one bothers to check anymore if it's true."

It wasn't until the color drained from her face that I realized I'd hit close to home. Well, at least she understood now. All it took was one word, a single lie dropped like dye into a bucket of clear truth, and the whole thing would be tinted. Tainted.

"I'm sorry, Daisy." She took my hand, and I was glad when she squeezed it because another cramp came on, and her hold helped distract me from the pain. "I'm sure Max will think of something. There's no way he's going to let you give up his baby."

I bit my tongue and lowered my head, staring at the impossible swell of my stomach. *Lucy*.

I couldn't tell her I'd already thought of a way to fix this—to fix everything.

Max was the leverage they held over me—over my heart. If he wasn't in my life, then their threats were empty.

If I left, Max would no longer be in danger, and Todd's parents wouldn't be able to find me.

"Daisy..." I lifted my eyes to Harper's. "Don't."

"Don't?"

"Don't run."

My mouth opened and then shut. "What are you talking about?"

How did she know?

In seconds, her eyes were awash with tears.

"Two years ago, Nox was in a relationship with someone. No one knew—well, I knew—but no one else did. Something happened...I found him upset. Angry. So angry." She shivered at the memory. "I begged him to talk to me. To Max. To Dad. *To someone*. The next day, he decided he was going to study glassmaking in

Italy. He didn't tell me until the day before he was leaving."

My breath hitched. Now, the chill between them seemed clearer.

"Nox had the same look when he told me he was leaving as you do now," she finished, her fingers curling into a fist. "He thought running was the answer, and so do you."

I didn't think it was the right answer. I thought it was the only solution. But I didn't say that. If this was what I decided to do, I couldn't tell her. She'd turn around and go right to Max.

"Isn't running what you're doing with Blaze?"

My question shocked her, but only for a second before she banded her arms over her chest and fired back, "Blaze never looked at me the way my brother looks at you."

And with that, she walked around the counter to wash her hands and then grabbed her bag. "I have to get to my hives, but if you need anything, just call."

My chin dipped.

"And Daze?" She stopped on her way to the door and looked back at me. "Max will be back soon, and he'll figure out a way to fix this, I promise. There's nothing he wouldn't do when it comes to protecting you."

My palm lifted to my throat, my heart nothing more than a rattle against my chest.

I watched her walk away. Heard the front door open and close. And that was when I let myself break.

Why was Max always the one protecting me?

I love him too, you know, I wanted to shout to her. *Why couldn't I be the one to protect him for once?*

Him and my baby?

My chest started to heave with deep cries, each one fitting between the increasing cramps in my stomach. Harder and harder. Each more painful than the last. I knew what they were, but they felt like my heart breaking. Each one cracking and splitting the seams of an organ I'd finally let feel.

Was it running when it was a choice? When it was to protect the man I loved?

There was a loud knock on the door, and my cries hiccuped to a halt. Swiping my eyes with my fingertips, I saw the basket still on the table.

Harper had forgotten them.

I picked up her things and went to the door, puffing out hard breaths through tight lips as the contractions intensified.

"Be right there, Harp!" I yelled, having to hold my stomach this time as I moved.

I wasn't expecting Braxton-Hicks to be this bad. Maybe I should call the doctor to check. To confirm. That was what they had to be, though. It was too early for anything more.

I didn't bother to look before opening the door. A mistake I'd realize too late.

"Harp—" I froze and stared at the face on the other side. "Oh my god..."

And then I felt a waterfall crash down my legs and drench my bare feet.

CHAPTER 30
MAX

"Mr. Obrien?" I stepped through into his office, my back as straight as a rod.

When I'd arrived at the hotel this morning to direct the cleanup, the night manager, who was on his way out, told me that Mr. Obrien wanted to speak to me before I left. I was sure he did. He'd called me on the drive home last night, and I ignored his call.

It wasn't important. Not compared to the woman sitting next to me in the car. However, that didn't absolve me of the consequences of walking out of the gala last night.

I should've known the McCormicks wouldn't let it go. Family and legacy, the image that provided was everything to them. I'd watched it shape my best friend from his earliest years. From the hobbies he had to the food he enjoyed, Todd was forever trying to cut the individualized pieces of himself off to fit into the shape his family wanted. As he got older, they gave him a leash, but it was only long enough to hang himself with. They played down his desire to work with me, to start

MaineStems. They made him believe we wouldn't have survived without his name and without their connections.

And Daisy...I knew from the moment I'd met her, not as her, but as Todd's girlfriend, that she was one more notch in his long string of attempted defiance. They let Todd work with me while slowly stripping away parts of his lifestyle that he'd been raised to rely on. And then, when Daisy got pregnant, they decided he had to marry her, that she had to leave school. *That she had to fit into their mold too.* Because of the baby.

I was sure now—I hadn't been before, but now, there was no doubt in my mind that Mary hadn't spoken to Todd. If she had, he would've been the one confronting Daisy at the fundraiser last night. Mary had lied to get Daisy to do her bidding, and she was doing it again.

Whatever power or control they thought they had, it was nothing compared to the hard work and dedication I'd put in over these last couple of years. Yes, their name had opened doors. Had garnered big clients with big contracts. But they weren't what made my business.

What made my business was individuals. Friends. Family. Local business. Word of mouth referrals. *That* was what had made MaineStems grow. Not the dozen or so political and corporate contracts. Those had benefited the company, to be sure, but they weren't the backbone.

In fact, if Mary knew anything at all, she'd know that was the one sticking point Todd and I perpetually disagreed on. All he wanted was to leverage his name and his family position to bring in business, and I wouldn't let him. Even then, I guess I knew better than to look a gift horse in the mouth.

Now, if only I could convince Daisy to trust me—that there was nothing they could do to me or my business that I couldn't withstand. The problem was convincing her would take time. I could see it written all over her beautiful face last night—the panic, the fear that she would be the reason I lose everything.

She was my everything.

"Please, come in." He motioned me forward, and I strode to the chair in front of his desk, sinking into the seat.

He finished whatever he was typing before closing his laptop and sliding his glasses off his nose. "Mr. Hamilton, your flowers were truly spectacular last night, as promised. And the perfume. Above and beyond."

Okay, maybe this wasn't going to be so bad.

"Thank you." I dipped my chin. "I'm grateful for the contract, and I hope we can work together this way again in the future."

His head bobbed. *Or not.*

"I'm not, however, pleased with the way you walked away mid-conversation with Mr. Grant." His eyes narrowed as his real reason for calling me in here came out. "I came back over with two other colleagues of mine to recommend you and your services, but you were gone. Mr. Grant was alone and annoyed." His lip twitched, his scrutiny holding steady. "I don't appreciate going out on a limb for a vendor only to be... stood up."

"I apologize, but my wife wasn't feeling well, and I had to take her home."

"I see," he murmured flatly, clearly expecting more of an excuse. "While I do understand, it was still—"

"Mr. Obrien." I sat forward, linking my hands. I didn't have time to be chided as if I were a child. If he didn't want to recommend me or do business with me anymore, I didn't care. "You may look at me and think my business is just pretty flowers, and that's okay. I'm sure there are guests who come to this hotel and think that your business is just rooms, but you know better. I know better. You aren't in the business of lodging. You're in the business of customer service and experience." My voice picked up a charge, sparking along every word in the hopes that one of them would catch in his mind and make him understand. "And I'm not in the business of flowers, but of love. Of care. What I provide shows the recipient, whether it's one person or a whole room of people, that someone cared enough to be thoughtful, to want to give them something beautiful because they are important. What kind of business would I be if I didn't give the same priority to my very own, very pregnant wife?"

I simultaneously rose from the chair and stepped down from my soapbox. "I'm sorry for my abrupt departure last night, Mr. Obrien, but my wife and baby will always come first." And then with a brief nod, I went to leave.

"Mr. Hamilton."

I stopped at the door because it was the polite thing to do. Even if we never did business again, I wouldn't purposely burn a bridge. As I turned, Mr. Obrien extended his hand over his desk, a steady smile drawing up his normally severe expression.

"I look forward to working with you again in the future."

I took it, knowing I passed some kind of test in his eyes, but when I walked out of his office, I couldn't find it in me to care. For the first time since I'd started pursuing my dream, since MaineStems was just a seed starting to sprout, its success wasn't at the front of my mind. Only she was.

My wife.

"AND WHAT IS THIS REGARDING?" THE SUITED secretary looked at me, his expression permanently wrinkled with displeasure that I'd shown up to Mr. McCormick's office without an appointment.

"His son and grandchild."

That earned a flicker of recognition.

The McCormicks could try all they wanted to keep the drama of Todd's disappearance under wraps, but there was no hiding that he walked out on a wedding. That they'd been forced to postpone the grand wedding reception they planned without even asking Todd or Daisy. *That he hadn't shown up since.*

"One moment, Mr. Hamilton. Let me check if Mr. McCormick can see you."

He would. Mary might've given me a hard time, but Todd Sr. would see me.

This was the real reason I left the house so early this morning.

To end this.

I waited impatiently in the hall while he went to check with Mr. McCormick, the walls claustrophobic with formal portraits of the McCormick family going back generations. Even Todd's photo hung among them, though it looked nothing like my childhood friend. I doubted any of them did. They weren't supposed to.

The portraits were commissioned to show how they wanted people to see them, not how they actually were. The oldest kind of filter for the rich and powerful. Even the one of Mr. and Mrs. McCormick, smiling together... a show. They weren't happy. And they weren't together.

Few people knew that Todd's parents lived mostly separately. They did their best to hide it from the world because they were more powerful together.

For all the time I'd spent in their orbit, even I hadn't known until a few years ago, when Todd let it slip, and only because he'd been drinking. Even for all the times he hated them, hated what they'd done to him, he never broke rank. Never betrayed the family image.

"Right this way, Mr. Hamilton."

His secretary led us along a rope of hallways, past Mr. McCormick's office that I'd been in a handful of times over the years, to the back corridor of the brownstone and into the more private rooms.

Wordlessly, he opened a door and announced, "Mr. Hamilton for you."

He shared a look with his younger secretary, and I had to wonder...

"Thanks, Jackson."

The door closed us in together.

"Max."

"Mr. McCormick." I walked up to his desk.

He motioned for me to take a chair, but I refused.

"What can I do for you?"

I braced my stance. "You can tell your wife to never speak to my wife again."

His eyes sparked. I wondered when the last time someone had spoken to him like this. He had the decency to shift uncomfortably before insisting, "I'm sorry, Max, but that's our grandchild, and it needs—"

"*She*, not it," I snapped, never feeling more pity for Todd than I did at this moment.

McCormick waved me off like it was a moot point.

"There are certain expectations for this family, Max. I don't expect you to understand, but unfortunately, if you are going to stay married to Daisy, you won't have a choice. There is a certain way our granddaughter needs to be raised."

I hated everything about how he spoke. How he sounded like he was in a business meeting discussing a contract. Not a baby. *Not my baby*.

I moved right in front of his desk and pressed my fingertips to the top.

"Except she's not your granddaughter, is she?" I said, my voice deadly low.

He didn't even balk, and that was how I knew I had him. How I knew I was right.

"Excuse me?"

"You heard me." I bent closer. "I know Daisy's baby isn't your grandchild because Todd isn't your son."

His parents' living arrangement wasn't the only thing Todd had let slip.

"How do you—"

"How do you think?" I charged, my voice low and taut.

He'd found out the night of his father's birthday party—the night Daisy and I had talked on the balcony. The night she'd gotten pregnant.

Todd had called me in a panic the next day. I thought it was because Daisy had told him what I'd said —what I'd suggested.

I remembered the way my heart clawed at my throat waiting for Todd to get to the farm. I didn't know what was going to happen, so I figured it was safest to talk where there was only a field of flowers to hear.

Except the fury—and alcohol—he'd shown up with wasn't for me. It was for his parents.

Apparently, earlier in the night, while he'd been roaming the house looking for Daisy—who'd been out on the deck with me—he'd walked in on his dad and another man together.

"I don't understand. I don't fucking...I don't under-stand." He'd trampled a path through the flowers, chug-ging from the bottle of vodka as he went.

"I asked him this morning. I asked, and he just brushed me off. 'We have an image, Todd. A happy family. We don't talk about what doesn't fit in that image.'"

"Does Mom know?"

"Of course, she knows. We have separate arrange-ments, but the family—our legacy—comes first."

"And me?"

"Enough. This conversation is over and is never going to be spoken of again. You know better than this, Todd. You know how our world works."

Todd had replayed the whole conversation, letting

me feel as though I'd been a fly on the wall the whole time.

Knowing his parents lived mostly separate lives hadn't been a tough pill to swallow. There were so many couples in that upper echelon that did the same. But learning his father was gay, it cracked something inside him that I couldn't understand.

Later that week, he'd done a DNA test.

Todd McCormick Sr. wasn't Todd's father.

"After the night after he found out you're gay, he took a paternity test," I said, watching his eyes dart around the room like some invisible microphone was recording me.

Todd got the results a few weeks later—a few days after Daisy realized she was pregnant. My resolution to keep my distance, to protect my heart, went up in smoke when my friend realized his family, the box he'd cut himself into pieces to fit into, wasn't actually his.

I told him to tell Daisy, but he wouldn't. Maybe he couldn't. But there was nothing else I could do except respect his wishes. Even now...even after the choices he'd made, I'd kept this part of his truth from Daisy. However, my respect for him ended at his parents— crashed and burned when they started threatening my wife and our baby.

"Goddammit, Todd." McCormick sat back in his chair, his ruddy face taking on a distinctly clammy sheen.

It wasn't my responsibility to wait while he processed the information. He didn't deserve that kind of compassion. He certainly hadn't shown it to me, let alone Todd.

"You want to threaten to ruin my business? Go ahead.

I don't know what Todd told you, but I never relied on your name or connections to make my business what it is. I guess maybe I always knew it was nothing but hollow support," I informed him coolly. "However, if you try to physically or legally insert yourselves into my daughter's life, I can promise you that the first thing that will come out is how little biological right you have to do so."

I straightened. McCormick looked like I'd set off a blasting cap on the desk right in front of him.

"I'm sure you'll let Mary know we've spoken." I rapped my fingers on the desk, making sure his eyes contacted mine before I went to let myself out.

"Max!" he called, and I stopped at the door, watching a man who I'd never seen falter, who I'd never seen unsure, bluster unsteadily, "You can't—"

"I just did," I said and walked out.

I told Daisy I was going to fix this, that I was going to protect her. Now, I was sure that I had.

MY BLOOD WAS BUZZING BY THE TIME I CLIMBED into the seat of my truck. The first thing I did was reach for my phone. I wanted to let Daisy know I was on my way back. I wanted to tell her it was finished, that she'd never have to worry about the McCormicks again.

In an instant, my heart, previously thundering with excitement, plummeted to the pit of my stomach, wrapped in a cold shroud. A message from Todd sat like a bright red warning flare on the screen. After all these weeks, what were the chances he'd message me today? Within minutes of my visit to his dad?

Maybe he had been in contact with them. Maybe as soon as I'd walked out of that room, Mr. McCormick had called Todd and leveled all his fury on his son. To me, it made no difference that there was no biological relation between the two of them, but to them, the image was all the difference.

I wished I could've talked to him before going to speak to his father. I wished I could've talked to him weeks ago when he left Daisy at the altar. Or when I offered to marry her. Or when we moved into my house. Not because I needed his approval, but because I wished I could know he was okay.

Now, we were here. I was married to his ex-fiancée, and I'd just threatened to expose his family's darkest secrets if they didn't leave us alone.

I didn't leave myself time to wonder whose side in all this Todd would be on. I simply swiped open the text and pushed through the tornado of emotions whipping through me. Anger. Concern. Frustration. Pity. My eyes collided with the message inside, and all those riotous emotions shattered like glass.

> Daisy's water broke. We're at Stonebar Hospital.

Nausea followed the whiplash as I read and reread the text. Like I'd stepped into a boxing ring with a heavyweight champion, each pass a harder hit than the last.

Daisy was in labor.

And Todd was with her.

Why—how? I should be there. I should be with her. My wife. *My baby, not his.*

I'd stood on the sidelines for years, ignoring how I felt because of how it could hurt others. I couldn't do that anymore. I wouldn't. Daisy was my wife. My future. *My heart.* And I was going to do whatever it took to make him understand that, even if it cost me our friendship.

I cursed myself every minute of the hour it took to get back to Stonebar. And I broke every speed limit on the way back to her.

CHAPTER 31
DAISY

This wasn't how this was supposed to happen.

Pain seared through my lower body, and I squeezed Todd's hand until his fingertips turned white. He didn't complain. I could've squeezed his hand straight off his wrist, and he'd have had no right to complain. Not after what he'd done.

The crest of the contraction dipped, and my thoughts collected into coherence again.

"Where is he?" I choked out, blinking back the tears that wanted to fall.

"He'll be here, Daisy. You know he will," Todd assured me, and for the first time in our entire relationship, I actually believed what he promised, and it had nothing to do with him and everything to do with the man we were talking about.

This wasn't how this was supposed to happen. I kept thinking it ironically because a few months ago, this was almost exactly what was supposed to happen. Me, giving birth, with Todd by my side. How could I have ever thought that was right?

From the second I opened the door and saw him standing on the stoop like an apologetic schoolboy, all I could think was, *how could I have ever chosen him?* I knew how. Because I'd grown up believing I couldn't be too close to anyone

So many times I'd thought it didn't matter if I never spoke to Todd again. I had nothing to say...and there was nothing I needed to hear. *Why would I want an apology for a decision that had been the right one?*

"He has to be here, Todd." I pushed out a breath and then sucked in another sharp one, feeling the clamp of another contraction starting. "Max has to be here."

"I texted him, Daisy. If he was in Boston..." Todd glanced over at the clock and frowned. "Do you want me to call him?"

I shook my head, my teeth locked as another contraction swept through me. This time, tears leaked free.

"Daisy," Todd said quietly once he felt my hand let up. "I'm sorry."

My throat tightened. I was surprised he'd held out this long before apologizing. Though, to be fair, my water had broken the moment I saw him, and after that happened, chaos steamrolled straight through whatever Todd had come to say.

"Don't apologize," I said, grabbing the cup of ice water and sucking down a sip. "You didn't want to marry me, and I didn't want to marry you." There was no room for anything but the raw truth.

"I know." He slid his hand through his hair, and I took a good look at him for the first time since he'd shown up at the house, seeing almost nothing of my fiancé who'd left me at the altar. Todd looked...good.

Maybe that should make me upset or angry, but it didn't. Not in the slightest. "But I want to tell you...I want to explain—"

"Really, you don't have to," I said, wishing I could pull my hand away, but the contractions hurt so bad, and it felt good to be able to squeeze something.

"Daisy—"

"I didn't love you, Todd. I don't think I ever did." I wasn't sure where the sense of urgency came from to tell him the truth, but it was there, and it was violent. And it felt like I had to get it all out before I gave birth. Like I needed to put this last piece of who I was—the woman who was too afraid to let people in—before my daughter saw that example set for her. "I just...You were safe. You didn't make me feel too much where I had to worry—" I broke off with a groan of pain, but the instant it let up, I forced myself to continue, "I shouldn't have agreed to marry you. Not when I wanted him. Not when I'd fallen for Max."

"I know, Daisy."

I whimpered, my head thrashing back. He didn't know. *He didn't know.* "No," I panted. "You don't know. You don't know, don't remember, but I said his name that night. The night I got pregnant." I didn't want to be harsh, but I was in no condition to be soft. "I want to be his wife, Todd, and I want this baby to be his."

His jaw flexed. "That's what I'm trying to tell you, Daisy, if you would just listen—"

"*Daisy!*" Max's deep voice charged into the room as he burst through the door, chiseled and chivalrous and heart-stopping.

He was here.

My heart leaped into my throat, and for the space of an instant, I felt no pain, only sweet, slow-motion relief. He was here, and just looking at his face, I knew everything was going to be okay. *And I didn't know how I could've ever doubted it.*

"Todd," Max growled.

"Wait, Max—"

"Get your hands off my fucking wife," Max said, and I'd never seen this side of him outside the bedroom —the side that stalked across the room and grabbed Todd's arm to forcibly remove his hand from mine. I didn't hate it. But neither did I love it at this moment when I was in labor.

"I'm sorry, Max—"

"Fucking right, you're sorry. How dare you come here after what you and your parents—"

An unearthly sound tore through the room. I never understood what they meant by a bloodcurdling scream until the moment it left my lips. It ricocheted around the small room and soured every drop of oxygen.

"Daisy!" Max was by my side, my hand wrapped in his big one as he brushed the hair back from my face. "What can I do?"

"Get the nurse," I said through sharp, practiced breaths. "The baby is coming."

"Already here, hun." Jennie strolled in and went right to the foot of the bed. "I'm going to check and see how dilated you are." She stopped and looked to Max and then over to Todd. "I'm afraid only Dad can be in here right now."

My heart raced straight off a cliff and then plummeted. Max was by my side, so of course, she assumed Max was the father. But...

"I guess that's my cue to wait outside," Todd's voice filtered in, and my eyes flung open, meeting those of my ex-fiancé. He gave me a small, tight smile and then walked out of the room as though...as though he didn't belong in it.

And he didn't.

"Told you that you were going to have this baby fast," Jennie said after her quick exam. "You're fully dilated. I'm going to go grab Dr. MacDonald, and then you'll start pushing."

I must've been more than fully dilated the way she jogged out of the room, but then another contraction hit, and all I could think about was the pain and the urge to push.

"You've got this, Daze," Max murmured, his face right next to my ear. "I'm right here. I love you so much, and I'm right here."

Air pumped in and out of my chest. Voices came through scrambled into my mind, encrypted into a code that spit out the same word over and over again. *Push.*

I blinked, and Dr. MacDonald was there, smiling and nodding like I knew what I was doing. I had no idea. Everything hurt. I felt like I was being split in two, but somehow my body knew what to do. Pain swelled, and I pushed. It retreated, and I breathed. Again and again and again. And in the space between, there was Max. His warmth. His touch. His voice. His scent.

"You're doing so good, Daze." *Push. Breathe.* "Almost there, baby. Almost there." *Push. Breathe.*

I grounded to him until it felt like I was made of nothing but searing pain and sweet words. And then, with a giant rush of relief, the dam released, and the world came rushing back with the sweetest, piercing cry.

Not mine.

Hers.

"She's here, Daze." Max smiled at me, tears in his eyes. "Lucy's here."

And then she was on my chest. Wiped and ruddy and crying. The most surreal minute of my life—that final minute when she'd gone from being inside me to lying on my chest.

"She's perfect," Max said hoarsely.

She was perfect, but I was too exhausted, too full of awe to do anything but stare. She was perfect and beautiful. And everything. And mine. I blinked to clear the fog of tears and looked at Max.

And his.

My daughter was his.

CHAPTER 32
MAX

"I can't believe how perfect she is." My voice cracked under the strain to keep it quiet so I didn't wake her.

The last two hours had gone by in a blur of doctors, nurses, weighing, holding, staring, *loving,* and with every moment, I just wanted more.

Turning, I looked at Daisy as I lifted her hand to my lips. "Just like her mother."

Her blush made my heart beat lighter.

"I was afraid you weren't going to make it," she said, and it was the first attempt to broach what had happened before the monumental, perfect moment that our daughter was born.

"There was nothing that could keep me from you— from both of you," I promised and kissed her knuckles. The back of her hand. Her palm. "It's over, Daze." She looked at me. "They're never going to come near you— come near Lucy again."

"Max..." Her eyes rounded, hope overflowing through them. "How?"

My jaw tightened, but before I could speak, the door opened.

"Sorry to disturb Mom and Dad." *I'd never get tired of being called Dad.* "Just wanted to check and see if either of you needed anything?" Jennie asked.

Daisy and I looked at each other and then said, "No," in unison.

"Okay." Her smile flattened. "Is it okay if I tell your family member it's okay to come in? He's been waiting..."

Family. *Todd.*

I looked to Daisy. "Your call, baby."

I was more than happy to tell him to take a hike, but maybe putting off this conversation was worse than getting it over with.

"Yeah, he can come in."

Jennie left, and there was a moment of privacy.

"We have to talk to him, Max." She stared at Lucy, but I could see the turmoil fighting through her expression. *He was her father too.*

"I know."

As soon as I heard the door, I stood and walked to the edge of the bed like a lion protecting his mate and cub.

My ribs strained against every breath, air cracking to reach the depths of my lungs, as my best friend walked into the hospital room where my wife had just given birth to his baby.

"Max."

Without my worry over Daisy clouding my gaze, I saw him clearly. Thinner. Nervous. But the bags under his eyes were gone. Same with the bloated look he always got when he drank too much. I wanted to ask if he'd stopped drinking, but that was a question for a different time. A different friendship.

"Congratulations, Daisy," Todd was the first to speak, tucking his arms over his chest as he came a little closer but not too close. Especially to me. "Max." Our eyes met.

The man who'd fathered Lucy and the man who wanted to be her father.

I brimmed with tension, every moment I'd been in the presence of his father earlier, hitting me like a freight train. If they sent him, if they thought I was going to let him anywhere near Lucy—

"If you're here because of what I said to your father earlier—"

"You talked to my dad?" Todd's arms dropped, and if I wasn't so skeptical of him and why he was here, I'd think he had no idea.

"Max?" Daisy's surprised gasp came from behind me.

"I did," I answered them both, but my gaze never left Todd's as my voice lowered an octave. "But if you didn't know, then why are you here?"

Every single question—assumption—hanging in the air between us.

Are you here to get Daisy back?

Are you here because you want to be a father to the baby you never wanted?

"I wanted to apologize to Daisy...and to explain." He looked briefly at me, but then his attention turned to my wife.

I wanted to step in front of him. I wanted him to explain to me first, but then I felt small fingers curl around my wrist and then slide to my hand.

Let him, her hold seemed to say.

"I know you said you didn't need my apology, Daisy, but I need to give it." He swallowed. "It's part of the program."

I stilled. How many times had I tried to get him to get help? To go to an AA program? He never would. Always said he didn't need it.

"I shouldn't have...left you...you both the way I did, but I just wasn't capable. Wasn't ready to...explain." Nerves shivered over him. He shifted his weight, his eyes losing some of their steadiness. He ran his hand along the back of his neck and then blew out a breath. "I'm just...I guess I'll just start at the root of it." He grimaced. "I'm gay, Daisy."

Daisy gasped, and I stiffened, Todd's truth hitting me like alcohol on the back of my throat, burning as it soaked in deep.

He was gay.

It wasn't that I'd never thought...never wondered... every once in a while...But I was his best friend, and we had plenty of gay friends, so I figured if he was, he'd tell me. Trust me.

"It wasn't you," he said, like he knew what I was thinking. "It was me. I was trying...not to be." He let out a bitter laugh. "My parents...what they wanted—"

"But your dad..." I croaked, and Todd's head snapped to mine.

I felt Daisy squeeze my hand, confused.

"Todd McCormick isn't my father," Todd rumbled. "Not in the ways that matter...nor the ways that don't."

"Wait, what? Todd, what are you talking about?" Daisy gaped.

"The night of my dad's party—the night we, ahh..."

He trailed off, and seeing that we all understood where he was going with that, he cleared his throat and continued, "You disappeared, and when you were gone for a while, I went to look for you. I thought maybe you'd wandered off into one of the quieter rooms of the house. I heard low voices—noises coming from my dad's study, but when I went inside, it wasn't you. It was him. With their neighbor, Matthew. They were...together."

Daisy's jaw dropped almost as far as mine had. "What?"

"I closed the door—left them. And that's when you found me, and all I wanted to do was forget what I'd just seen." He paused and drew a steadying breath.

Daisy sat forward. "You never said anything."

"Honestly, I was a mess. I wanted to forget everything about that night, but I couldn't," Todd said, rocking back on his heels. "I confronted my dad the next morning, and he...acted like it was nothing. Told me it was nothing. That this was how his life—my mom's life—had been from the start. That it was how our life went. That legacy came first."

"Oh, Todd." Her voice carried every emotion with it that I'd felt the night he'd told me this.

"I was in a fog. Spiraling. I hate to say it, but I wasn't even thinking of you, Daisy. I was just thinking of how blind I'd been. I had this pit in my gut, so I took a DNA test." Even the memory looked like it was a fist to his gut. "I'm not his son. Not biologically, anyway. Which was ironic because that night I caught him, my first thought wasn't 'holy shit, my dad is fucking another guy,' it was 'holy shit, maybe this is why I feel...why I like...'" He shook his head. "I know that's not how it works, obviously, since we're not related."

"Oh, Todd..."

"I got the results right after you told me you were pregnant," he went on like he hadn't even heard her. Maybe that was the only way he could keep going. "I know I was a mess after that, Daisy, and I'm sorry. All I can say is...it wasn't you." His shoulders fell with a sigh. "I'd just learned my dad was basically in the closet. And then that you were pregnant, and I was going to be a dad. And then that my dad wasn't my dad. And I just...I did what they told me to do because I was too lost to do anything else."

I glanced at Daisy then and saw tears streaking down her face. Only my incredible wife would be able to feel pity for the man who'd left her at the altar.

"Anyway, I tried to convince myself it was going to be okay. That I cared about you—loved you in a different way. That I wanted to do the right thing for our baby." His chin dipped. "But the weight of...hiding who I was, I couldn't..."

"The drinking," I filled in the blank he'd left open.

Looking at me, he nodded. "I thought I could drown it out. I mean, we'd been together for four years, and I'd mostly buried that part of me for longer. I thought I could do it again."

"But you couldn't."

"Can't stop a seed from searching out sunlight." His expression was sad but without regret. "Maybe I could've buried it deeper if I hadn't...if he hadn't..." Todd's face reddened, and he shoved his hands in his pockets.

"You met someone," Daisy breathed, and Todd's head snapped up.

"Not met. We already...knew each other."

"Scott." I hadn't realized I'd been seeing my friend through a fog all these years, but as soon as he started to clear it, I began to recognize all the signs. How close they'd been in college. Why Scott reappeared when he did...after Todd's wedding was announced.

"We were close in college, but especially back then, I ignored the way I'd catch him looking at me...and the way it made me feel. And after we graduated, I think that's why we lost touch. Anyway, when my parents announced our engagement, he showed up at the country club." Todd lowered his head. "I thought I could ignore how I felt." His words echoed my mindset about Daisy. *I thought I could ignore how I felt about her.* And like him, I'd done everything I could to hide it, and like him, it had wrecked me. "But he kept showing up—wouldn't give up—and with everything that happened, he was the only place that felt safe."

"You could've told me," Daisy said, her tone both sad for him and hurt that after everything, he hadn't trusted her with this.

I felt the same.

"I know." He pared me a guilty glance. "I could've told both of you." He sighed. "It wasn't you. It was me. I was drowning in everything I was trying to figure out. I wouldn't have known what to say or how to say it."

"You could've called off the wedding or at least postpone it..."

"I tried," he said, and I felt Daisy's ripple of shock. "Before the rehearsal dinner, Scott and I argued. He said he couldn't be with someone who was fine with hiding who I really was—who I really loved. He told me..." His voice choked. "He asked if that was the example I wanted to set for my daughter.

"I went to my dad after dinner and told him I was going to call off the wedding. I thought of all people, or at least out of the two of them, he'd understand. I told him how I felt—that I was gay. He responded..." He let out a strained laugh. "He wasn't unsupportive. I guess I can give him that. But I guess I was hoping for a little more understanding than 'I don't give a shit who you fuck behind closed doors, but in public, you're a McCormick, so you're going to marry the girl you knocked up, and you're going to continue this legacy, just like I have.'"

"Did you tell him that you knew the truth?" I asked, a not-so-small part of me wishing I was crueler to the man I'd threatened earlier.

"No." The sound he made then was the ragged groan of hope being buried alive. "Even if I thought it would make any kind of difference, he didn't give me the chance. He said if I called off the wedding, he'd disown me, and without anything, Daisy...with the pregnancy and the baby...I wouldn't have been able to support you." He speared a hand through his hair. "I didn't know what else to do. I didn't want to hurt you. You have to believe me. You deserved better than this... than me. You deserved...the man who'd always wanted you."

There wasn't even a shadow of malice in his gaze as it steadied on me. He knew how I'd felt about her...just like he knew I'd never do anything to betray him.

"So you disappeared." I wanted to blame him, be angry, but it was hard to.

"Maybe there were other options, Max, but at that moment, I was drowning in alcohol and fear that I was about to trap myself into a life of being someone I wasn't, and I was going to take Daisy and the baby down with me. So I disappeared." His expression shuttered. "I knew my parents would want to avoid a scandal, so they'd make up some excuse for me—for what happened. In the meantime, you would've still had the house to move into and access to my credit card."

"Did you really think I'd use them after you left?" Daisy demanded, and Todd had the decency to flinch.

"No. I mean, if there were no other option, I knew you would, for the baby. But I knew it wouldn't come to that," he admitted, looking to me again. "I knew Max would never let it come to that."

"So why come back now?"

Todd blew out a breath. "I wasn't planning on it," he admitted. "I thought it would be better—easier if I were just gone, especially after I learned from my mom's ranting voicemail that you'd gotten married. I guess she thought that would provoke me to return or to at least reply. When I didn't..."

"She approached me at the fundraiser."

"I tried to make it in time, but my flight was delayed twice. By the time I landed early this morning, she'd left me another voicemail that they were going to ruin Max's business and then fight for custody of the baby. I came straight here to tell you everything and figure out a plan, but it sounds like I'm too late for that as well."

I tightened my teeth and nodded. "They won't be coming after us anymore."

Todd's throat bobbed.

"I told him if they tried to make a claim for the baby, they'd have to submit to a DNA test, and I was pretty sure he wouldn't want the results of that made public."

He nodded again.

"I'm sorry," I said roughly.

"Don't be." His expression was pained. "They...did this. I'm just glad you're both okay—happy." The hurt started to wash away.

"What are you going to do now?" Daisy asked, her voice soft.

"Go back to Providence with Scott. Finish my program. Heal." A half-smile appeared on his face. "Figure out how to...be."

Lucy let out a small whimper then, and all of us looked to the tiny human who tied us all together.

"One day I'd like to know her," he said, giving a brief but slightly sad smile. "One day, when I know myself a little better."

There was another knock at the door then, and Jennie popped her head inside. "I'm sorry to bug you again, but I have the birth certificate ready to fill out. It'll just take two minutes."

Daisy's hand tightened, but I couldn't look away from Todd.

"It's no problem. I was just leaving anyway," Todd said, and then, with a look to Daisy and me that spoke volumes, added with a poignant tenor, "Congratulations again. Lucy couldn't have asked for better parents."

There were a lot of things that were clear in what he said. His happiness for us. His relief that it had all worked out. And the subtle expectation that it was my name going on that birth certificate under *father*, not his.

Daisy and I shared a look, and then as soon as

Jennie moved by me, I was out the door and calling for Todd.

He stopped just a few steps from the room, surprised to see me. It took me a beat once I caught up to him to figure out what I wanted to say.

"Are you okay?"

His head tipped, and then he smiled, and it was probably the easiest smile I'd seen from him in a long time that wasn't alcohol induced. "I'm figuring out how to be okay, but in the meantime, I'm happy."

I smiled back. "Good."

"Sorry I never told you," he repeated and let out a deep breath. "I should have. It wasn't you. I just...I knew you'd never let me continue being something I wasn't, especially with Daisy, and I didn't know what I was. Who I was. I guess I just thought keeping it to myself would help me figure it out."

"To be fair, I never figured out how to tell you how I felt about Daisy."

"True." His chuckle sifted into silence. "I'm happy for you, Max. For both of you." He extended his hand, but instead of shaking it, I took it and pulled him in for a hug. It was the only thing that felt right.

"I'm happy for you too," I said. "If there's anything I can do...anything with your parents."

"Thanks, but I can handle them. Finally." He smiled tightly and drew back. "Take care of Daisy and that beautiful little girl of yours."

My chest strained. "Always."

I watched him walk away until the end of the hall, and then he turned the corner, and I turned back to Daisy. To my daughter. *To my future.*

CHAPTER 33
DAISY

I didn't think I could love Max any more than I did the day he surprised me with Lucy's Narnia nursery and the handmade crib. But every time I saw him gently lower our daughter into it so as not to wake her, I managed to love him even more.

Maybe it was my new perpetual state of exhaustion, but the last six weeks since we'd brought Lucy home from the hospital had been the happiest of my life.

We came home to the house Max had bought for us. The house that had been fingerprinted with my things. Lucy's things. Transformed every day by the new memories we were carving into its fabric. And for the first time, I felt like I was exactly where I was supposed to be.

"I don't know how you always manage to get her down without waking her," I whispered when Max came back over to me, where I stood watching him from the door.

"I have a magic touch," he teased and pulled me into his embrace, adding low, "I have one for you too."

I hummed as his head lowered, and he kissed me slow and sweet—a stolen second in days that sometimes devolved into chaos. Somehow, he always managed to steal a second or several for me. For us. To hold me. To rub my back. To play with my hair. To massage my feet.

Laughter floated upstairs from the kitchen, and Max groaned as he pulled away. "Can I kick them out?"

"Absolutely not." I chuckled and took his hand, leading us to the stairs.

Max's family—in any and all combinations—had been at our house in some capacity almost every day since we brought Lucy home. To bring food. Gifts. Clean. Do laundry. Hold the baby so I could take a power nap.

They always said it took a village, and I'd never been more grateful to have one. There was no world where I'd let Max kick them out—even if it was for a delicious reason.

Max grumbled all the way downstairs, where we joined his family—and our belated Thanksgiving celebration.

I'd given birth the week before the holiday—discharged only days before. Without even asking, Ailene and Gigi came to visit us at the house and informed us that the big Kinkade-Hamilton Thanksgiving would be postponed and joined with Christmas. So we planned a Christmas brunch followed by a turkey dinner.

As I walked into the kitchen where everyone was gathered, I couldn't help but think how I'd gone from basically no family to...all this. A house brimming with people and stuffed full of love, and my heart had never been fuller.

Back downstairs, we joined the jovial crowd, my phone with the video monitor app always in my hand and Max always by my side.

"Daisy, come open your presents." Frankie swooped her arm through mine. "Max, you're going to have to let her out of arm's reach for a few minutes."

"A few minutes. I'm timing you," he said as she led me toward the tree Jamie and Kit had put up two weeks ago when we'd taken Lucy to her doctor's appointment.

Within moments, my hands were filled with food and presents. Lou shoved a blueberry muffin in one hand, and her twin made me open a present with the other. New pajamas—matching ones for me, Max, and Lucy. A gift certificate for a massage. Gift cards for restaurants. Several of them. And then at least two dozen outfits for Lucy...on top of all the hand-me-downs they'd already dropped off.

In return, I doled out all the presents Max and I had ordered while we'd been up in the middle of the night with Lucy. I'd rock the baby, and he'd throw out present ideas for his family.

"Harper's Christmas gift arrives right after the holiday," Frankie teased when I set a large box in Harper's lap, the contents a large fuzzy blanket that she told me she'd been eyeing. The cottage she lived in on the Hamilton farm never got warm enough in the winter, or so she said. "Blaze Stevens and daughter. Residents of Stonebar Harbor."

"Not funny and not my present," Harper returned, and to her credit, her voice came out practically emotionless.

"So you aren't pining for him anymore?"

"It was a high school crush, Frankie," Harper

groaned. "I'm sure you had plenty of those and that Chandler wouldn't appreciate it if I started teasing you about them."

I watched as Frankie opened her mouth to reply, but then snapped it shut as her eyes narrowed.

"Are you...dating someone?" she asked, her voice dropping to a whisper.

Harper's eyes bulged like she'd been caught, and I waited for her answer too. She hadn't said anything to me about a boyfriend, but to be fair, every single moment since Lucy had been born, I'd been selfishly focused on my sweet baby, and so had all my conversations with my sister-in-law.

Before Harper had a chance to answer, she turned and looked above me just as a warm voice rumbled over my shoulder.

"Don't forget my gift," Max rumbled, joined on either side by his dad and Ailene, who was holding Lucy.

"She's up?" I gaped and reached for my phone, panicked that I hadn't heard the video monitor.

A moment later, Max held my phone in front of me.

"I took over Lucy-cam watch so you could have a few minutes."

Every time I thought I couldn't love him more, he did something that dared me to try.

"For you, Daze." He handed me a small, elegantly wrapped box.

"Max..." We'd agreed not to get each other anything, which wasn't to say I didn't have a present for him, but it was the kind of present that was *private*.

"Open it, my little wife," he encouraged, kissing the side of my head.

I peeled open the paper as he sat next to me on the couch.

The box was plain, with no markings. A maroon cloth that suggested whatever was inside was expensive.

I lifted the lid, peeled back the tissue paper, and found an elegant glass bottle nestled into the packing.

It wasn't until I lifted it out that I realized everyone was watching me.

"Max..." My finger roamed over the label, the edges hand-painted with a string of peonies that wove around the edge, framing the scraggly, cursive word in the center.

Daze.

There was no level of exhaustion that would've made me question what this was.

It was my perfume. Bottled in hand-blown glass from Nox, the label painted by Kit.

After Lucy's birth, my perfume-making continued, but at a slower pace, and Max seemed hesitant to talk about incorporating it as a permanent offer from Maine-Stems. I thought it was because he worried I was taking on too much, but now I knew the real reason.

Because he was making one more of my dreams a reality.

"It's official now," he murmured. "Daze, eau de perfume, will be coming to MaineStems as soon as you're ready."

"Max..." I tried to blink back tears, but it was impossible. They rolled down my cheeks as he pulled me to him, a hum of excitement buzzing through his family.

"I love you."

I felt him smile against my cheek. "I love you too, my little wife."

"I can't believe you did this." My voice wobbled. "You didn't have to..."

"Oh, he did, dear." I looked over my shoulder at Gigi, who wore the biggest smile on her face.

At my confusion, she motioned for me to hand her the perfume, and when I did, she stared at it, lovingly running her fingers over the front.

"Don't you recognize it, dear?" She turned the bottle to me, but even with another close look, I didn't understand what she was talking about.

When I looked to her to explain, she poked Max. "Tell her."

My eyes met my husband's.

"This," he paused and ran his thumb over the label. "Gigi gave it to me...the day I met you."

My mouth dropped open, and my eyes snapped to the handwriting. *How had I not recognized the handwriting?* Even if I had, it wouldn't have crossed my mind that this was Max's label from his grandmother. While mine had said *peony,* Max had been given a label that said Daze...four years ago. For this moment. *For me.*

"You were always meant to be mine," he said softly and passed the perfume bottle around for everyone to smell so he could take Lucy from his aunt and steal another moment for us. "The first bottle of the first batch of Daze perfume."

"I love you," I murmured, staring at the two of them.

My daughter and my husband.

My daughter and her father.

"I love you too, my little wife."

I could almost forget we were surrounded by his

entire family until we kissed, and the crowd broke out in cheers.

Later that night, after his family had left and we'd sung Lucy to sleep with Christmas carols, I led Max to our bedroom and let him open his present.

With love and wild hunger in his gaze, he unwrapped my pajamas from my body like a gentleman. And when he saw the black lace lingerie I had on underneath, he shed his gentleman and made love to me like the man who was made for me. My king of flowers.

The king of my heart.

EPILOGUE

DAISY

TWO MONTHS LATER...

"Ready?"

"I think so." I smiled at Lou and turned my gaze around the living room at the Lamplight Inn, which looked nothing like a living room right now, but a secret garden.

"We did a pretty good job, if I do say so myself," Frankie said, coming to stand at my left with a grin. "And I don't think Max has any idea."

It was just about as hard as it sounded to pull off putting together a wedding without the groom knowing when it was his flower company that was supplying the flowers.

"Oh, no." Lou shook her head. "He's definitely convinced one of our guests is getting married today. I think the fake contract Wade typed up and signed really sealed the deal."

After Lucy's birth and then Christmas, Max and I settled into a routine that felt as familiar as it did comforting, but there was one thing that nagged at me. After how wild the last six months had been, I couldn't believe how I'd walked out of chaos and into a fairy tale. Every day I woke up next to him, every day he went and picked up our daughter from her crib and brought her into bed with us. I couldn't believe the dream I was living.

I couldn't believe the dream I was living with him.

But there was one tiny, tiny thorn that kept pricking at me as the days and weeks went on. I'd never regret a single moment of the path that brought us here, but that didn't mean there weren't things I wanted to give Max —parts of his dream that he'd happily hopped and skipped over to protect me.

Like a wedding surrounded by his family.

"Chandler just texted. They're on their way." Frankie slid her phone back into her pocket and lifted her mimosa glass. Mine, filled with just orange juice, clinked with hers and Lou's. "Have I mentioned how much I love that they decided on this whole 'Dad day' idea?"

Right after Christmas—though Jamie claimed he had the idea on Christmas and he and Kit bickered about it—the dads in the family, Jamie, Kit, Chandler, Wade, and Max, came up with the idea of a 'Dad day' that they took every other week. They'd take all the kids and go out for the day, or most of it, and do something fun. They'd done bowling days, hockey games. One time, Kit plastic wrapped his entire studio, and they did something that was more making a mess than it was painting, but Max had brought home a small canvas of Lucy's footprints that Jamie then made a frame for.

"Such a great idea," Violet said and joined us, but over by the window, where she could keep lookout.

Meanwhile, on Dad days, the moms got to play. Or, more accurately, relax.

"They're here!" Ailene announced, beaming as she whisked my orange juice from my hand, and then my father-in-law offered me his arm, leading me to the end of the short, rose-petal-lined aisle.

George was performing the unofficial ceremony, keeping the entirety of the event contained to family members only.

"You sure you want to marry Max again?" His eyes twinkled at me in jest.

"Every day." I smiled back and then looked to the entrance into the room, my heart rioting in my chest like I wasn't already married to the man about to walk through it.

I heard the front door open. "Lou, I'm here. What's wrong? You said—"

His determined stride skidded to a halt when he reached the threshold and saw the room we'd turned into nothing short of a secret garden. My smile of happiness cracked, wanting to split wider when I saw Lucy sleeping in the carrier strapped to his chest. That little girl couldn't have been more *his* even if it had been his genes woven into her DNA.

"Daze...what's going on?"

Ailene went to him and slid her hand through the crook of his elbow, guiding him down the aisle. "Of all people, Max, I think you'd recognize your own wedding."

"What's all this?" he murmured, lifting his hand to

trace my cheek as I bent forward and kissed the soft hair on the back of Lucy's head.

"You've given me all of my dreams, Max. I wanted to give you one of yours."

He looked painfully handsome the way he stared so intently at me. "You already did."

I groaned and brushed away the happy tears that danced down my cheeks. "Marry me again, Max. Please?"

Max chuckled and looped his arm around my waist, pulling me close. "Every day, Daze. I'll marry you every day if that's what you want." And then his mouth dropped to mine.

"Hey! That part happens at the end," George protested to a ripple of laughter through the room.

"Backward...forward...in any direction, I'll always end up with you," Max said, looking only at me, and then kissed me again.

At some point after that, his dad started the short ceremony, and we said "I do" over the small, sleeping whimpers of our daughter between us. I cried. His family cheered. Heaps of pastries appeared from the kitchen, and we ate and laughed and celebrated together until the babies started to get hungry and tired.

After rounds of hugs and congratulations from everyone, we went home exhausted and happy. After I fed Lucy and we put her to sleep, I led Max into our bedroom and looped my arms around his neck.

"I have another present for you."

"Another one?" His brow lifted, a hungry look already infusing his stare. "Is it like my Christmas present?"

I tipped my head, giggling when his mouth

instantly latched to my neck just below my ear. "Not exactly." I wiggled out of his hold and spun around. "Can you unzip me?"

His answer was those big hands framing my shoulders, and then the slow peel of the zipper opening along my back.

"You know I love this present," he rumbled and pushed my hair to the side so he could kiss the base of my nape, his knuckles skating up and down my bare spine.

A hum filtered through my lips. "Me too," I said with a shiver and then took a step away before I got lost in his touch. "But I think you'll love this one even more."

I faced him and placed my hands on either side of my stomach, the swell not even gone from Lucy's pregnancy. Max stared at me, stared at my stomach, and then back at me again.

"Daisy..."

"I'm pregnant, Max," I said, still slightly in disbelief that it had happened so soon, though I knew it was possible.

"You're..." His throat worked, the whole of him gone stiff, like he was about to shatter.

I flushed. "My due date is the week of Thanksgiving...again." Technically, it would be possible for Lucy and this baby to share a birthday exactly a year apart. Unlikely, but feeling more and more possible after the *unlikely* things we'd been through.

Max let out a growl, and the next thing I knew, I was crying out as he lifted me into his arms with a loud whoop, spinning me around even as he kissed me.

"You're pregnant," he repeated, allowing me only to

nod before he kept kissing me. Harder. Deeper. Tangling the two of us until we fell together onto the bed, me on top of him. "Fuck, Daze." He beamed up at me. "We're going to have another baby."

My chest caved with a happy sob. "Yeah, we are." He pulled me down to him, kissing me until my head spun. "You said you wanted a lot of babies."

"All the babies, Daze," he rumbled, spearing his tongue against mine. "I want a dozen babies with you."

"A dozen?" I choked out, laughing. "That's...a lot of babies."

He grinned wickedly up at me and then rolled me underneath him. Using one hand, he opened the waist of his pants and drew out his cock, teasing it along my entrance.

"And all the reason we should keep practicing," he said as he thrust inside me, the promise an end to our conversation...and the beginning of everything.

A LOOK AT BOOK SIX:
THE BEEKEEPER

There's nothing more important to Harper Hamilton than her honey.

Literally. Her beekeeping hobby blossomed overnight into a full time honey-making business, and she couldn't be happier.

Well, she could be. If the next step in her success didn't involve Blaze Stevens.

Blaze is everything a Hollywood actor should be. Jaw-droppingly gorgeous. Mind-numbingly arrogant. And stereotypically careless. At least he was the last time he was in Friendship. This time, there's something different about him... and it's not just the little girl clinging to his ankles.

Blaze has made some mistakes. Okay, many, but who's counting? However, there's only one mistake he won't regret, and it's the one that gave him his daughter. Unfortunately, all the regret in the world won't protect them from media scrutiny. So, he's back in Friendship and ready to beg the beautiful beekeeper to shelter the two of them on her farm. In return, he'll use his fame to help market her business.

They say you draw more flies with honey, and Harper would agree that this business arrangement is just that. Small-town shelter in exchange for movie-star marketing. Until she finds something even sweeter in Blaze's kiss.

AVAILABLE OCTOBER 2026

Rebecca Sharp is a contemporary romance author of over thirty published novels and dentist living in Pennsylvania with her amazing husband, affectionately referred to as Mr. GQ.

She writes a wide variety of contemporary romance. From new adult to extreme sports and forbidden romance to romantic comedies, her books will always give you strong heroines, hot alphas, unique love stories, and guaranteed happily ever after. When she's not writing or seeing patients, she loves to travel with her husband, snowboard, and cook.

www.drrebeccasharp.com
Rebecca Sharp's Sexy Little Sharpies